Beyond Michelangelo

ALSO BY NICK J. MILETI:

CLOSET ITALIANS: *A Dazzling Collection of Illustrious Italians with Non-Italian Names (2004)*

Beyond Michelangelo

The Deadly Rivalry Between Borromini and Bernini

Nick J. Mileti

Library of Congress: 2005902865

ISBN: Hardcover 1-4134-9170-7
Softcover 1-4134-9169-3

Copyright © 2005 by Nick J. Mileti.

All rights reserved. No part of this book may be reproduced or transmitted in any form or by any means, electronic or mechanical, including photocopying, recording, or by any information storage and retrieval system, without permission in writing from the copyright owner.

This book was printed in the United States of America.

For more information visit
www.closetitalians.com

Or contact
njmileti@aol.com

To order additional copies of this book, contact:
Xlibris Corporation
1-888-795-4274
www.Xlibris.com
Orders@Xlibris.com

25308

INTRODUCTION

This book was inspired by the city of Rome.

Living in the Eternal City, I quickly came to realize that Rome was basically a Baroque city, which meant, I quickly learned, that Rome was basically a GianLorenzo Bernini city (spiked by Francesco Borromini, one of the most innovative, and copied architects of all time).

But what about Michelangelo? Before I moved to Rome and discovered Bernini, I thought Michelangelo was the dominant artistic force in all of Italy.

The matter consumed me.

I compared Bernini's sculptures with those of Michelangelo, and found that Bernini was clearly a superior sculptor (to confirm this, one need only examine the masters' respective statutes of 'David').

The Michelangelo myth was unraveling.

Regarding architecture, I found that Bernini (and Borromini) also far surpassed Michelangelo (compare Bernini's Colonnade, which creates

Piazza San Pietro—considered by many the most beautiful public square in the world—with Michelangelo's Campidoglio, *which he didn't even finish*).

Speaking of not finishing a project, a Michelangelo trademark, I uncovered the truth behind who actually designed the dome of Saint Peter's you see today—and, contrary to common belief, it wasn't Michelangelo.

On the painting front, although Bernini reportedly completed hundreds of paintings, only a handful survive—all masterpieces, but relatively insignificant in comparison to the Sistine Chapel—so that palm must go to Michelangelo, at least until Bernini's other paintings are (hopefully) found.

Conclusion: A close examination of all the facts leads to the inescapable conclusion that Bernini was the single greatest all-around artist in history. Sadly, however, only a handful of scholars know this about Bernini. In fact, "who?" is the usual response I receive when I mention the great man's name to a layman.

But why is Michelangelo so much better known, and admired, than Bernini? (Have some fun—survey a room, any room, and ask who was the greatest all-around artist in history. I predict you will invariably hear "Michelangelo").

Here's what I think. I think the power of a best selling novel and blockbuster movie ('The Agony and the Ecstasy') are to blame for this misconception.

And—no surprise here—Borromini is not only much less known than Michelangelo, he is even less known than Bernini.

The delicious irony of all of this is that Michelangelo was the idol of both Bernini and Borromini.

—

As I progressed in my research, I discovered an unusual fact. Every author (and there are some great ones), whether writing about Bernini, Borromini, or the Baroque, mentions the rivalry, but no one elaborates. There is a dissertation in Germany, and a recent book, which both have titles that look like they will discuss the rivalry in detail, but, unfortunately, they shed no new light on the subject, nor do they probe beyond the obvious.

For me, however, in the course of the ten plus years of research and writing, the most exciting moments were when I connected the dots (perhaps it's my lawyer's training).

For example, among other things, I pieced together:

How Pietro Bernini arranged for the papal commission that took his family to Rome;

What the initial cause of Borromini's hatred of Bernini was, and what fueled it;

Why Bernini recommended Borromini for the position of architect of the Sapienza;

Why Pope Innocent X ordered Bernini's magnificent bell-towers on Saint Peter's torn down;

Why Bernini left Rome for the first time and went to Paris at age sixty-seven (and why his plans for the Louvre were rejected);

And, of course, most importantly, what triggered Borromini's suicide?

—

Bottom line:

I have written BEYOND MICHELANGELO to explain the rivalry, but mostly to help set the record straight about these two towering geniuses.

Everything in the story is based on historical fact, but a number of my conclusions, based on those years of research, differ substantially from those held by many well-known historical experts.

I have given this considerable thought of course, but I eventually decided that my conclusions are logical—and more than justified by the facts.

In fact, after reading the book, I believe many of today's Bernini, Borromini, and Baroque scholars (not to mention Michelangelo and Renaissance scholars) will be forced to re-evaluate their positions.

When you tell the truth, it's not bragging.

Prologue

The 16th Century was one of unprecedented change. New countries were being discovered, scientists were opening new sources of knowledge, and the dissemination of that new knowledge (and the knowledge of the classicists) through the printed word brought the masses into the mix.

In response to what it viewed as challenges to its authority, the Catholic Church initiated several unfortunate—infamous—actions. The Inquisition, the Index of Forbidden Books, and the creation of the Jewish Ghetto in Rome (the capital of the Papal States), were just three of the Church's stratagems.

But these inhuman tactics couldn't stop the general upheaval, which was rapidly lessening the authority of the Church. Clearly, something more needed to be done.

—

Before discussing the Church's positive solutions, let's look at what triggered all of this activity.

In the early 1500s, a Catholic priest from Germany took a trip to Rome. While in the Eternal City, the cleric was outraged by many of the

Church's practices; he was particularly incensed by the blatant sale of Indulgences—a tactic Pope Julius II was employing to finance the new Saint Peter's basilica.

Finally, in 1516, the priest, named Martin Luther, who was also a Professor of Biblical Theology at Wittenberg University, had enough. He wrote a list of ninety-five 'Theses' (articles for academic debate) and posted them on the university's bulletin board, the door of the Wittenberg Castle Church.

The result of his actions was eventually labeled the Reformation, and unwittingly, as we all now know, the naive priest changed the Catholic Church, and the world, forever.

—

The Catholic Church was slow to react. In fact, it wasn't until some thirty years later that it began to fight back in an organized way. The key vehicle of the counterattack was the Council of Trent, which was convened in 1545 by Pope Paul III to deal with the questions raised by Luther. In the eighteen years it was in session, the primary accomplishment of the Council was to recommend numerous reforms in the Church.

Equally important, however, the Council used the opportunity to promulgate a long-term offensive strategy, which came to be known as the Counter-Reformation. In fact, the second half of the 16th Century was dominated by the Counter-Revolution, stressing piety and submission to the authority of the Church.

Beneath the rhetoric, the Church understood that the Protestant Reformation was a cold, born-in-Germany movement that condemned art (which it labeled sensual and licentious) and disregarded the needs of the senses. Happily for art lovers over the centuries, the Church fathers decided to employ the power of art to deliver its message to the world.

The Church, however, faced a major problem. The art scene, of which Rome was the epicenter, was, relatively speaking, in the doldrums. Michelangelo, Raphael and Leonardo were dead, which effectively ended the glorious artistic period now known as the High Renaissance. The austere style that followed, called Mannerism, did not suit the needs of the church, and therefore was not a real force.

The Roman Catholic Church prayed for a miracle: "Please God, send us a few extraordinary men with artistic talent—men who have the artistic talent to convey our mission to the faithful."

—

The first signs that its prayers were being answered appeared in the form of Annibale Carracci and Michelangelo Merisi, known as Caravaggio. These two artistic geniuses worked in and about Rome at the turn of the 17th Century, creating revolutionary paintings and frescoes. While these masters worked their respective magic, the Church's prayers were answered. A flood of world-class artists, sculptors and architects were born within a short period straddling the turn of the century. They all lived in, or were influenced by, Rome.

Among the best were Simon Vouet (born in 1590), Guercino (1591), Jusepe de Ribera (1591), Georges De La Tour (1593), Artemisia Gentileschi (1593), Nicolas Poussin (1594), Francois Duquesnoy (1594), Alessandro Algardi (1595), Pietro da Cortona (1596), GianLorenzo Bernini (1598), Francisco de Zuberan (1598), Sir Anthony Van Dyke (1599), Andrea Sacchi (1599), Diego Velazquez (1599), Francesco Borromini (1599), Claude Lorraine (1600), Philippe de Champaigne (1602), Rembrandt van Rijn (1606) and Pierre Mignard (1612).

These men created paintings, sculpture and architecture that was seductive, exuberant and dramatic; works that created a close, personal relationship with the faithful. Their art was filled with a richness of illusion and suggestion that told the church's story in a provocative, yet delightful manner. In other words, it was art that appealed directly to the senses. Later labeled The Baroque by art historians, the new art movement was the answer to the Church's prayers.

—

But, there was one more problem. The Church—the quintessential organization that understands the need for strong leadership—knew that a leader was needed to inspire and direct these strong-willed artistic geniuses.

The checklist for the leader-to-be was daunting. He had to be talented enough to command the respect of his contemporaries, smart enough to withstand the pressures of leadership and rivals, personable enough to command the respect of his patrons, and dynamic and articulate enough to capture the imagination of the public.

Again the church prayed for a miracle and again its prayers were answered. The leader quickly emerged from the pack. He was a true child prodigy. His name was GianLorenzo Bernini.

Here is the noted art historian, Rudolph Wittkower, describing Bernini:

"He was, to be sure, an artist of all-around performance, an 'uomo universale,' in line of succession to the great Renaissance artists—and probably the last link in that chain. Here was an artist with an immensely fertile imagination, an unlimited working capacity, an unequaled facility of handling marble, a gift for organizing sculptural tasks on the grandest scale, and he was given opportunities without parallel in the history of art through the lavish patronage of the great 17th Century Popes and their families. Compared with the extent of his production, even the life work of a Michelangelo or a Rodin appears small. It was he more than any other artist who gave Rome its Baroque character. And it was his new conception of the saint, of the portrait bust, of the equestrian statute, of tombs and fountains, among other new creations, that determined the development of Italian and even European sculpture for more than a hundred years."

—

In addition to the mandate of the Council of Trent, the unprecedented plethora of artistic talent, and the emergence of Bernini as the dominating force, there were several additional reasons art became the dominating factor in the 17th Century.

Popes, who were coming to terms with their diminishing role in international affairs, began to turn to art and architecture to help fill the void. When a new Pope was elected, in spite of the early, inevitable protestations to the contrary, sooner or later he would try to surpass his predecessor with his own wealth (and power). For this reason, the 17th Century Popes became the greatest art patrons in history.

Not surprisingly, the papal court and papal families emulated the all-powerful leadership of their Popes.

In addition, the relatively new religious Orders—especially the major ones; the Jesuits, Oratorians, Dominicans and Theatines—were eager to establish their importance. They saw art as the vehicle that could most easily help them accomplish their goals, so they too became major patrons of the arts.

Lastly, private citizens, such as the nobility, did not want to be left behind nor considered out of step, so they also commissioned art and architecture to honor themselves and their loved ones.

—

So, the stage was set. But as the story unfolded, it was Bernini who had the problem.

Since the beginning of recorded history, rivalries and intrigue have been a part of the fabric of every community, and 17th Century Rome was no exception. As the man on top, Bernini—the greatest overall artist in history and the artistic leader of the Counter-Reformation—dealt with jealous rivals throughout his long, unprecedented career.

But there was one man who was more than a rival. This man was obsessed with GianLorenzo Bernini and everything about him. His name was Francesco Borromini and he made it his life's work to topple the master.

That is the story I have chosen to tell. The life-story of the great GianLorenzo Bernini, intertwined with that of Francesco Borromini, the brooding architectural genius who tried his best to destroy Bernini, but destroyed himself instead.

Major Dramatis Personae

(In order of appearance)

GIANLORENZO BERNINI. Child prodigy, and the greatest artistic genius in history.

PIETRO BERNINI, his Florentine father.

MISTER GALANTE, his Neapolitan grandfather.

ANGELICA GALANTE BERNINI, his Neapolitan mother.

FRANCESCO BORROMINI. Innovative architectural genius and architect of bitter, one-sided rivalry with Bernini.

PETER PAUL RUBENS. Famous Flemish Baroque artist. Friend of Bernini's father.

ANNIBALE CARRACCI. Famous classical painter from Bologna, where he ran a well-known school for artists. Friend of Bernini's father and idolized by young Bernini.

CARDINAL SCIPIONE BORGHESE. Cardinal/Nephew of Pope Paul V, and Number One patron of the arts. Commissions Bernini's most famous sculptural groups, including Rape of Proserpina, David, and Apollo and Daphne.

POPE PAUL V (CAMILLO BORGHESE). Publicly proclaims Bernini's genius when artist is only ten years old. Becomes patron of Bernini.

CARDINAL MAFFEO BARBERINI. At the request of Pope Paul V, the refined, cultured and artistic cleric personally tutors Bernini from age ten to age twenty-five—from 1608 until 1623—until he himself is elected Pope (see below).

LEONE GAROVO. Borromini's cousin, who helps Borromini when he arrives in Rome.

CARLO MADERNO. Number One architect in Rome before Bernini. Supporter and idol of Borromini.

POPE GREGORY XV (ALESSANDRO LUDOVISI). Aged cleric becomes Pope in 1621, serving only 2 + years. He is so pleased with the papal busts Bernini carves he bestows knighthood on the twenty-three year old genius.

POPE URBAN VIII (MAFFEO BARBERINI). Elected Pope in 1623, serving twenty-one years. One of history's greatest patrons of all the arts. Close friend and patron of Bernini.

GIULIO MAZZARINI (JULES MAZARIN). Best friend of Bernini, Prime Minister of France, secret husband of Queen Anne of Austria and father of King Louis XIV.

JUAN SAN BONAVENTURA. Head of Trinitarian Order, Borromini's first client as architect. Revolutionary church and cloister of San Carlino are the result.

GIUSEPPE. Bookstore owner. Aggressive salesman and 'town crier'. The book's only fictitious character.

CARDINAL VIRGILIO SPADA. Architectural dilettante. Number One supporter of Borromini, and secret enemy of Bernini. Artistic advisor to Pope Innocent X.

COSTANZA BONARELLI. Bernini's fiery mistress.

MATTEO BONARELLI. Her husband.

GALILEO GALILEI. First modern scientist. Miscalculation—making fun of friend, Pope Urban VIII—leads to condemnation by Inquisition for advocating earth moves around the sun and is not the center of the universe.

CATERINA TEZIO. "The most beautiful girl in Rome." Bernini's smart and loving twenty-one year old (half his age) wife who changes his life.

POPE INNOCENT X (GIAMBATTISTA PAMPHILI). Elected in 1644, serves eleven years as Pope. In vendetta against Bernini because of his close ties to Barberini family, he ceases papal commissions to Bernini and orders Bernini's bell-towers of Saint Peter's torn down.

DONNA OLIMPIA MAIDALCHINI, his sister-in-law. Disliked, greedy and scheming manipulator of the Pope.

JOHN EVELYN, English traveler and diary writer.

DIEGO VELAZQUEZ. Famous Spanish Baroque painter and friend of Bernini.

SISTER MARIA ALALEONE. Commissions family chapel from Bernini.

CARDINAL FABIO CHIGI. Member of famous Sienese family. Friend of Bernini. Later elected Pope.

POPE ALEXANDER VII (FABIO CHIGI, see above). Bernini's greatest patron.

QUEEN CHRISTINA. Queen of Sweden. Abdicates throne and moves permanently to Rome. Most famous convert to Catholicism in history. Great friend of Bernini.

GIOVANNI PAOLO OLIVA. Superior General of the Jesuit Order and close friend of Bernini.

PAUL FREART, SIEUR DE CHANTELOU. Bernini's host in France appointed by King Louis XIV and ordered to treat Bernini like royalty.

JEAN-BAPTISTE COLBERT. Superintendent of the King's Buildings. Secretly undermines Bernini whenever possible.

LOUIS XIV. King of France.

FRANCESCO MASSARI. Borromini's young servant.

BERNARDO BORROMINI. Borromini's nephew. Tries to save Borromini from himself.

POPE CLEMENT IX (GIULIO ROSPIGLIOSI). Elected Pope in 1667, serving only 2 + years. Old friend of Bernini's who invented comic opera form, for which he wrote the librettos and Bernini designed the sets.

POPE CLEMENT X (EMILIO ALTERI). Elected Pope in 1670, seventy-nine year-old cleric serves for six years. Close friend of Bernini.

POPE INNOCENT XI (BENEDETTO ODESCALCHI). Last of eight Popes Bernini serves. Squelches malicious attack on the eighty-one year old master.

Chapter I

Nick J. Mileti

Seven year-old GianLorenzo Bernini was so skinny and small he had to stand on his toes to see inside the house. The wiry, snap of a boy was peeking through the lace curtains of the front windows of his grandparent's home in Naples, the biggest, best-designed house on the lava-paved street. The sun was unbearably hot—a typical summer day in southern Italy—but the child was comfortable. His boots protected him from the steaming rocks, and he wore the blouse he had his mother cut the sleeves off of so he could have full movement of his spindly arms.

GianLorenzo always wore that particular blouse when he played the game he invented. He called it Seguire and he made the rules simple—follow old people around and find unusual motions or poses to sketch; the most dramatic drawing earned ten points on his made-up scale. On a good day, the little boy would rack up thousands of points following everybody and anybody around. Most neighbors thought it was cute.

This blistering day, a Sunday, in the Year of our Lord 1605, was painfully boring however. *I love my father and nonno, but what fun is it watching them just sit and talk? I'm going home to read my new book.*

The child gathered his crayons—he was anxious to study the book of engravings he received from his father for his birthday in December—when something wonderful exploded in front of him. *Nonno is shouting and waving his arms. Finally, something to draw.* The little boy immediately started sketching. Page after page flew to the ground—the faster he sketched, the more points he was accumulating. *What luck I'm having. I hope this goes on all day.*

Suddenly, the words "Moving to Rome" filled the air, spreading their venom over his mind like hot molasses dribbling down a crystal goblet. *Did I hear father say 'Moving to Rome?' I love it here in Naples, I don't want to move anywhere.*

The startled child dropped his crayon and paper and jammed his wet cheek against the windowpane.

—

"Moving to Rome?" Mister Galante screeched in the loudest voice the youth had ever heard him use. "Nobody in his right mind would move from Naples to Rome—not voluntarily at least."

Mister Galante quickly emptied his goblet and immediately refilled it; unmindful of the copious amount he spilled. With one gulp, the goblet was drained once again.

The child was transfixed. *Nonno may be smaller than father, but he can holler a lot louder.*

GianLorenzo scooped-up his crayons and papers, and with a few bold strokes captured his nonno—bald, trim, and about the same height as everybody in Naples (even though he had large bones)—strutting around the room, providing the young artist innumerable action scenes to draw, not to mention hundreds of points.

When his nonno finally sat down (to GianLorenzo's dismay) his voice returned to its normal Neapolitan level, that is to say, semi-controlled screaming. Mister Galante fought back a grimace, but he couldn't control his index finger, which punctured the air and underscored every word.

"Pietro, I understand this papal commission is the highlight of your distinguished career." More drinking. More yelling. "Hell, a papal commission would be the highlight of any career. But think about it. You're not yet fifty, you're an extremely successful sculptor here, and your reputation is impeccable. Everyone respects you as a person and as an artist, and your family is here."

Pietro sipped his wine. Mister Galante gulped his.

"Besides," he said, giving his son-in-law his best shot, "Naples has the best food in Italy."

Pietro Bernini couldn't help laughing. While gathering his thoughts, he sipped the wine he had made the year before. He examined the color; it was the deep red that characterized the hearty wines of the area.

Pietro was considerably taller than his father-in-law. Always impeccably dressed and well-groomed (thanks to his wife, Angelica), Pietro's perfectly trimmed mustache framed his full lips and was complimented by a perfectly trimmed, soft, tufted goatee—which he now stroked with the index finger and thumb of his left hand. Pietro swirled the wine slowly, and took another sip. He admired the color once more, smacked his lips and finally fixed his father-in-law with a penetrating gaze.

GianLorenzo was mesmerized. *Uh oh. I've seen that look on father before. Last year when I tried to drive and smashed the carriage into the barn. Dumb horses. One look's all it took. He didn't say one word but I haven't tried to drive since. People say I have father's eyes. I hope that's good.*

Pietro Bernini was a man whose friendly manner masked a keen intellect, but this fateful day he spoke in an exceptionally soft, conspiratorial voice. The child was afraid he was going to break the window straining to hear what his father had to say. Pietro arose, and put both of his hands on the smaller man's shoulders—his gaze was so intense, it took a Herculean effort on Mister Galante's part to keep from looking away.

Pietro decided his father-in-law deserved an explanation.

"Mister Galante," Pietro said, "please try to understand. My motives are noble. I'm closing my workshop here in Naples and moving my family to Rome for my son."

GianLorenzo captured his nonno jumping out of his chair, slamming his goblet on the table, splattering the room with wine, banging his way around the room, trying to decide what to do with his clenched fist—which he was smashing into his open left hand.

GianLorenzo was torn. *It's fun drawing this, but it looks like nonno's going to hit father.*

Pietro had the highest regard for his father-in-law and hated to upset him this way—but he decided the situation cried out for the truth. He plowed ahead.

"You heard me right. I'm doing it for GianLorenzo. That is the reason. There is no other reason."

Mister Galante was dumbfounded. He raced to his son-in-law, placing his flaming crimson face within an inch of Pietro's face, his voice rising to previously unheard levels. "You would uproot your entire family—and upset ours as well—for a seven year-old child? Have you gone mad?"

Pietro took another sip of wine. "That amazes you? Then you better drink the rest of that bottle of wine because you're going to need it. Ready?"

GianLorenzo made ten sketches of his nonno during the few seconds it took the suffering old man to drain the half-empty bottle.

"Ready as I'll ever be," Mister Galante said, refusing to raise his head, staring, rather, into the bottom of the empty wine bottle.

Pietro continued, in a voice that was a cross between the somber tone he employed at confession and the captivating tone he used in the bedroom.

"To make the move from Naples to Rome feasible," he said smiling, happy, in a way, to share his extraordinary secret with someone he knew he could trust, "I was able to, personally, 'arrange' to receive the papal commission."

Chapter II

GianLorenzo Bernini was the most confused little child in the Kingdom of Naples. He felt woozy. He put his hands over his ears. *I don't want to hear any more—what does all this talk mean?* When his grandfather started shouting again, the child quickly relented and listened more closely than ever; sketching, sketching, sketching.

"What are you saying, Pietro?" the incredulous Mister Galante asked his son-in-law. "I know you are a cool, calculating Florentine, but how can you, or anyone for that matter, arrange a papal commission—from the austere Pope Paul V no less?"

"I'm not going to tell you how I arranged it," Pietro replied, pleased by the left-handed compliment. "That is much too sensitive a subject, as you can imagine."

GianLorenzo strained forward. *I know father favors me over my sisters—everyone know that. But what's this about?*

Pietro took a deep breath and walked around the room—as if making certain there were no foreign spies in the area. Books filled the wall-to-ceiling wooden shelves on two of the walls, while paintings covered every inch of the other two. Pietro straightened one of his father-in-law's paintings of Mount Vesuvius and slowing turned to face him. He spoke forcefully, but with caution.

"One night, about three years ago, a revelation came to me during my evening prayers. Or maybe it was a sensation. I wasn't asleep, so it could not have been a dream, and . . ."

"Pietro," Mister Galante said, "what are you talking about?"

Pietro flashed a warm smile. "I know this is going to sound strange, maybe even weird," he continued, "which is why I hesitated to tell you about it. Matter of fact, I haven't mentioned this to anyone else, not even Angelica. I'm telling you now because of the impact my plan has on the family." His voice, when he finally spoke, was soft and full of compassion. "Yes—I believe you have a right to know my thinking."

To keep busy and hide his curiosity, Mister Galante opened another bottle of wine. He carefully poured two full goblets, which both men sipped as they drifted into deep thought. The silence in the room was eerie—the kind of silence only a metaphysical discussion can trigger. The wine had no effect on either man.

Pietro finally continued—speaking slowly, in a trance-like monotone. He was barely breathing, but his dark brown eyes were alive as he relived his life-altering moment.

"I was praying that night, three years ago. During those prayers, my son appeared to me. And all around him, he had an aura. Not just a regular aura, whatever that may be, but an aura of greatness. To say I was startled would be an understatement of monumental dimensions. Now here's the weirdest part—since then, whenever I see GianLorenzo, whenever I see my son, I see this aura of greatness surrounding him."

A wide-eyed GianLorenzo held his breath. Mister Galante wiped his brow with his kerchief. He watched his son-in-law with a mixture of suspicion and wonder.

Pietro raised his goblet in a semi-toast and continued. "It's some sort of miracle, of course. Normally I don't believe in miracles, but there you have it. As you can imagine, from that moment on, planning my son's future has been an obsession with me. And, as you've probably guessed, it took me the last three years to arrange that papal commission but finally, it's done."

GianLorenzo's mouth was dry and his heart was pounding. *What's a revelation? What's an aura?*

Mister Galante's mind was whirling, but his efforts to maintain his composure met with success. Considering what he was hearing, he felt composure was important. "Pietro, you are the most steady and sensible man I know. That's why I was so pleased when you asked for my daughter Angelica's hand in marriage. But this, this is . . ."

In spite of his great respect for his father-in-law, Pietro couldn't help interrupting. "I tell you, the aura is tangible. It's real. At least it's real to me. Now here is the best part. I see something *within* this aura of greatness. I see the child surpassing me as a sculptor. No, I must be truthful with you, Mister Galante. I see more than that."

Pietro stopped and nibbled at his left index finger. He gulped down his wine. His father-in-law laced his hands together, placed his elbows on the arms of his chair, placed his chin on his hands and stared at Pietro. He gave a slight nod, indicating he was finally ready for whatever Pietro was about to say.

Not a bit surprised by his father-in-law's reaction, Pietro soldiered on, actually happy to be sharing the secret he'd been harboring for three years. "Here's what else I see. I see GianLorenzo taking the arts—all of the arts, all of them—to places no one has gone before. No one."

Mister Galante's head fell against the back of the chair; he wasn't sure he could handle anything more. He raised his left hand to his left eyebrow and rubbed it. He drained his goblet and finally spoke—his voice mild, and, now, transcending awe, full of respect. "No One? Good God . . ."

"You are right," Pietro interrupted, heaving a sigh of relief, welcoming the inadvertent help. "God is good. Actually, God is not only good, I believe that through His Grace—the Grace of God—my son will soar beyond everyone. Even beyond the great one. Beyond Michelangelo."

—

Seven-year-old GianLorenzo Bernini wanted to run into the house and hug and kiss his father but thought better of it—instinctively realizing he'd just heard a secret he wasn't supposed to hear. Instead, he wrapped his arms around his trembling body and scratched at the goose bumps on his bony legs until they bled. *How could father know what I've been dreaming since I was a little boy?*

Chapter III

"There is nothing wrong with Naples," GianLorenzo heard his nonno persist, and he agreed with him. "You found your wife here and you've established yourself as a first-class sculptor."

"You are absolutely right about Angelica," Pietro said, his outgoing smile lighting up his face and highlighting his strong cheekbones. "Your daughter is the best thing that ever happened in my life. She is a loving wife, a caring mother, and, most importantly, she gave me GianLorenzo. Who could ask for anything more? As for my talent, I don't delude myself. I'm one of the best among a group of mediocre artists and you know it."

Mister Galante studied his lanky, good-looking son-in-law. *It must be his high forehead. People say that's a sign of intelligence. Whatever it is, this man makes too much sense whenever we talk.* "I don't know," he replied, studying his wine and avoiding Pietro's eyes. "There has to be more to this Rome move than you're telling me."

Once again, Pietro couldn't help laughing. He really did like his father-in-law, and he fully understood why the old man was trying to talk him out of taking his family away.

"You don't convince easily." Pietro smiled an honest smile. "Okay. Let's take it one step at a time. First-of-all, where do today's greatest artists live? In Rome, of course. They are all over the city, like marble on the Coliseum. I want the boy to meet these important artists and learn from them. Secondly, how about ancient sculpture and painting—there is probably more great art in the Vatican than the rest of Italy, maybe even the rest of the world, combined."

Mister Galante clung to his arguments, like barnacles on the bottom of a boat. "There are good artists living in Naples, even a few great ones. Caravaggio was here for a short time, and we have hundreds of important churches, and . . ."

Pietro was too worked-up to acknowledge his father-in-law. He tapped the arms of his chair with the fingers of both hands, subconsciously structuring his next set of arguments. "Then there is architecture. In Rome he can study innumerable ancient ruins. And, don't forget current architecture. The city is bursting with building activity like no other—new churches and palaces are going up every day."

After a long pause and a moderate drink of wine, Pietro switched tactics.

"Look, Mister Galante, since the Inquisition burned Giordano Bruno at the stake five years ago, I know what you think of the Papal States. That also appalled me. But, like it or not, Rome is the center of the Christian Church—the most significant religious movement in history, at least in this Year of our Lord, 1605."

"I grant you that, so what?" He knew his response was feeble, but, hopefully, it wasn't edgy.

"I'll tell you so what," Pietro answered, inadvertently giving his remarks an attitude and regretting it immediately. He continued, making it a point to speak in his usual friendly tone. "With all due respect, think about who lives in Papal Rome? Think about it. Art patrons and collectors, isn't that who lives in Papal Rome? Start with the papacy. It is literally impossible to overstate how important the Pope is to artists. Add to that the rest of the clergy, not to mention the nobility, the private individuals—all inspired by, or emulating, the Pope and his court—and I think it's safe to say there are more art patrons and collectors in Rome than any other place on earth."

GianLorenzo could see that his nonno was exhausted. *He looks like he chased his horse Thunder all over the yard for a whole month.*

"Pietro," Galante said, offering his goblet of wine in a toast of surrender, "you argue so well you should be a lawyer."

"Then allow me to summarize," Pietro said, "like the lawyers do. I firmly believe Rome is the environment GianLorenzo needs. And equally important—even more important I should say—your daughter agrees."

GianLorenzo captured the victory—his father relaxing his gaze and his body—in several sketches. Then he drew his grandfather—beaten, but still a proud little Neapolitan. *Poor nonno—he looks so sad.*

—

Without realizing it, in the course of his eavesdropping the child was drawn, argument-by-argument, to his father's viewpoint. When GianLorenzo heard that his mother agreed with his father, he became positively enthusiastic about the move.

The child ran all the way home with his stack of sketches and a record number of points. *I can't wait—Rome sounds really, really nice.*

Chapter IV

Angelica supervised the packing for the five-day trip from Naples to Rome. She reluctantly agreed with Pietro that they had to leave their furniture and would buy new pieces when they reached Rome.

While her daughters packed, Angelica put on several petticoats, a boned-stiff bodice, a full skirt, and a red and gold colored blouse with a scalloped lace collar. She brushed her silky black hair, gathered it in a bun, and put a purple flower in it.

The amazed girls followed their graceful mother as she walked slowly, but fluidly, through the house. She studied each vase, each sculpture, each painting—but the tables were her personal favorites.

Angelica ran her long-shapely hands over each table—some were round, some square—but she lingered over the tables with rare wood inlays in their solid walnut. Some of the tables had inlay of small flowers, and some had threading, but all were beautiful and brought back pleasant memories; especially the long, rectangular hand-painted table with the caryatids for legs—the one that Pietro himself made for her.

Angelica shooed the girls away and sat in one of the delicate chairs—the one with the scroll-shaped legs—and sighed. *I pray to God Pietro knows what he's doing.*

—

Angelica and Pietro rode in the first carriage, the girls rode in the next two, and the servants rode in the fourth. The belongings Angelica allowed to be taken along were piled atop the carriages, which were extra-large, had a seat in the middle, and were pulled by four horses. The carriages were each driven by two men hired to protect the family from the bandits who roamed the countryside between Naples and Rome. The drivers carried inlaid ivory, German-made muskets and pistols.

After an hour of tearful goodbyes, a proud GianLorenzo, on the horse Thunder—a gift from his grandparents—led the impressive caravan out of Naples. Although the road of hard-packed, compact dirt was dusty and filled with bumps and potholes, it was straight and swarming with other travelers headed in both directions. The poorly cultivated fields depressed GianLorenzo, who could find little of interest to draw, but the girls didn't notice—they giggled and teased each other while their parents dozed.

After passing through the pleasant little town of Aversa, the group stopped for the night in the town of Capua. After checking to make certain the family was asleep, the child slipped into the tavern attached to the Inn. Before they left Naples, his mother had warned him that he was not allowed in any of the taverns, so the youth carefully avoided the busy innkeeper. GianLorenzo found an alcove, took out the chalk and paper he'd hidden in his breeches, and started sketching. The pages flew.

The youth sketched a man and woman dancing to the music from the little band, and later the same couple weaving on the dance floor, moving to the music in their heads. He captured a boisterous dice game that never ended. He enjoyed the look of the beautiful girls with flowing black hair and white gowns, sitting on men's laps, kissing and rubbing their necks. On and on it went. The child had never seen anything like it—the chaotic scene played over and over in his mind as he drifted off to sleep, chalk clutched in hand.

—

Dawn brought the innkeeper sweeping the floor. He stumbled on GianLorenzo, who was sketching. "What's this?" he barked. His teeth—those that were left—were black and his left cheek had a long, red scar. "Who are you, you little shit-face? What are you doing here?"

The child grabbed his drawings and tried to run away, but the burly innkeeper, who was built like a pear, grabbed the little boy around the waist and pushed him against the wall. His breath almost caused GianLorenzo to faint. *I wonder why he smells like that? Not even Thunder smells like that.*

"You're not going anywhere, you snot-faced punk." He grabbed the sketches.

GianLorenzo stood straight and tried to look contrite. The olive-skinned youth with the sharp features ran his hand through his full head of black hair and flashed a radiant smile. *This man isn't nice—and his hair goes down to his waist. I've never seen that before. If he hits me, I'll pull that stringy hair.* "Did I do something wrong, sir?" the good-looking little boy asked, trying to strike just the right note between humility and confidence. "If I did, I'm very, very sorry."

The innkeeper didn't hear the child; he was concentrating on the massive pile of drawings, studying each one carefully. He spoke in a slightly more civil tone. "You . . . you. Did you draw these?"

GianLorenzo nodded, never taking his eyes off of the enemy.

The innkeeper continued examining the drawings. He was fascinated, and in spite of himself, the innkeeper's tone softened. "There are so many sketches here and they're all so good," he said, now speaking in a normal tone of voice. "You must have been hiding in my tavern for weeks. How long does it take you to draw each one? Be honest. Do you know what that means?"

"Mother and father talk to me about being honest most every day, sir." *I'm glad he stopped hollering.* The child fought the urge to cover his nose with his kerchief. *I've never smelled anything like this.*

"Good. Be honest now. How long does it take you to complete sketches like these? Exactly?"

"I don't know exactly," the child replied. *I don't know what he's getting at so I'd better not lie.* "A few minutes for each I guess."

The innkeeper was stunned. Painters and artists frequented his tavern all of the time, but he'd never seen quality like this produced with speed like this. His eyes traveled from the drawings to the little boy. From the drawings to the boy. Back and forth, back and forth his blood-shot eyes roamed.

He finally focused on the child, who was dressed in his traveling costume of tan calf-length breeches, over-sized white blouse with red sash and wide-brimmed black felt hat. The innkeeper smiled in spite of himself. *He looks like a darling Christmas tree ornament.* "How old are you, young man?"

"Seven, sir."

"Wait right here, the innkeeper said. "Don't move." He made fresh lemonade and brought a huge goblet to the child. "I hope my wife doesn't find out, but I'm giving you this drink free in exchange for these sketches. And wait a minute. To be fair, I'm not going to charge your parents for your food. Now tell me your name."

The youth suppressed a smile. *I've never seen anyone change like that—he was so mean and now he's nice.*

"GianLorenzo, sir. GianLorenzo Bernini."

"I don't know if I should spank you or hug you GianLorenzo Bernini, but I know one thing—I'll never forget you. You are a rascal, and that's putting it mildly."

The innkeeper started to hug the little boy, but GianLorenzo stiffened, so he pinched the child on both cheeks instead. "Now finish that drink and get out of here."

Chapter V

Beyond Michelangelo

"From Capua," Pietro announced to his family, "we ride the 130 miles to Rome on the famous Appian Way—built by the Romans over a thousand years ago." He loved educating his family and his family loved being educated by their father. Especially GianLorenzo. "Will I see interesting things to draw?"

The group approached the town of Fondi. "This is the last town in the Kingdom of Naples," Pietro said. "After this, we will be in the Papal States."

The news excited GianLorenzo—they were really on their way now. But, were they? Ahead, the youth spotted a long snaking line. He was heartbroken. *We'll be here forever.*

Suddenly, a guard in full military dress appeared, saluted Pietro, and escorted the Bernini party past the crowd and the checkpoint, without asking for any papers. The child asked his father about this.

"What's the sense of being a celebrity," Pietro said, "if you don't have the emoluments."

GianLorenzo made a mental note to look up the word when he unpacked his dog-eared dictionary.

To the young boy, the sights along the way were spectacular, but frustrating—ancient viaducts and other ruins dominated every view. He begged the drivers to stop so he could sketch them, but they would seldom stop. "Too dangerous," they would say, fondling their weapons. "Way, way too many bandits."

GianLorenzo had never been so excited in his life. *Good, I want to see a bandit so I can sketch him.*

A rest stop provided GianLorenzo the opportunity to sneak away from the traveling party. He wondered off into an orchard and picked the biggest orange he could find. "This is heaven," the child said to Thunder, as he sucked on the best piece of fruit he'd ever eaten. The youth ran his strong little hands along the horse's massive jet-black neck, as if searching for the hinges that held the animal together. Pure pleasure.

A sharp click interrupted young Bernini's daydreaming. A beautiful bandit—in the child's eyes, at least—was pointing a rusty musket at him. Actually, the robber was an ugly youth with straggly hair. He was dressed in rags, with legs wrapped in canvas and tied with cord, wearing a hat that looked like his victim's.

"Freeze," GianLorenzo ordered.

The young thief was flabbergasted as he watched his intended victim pull crayons and paper out of his pocket. The brigand scratched his head. *Something about this isn't right.*

The child quickly sketched the flummoxed bandit and then threw his orange at him. The missile hit the outlaw in the eyes, causing him to fire his rifle harmlessly into the air.

GianLorenzo slapped his horse on his hind-side. "Go Thunder. We better get a musket."

The young bandit jumped on his skinny horse and started after the boy—he was mad as hell and wanted to teach the little snake a lesson.

"Robber, robber," GianLorenzo cried as he approached his family. "Quick, throw me a weapon."

Muskets and pistols started blazing away from the carriages, forcing the out-manned robber to turn and flee.

"We had him on the run, didn't we Thunder," the exhilarated child said, giving his horse a well-deserved pat on the neck. "I wish he'd come back though, so I could draw him some more. He had a really interesting face."

CHAPTER VI

When the party reached the town of Terracina, GianLorenzo immediately presented his sketch of the brigand to the owner of their inn. "This is the bandit I scared off," he announced proudly. "Notice the look on his face. That's cause he was afraid of me and Thunder."

The proprietor studied the drawing. "Did you say you drew this?"

"Of course. But you better post it here in the lobby. That way, if your customers see him somewhere they can arrest him. If you want, you can reward me."

The grateful proprietor laughed. "That's some remarkable little boy," he said to Pietro and Angelica. "Would a free supper for the child be sufficient payment for his sketch?"

"It'll do okay," GianLorenzo answered before either of his parents could speak.

Angelica took the child aside. "'It will be appropriate' would be better grammar, young man. And what happened to your manners? Don't you think a 'thank you' is in order?"

The young boy rushed back to the proprietor. He stood straight and looked the man in the eye. "Excuse me sir, but I forgot to say thank you. I'm so embarrassed—my father taught me that word last week—you may forget giving me that free meal."

———

That night, after supper Pietro and Angelica lay in bed. The couple shared a bottle of wine from the region and reviewed the tumultuous day.

"That son of ours is more trouble than our six daughters combined," Angelica said as she snuggled up to her handsome husband. "Is it because he's a boy?"

Pietro stroked his wife's long, silky black hair and examined her supple body. *I can't believe she has retained her perfect shape in spite of bearing seven children.* "I think it's your hot Neapolitan blood," he said, his eyes full of anticipation.

Beyond Michelangelo

"Stop that, I'm serious," Angelica said, sitting up. Although the beauty's dark eyes gleamed with mischief, she had a strong sense of duty when it came to the family and she never hesitated to express it. "GianLorenzo truly worries me. Truly. He hardly sleeps. He would never bother to play with the other children in Naples. All he wants to do is draw and eat fruit. Is that healthy? Is that normal? And look at that robber business today. We almost had a disaster on our hands."

Pietro sighed internally. *Always the same discussion. Under the circumstances, I'd best be a little more patient tonight.* "Sweetheart, in my opinion, GianLorenzo doesn't sleep more than three or four hours a night because he is fascinated with life. Frankly, I think he's afraid of missing something interesting or exciting. As usual, you are right. The child would rather read and draw than kick a silly ball around. Is that so bad? Yes, he eats fresh fruit almost exclusively, but the doctors insist that's okay. And yes, he's impetuous and passionate—but so are you my love."

Angelica slowly relaxed, deep in thought. She rubbed her thin, long fingers down her slim, lithe thighs, an inadvertent move that excited Pietro. Now she spoke in a soft, but challenging tone. "But where is your cold, placid, Florentine influence? He's your son too, you know."

Pietro laughed out loud. "Oh, I think GianLorenzo is cool and calculating enough. Think about what he did. First he tangled with a robber and then he sold a sketch of the thief. You'll notice that his drawings have paid for all of his food and drink on this trip. In fact, did you see how his 'thank you speech' got a second free meal earlier from the startled proprietor? To me, it looks like our little boy is an amazing combination of artist, adventurer and businessman. What do you think my dear?"

The beauty pushed her hair—which was parted perfectly in the middle—away from both sides of her narrow face and gave her husband a warm hug and kiss. She pulled away for a moment.

"I think you always take GianLorenzo's side no matter what. That's all well and good, of course—one of us should probably spoil him. But I'm still worried about what will become of our baby," Angelica said, closing the matter before melting into her husband's arms.

Chapter VII

T he Bernini family cheered when they spotted the Porta di San Giovanni in the Aurelian Wall. "That gate has served as the prime southern entrance to the city of Rome for several thousand years," Pietro told his happy band of travelers. "That is the Aurelian Wall, and it encircles the entire city of Rome."

The wall fascinated GianLorenzo. The curious little boy rode ahead of the group, past the long lines waiting to show their papers. He touched the wall in several places. *Father said this wall was built to keep people out, but it feels nice to me. I like how the brick shows through the crumbling stucco—there's more to it than I can see. Like father, I think. Right now I've got to get inside Rome.*

Horse and rider tried to enter the actual gate, but a colorfully clad papal guard stepped out of a guardhouse and blocked the way. "Where do you think you're going, you little monster," he growled. "Get to the back of the line."

"It's okay, sir," GianLorenzo answered. "Our family is moving to Rome. My father knows the Pope."

The papal guard roared with derisive laughter. He held the little boy and his horse until Pietro and Angelica arrived, breathless and apologetic. With the haughty air of a typical minor functionary, the guard told the pair what the child claimed. Hating to embarrass the guard, but unwilling to allow his son to be humiliated, Pietro flashed his papal commission. The guard almost fainted.

"Mister Bernini, come this way, please. Please," said the guard. He sent his partner for the rest of the traveling party, and then led the group through the gate—ahead of everyone in the line, and without need for documentation.

This time GianLorenzo understood why they were receiving preferential treatment. *Love those emoluments.*

—

The Bernini's wove their way through the medieval streets, past great churches situated on squares large and small, past magnificent palaces with shops on the street level, past restaurants and cafes jammed with diners and revelers—all contributing to the general chaos. Vendors selling every kind of food worked the crowds on the narrow streets and slowed the group's progress; all of which suited GianLorenzo just fine. He loved the excitement and drew it with more enthusiasm than usual.

The traveling party finally reached its goal—a stately multi-storied house, even bigger than their home in Naples. "Here's where we are going to live," Pietro said. "And that's Santa Maria Maggiore, where I'm going to work. On the Pauline Chapel—for the Pope."

The family was so intent on studying their new home, they hadn't looked around. They now all followed his gaze. Diagonally across the road stood the largest church any of them had ever seen. "Wait until you see the inside the church—the ceiling of the nave, the long main aisle, is gilded with the first gold brought back from the New World."

Seven year-old GianLorenzo was so excited he almost wet his pants.

Chapter VIII

The village of Bissone, is situated perfectly. The little town lies on the shore of charming Lake Lugano, and since it reflects the lake's clear blue waters, Bissone sparkles like a polished diamond. Immediately behind the hamlet, there are rugged mountains, with incongruous snow-capped peaks that seem to mock the sand and surf below them. To cap off the town's ideal location, even though it's located in the north at the Swiss-Italian border, Bissone enjoys a relatively mild climate.

The tiny fishing village of Bissone is where Francesco Borromini (known as Francesco Castelli at that time) was born on September 27, 1599.

Inexplicably, this Lombard region is where an inordinate number of the world's most talented stonecutters and masons have been born over the years. Because there was basically no work for them in the bucolic environment, however, the artisans—and architects and sculptors—spread throughout Italy and Europe, where many achieved considerable fame and fortune.

—

Francesco's father, Giovanni, who was an architect, came from a family of masons, while his mother, Anastasia Garovo, was descended from a prominent family of masons and builders. Francesco's parents did not want their son to be a stonemason nor architect. They dreamt their boy would become a sculptor.

The ten-year-old Francesco was tall and well built for his age. His face was tanned from constantly being outdoors, and his arms and hands were muscular—all due to his youthful work helping the local stonecutters. His hair hung down to his shoulders and his nose was finely chiseled but not long. He looked comfortable in his wrinkled clothes, which, to his mother's consternation, always looked like he slept in them.

Francesco was sent by his parents to Milan to apprentice with the sculptor Giovanni Andrea Biffi, a blond, blue-eyed hard working northerner who was happy in his work. The twenty-eight year-old sculptor had an active studio, which was primarily producing works for Milan's monumental Cathedral, known as the Duomo.

When Francesco's father introduced his young son to his tutor, the amiable sculptor patted the child on the back. "You may call me Gian," he said. "That's what my friends call me. Gian."

Biffi led the child and his father to the rear of his studio. "Here's the bench you will work at, Francesco. Three other boys will share the bench with you—they arrive later this week."

Young Borromini never hesitated—he grabbed a loose piece of wood and drew a circle around the workbench in the marble dust that covered the floor.

"What in the world are you doing," the startled Biffi asked.

Francesco spoke for the first time since meeting his new mentor. "This is my workbench *Gian*, and nobody better cross that line. Only you could. Let the others find their own place to work, *Gian*."

—

After a good deal of arguing and haggling, young Borromini's father paid the tutor four times his usual fee—to cover the extra places for his son.

"Francesco needs the extra room for his books, and for his collection of shells," he explained to Biffi. "When he's not cutting stone, the boy likes to read. Either way, he likes to be alone so he can concentrate."

Biffi wasn't sure whether he should laugh or cry, but he certainly was impressed. *A ten-year-old who reads books—that's a first for me. I wonder what kind of books he reads. Probably pornography. And that circle around his workbench. How will the other boys react to it? I fear for the worse.*

Chapter IX

Beyond Michelangelo

Twelve hours a day, and often more, Francesco and his fellow apprentices developed their skills as decorative sculptors under the capable hands of Gian Andrea Biffi. Although their duties mainly related to Milan's Duomo, one of the largest churches in the world, they also spent time on other projects.

Evenings, and the odd day off, Francesco's fellow apprentices inevitably celebrated their free time together. They played sports, and made as much mischief as possible in Milan.

Young Borromini on the other hand, spent his free time reading and seeking out the religious and other structures of the city.

Much to Biffi's surprise, the circle young Borromini drew around his workbench—which looked like a moat surrounding a castle—became a joke among the other boys, rather than the source of a problem. The worse mischief it inspired was the apprentices stepping back and forth over the line when they passed Francesco's desk, pretending not to see it.

The divergent life styles, on the other hand, fueled spats among the young apprentices. The youths taunted Francesco for not joining in their games. Young Borromini, who was naturally shy and preferred quiet at his workbench so he could concentrate on his stone cutting, ignored them—which endeared him to his mentor but irritated the other boys even more.

—

In later years, as the boys reached their teens, the tormenting remarks took a different, more serious turn. The taunting now invariably centered on Francesco's relationship, or rather lack of relationship, with women. For some reason, the apprentices couldn't—or wouldn't—understand what young Borromini was talking about when he explained that he had decided to be celibate in honor of God.

Francesco worked as hard at ignoring his tormentors as he did at his carving, but he found the harassment harder and harder to disregard. Not surprisingly, the more upset Francesco became, the more the other apprentices baited him.

Mentioning girls became a kind of sport among them. Sometimes, the troublemakers would hide Francesco's marble and replace it with a woman's hat. Or, they would draw pictures of copulating men and women on his marble. Childish things like that.

At the end of one particularly long day, as Francesco left the studio, one of the apprentices, who was dressed like a woman, threw himself at Borromini, kissed him full on the lips, grabbed his crotch, and ran away. His fellow agitators, watching from the bushes, cheered. Biffi was thrilled that Francesco continued to ignore the childish behavior, but the battle was clearly escalating.

—

The foolishness culminated one night when young Borromini was walking home in the dark. A group of the apprentices jumped Francesco. "Maybe you prefer this to girls," the juiced-up tormentors shouted as they tried to sodomize him with a metal rod from the workshop. Borromini, who had developed into a well-built, strong young man, was able to escape his attackers.

—

Francesco stayed home for two days nursing his not inconsiderable wounds. *That's it. I guess turning the other cheek is not going to work. I just wanted to be left alone.*

Since Borromini told his mentor nothing, the tormentors thought he had quit the workshop—which was exactly what Francesco wanted them to think.

On the night before his return to the studio, Borromini followed the ringleader home. He surprised his main instigator and hit him over the head with a metal pipe, knocking him unconscious. Francesco then rammed the metal pipe into the youth's rear end, and jammed a second piece of pipe into his mouth. He then wrapped his antagonist in cord, carried him to the workshop, and propped him up against the front door.

With the piece of metal sticking out of each side, the young man looked like a sausage ready to be placed on a spit.

Based on the statements of the other apprentices, Borromini was arrested. "It was Francesco," they said. "He did it, we saw him do it."

Borromini was quickly set free, however, when his mentor, Biffi, explained to the police that Francesco was with him at his house the entire night in question. Studying. "He even slept over, so he couldn't possibly be the perpetrator of this despicable deed."

Not surprisingly, peace and quiet reigned thereafter, and the studio's output rose dramatically, in direct proportion.

Chapter X

In his never ending prowling around the city, Francesco discovered that Milan was inordinately rich in Medieval, Romanesque and Renaissance churches.

Because the decoration of these ancient buildings was sparse, young Borromini found himself concentrating on the architectural and structural aspects of the churches, such as arches, vaults, and facades. He found the two-level façade of San Giuseppe, with its pilasters and columns, particularly intriguing. Francesco was also impressed with Bramante, especially his church known as Santa Maria presso Sant' Satiro. To Francesco, Bramante's work was logical and orderly—traits he admired.

Little by little—day-by-day, week-by-week, month-by-month and year-by-year—Francesco became more and more fascinated by the architectural demands of construction, and how architects solved those issues. There seemed to be a pattern, but young Borromini couldn't quite put it all together.

—

"Do you have any books on mathematics," Francesco asked his mentor one day. "I'm wondering if it's possible that mathematics and architecture are somehow related."

"From the little I know about architecture," Biffi said, "I'd say that it's entirely possible that mathematics and architecture are related—they certainly are in sculpture. Yes, you may take home any of the mathematics books from my desk—Gerolamo Cardano's writings are the best I've ever read on the subject. Just be sure to return any book you borrow."

The sculptor had come to like the serious young man. *He's a loner who doesn't speak much, but he wants to learn. I can't believe I thought all he wanted to read were pornographic books. And his carving—he's getting better and better at carving but it looks like he's more interested in architecture than sculpture.*

—

After seeing the church of Santa Maria delle Grazie—and Leonardo da Vinci's 'Last Supper' in the adjoining convent—Francesco launched into a study of Leonardo's life. He learned Leonardo had written something called 'Architectural Sketchbooks,' and asked his mentor if he had a copy.

"Leonardo's writings I won't let out of my studio," Biffi said to Francesco, "they are among my most precious possessions. But, I have not objection if you want to remain in the workshop and study them at night."

Young Borromini read Leonardo's writings every night, often remaining in the studio for twenty-four hours at a time. When he found the drawing by Leonardo of the 'Vitruvian Man' in Leonardo's writings, he was intrigued. "Who was this Vitruvius person?" Francesco asked his mentor.

"Perhaps the most important man in the history of architecture—not as an architect, but as a writer. His major writing is called 'De Architectura libri decem,' which I understand means, in Latin, 'Ten Books of Architecture.' The treatise is considered a masterpiece by all learned men, and is the only complete treatise on architecture to survive from Roman times. Who was this Vitruvius person? Even the great Michelangelo, was influenced by Vitruvius."

Francesco begged Biffi to loan him a copy of 'De Architectura.' "I promise I will handle it gently."

"I only wish I had a copy," Biffi said. "Leonardo's writings were much more helpful in my work, so I spent my hard-earned money on them. Vitruvius's ten books on architecture, on the other hand, cost more than I can afford—plus they are mainly oriented to architects and engineers, not sculptors."

Francesco turned and sulked off, but his mentor called him back.

"Besides," Biffi said, "Vitruvius lived about fifteen hundred years ago and wrote in Latin, which, I'm embarrassed to say, I am unable to read."

Francesco ran to the nearest bookstore and purchased a used dictionary on the Latin language.

He studied the book every night and into the early morning. The project was so difficult, the frustrated and depressed young scholar would absolutely, positively abandon his near insurmountable project every night.

The next night, however, the highly motivated and determined young man would return to the task of teaching himself Latin.

As soon as he felt comfortable with the new language, young Borromini approached Biffi about the Vitruvius treatise.

"Sorry, Francesco," his mentor said, "I've checked with every architect and bookstore in Milan, and no one has a copy. Actually, I've tracked down a copy—the Vatican in Rome has one—but that's not much help, is it?"

Young Borromini got a glint in his eye, but his demeanor quickly turned sour. Biffi missed the glint, but caught the mood.

"I understand your disappointment," he said, "but I do have some good news. I know where to get you a copy of Leone Battista Alberti's 'Ten Books on Architecture'."

"Why should I care about somebody named Leone Battista Alberti," the dejected youngster said. "I never heard of him."

"Well, then, I guess you aren't interested to know that Alberti was a famous architect and writer who lived about 200 years ago and was directly inspired by Vitruvius. Or, that Alberti is the man from whom Leonardo learned about the mathematical principals of architecture. And, that Alberti believed—and wrote—that architecture is governed by mathematical laws and proportions. Just like you suspected."

"Where did you say I could find Mister Alberti's book," a beaming Borromini said to his mentor,

---

Borromini walked home from the studio deep in thought. *Rome. I've got to get to Rome to see those Vitruvius books, but that will take money. How can I raise money? Let me think. Hmmmmm.*

Chapter XI

Beyond Michelangelo

Twenty-year-old Francesco Borromini felt good. His ride, from Milan to Bissone, and his break-in to his father's architectural office, both under cover of darkness, had gone well.

Francesco laughed to himself as he fingered the most promising overdue notice in the pile. *Who would have thought that my prize would be sitting on father's desk in plain sight? And to think I was afraid I wouldn't be able to find the box containing his account's receivable—how stupid of me.*

Borromini picked up a pen and paper and scribbled a hasty note, which he placed on his father's drawing board.

> "Dear Parents. I had to go somewhere. Sorry to miss our annual get together on my birthday. Your Son, Francesco."

The note fell to the ground off the slanted board, but Borromini didn't bother to pick it up. He was in a hurry.

—

Borromini sat on his horse, watching the sun as it rose over a large construction site in the nearby town of Lugano. The air was freezing cold, but the energized young man felt comfortable in only a cotton blouse, with a scarf tied around his neck.

As Francesco waited, he thought about his mentor, Gian Andrea Biffi. *I liked the man and not even a goodbye—I couldn't risk it. Oh well, I got to look forward, not backward.*

Borromini smiled when he saw a well-dressed gentleman arrive in a fancy carriage, drawn by two horses. *Just as I figured—Mister Maroni is personally checking on his workers first thing every morning. Now don't lose your temper, Francesco. That's the main thing for you to not do.*

The youth rode up to the carriage, and spoke to his mark before he could alight. "Mister Maroni, my name is Francesco and I believe you got something that belongs to my father, Giovanni Castelli. I'm here to collect it for him."

"Who are you," the startled businessman shouted, causing the horses to rear up and the driver to draw his pistol. "Who are you . . . What do you want? Leave immediately, or I'll go to the authorities."

The driver cocked his gun.

"Perfect, you can save me the trouble," Francesco said, smiling broadly. "The police are always interested in people who don't pay bills—that were due and payable one year ago. And tell your driver to put that gun away or my friends hiding in the bushes will take care of both of you."

The Very Important Man looked from his tormentor to the nearby bushes and back again. *I don't see anyone in the bushes, but who can take that chance? Besides this boy looks strong and mean and determined. And public discussion of my finances is the last thing I need.* He waved his driver off. *I should at least try to avoid this debt one more time—it's the principle of the thing.*

"How do I know you are Castelli's son," he asked, in a slightly less challenging tone.

"Here. This could interest you," Borromini said as he handed the flustered debtor the purloined invoice for architectural services rendered.

—

Francesco suppressed a smirk as Maroni paid him the full amount and shook his hand.

Borromini rode off, waving to his non-existent friends to join him.

"Give your father my best regards, Francesco," Maroni called out. He walked to the field office mumbling to himself. *I should know by now that it's not unusual for people to send their servants, or sons, to collect monies due them. It is, after all, a dignified way to handle the situation.*

Chapter XII

Borromini rode south non-stop, pushing his horse to his limit.

When he reached Bologna, Francesco finally felt safe enough to stop for the night. He was reluctant to spend the money, but his mentor Biffi had once mentioned that Bologna probably had the best food in Italy, and therefore the world. Francesco ordered spaghetti for supper. When it was served, the pasta overflowed the bowl. It was covered with a thick tomato sauce that was fortified with a copious amount of meat. The waiter sprinkled a cheese all over the pasta. "It's called Parmesan, and it's produced in a nearby town," he said.

Although he was a skimpy eater, Borromini devoured his dish of pasta, skipped the meat course, and ordered a second bowl of spaghetti. "Lots of that cheese," he said to the waiter. *I can't believe how much better this pasta is than our rice.*

Francesco went to his room and fell into a deep, luxurious sleep—his first in a week.

—

Florence was a revelation to Borromini. There were palaces everywhere. And churches. And sculpture. When Francesco saw Michelangelo's massive statute of David in the Piazza della Signoria, he understood why his mentor was always praising Michelangelo.

Captivated, Francesco sought out every work of the master in Florence. The discovery of Michelangelo's tomb in the immense Franciscan church of Santa Croce was the culmination of Borromini's search. The youth was overcome with emotion. *He's in there? I want to lie next to my hero.* Francesco climbed onto Michelangelo's tomb.

It took every one of the eight friars visiting from Pisa to ply Francesco off the monument.

—

Borromini spent considerable time in Florence's skyline-shattering Cathedral, also known as the Duomo. Day after day, Francesco lay on the floor of the church and studied the massive copula towering over him. A local monk, who had seen this kind of passionate, intense reaction many times, befriended Borromini.

Beyond Michelangelo

"I thought Milan's Duomo, where I worked a lot, was really a good job," Francesco said to the Holy Man, "but this job's even better."

The monk laughed. "Every builder and architect in Tuscany tried to develop a workable design for the dome and receive the commission," he explained. "They tried for over ten years, if you can believe it, but they all failed. Brunelleschi, however, was smart. Before he submitted his scheme, he went to Rome and studied classical building techniques and architecture. I believe that is why his plan was selected and I believe that is why his plan was successful."

———

"I'm going to Rome, just like that Brunelleschi did," Francesco said.

"That's nice," the cleric replied. "Are you an architect?"

"Not yet, but I'm gonna be. I plan to be better than Brunelleschi. I plan to be like Michelangelo."

The monk made the Sign of the Cross. *Another one.* "Good luck, and go in peace, my son. May all your dreams come true."

"My mentor in Milan said I should dream no little dreams. He said they stir the imagination of nobody. So maybe I can do more better. Maybe I can go someplace . . . maybe I can go . . . beyond Michelangelo."

The monk smiled and walked away. Borromini was studying the cupola so intently he didn't notice.

Chapter XIII

At Monterotondo, Borromini left the Via Salaria and joined the Via Flaminia. He followed the ancient route until he reached the northern entrance of Rome, the Porta del Popolo.

After waiting in line for what seemed like forever, Francesco showed the papal guards the papers he had taken, and altered, from his father. The guards huddled. They passed the documents back and forth, eyeing Francesco all the time. They didn't like what they saw. The young man's clothes were tattered and filthy, and his few possessions were in a roll tied to his saddle, next to a musket and sword. Yes, he definitely looked like a brigand.

"What is the matter with you people," Borromini said. "I been waiting all day."

"Your business? Why are you coming to Rome?"

"If you must know, I have ta joining my cousin Leone Garovo. I'm a important decorative sculptor."

The guards looked questioningly at each other, raised their eyebrows and shrugged. "We've never heard of this Garovo. You'll have to come with us for further questioning."

Borromini straightened in saddle. Emboldened by his recent success with The Big Lie in Lugano, he tried the same tactic. "If you touch me, my uncle will have your jobs."

The guards starred at the ragamuffin, eyed each other and nodded; they decided to teach this bandit a real lesson. They started to pull Francesco off his horse, but Borromini hung on and shouted at the top of his voice, "My uncle's name is Carlo Maderno and he's the Pope's advisor."

The guards stopped in their tracks. Carefully, they released their prey. They exchanged furtive glances. Finally the senior of the two spoke, his voice now carefully guarded. "You don't mean Carlo Maderno, the Architect of Saint Peter's?"

Borromini merely smirked as he smoothed his cape.

The nervous guard continued. "The most important architect in Rome—that Carlo Maderno?" Borromini broke into a broad smile, he knew he had won.

The flustered sentinels exchanged furtive glances. "We must go—we're already late for the changing of the guard. God speed, and enjoy your time in Rome."

—

Borromini rode slowly through the Piazza del Popolo and came to a halt at the gigantic obelisk in its center. *I've never seen anything like this. I wonder what it is.*

A priest stopped and talked to the wide-eyed Francesco. "Isn't it beautiful?" he said. "By the way you look at the obelisk, I can tell you just arrived in Rome so allow me to explain. This obelisk is a 3,000 year-old pagan symbol—Emperor Augustus had it brought to Rome after he defeated Egypt. Our beloved Pope, Sixtus V, had it placed here in the Piazza del Popolo a few years ago, and, of course, had it consecrated. It is beautiful, isn't it?"

"Beautiful? It's not only beautiful," Francesco replied, "It's interesting. The obelisk is so straight, and reaches so high, it's like a signpost to heaven."

The priest kissed Borromini's hand. "You must be a very religious man—or a poet. We need more of your kind in Rome. Welcome to our Eternal City."

Francesco beamed. *Rome looks like a world apart from Milan. Maybe I found a home.*

Chapter XIV

The Bernini's first morning in Rome was clear and crisp, and the air was filled with the scent of orange blossoms and jasmine. Pietro arose at dawn and went to awaken GianLorenzo, only to find an empty bed. In Naples he knew exactly where to find his son under these circumstances, but in Rome?

On a hunch, Pietro crossed the road and walked along the side of Santa Maria Maggiore.

When he reached the square in front of the church, he found chaos. Clergy and nuns in colorful vestments were everywhere. Several Cardinals, with their entourages, strolled by. Costumed altar boys kicked a ball around the piazza. *Is every single person in this city associated with the Church?*

Pietro plunged into the crowd, elbowing his way past several obnoxious beggars. Sure enough, GianLorenzo was there, squatting in the center of the square, sketching the church. Unobserved by the little boy, Pietro sat on the pavement next to his son. *How can he concentrate in the middle of this bedlam?*

GianLorenzo finished a sketch and looked around for another sheet. When he saw his father, he jumped on him—hugging him, and kissing him on both cheeks. Twice.

"What are you doing here," the youth asked. Pietro lifted the child onto his broad shoulders.

"I thought you'd like to go into the church to see where I'll be working—and to see that gold leaf."

GianLorenzo and his father walked down the stairs of Santa Maria Maggiore. The little boy could barely contain his enthusiasm. "Those mosaics were the best—and I couldn't take my eyes off that floor."

He ran ahead to get a drink from the fountain in the square. Out of nowhere, a beggar appeared and accosted GianLorenzo: He waved his arm stumps in the child's face, demanding money. The little boy stood his ground and waved his arms even more wildly in the beggar's face. The confused tramp ran away, screaming.

Pietro ran up and took his son in his arms. "It's okay. I'm here," he said, trying to sound calm.

"Don't worry, father, he didn't scare me," GianLorenzo said. The hyped-up child bounced up and down on his toes, anxious for another encounter. "Why are there so many beggars in this square?"

"Good question, son. Probably because when people leave this awesome church, they feel charitable."

GianLorenzo turned the explanation over in his mind. "If that's the case, why are the beggars so pushy?"

Pietro studied his handsome, but skinny, little son. *He's fearless—that must come from his mother's Neapolitan blood. And how he can be this logical at his tender age—I take credit for that.* "My guess is that they don't want to leave anything to chance."

"What does that mean?"

Pietro smiled, always relishing the chance to teach his son a valuable life-lesson.

"You see, GianLorenzo, there are certain times—certain situations—when a little pressure in the right place is necessary, perhaps even critical."

Chapter XV

On the way to the Chiesa Nuova, Pietro explained that the Oratorians owned the church, and Filippo Neri founded the Oratorian Order.

"Neri was a wonderful, warm and patient man," Pietro said to his son. "I wish he were still alive so that we could meet him. Do you know the word 'reformer?' That's Neri."

"What makes him so special," the child asked.

"Fair question," Pietro replied. He thought for a minute. "Here's an example. See those little boys over there, searching through the garbage? They're called urchins. Well, Filippo Neri was the only one who cared for them when he was alive. Not only that, he had lots of followers who were of noble birth. One time, he had them parade down the Corso wearing rags and foxes tails. In other words, Neri was like a birddog, pointing out to the world that the Church still believed in, and practiced, the basic values of Christianity—like charity and humility—which many claimed had been forgotten by the Church."

"Mother always makes me get cleaned up and dress nice when I leave the house—she'd kill me if I ever went outside in rags," the child said. GianLorenzo saw the confused look on his father's face. "But that's different, isn't it?"

The pair tied their horses in front of the Chiesa Nuova.

"I love the construction going on all over Rome," Pietro said, pointing to the façade of the church. "It's good for all us artists. By the way, Filippo Neri also had his noble-followers help build this church. Let's go in, I want you to meet someone."

GianLorenzo and his father walked the length of the church. Pietro's friend, who had been painting, made his way down the scaffolding.

"This man is a remarkable artist," Pietro whispered to his son, "even though he's Flemish, not Italian. His use of color will remind you of those great Venetian painters I've told you about. Tintoretto, and especially Titian."

The little boy was confused. "It he's not Italian, why does he use Italian colors?"

Pietro couldn't help laughing. *I hope the boy doesn't think I'm laughing at him, but that is an interesting way to say it.* "Because," he said, "the man moved to Italy about seven years ago and is studying how we do things. He told me he wanted, 'to study at close quarters the works of the ancient and modern masters.' So, this artist 'uses Italian colors' because everyone is influenced by what he studies."

The child thought about that for quite a while. "I'm glad we moved to Rome, father."

—

"What a pleasant surprise," the artist said as he embraced Pietro. "And who is this handsome lad? It must be your son. There's no denying him—he looks exactly like you."

"Peter Paul Rubens, meet my son, GianLorenzo Bernini. Son, meet Peter Paul Rubens, one of the best painters working today."

As the child shook Ruben's outstretched hand, he studied the man. *I can see he's not Italian—his nose is pointy, his hair is reddish and curly, and his mustache and beard look different. But he has piercing eyes, like fathers. I don't care that he's not Italian; I'm meeting a real, honest-to-goodness artist. That's what I care about.*

Rubens picked the little boy up and spun him around three or four times. "Goodness, son, you're light as a feather. Doesn't this man feed you?"

"Yes sir. My father does everything for me—he's the best father in the whole world. It's just that I don't like to take time to eat, so I mostly nibble. I love fruit."

The little tyke fascinated the thirty-year-old-artist. "Dare I ask what it is that keeps you so busy young man?"

GianLorenzo peeked at his father to see if he should respond; his father's discreet nod signaled yes.

"I draw a lot, sir. And I study. I love to study and learn things. In fact, I see you're only starting here. Can I come back to see how you're doing?"

Pietro gave his son a stern look for his awkward choice of words, but Rubens laughed heartily.

"You sound like my patrons," he said. "Of course you can come back. Come see me anytime. In fact, why don't you come at dinnertime someday—we'll 'waste some time' and dine together. Now, Pietro, how goes the business of the Academia di San Luca?"

"Fine, Peter, although I haven't had much time to devote to my duties since being elected President. Actually, not so fine. Keeping a professional association of artists interested is practically a full-time job. You can help, though."

"Name it."

"Come to our next meeting and speak. Tell us about your experiences in Italy and describe the conditions you had to meet in order to receive this commission from the Oratorians."

Rubens flashed a half-smile. "What have you heard?"

"It's common knowledge that Cardinal Jacopo Serra agreed to pay the cost of painting the altarpiece if they hired you."

Good grief, this is a small town. "And the conditions the Oratorians imposed," Rubens asked. "What do you know of them?"

"That's what I want you to share with the others. How you had to paint exactly what they told you, and so on. Tell the group, in detail, the Order's endless conditions. The fact that they made you contribute to the cost, you can leave that part out of your talk."

"Good grief, this is a small town," Rubens said in a measured voice.

GianLorenzo had been quietly listening to the conversation—just like his mother told him to act when old people talked to each other—but he couldn't restrain himself any longer.

"Why would you pay part of the cost, Mister Rubens? I thought the patron was supposed to pay the artist? Isn't that what you told me, father?"

Rubens patted GianLorenzo on the top of his head. "I like the way you think, young man. Truthfully, there was no risk—I knew my paintings would please the patrons. It all comes down to confidence. If you believe in yourself, and have the talent to back up your confidence, you can accomplish anything."

"GianLorenzo," Pietro said, "pay attention when this man talks—he is wise beyond his years."

"Allow me to mention the other side of the coin," Rubens said, glancing around the church to insure no one was within earshot. "I feel very sorry for any artist who has low self-esteem and works for these Oratorians. They will eat him alive."

Chapter XVI

"So, how do you like this side of the river," Pietro asked his son. "This area is called Trastevere, which means across the Tiber." GianLorenzo found himself in a maze of twisting, turning, narrow streets and alleys. Laundry hung from most of the old brick and stone buildings, and there seemed to be boisterous people everywhere. He loved it.

"I thought the streets of central Naples and Rome were great," the child said, "but this . . . this . . . is wonderful. Why can't we live around here?"

"First of all," Pietro said, "I'd be worried about your mother and sisters in this neighborhood. Besides, I want to be close to the church I'll be working in."

As the youth and his father rode through Trastevere, GianLorenzo became more and more confused. "This area looks fine to me," he said. "I really like it."

Pietro gave his son a look of understanding. "In the morning, yes. But this is the toughest part of Rome. Laborers and workingmen live here, and it can get rough at night. You can see for yourself there's a tavern on most every block, usually more than one. Truthfully, son, Trastevere has almost nothing in common with the Rome you know—it's like the waterfront area of the toughest port city in Italy. Like Genoa, maybe."

"Genoa has to be good. I remember you said that's where Cristoforo Colombo lived when he was young. He was a brave man, wasn't he father?"

Pietro thought about the incidents with the robber and the beggar and gave his son a hug so powerful it even surprised GianLorenzo.

—

The pair arrived in a large piazza, which was almost a perfect square. They dismounted.

"There it is son, Santa Maria in Trastevere, probably the first official Christian Church in Rome. It was founded prior to Christianity's acceptance, when it was still an outlaw, minority cult, way back in the third century. It's famous for its mosaics."

GianLorenzo raced across the piazza to get a better look at the dramatic mosaics, which extended across the top of the outside of the church.

"Stunning, aren't they," Pietro said when the youngster returned. "Nobody is certain who laid them. Or when they were laid."

The child was overwhelmed. "I'm trying, I really am, but I can't decide which mosaics are more magnificent, these or the ones inside Santa Maria Maggiore."

Pietro nodded, pleased at his son's perspicacity. "You don't have to decide, son. Enjoy each for what it contributes to the whole. Remember I told you that for art to have meaning and make an impact, every element—whether it's painting, sculpture, or even architecture—must work together. Otherwise, you merely have a bunch of pretty things."

"I think I understand," GianLorenzo said. The child paused, and when he continued, he spoke deliberately. "You are saying that even though the mosaics are beautiful on their own, unless they make the church more beautiful, then they are not so beautiful."

The euphoric Pietro was so moved, two tears trickled down his face. He wiped them away before his son could see them.

Chapter XVII

"This beautiful square is called Campo de' Fiore, because it's a flower market," Pietro said. GianLorenzo looked around the teeming piazza. There were stalls everywhere, covered with umbrellas. Elderly women, selling fruits and nuts but mostly flowers, staffed them all. The child had never seen such a profusion of bright and contrasting colors. He immediately sat down on a curb and started to sketch the exciting scene.

Pietro decided his son was mature enough to learn a serious lesson. "You'd never guess that sometimes the Church uses this piazza to punish its enemies. I assure you, son, that's a scene you wouldn't want to draw."

"Punish? What does that mean?" Reluctantly, the confused child laid his crayons down.

"It means that a few years ago, Giordano Bruno, a Dominican monk and a brilliant philosopher, was burned at the stake while he was alive. Right over there, where the fresh fish stand is."

GianLorenzo was repulsed and rattled, in equal parts. "Burned dead? The Church did that? Why? Why would the Church burn somebody to death? I can't believe it."

"What happened was, the Board of Inquisition—that's a tribunal established by the Pope to seek out and punish people who disagree with him—ruled that Bruno was guilty of heresy. Heresy is when somebody says something that is different from what the Church thinks you should say. That's one of the reasons your nonno hates the Church."

"What did Mister Bruno say that made them mad enough to burn him alive?"

Pietro plowed on, like a priest delivering a favorite sermon to a responsive audience. "You must understand son, things are changing. New lands have been discovered. Men are finding out things about our bodies and minds—about our whole wide world—that are different from what people used to think. In any event, Bruno was an outspoken man who said out loud what he believed in his heart . . ."

"But what did Mister Bruno say?" the child asked, reluctantly interrupting. He was on the verge of tears.

"What Bruno said was, our earth revolves around the sun. Unfortunately for him, however, the Church says our earth is the center of the universe. For that belief, the Inquisition condemned the monk to death. The tragedy is he was only fifty-two years old and still had a lot to offer—he was a writer and intellectual. The world lost a fine man."

"How can the Pope and Church do that? Is it legal?"

"GianLorenzo, in Rome—actually, in all of the Papal States—whatever the Pope and the Church *say* is legal, *is* legal. Do you understand that? What does that tell you?"

Without missing a beat, the child cried out, "I hope no Pope ever gets mad at me."

Chapter XVIII

Pietro led his son to the Moses Fountain, located near the ruins of the Baths of Diocletian.

"This is the terminal," Pietro said, "of the Aqua Felice aqueduct. It's named for the great Pope Sixtus V, who's real name was Felice Peretti, because he brought fresh water to this area for the first time. What do you think? Of the statute in the center, I mean?"

GianLorenzo studied the ground in front of him and shifted from foot to foot. *Why did father bring me here? I'd like to go home.*

"Well?" his father said.

"I like the three arches a lot," the child said, desperately searching for a way out. "They have symmetry. I like that word you taught me. Symmetry."

Pietro knew exactly what his little boy was up to and enjoyed watching his mind work.

"I'm glad that your vocabulary is improving, GianLorenzo, but I'm asking you about that over life-size statute of Moses. Be honest now."

The child hesitated: He hated to hurt his father, whom he assumed loved the statute. *But mother would kill me if I disobeyed father.*

"I think it's really ugly," GianLorenzo said, resigned to a bad day. "It looks like somebody was mad when they carved it. The worse thing is—the proportions are all wrong. How can that happen? Was the sculptor man copying something? You know the bell-towers at Santa Maria Maggiore and Santa Maria in Trastevere? I think they are in proportion. This isn't."

Pietro grabbed his son, who pulled back. But to the little boy's surprise, his father hugged him and kissed him on both cheeks.

"What's going on, father?"

"Son, I'm so proud of you. Not only were you honest, you were right. The statute is pathetic. I showed it to you because one can also learn from bad art."

The relieved child showered his father with kisses. "You are the best father."

"Now, son, what if someone—say a Pope, or anyone—asked you to comment on a rival's work. Can you think of something you might say that was honest, but didn't get everyone upset?"

GianLorenzo thought for a moment. "I'd look at the work for a long, long time—pretending to be studying it. Then I'd say something like, 'Great isn't the word'."

Chapter XIX

One night when GianLorenzo went to the supper table, he noticed that his sisters were dressed prettier than usual. *What's going on? Mother and father look like they're going to church.*

When the meal was over, Pietro brought a triple-tiered cream-filled cake from the kitchen topped with white candles and placed it in front of the boy. "Your mother gave me the honor of presenting her masterpiece," Pietro said. He lit the candles.

GianLorenzo broke into a smile that lit his face as bright as the cake. *And I thought they forgot my birthday.* "But I'm only ten years old," he said, smiling ear to ear. "Why are there eleven candles?"

"The extra candle is for good luck," Angelica said, "and for once in your life, I want you to eat a sweet. I'm serious. If you don't eat a piece of cake, it could be bad luck. Now blow out the candles."

One puff, and the room went dark. Following the applause and the family's singing of Happy Birthday, the little boy held out his plate.

"I'd better eat two pieces," he said, "just to be safe."

—

Later that night, GianLorenzo and his father had their regular evening chat. The youth decided this was a perfect time to discuss his recurring dream.

"Father, I know that I still have a lot to learn. I'll never stop learning. You taught me that. But, I have something I can't get out of my head. More than anything . . . at this point in my life . . . I want to create something of my own. After all, I'm ten years old now. Am I being ungrateful? I promise, I won't stop learning but I want to see what I can do."

"Come down to the studio with me," Pietro laughed.

Arm in arm, the pair walked to the workshop. Once inside, they moved past the office, past the tool storage, past the showroom, past the casting area, past several benches used by stonecutters and stopped at the last bench in the rear of the studio.

Pietro retrieved a large object, which was wrapped in canvas, from under the workbench. He bowed as he presented the package to his son.

"Happy tenth birthday, GianLorenzo."

The child untied the thick string and ripped the covering off. He found himself face-to-face with . . . a face. "I know it's a death mask," the confused child said, "but who is this man. I've never met him. Why are you showing me this?"

"His name is Giovanni B. Santoni," Pietro said. "He was a Bishop who died about fifteen years ago."

Pietro patted a square piece of marble that was sitting on the bench. He was thrilled the surprise was going so well. "How long do you think it will take you to carve Santoni's portrait in this beautiful block of marble?"

GianLorenzo gasped. *What a dunce I am. I was so excited I didn't even notice the marble.* The youth caressed the stone—he felt like he was absorbing the marble into his body, like the cream his mother rubbed on his face before he went to bed at night. *It feels like marble, but it looks like those diamonds I see displayed in the Vatican.* He laid his wet cheek on the marble. He kissed it.

Then, to his father's amazement, and delight, GianLorenzo picked up the death mask and spoke directly to it.

"Mister Santoni," young Bernini said, "I love you—you are mine."

Pietro slipped out of the workshop unnoticed. He whistled a Neapolitan tune on his way to the bedroom.

Chapter XX

GianLorenzo stared at the death mask. *You may be dead Mister Santoni, but I must find your inner soul—just like father taught me.*

The little boy carefully placed his model on the bench and fondled the block of marble once again. *As for you, Mister Marble, I promise to treat you right. I'll be subtracting pieces from you, not adding lines like when I draw. But don't you worry; I know I have to be extra careful.*

GianLorenzo lit half-a-dozen fresh candles, nibbled on a hard pear, grabbed a hammer and one of the tiny chisels his father had made for him, steadied himself, and raised his right hand to strike the first blow on his first trip to heaven.

Young Bernini stopped abruptly and fell to his knees.

"Please God," the child said, praying out loud, "make it possible for me to make my phenomenal father happy—I hope you don't mind, but I really love that new word I learned."

GianLorenzo jumped back to his feet and raised his hammer once again. *This must be what mother feels like when she has a baby.*

—

Mario, the newest apprentice, arrived at Pietro's workshop at dawn, as he did every morning. His duties included opening the studio and preparing it for the others. When he saw GianLorenzo, he panicked. "What are you doing with that piece of good marble? You're supposed to practice on left over chips. Your father will kill you."

The apprentice grabbed the child's arm. GianLorenzo instinctively swung at him, opening an ugly gash in Mario's cheek with his chisel. Blood gushed from the wound.

"Let that be a lesson to you," young Bernini said. "Don't ever touch me when I'm working. Understand? Now clean that blood off of the floor."

—

'Why are these men all so quiet,' Pietro wondered when he arrived at his busy studio. "And you," he said to Mario, who was holding a kerchief to his face, "what happened to you?"

"Nothing," the young apprentice said. "GianLorenzo and I were fooling around and I fell and cut myself. It's nothing—just a little scratch."

"That may be, but I prefer that you go and have Angelica look after it," Pietro said, to everyone's relief.

Pietro noticed that GianLorenzo was the only one in the workshop working assiduously and ignoring the drama. He was certain there was more to the story than Mario was letting on, but decided not to pursue the matter. *I must remember, my role is to guide the child's God-Given enthusiasm without crushing it. As my Neapolitan wife says, 'Nothing great has ever been achieved without enthusiasm.'*

Chapter XXI

Beyond Michelangelo

"There's a child prodigy in our midst!!!!!"

The words flashed through Rome like a sudden hailstorm on a placid summer evening.

Tongues wagged all over town: "Is such a miracle possible? I doubt it." "A true child prodigy? Not likely." "It has been forever since we've had one—why now?" "A skinny little ten year old is a sculptor? Impossible." "He probably can't even lift the carving tools." "I hear he has wild hair and even wilder eyes."

Over night, Pietro's workshop became a beehive of activity. From miles around, every person of consequence—including men from the academies and guilds, clergy, collectors, patrons, nobility, and even jealous artists—rushed to the studio on the Esquiline Hill to see if the rumor was true.

They arrived alone, and skeptical, but after they saw G. B Santoni—looking life-like with hollowed-out pupils and bones indicated under his skin, straining to escape from his block of marble—the skeptics left believers.

Actually, they became more than believers; they became admirers, and then advocates.

One by one they returned with their friends, sweethearts, wives, and even mistresses to show-off their find. The bright, polite little boy—with the wild hair and wild eyes—became the talk of the town and everybody's darling.

The Romans felt especially good. "An honest-to-goodness child prodigy, right in our own hometown." "I've never seen such talent anywhere—not at his age." "I don't care where he was born, the child is a Roman now." And the ultimate compliment: "Nothing like this has happened since that Michelangelo person was discovered in Florence."

Chapter XXII

"I have exciting news, GianLorenzo," Pietro said. "My friend, the great Annibale Carracci, is coming tomorrow to see your portrait of Santoni. Do you know who he is?"

The child was crushed but tried, in vain, to hide his feelings. "Father, don't you know how much time I've spent studying Mister Carracci's frescoes in the Villa Farnese? I am familiar with every figure he painted, every inch." *A real artist is coming to see my very own project. Now we're getting somewhere.*

The honored guest knocked on the front door. "Stay out of sight," Pietro said to his son. "I don't want Annibale to feel obligated to say nice things. I want his honest opinion."

GianLorenzo hid in a closet in the studio. *It seems like only yesterday I was spying on father and nonno in Naples—now here I am hiding at father's request from one of the world's greatest painters who has come to see my work. I think that's what father told me was called irony.*

From his vantage point, the youngster studied the artist who was studying the bust of Santoni. *Mister Carracci's squarish face is interesting. I've never seen short-cropped hair going down the side of a face like that, but the hair does help hide his big ears. I like his smile the best—it tells me Mister Carracci is a nice man, although I wonder why he looks so tired. He looks like a tree that has been battered by wind and is about to fall over.*

It was difficult for GianLorenzo to hear what the artist was saying, but then Carracci raised his voice. "Know what I see, Pietro? I see talent. Not just talent, but remarkable talent. Talent at the ripe age of ten years that most artists hope to attain in old age."

The eavesdropping child couldn't contain himself—he burst into the room and jumped into Annibale Carracci's arms. He wrapped his arms and legs around the famous artist, knocking him down.

"GianLorenzo, behave yourself," the mortified Pietro screamed.

The great man untangled himself from the child and gave him a pat on the head.

"No, Pietro my friend, you are wrong. The boy is definitely not misbehaving; he's displaying something essential to any great artist—emotion. Don't bottle it."

—

On the way out of the studio, Carracci put his right arm around the elder Bernini and held GianLorenzo's hand with his left one. "Tell me, Pietro, as old friends, did you work on the portrait?"

"If you're asking if I helped, of course I did," Pietro said. "Advice, mostly. Other than that, I touched up the hair and beard, but that's it. GianLorenzo designed and carved the bust himself."

"Has Scipione seen the piece?"

"No," Pietro replied. "Not yet. Good point. I'll look after it immediately."

Annibale Carracci looked down at the little boy clutching his hand.

"One more thing, Pietro my friend. With all due respect, I think you should cease touching up your son's work. Let me put it this way—with all due respect, in my opinion GianLorenzo doesn't need your help in carving." *I hope Pietro doesn't mind but this is the most remarkable child I've ever seen.*

Chapter XXIII

"Who is this Scipione man?" GianLorenzo asked his father as soon as Annibale Carracci left.

Pietro was happy to have the chance to tell his son about Cardinal Borghese. "He's the second most important man in Rome—after the Pope, of course."

"What makes him so important?"

"Scipione Borghese is Pope Paul V's favorite nephew. To give you an idea of the esteem in which the Pope holds him, he made Scipione a Cardinal just two months after he was crowned Pope. Not only that, the pontiff even gave Scipione his last name—Scipione Caffarelli became Scipione Borghese. Furthermore, the Cardinal serves as Secretary of State, which means that he's in charge of all matters that affect the Papal States."

"He's rich, isn't he?" GianLorenzo said. "I remember hearing that people around the Pope were given lots of money and things."

"You heard right, son. Cardinal Borghese's yearly income is in excess of 100,000 scudi, which enables him to live lavishly, as well as be a great patron of the arts. He's a robust, heavy-set man, with a round, chubby face. I tell you that because his soft features tell you about his life style—the Cardinal loves to party and have a good time."

"He sounds like a big teddy bear to me," the child said, "like the one mother gave me when I was small."

Pietro smiled. *This child never ceases to amaze me.* "Unfortunately," he continued, "when art is involved, the Cardinal's likeable and friendly traits disappear. He is such a passionate collector, when he wants a certain piece nothing stands in his way. Nothing. I'll give you an example. You've heard of Cavalier d'Arpino, I know. Many—not me, but many—consider him to be one of the most important artists painting today. Not long ago, even though Arpino is one of his favored artists, Scipione had the Cavalier arrested on trumped-up weapons charges and sequestered his assets. That means that even though the charges were not true, all of the paintings in the artist's collection—and they were considerable—were commandeered by Cardinal Borghese. Why did he do this? Simple. The Cardinal had his eye on Arpino's substantial Caravaggio collection. The result? All of Arpino's Caravaggio paintings are now the property of Cardinal Scipione Borghese."

The child thought about this for a long time. "I love the way Caravaggio uses light—he's one of my favorites. Even though he does bad things, are we still going to go to see this Cardinal Scipione Borghese?"

"GianLorenzo, in addition to being the Pope's Cardinal/Nephew, Cardinal Scipione Borghese is the most important patron of the arts in Italy, and maybe in the world. Now, can you think of anyone you'd rather show your work to?"

The youngster got a gleam in his eyes. "It's easy to understand when you put it that way father."

"Besides," Pietro said, being careful not to sound preachy "everybody does bad things sometime in his life. I'm sure someday you will too, my little angel."

Chapter XXIV

"This must be the genius the entire city is gossiping about," Cardinal Scipione Borghese said as soon as Pietro and GianLorenzo Bernini were led into his spacious office in the Quirinal Palace. "And I finally get to see the portrait of Bishop Santoni. I knew him well when he was majordomo to Pope Sixtus V."

Pietro glanced nervously at his son, but GianLorenzo appeared unmoved—or did not understand—the Cardinal's semi-veiled threat.

Cardinal Borghese was a big, earthy man with a thick chest and waistline to match. His face was large and round and almost always full of smiles. Although he was squat in appearance, he moved with authority and commanded respect.

When Scipione lifted the cloth from the portrait bust he was stunned and visibly flustered, a condition which occurred in this connoisseur most infrequently. "Pietro," the Cardinal stammered, "this is extraordinary. We must take this young man to my uncle at once."

The Cardinal led the pair through the richly decorated halls of the palace to a sumptuous salon. Beautiful music greeted the group. "It's a new piece by Monteverdi, a madrigal, I believe," Scipione said. "We'll wait here until the concert is over."

GianLorenzo surveyed the room—the elaborate decor seemed to him out of proportion to the delicate pilasters and casework. His view of the Pope was unhindered. *He is a handsome man. I like his neat mustache and small triangular beard.*

An aide to Cardinal Borghese placed the Santoni bust to the side of the Pope, who immediately signaled the concert was over. GianLorenzo noticed that nobody in the audience moved as the ensemble quietly departed.

Scipione and his guests wove their way past the seated Cardinals to join the pontiff at the front of the room. Paul V stared at the portrait without saying a word.

Pietro wasn't certain where he should look, so he looked at his son. *That Angelica—she has dressed GianLorenzo so well, he looks like a little angel in his white shirt with broad scalloped-lace collar, calf-length breeches, and black jacket with buttons all the way down the front. She is amazing—the child not only looks great, she dressed him perfectly for this occasion. And what an occasion. A personal audience with the Pope. The ultimate honor for any artist, and it's happening to my son at ten years of age. How can such a little boy possibly understand the significance of this moment?*

—

Paul V finished studying the marble portrait of Bishop Santoni and sat down with a sigh. The entourage searched the pontiff's face, eager to learn his opinion of the piece.

"Pietro, how nice to see you," the Pope said, shattering the silence. "I've known of your talent for some time, of course, but I can see there is another talented sculptor in the Bernini family."

"Your Holiness," Pietro said, "may I present my son, GianLorenzo."

The pontiff's piercing eyes locked on the child, who recoiled slightly; but Pietro discreetly pushed the youth forward. GianLorenzo approached the Pope, knelt and kissed his ring, as instructed—and rehearsed—by his mother.

"GianLorenzo, is it," the Pope said. "But why do you have two first names? That's a big name for such a little boy."

"Having two first names is the result of being preceded by six sisters," the child said.

Pietro looked for a hole to crawl into. The entourage stared at the Pope. The pontiff studied the little boy for some time, and then burst out laughing. The Cardinals, naturally, followed suit.

"Is that the only reason," the amused pontiff asked.

"No sir. I am called Gian for my great-grandfather, whose name was Giovanni, and I am called Lorenzo for my nonno. Saint Lawrence is my namesake."

"Well son," the Pope said, obviously enjoying himself, "with two first names, you must be twice as talented as anyone your age, which I understand is ten."

"That could be," young Bernini replied, "or, I could be as talented as anyone who is twenty years old."

Paul V, clearly enthralled with the child, slapped his knee and laughed so hard he almost fell out of his elevated, highly decorated chair. The Cardinals joined in the merriment and Pietro almost relaxed. GianLorenzo wasn't sure why everyone was laughing, but he was enjoying his talk with the Pope. *I can't wait to tell mother.*

"Now," the pontiff said, "I must be serious for a minute. I have heard of your talent from various sources in addition to my nephew, and now I have seen the portrait bust of Bishop Santoni. The bust is outstanding, but frankly, it is difficult for me to believe that anyone could have the talent they say you have at ten years of age. Are you certain you carved the Bishop's bust?"

GianLorenzo remained silent, as he was instructed to do when he wasn't sure what to say. *Was that a compliment?*

The Pope studied the little boy standing before him, straight as an arrow, for a full five minutes. To Pietro, it seemed like five hours. The entourage was perplexed, but remained silent.

Finally, the pontiff decided that the way to verify the rampant rumors that the child hadn't carved the Santoni portrait was to force the issue. He spoke, his strong voice cracking the silence, like a church bell signaling the first mass on a crisp morning.

"Would you mind drawing something for me," the Pope asked, his tone more of a command than a request.

"Of course not," the child answered. "What will please you, Holy Father?" he quickly added, remembering his mother's instructions to relate whatever he said to the desires of the Pope.

The Pope's smile carried a look of surprise. "A head. A head will do nicely."

One of the pontiff's secretaries handed GianLorenzo a pen and paper. He was shown to a seat and immediately started to draw a head but stopped abruptly.

An audible gasp rang through the room—the Cardinals assumed that the child had either panicked or didn't really have the ability to draw. Pietro was concerned by his son's action, but remained still. All eyes were on the youngster.

GianLorenzo took a deep breath, and then spoke in a load, clear voice.

"What head does Your Holiness wish? A man or a woman? Young or old? With what expression? Sad or cheerful? Scornful or agreeable?"

Paul V was delighted. "In that case," he said, "you know how to do everything."

"I should," the ten-year old answered, "I've been drawing all my life."

Without waiting, the Cardinals laughed as hard as the Pope; they had never seen the ex-diplomat and jurist this animated. Scipione hadn't had this much fun since his last all-night party. Pietro was laughing and crying at the same time.

"In that case," the Pope said, "please sketch my namesake, Saint Paul."

Silence engulfed the salon. All eyes were on young Bernini, who was totally oblivious to the distinguished audience watching him draw. After a few bold strokes—in less than five minutes—GianLorenzo handed the drawing to the Pope. "I hope it pleases you, Holy Father."

Paul V studied the sketch. He was astonished by what he saw. *How could this young child create such a dramatic drawing in no time at all?*

"Look at this gentlemen," he said, passing the sketch to his aide. "You won't believe what this little boy has accomplished. This sketch is not only remarkable; it proves to me that this child prodigy did indeed carve the portrait of Bishop Santoni."

Ohs and ahs followed the paper as it moved from manicured hand to manicured hand.

"Maffeo," the Pope said to Cardinal Barberini, a member of the entourage, "I implore you, as a great devotee of the arts, not only to attend with every care to this child's studies, but with fire and enthusiasm. You are the guarantor of the brilliant result that is expected of him. Do you accept this challenge?"

"Gladly, Holy Father," Cardinal Barberini said. He concentrated on the child, who was now standing at attention, smiling. "In fact, based on what I observe here today, I predict it will be an absolute pleasure."

Pietro's knees buckled. *How can we be so lucky? Maffeo Barberini is the smartest man in Rome, he loves artists and scholars, and best of all, he is a close, personal friend.*

GianLorenzo shifted his attention from the Pope to Cardinal Barberini. *He has sleepy eyes and his brow is creased all the time. He has a melancholy look—love that word father taught me—but he looks like he's going to smile at any minute. I think I'm going to like this Cardinal Barberini.*

—

A smiling Pope Paul V rose—and the others immediately followed suit. The pontiff faced the group, holding his arms straight out, parallel to each other, palms inward. Benediction style. From the far-away look in the Pope's eyes—indeed, from his entire demeanor—the Cardinals felt the Holy Father was speaking not only to them, but also to the world.

With each word—which seemed to reverberate throughout the palace—the pontiff raised and lowered his arms for emphasis.

"I . . . believe . . . this . . . child . . . will . . . be . . . the . . . Michelangelo . . . of . . . his . . . age."

The room filled with spontaneous applause. Pietro watched in wonderment as the pontiff descended from his chair and approached his son.

"Put your hands together and hold them out, like this," the Pope said, cupping his hands in example. He then filled the little boy's hands with gold coins. "I present these to you as a token of my esteem. Spend them in good health."

To everyone's delight, except Pietro's, GianLorenzo solemnly counted the money—twelve gold coins. He gave them all to his embarrassed father.

"Father," the child said just loud enough for everyone to hear, "please give six coins to mother for the family, and save six for me."

—

For years afterward, everyone in attendance, including the Pope, reveled in recounting ten-year-old GianLorenzo Bernini's extraordinary audience with Paul V.

Chapter XXV

Beyond Michelangelo

Time flew, which totally frustrated young Bernini. So much to learn and accomplish, so little time. Most every day, the cultivated Cardinal Maffeo Barberini met with GianLorenzo and tutored him with the enthusiasm ordered by Pope Paul V on that historic day in 1605. No subject was overlooked.

Geography: "In Italy, there are eleven separate domains, of which the Papal States are the most important;"

Music: "Baltazarini di Belgioioso invented ballet as we know it, and the most notable composers working today are Cladio Monteverdi and Girolomo Frescobaldi. Monteverdi is perfecting a new art form, which is called opera, and Frescobaldi is the new organist at Saint Peter's;"

Explorers: Marco Polo, Giovanni Caboto (father and son) and Cristoforo Colombo;

Poets: Virgil, Ovid and Tasso;

Literature: Petrarch, Dante and Boccacio;

Science: Pliny the Elder, Leonardo and Galileo;

Art: Giotto, Titian and Raphael;

Philosophy: Politian and Julius Caesar Scaliger (father and son);

Politics: Pliny the Younger, Machiavelli and the Medici's;

Architecture: Brunelleschi, Vitruvius, Palladio and Bramante;

Sculptors: Ghiberti, Donatello and Michelangelo;

Language: Italian and Latin;

Physicians: Fallopius and Fabricius,

And, of course, Saint Thomas Aquinas and religion.

The study sessions each lasted at least a full half-day, always ending too soon for both tutor and pupil.

"GianLorenzo," Cardinal Barberini said one day, "I have absolutely never seen anyone quite like you. Why do you think you have so much energy?" He was truly curious.

"My diet of fruit," young Bernini said playfully. "Seriously? I think God put me on earth to do good things in His Honor, and I figure the way to make Him happy is to do as many things as I can, as well as I can, as often as I can. Sleeping interferes with that."

The Cardinal couldn't think of an appropriate response, so he changed the subject. "I understand you and your father are working on a series. A series of what?"

"Four small statutes," the youth replied. "Each figure represents one of the seasons. I designed the poses and cut the figures, and father carved the faces. It was fun working with father."

"GianLorenzo, I must tell you something else I find unique about you. I think you and your father have the most idyllic relationship I've ever seen."

"Idyllic?"

"Pleasing. It means you get along with each other. No jealously. Just love, and mutual respect. Believe me, it's a rare situation and something you should cherish."

"Isn't that normal," a perplexed GianLorenzo asked.

Cardinal Barberini shrugged. "Actually, sometimes I think the opposite is true. Here's an example. Remember when you studied Benvenuto Cellini? Of course you do. Well, he and his father fought constantly because Mister Cellini wanted his son to be a musician, not a goldsmith."

GianLorenzo thought this information over. "I'm happy Cellini became what he wanted to be. Excuse me now sir. I've just had an idea for the face of Saint Lawrence."

It was Cardinal Barberini's turn to be perplexed, which young Bernini observed.

"I'm talking about your commission, sir. So far, I'm satisfied with the fire, the pose and the body, but what I'm not satisfied with is the expression on the Saint's face. I'm showing pain, but I'm not sure I'm capturing his feeling at the moment of his martyrdom. I need to show the effect the fire had on the Saint's mind, and so far, I fear I'm not accomplishing that."

—

When young Bernini arrived at his father's workshop, it was deserted. The youth lit a candle and searched until he found what he was looking for—a brazier. He filled the brazier with coals, and when they became white hot, he quickly removed his britches, tunic and underwear—to be naked like Saint Lawrence was.

The youth then lay down on his workbench and strategically placed a mirror, so that he could see his face in it. Without any hesitation, GianLorenzo placed his naked thigh and leg against the blazing brazier. He held that position while he sketched his reactions to the searing heat—reactions he saw reflected in the mirror.

The smell of burning flesh went unnoticed.

When he was satisfied with his drawings, young Bernini jumped off the bench and examined his charred leg. He rubbed salve on it. "I wager you're happy I can draw fast," he said to his leg.

After putting his clothes back on, GianLorenzo examined the sketches and immediately saw the solution to his problem. *No wonder I couldn't get the expression I needed—I thought the Saint was in pain at the moment of his martyrdom. Looking at these sketches, however, I can see that even though I thought I was drawing pain, my mind perceived he was in ecstasy, not pain—and that is the look I shall give him.*

Chapter XXVI

Beyond Michelangelo

Most days, after his lessons with Cardinal Barberini, GianLorenzo ran to Saint Peter's to meet Annibale Carracci, the burnt-out artistic master who attended Mass at the basilica every evening trying to bury his disillusionment.

The two unlikely friends would saunter through the church; the child outlining his dreams, and the middle-aged genius rambling on about problems with his patrons. To the adoring public monitoring the master's every move, Carracci managed to appear serene—like a ship in port having escaped a killer storm.

—

"Why," GianLorenzo asked his friend one night "why is this basilica so bare? I know Saint Peter's is the biggest and best church in the world, but wouldn't everyone love it more if it looked nicer. Why doesn't the Pope hire you or somebody to decorate it?"

Carracci never ceased to be amazed by his little friend's inquiring mind. *This youth sees things only grown-ups usually see. He's absolutely right, of course, but the issue of decorating Saint Peter's is not as simple as it appears. I could be commissioned—and I would love it if I were—to paint painting after painting, fresco after fresco, but this church is so vast, I must admit that much more is needed. Much more.*

"Allow me, my brilliant young friend," Carracci said, "to explain something to you." He took the youngster by the hand and led him to the Crossing. "What do you see?"

GianLorenzo looked at the four monumental pillars holding up the immense dome. "When I look around, I see a really big space here over Saint Peter's tomb," he said. "It's huge and it's empty. Nothing is here—even the gigantic pillars are bare. Then, when I look up, I see Michelangelo's dome being frescoed."

"Forget the frescoes—they are by Cavalier d'Arpino and are not his best work. And the dome is by Giacomo della Porta, not Michelangelo. But no matter—now look at the apse, what do you see?"

"I see the end of the church. It's also empty—bare I mean."

"Believe me," Annibale Carracci said, bending down and smoothing young Bernini's erratic hair, "the day will come, when, no one knows, that a prodigious genius will make two great monuments in the middle and at the end of this temple on a scale in keeping with the vastness of the building."

GianLorenzo tried to remain calm, but he was bursting inside. *Why is he telling me this? Can he mean me? I feel like I'm about to burst.* "Oh, if only I could be the one," young Bernini blurted out.

The excited child started to jump into Carracci's arms but caught himself—he remembered knocking the master down the first time they met. "Forgive me for being so bold, Mister Carracci. I shouldn't have said that."

"Nonsense," the master said. "Passion and emotion. All great artists have passion and emotion. Never apologize for having passion and emotion—they give you confidence. I wish I'd had a little more—like Caravaggio. Maybe then I would have challenged Farnese when he cheated me." The thought of the injustice caused Carracci to shake from head to toe.

Tears filled GianLorenzo's eyes as he watched the great painter struggle to stop shaking.

"Promise me," Carracci said to the child, "promise me you will never apologize for your God-Given enthusiasm. It's one of the traits that will make you a greater artist than I am."

"No sir. I mean yes sir. I promise."

The child watched his friend's anguish and cried openly. Annibale Carracci dabbed young Bernini's face dry with his kerchief. A few deep breaths and the master stopped shaking.

"It's getting late," Carracci said, "but I must tell you one more thing before you go." He flashed the warm smile the little boy loved so much. "You guessed right—you are the one. You are the prodigious genius I was talking about. Now get home to supper. Your father would be distressed and disappointed if you were late."

"And mother would finish the job," GianLorenzo said.

Chapter XXVII

GianLorenzo enjoyed his regular visits to the Vatican (to study) and Saint Peter's (to meet his friend), but every day he had to work harder to concentrate—Mister Carracci hadn't shown up in some time. The child asked his father if he had seen him.

"Annibale has had a stroke and is confined to bed," Pietro said. "At least I think it was a stroke. I went to visit him at his home but he couldn't speak—I fear his time is near."

—

Young Bernini ran out of the studio and didn't stop running until he reached Carracci's home. The house was surrounded by carriages and filled with people.

The child pushed his way through the crowds on the first two floors. At the third level he found Annibale Carracci in bed, surrounded by priests, doctors, nuns, family and friends. The room was quiet and the mood was somber.

When the master saw GianLorenzo, he reached out to him with out stretched arms.

The mourners were flabbergasted because it was the first physical move their patient had made in weeks. The child realized his friend was trying to tell him something so he leaped on the bed and placed his ear next to Carracci's mouth. The astonished doctors tried to stop young Bernini but they were too late. Resigned, they watched in awe as the little boy nodded. Could he understand what Carracci was whispering? Impossible. They looked around—it was clear that no one else in the room could make out the words. And yet . . .

Even though Carracci was struggling to articulate every word—every syllable—young Bernini had no problem understanding his dying friend who struggled to articulate each word. "Ten years work . . . on the Farnese Palace . . . for five gold scudi. Do not . . . ever . . . let that happen . . . to you."

The doctors had to physically remove the hysterical youth from Carracci's bed.

—

Annibale Carracci died that evening at only forty-nine years of age. In the block requesting 'Cause?' the Death Certificate listed 'Stroke.'

—

"He died of a broken heart," GianLorenzo said when his father informed him of Caarracci's death. "The Farnese killed him."

Pietro was astonished at his son's remark. "Why in the world would you say that?"

Pietro waited while the child composed himself. *I can't tell father Mister Carracci looked like a man who had been crushed by a falling obelisk when he died. That wouldn't be respectful.* "I just know," the child said. "He was my friend."

"GianLorenzo," Pietro said, "we need to talk."

—

After finishing his prayers that night, young Bernini remained kneeling. The youth gathered his thoughts as he gazed upward. Finally, the youth spoke out to his friend in a clear, powerful voice.

"Mister Carracci, my father gave me a serious lecture tonight. He told me that even though you had problems with your patrons, I must always respect my patrons. So, of course, I will. He said it was very important for me to remember that. He used the word critical. But even though I will respect my father's wishes, I swear to you—I swear on your grave, Mister Carracci—I will respect your dying wish. I will never, ever, allow a patron to cheat me, or kill me."

The little boy was feeling a little better as he eased his bony body into bed, but a horrible thought crossed his mind. He quickly knelt back down and crossed himself. He gazed skyward once again.

"Please God, don't let the Pope get mad at me for swearing. I don't want to get burned at the stake."

Chapter XXVIII

P ietro Bernini burst into his studio. "Gentlemen, I have an extraordinary announcement."

All work stopped. "Cardinal Scipione Borghese has commissioned a sculpture. A mythological piece."

GianLorenzo and the other workers burst into applause and rushed to shake Pietro's hand and pat him on the back. "Don't get too excited," Pietro continued, purposely downplaying the commission. "It's only a small marble group that he wants—a table-top piece really."

"I don't care how small it will be," Mario, the apprentice said, "a commission from Cardinal Borghese is significant. Did he select the subject or will you?"

Pietro paused for effect, scrutinizing the smiling faces, all of which were dreaming they would be chosen to work on the piece. He finally spoke. "The Cardinal left the subject to GianLorenzo."

All eyes shifted from father to son. What the hell was going on?

The child was equally confused. "Me? Why me?"

"Because." Pietro said, pausing for effect. "Because the commission is for you. Congratulations, son, on your first commission."

GianLorenzo jumped into his father's arms. The workers fought each other trying to be the first to congratulate young Bernini on this historic occasion. The scene resembled a rugby scrum.

—

Pietro untangled himself from the group and pulled the child aside.

"I want you to be careful," he said. "Cardinal Borghese didn't specify the exact dimensions or the subject, which he invariably does when he grants a commission. Frankly, I think it's a test. Remember, he saw your technical artistic talent in the Santoni bust, which was, after all, a copy of a death mask. Now, I wager, he wants to test your imagination—your creative powers."

"How does it work," GianLorenzo asked, jumping around as if engaged in a sword fight. "Do I need to accept the challenge in some way? Like in a duel?"

Nick J. Mileti

—

    Angelica and her daughters, who were waiting outside the door, came into the workshop, carrying enough bread, wine, salami, olives, dried fish, fruit, and cheese to feed the entire neighborhood—which quickly arrived to share in the joyous occasion

    Angelica grabbed her little boy and hugged and kissed him. "Please eat more than just a little fruit, GianLorenzo," she whispered in his ear. "How will you have the strength to cut the marble?"

    "Mother, I'm so excited, I think today I could carve marble with my fingernails."

Chapter XXIX

After supper, GianLorenzo showed his father the sketch for his first commission.

Pietro studied the drawing of a goat and two figures. The lines were bold and vigorous. He liked that. Pietro started to speak but stopped and picked his words carefully—walking that fine line between teaching and badgering. "It's very interesting, but I need some explanation, especially about that third figure. Tell me what you're thinking."

"Amalthea, the goat, will be looking back over its right shoulder, questioningly, at Zeus."

"Questioningly? My, my." Pietro thought for a minute. "That's clever. That is extremely clever. And what will Zeus be doing?"

"I'm not sure. What do you think Zeus should be doing, father?"

Pietro was pleasantly surprised that the child was actually asking his advice. "Either drinking the goat's milk . . . or perhaps milking the goat . . ."

"Stop. That's it." GianLorenzo easily amended the drawing. "I don't want to show the actual milking though. You asked about the third figure. I've given the infant Zeus a friend, a satyr. He'll be drinking the milk—after all, the God Zeus must be benevolent."

"My, that's a big word for a little boy. Where did you learn it?"

"From Cardinal Barberini. He's the best teacher there is—after you, of course."

—

Things were moving fast.

On one of the best days of his life so far, GianLorenzo received a personal workbench, which his father made for him. "The top revolves, so you can work on all sides without moving the piece you're working on. Also, the table makes the marble waist-high, the perfect height for you."

Pietro also made the child some new tools. "These fine chisels, rasps and files will prove useful for the delicate piece you're planning. So will the scriber, and the three kinds of hammers, one with an iron head, one with a brass head and one with a lead head."

Beyond Michelangelo

The youth fingered the tools one by one. *I never dreamed that my very own commission would have so many emoluments.*

—

The highlight of the child's day, of course, was when the actual marble block arrived. Pietro watched with pride, and just a touch of apprehension, as his son tested it.

GianLorenzo followed the procedure his father taught him. First he tapped the block with a metal carving hammer. *Ah, a clear. Ringing sound.* The youth then wetted the block down and checked it for any imperfections. *I knew I wouldn't find any.* He then took a hardwood mallet and a pitching tool and struck off a small corner piece. The fresh fracture was sharp and clean.

The child hugged and kissed Pietro. "It's perfect father. It's the most perfect block of marble there ever was. But I wouldn't expect anything less from a perfect father."

"Why should you have less when you are working for the most important collector in Rome . . ."

"And maybe the world," the child said. "And the world is getting smaller every day."

I must be careful what I tell him—this little boy remembers everything.

—

Young Bernini placed straw under the block of marble, but before he could strike a blow, Pietro lunged forward and grabbed his son's arm. "Sorry, but before you start roughing out the marble, may I see your clay model of the group?"

GianLorenzo was shocked and dismayed over his father's interference. "I didn't make a model out of clay, or anything else." *I wish father would holler at me and get it over with. I want to start carving. Right now.*

"Watch your tone, young man. Shall I assume you also did not make a large model from which you can take measurements? If I assume correctly, how do you know what to carve?"

"I'm sorry if I made you angry father. I was so anxious to get started, I didn't bother with any models. Besides, I know what to carve because it's all here," the child said, pointing to his forehead.

"GianLorenzo, I have no doubt you can see the finished piece in your mind. But what if you change your mind along the way? Even a little bit. Remember, once you cut away a piece of marble from the block, no matter how small it may be, Alia Iacta Est—the die is cast, so to speak."

The boy remained silent as he mulled this over in his head.

"Look son," Pietro continued. "Based on the drawings I saw, I'm confident your group will be wonderful. The question is, will it be the best you can do? More planning on your part gives you that chance. Here's an idea—think of the models, along with the sketches and drawings, as a map."

"A map? What's a map?"

"Remember our trip here, from Naples? We knew exactly which way to go because we had a map. Remember how smooth everything went?"

GianLorenzo quickly grasped the analogy. On his way to the clay pot, the child stopped and turned.

"Except for the brigand with the interesting face," he said. "Poor bandit—he never had a chance against Thunder and me."

Young Bernini was pleasantly surprised as he studied his marked-up scale model. *I can't believe how much the group has changed from what I thought were my final ideas. That father of mine—he knows everything.*

The child moved the block of marble into position. "Finally," he said, kissing the stone. Chips flew, and dust settled onto the clean smock his mother had made especially for this moment. GianLorenzo Bernini gleefully licked his hands clean, rubbed them in the debris from his cuttings, and then spread the slightly warm chips and marble dust all over his face. He licked his smiling lips clean but didn't touch the rest of his face.

Chapter XXX

Both Cardinal Maffeo Barberini and Pietro Bernini enjoyed their periodic private dinners.

Pietro studied the man who had become a good friend. He had a warm and kind face with full lips. His bushy eyebrows and thick mustache reminded him of his own except the Cardinal's beard was twice as wide as his and therefore seemed to pull the mustache down. The future Pope's large blue eyes signaled his Florentine birth: They always seemed to be covered by half-closed lids, giving Maffeo a perpetual sleepy, but forceful, look.

The lively conversations ranged from literature to philosophy, and most nights the cultivated and learned cleric, who was educated by the Jesuits, read the latest poems he had written. Pietro understood the verses that were written in Italian and Latin, but Cardinal Barberini had to translate those he wrote in Greek.

Inevitably, however, much to Pietro's joy, the discussions turned to GianLorenzo. The Cardinal enjoyed citing examples of how brilliant GianLorenzo was, and how well the boy was doing with his schooling.

"Your son is like a sponge," Maffeo said one evening. "As soon as I tell him something, he absorbs it and asks for more. Not only that, the youth is interested in everything—and he forgets nothing. Now, Pietro, if you don't mind, I can't stand the suspense any longer. Did you bring it?"

—

Pietro lifted The Goat Amalthea and Infant Zeus with Satyr—as GianLorenzo named it—from behind his chair and removed the covering. Cardinal Barberini gasped. His eyes widened. He fingered the group lovingly, with the practiced hands of a connoisseur.

"I had no idea the boy had progressed to this level," he said. Then, almost under his breath, the Cardinal added, "I'm glad I was smart enough to commission something from him before Scipione did."

"In fairness to you," Pietro, said, "you have been—understandably—focusing on his intellectual growth rather than his artistic growth."

—

"What do I like best about the piece? Everything," Cardinal Barberini said. "First of all, it's perfectly proportioned. And the treatment of the surfaces—it's startling. The goat's fur looks soft as silk, but Zeus and the Satyr look hard as porcelain. And all of their expressions. Enchanting is the word that jumps to mind."

"You are very kind," Pietro said.

"Believe me, my friend, I don't say these things out of kindness, I say them from the heart. Tell me, did you help the boy?"

"Only with advice. I did not touch the piece."

"In that case, I have what you may consider bad news,' the Cardinal said, "but I hesitate to be the messenger. I don't want you to become angry with me."

Pietro's mind was racing. *What can my esteemed friend be talking about? The bad news must relate to GianLorenzo's group, and yet he said he loved it.*

Pietro wiped a few drops of sweat from his forehead. "You know the affection I feel for you, Maffeo, I could never be angry with you. Tell me, please, what is wrong?"

Cardinal Barberini drained his wine goblet and cleared his throat. "Pietro, my friend, I take pride in the fact that I have never been less than honest with you. So tonight, I feel compelled to tell you something you may not want to hear."

Maffeo Barberini studied his friend and wondered how he would handle what he was about to say if he had children. He was about to change the subject when he locked eyes with his friend. Pietro's eyes were filled with love. *Oh well, what are friends for? What I have to say is for his own good.*

"With all due respect, Pietro, your son has surpassed you."

—

Pietro fell back in his chair and took a long swig of wine. As he stared at the drink, his mind flashed back to Naples and the first time he saw the aura of greatness surrounding his son. *I knew I was right.*

Pietro, his face aglow, smiling ear to ear, held his goblet high.

"A toast, Maffeo. You were afraid I'd be upset when you told me my son has surpassed me as a sculptor, weren't you?"

Cardinal Barberini nodded. Pietro Bernini couldn't stop smiling.

"Why am I not upset?" the proud father of the young genius asked. "Don't you see, my dear friend, in this game, he who loses, wins."

Chapter XXXI

Cardinal Maffeo Barberini heard on impeccable authority that his friend (and artistic rival) Cardinal Scipione Borghese planned to award young Bernini a major commission.

Since everyone in Rome was aware of Scipione's notorious hunger for control of artistic talent, Cardinal Barberini acted fast and immediately commissioned another piece from the budding genius. The Cardinal selected the subject—Saint Sebastian, a Saint he particularly revered—but left the other aspects of the piece to the youth.

Young Bernini decided to place the martyred Saint in a totally new pose. He slumped the Saint's body and head against a tree trunk, and dangled his muscled arms and legs. "I made his face shine," GianLorenzo said when he presented the sculpture to his patron, "because I wanted it to reflect the miracle that occurred when Saint Sebastian met his God."

Cardinal Barberini was overcome with joy. "This magnificent statute will remain in my personal collection forever."

The words so excited young Bernini he moved toward his mentor to hug him but caught himself in time. *Mother would kill me if I grabbed a Cardinal like that.*

"Thank you sir." The youth paused while he searched for the words that would be appropriate for this extraordinary compliment. Finally, he shook the Cardinal's hand. "Thank you," he said, "Thank you for everything."

—

"If you don't mind," Cardinal Barberini said, "I feel that the time has come to ask you a very personal question. If I may."

"Sir, with the question coming from you, the more personal, the better."

"You do have a way with words, young man. Now, if I'm not mistaken, you are exactly eighteen years of age, and have been creating masterpieces for over ten years. How is my arithmetic?"

Young Bernini hadn't paused long enough to think about his life—he was much too busy—but he certainly enjoyed hearing the analysis. Since he wasn't sure what his mentor was getting at, however, GianLorenzo remained silent.

Cardinal Barberini continued. "Did your father help you carve this sumptuous Saint Sebastian?"

"He gave me advice, which I solicited, but didn't touch the work. Why do you ask?"

"This matter is so important, I've even discussed it with the Holy Father and Cardinal Borghese. What I'm saying is, GianLorenzo Bernini, have you thought about establishing your own studio?"

Young Bernini was too stunned to speak. He walked around the room, thinking, close to tears. He finally decided to be perfectly honest.

"Thought about it? I've been dreaming about it. The problem is, I don't know how to tell my father. He's the best father in the world, and I don't want him to think that I'm not grateful for what he has done for me. Truthfully, sir, my father has done everything conceivable for me."

"Everything?"

GianLorenzo's mind flashed back to the conversation he overheard more than ten years earlier at his nonno's house in Naples. *I'm closing my workshop here in Naples and moving my family to Rome for my son. That's right, I'm doing it for GianLorenzo. Period. No other reason.*

The smile fell off of young Bernini's face. His expression turned serious—his eyes falling to half-mast—and he spoke deliberately. "Yes, sir, everything is the correct word, but maybe it's not a strong enough word. My father has done more for me than anyone will ever know. Teaching me about the art of sculpture is only a part of the everything."

Cardinal Barberini had seen his young prodigy emotional many times—but he had never seen the emotion encased in such serious reflection. *I have obviously touched a nerve. Perhaps I can help soothe his melancholia.*

"GianLorenzo, I may have a solution for you, and here is the personal question. Would you grant me the privilege of proposing it to him? May

I suggest to your father that it may be time for you to strike out on your own?"

GianLorenzo grabbed his mentor's hand and kissed his ring.

"Don't do that," the embarrassed Maffeo Barberini said. "I'm only a Cardinal, not the Pope."

Chapter XXXII

Borromini spent his first days in Rome searching for Leone Garovo.

Fortunately, shortly before his money ran out, he found his cousin working in Saint Peter's basilica. Leone, a thin, lanky and industrious man in his early twenties, was thrilled to see someone from home. He took Francesco to the nearest bar for a coffee and conversation.

"Honestly, I don't have the slightest idea how we're related," Leone said. "I think we're first cousins . . . maybe second or third. But what's the difference? We're family and I want to do whatever I can to help you get started in Rome."

Francesco was going to make polite conversation, but instead, decided on a direct approach. "A job, that's what I need right now. I need ta work."

"First, you must leave that pensione and move in with my wife and I," Leone said. "That will save you some money. Tomorrow, you can begin work as a stonecutter—lucky for you I'm in charge of those men at Saint Peter's. That way you can start to make money."

Borromini was overwhelmed by his cousin's generosity. "I dunno how can you hire me? Without seean the marble I cut."

"I know the situation in Milan very well Francesco. If you worked in and around the Duomo for ten years, you have to be an excellent stonecutter."

Leone put his arm around his cousin's broad shoulder as they walked out of the café. "Besides, we are family, did you forget? Now, let's go pay your account at the pensione and get you settled in my home. After you've worked for a short time, you'll be able to buy some new clothes."

"I like my clothes," Borromini said without smiling.

—

Once Leone saw the quality of Borromini's marble cutting, he treated his younger cousin more and more as an equal, steadily easing his supervision of him.

For Borromini, even though the jobs he was assigned were extremely modest, he loved working in Saint Peter's and for Leone, who had become a friend.

In the evenings and on weekends, Leone showed Francesco the sights of Rome.

"I thought Milan had good artistic things," Borromini said. "But compared to Rome, Milan's nothing—like Bissone, if you know what I mean."

Leone knew exactly what he meant—he left the Lombard region and moved in Rome for precisely the same reason.

—

"The Duomo in Milan—I like it," Borromini said to Leone one night over supper, "but just being in Saint Peter's is better. It makes me feel more closer to God."

Leone understood his cousin's comment when he placed it in the context of Francesco's celibacy. Out of love for Francesco, he felt that he should nurture his religious fervor.

"We're only just beginning the decoration," Leone said. "Imagine how powerful the religious experience will be when the decoration is complete."

He watched his cousin devour a plate of spaghetti doused in a meat sauce. Francesco was obviously too occupied to speak, so Leone talked on.

"Actually, Saint Peter's was started about a hundred years ago, but my father-in-law's recent work has really set the tone of the church."

Borromini jumped from the table, knocking over the pasta, which splattered on the ground. "Your father-in-law? Did you say father-in-law? Don't tell me your father-in-law is . . ."

"Yes, Carlo Maderno. The man who completed the nave of Saint Peter's. The man who built the façade and the portico of Saint Peter's. The man Pope Paul V appointed Architect of Saint Peter's. That man."

Borromini was thunderstruck. His mind was reeling. *I have been living in the same house with relatives of the most famous and important architect in Rome, the man I would kill to meet, and I didn't know it.*

By the thinnest of margins, Francesco overcame the urge to strangle his cousin. He gasped for air and drank two goblets of water trying to settle down. This worked to a point, but he was unable to steady his hand or his voice.

"Would it be possible to meet Carlo Maderno?" Francesco managed, without a trace of hope.

"Of course," Leone said. Looking at the veins pulsating in the forehead of his cousin's flushed face, he felt terrible. "Sorry, I don't know why I didn't think of that myself."

Chapter XXXIII

F rancesco and Leone walked along the nave toward the front of the immense basilica of Saint Peter's. Borromini was nervous and excited in equal parts—he was sweating like a man in a Roman bath.

"Don't fret, Francesco," Leone said. "I'm sure the meeting will go fine. Carlo Maderno has a reserved manner, but he is the nicest person alive— and I don't say that just because he's my father-in-law." *If you had gone to University, you'd recognize him as one of those thoughtful and quiet professor types—the gentlemen who care about their pupils but also have strong personal pride and substance.* "You'll see," he continued. "Come along, he said he'd be at the Crossing."

The pair ambled down the longest nave of any church in the world. Borromini asked the obvious question. "Why did that Maderno man change Michelangelo's design from a Greek Cross to a Latin Cross?"

"That's a question for Carlo, but I wouldn't bother him about that today. He's inundated with meetings, so we should just say hello and leave. Ah, there he is, pouring over drawings."

—

While Leone waited for an opportune moment to interrupt the master, Borromini studied Carlo Maderno. *He certainly is a distinguished looking gentleman, and his mop of wavy gray hair sets off his lined face—which tells me he works outside a lot. He's probably over sixty, but his solid build makes him look much younger.* Borromini noticed that Maderno's shoulders slouched and head hung slightly, even when he straightened up.

Must be from studying drawings over the years.

"You must be Francesco," Carlo Maderno said, flashing a warm, welcoming smile that made him look ten years younger. "It's amazing, you look exactly like your mother. How are your parents? I've known them from years ago. What do you hear from back home? It is Francesco, is it not?"

Francesco wiped his brow with his kerchief. "Fine, Fine. They're fine. Everyone's fine. Yes, it is Francesco." *This isn't going the way I hoped, but I may never have this opportunity again.* He took a deep breath and cleared his throat loudly. "May I ask you a question, sir?"

Leone glared at his cousin in disbelief and anger. *After I told him not to bother Carlo today.*

Maderno stood erect. He looked at Leone, at the work on his desk, and at the young man he'd just met. *I mustn't think badly of him—after all, he is a neighbor from up north. The work will have to wait.*

"Certainly," the benevolent master said in a soft and even voice. "Anytime. What is it?"

Borromini glanced at Leone but chose to ignore the slight shake of his cousin's head. *I've got to get this out fast.* "Vitruvius. I wanna read his ten books on architecture and there's a copy in the Vatican Library and since you are the Papal Architect you can get me to read that 'De Architectura and . . .'"

"You may stop," Maderno said. "I've heard enough."

Borromini was stunned. His face froze as all hope fled from his body. *Shit. I came all the way to Rome for nothing.* He turned his back so that Maderno could not see the tears rolling down his ashen face.

Maderno instantly realized he sounded cross. "Relax, Francesco, please," he said in his most soothing tone. "What I meant was, I have a copy of all of Vitruvius's writings and you are welcome to borrow them. Leone, please see to it. Now, allow me to continue my work. Francesco, Leone tells me you are an excellent stone-cutter."

Borromini spun around. Later, all he could remember was hugging Carlo Maderno and kissing him on both cheeks—something he heard the people from the South did regularly, but he had never done before.

—

Not long after the meeting with Maderno, Leone and Francesco examined some new scaffolding. It had taken a full week for Leone's carpenter crew to erect it, so he was anxious to get to work.

"I'll check the scaffolding," Leone said to Francesco, "then you come up. I want to show you how stucco-makers patch damaged areas."

With practiced steps, Leone scrambled up the enormous maze of wooden planks and slats. When his cousin reached the top, he was so high, Borromini could barely see him.

Leone then signaled for an aide to send up his tools. When the bag of tools reached Leone, Borromini saw his cousin strain to grasp it. For some unknown reason—which Francesco later replayed over and over in his mind—the bag eluded Leone's outstretched hand, and when he leaned over and grabbed for the tools, he slipped.

Leone fell off the scaffolding, his body spinning wildly until it hit the marble floor with a sickening thud. Borromini's scream echoed though out the basilica.

Leone Garovo—a handsome young man still in his twenties—died instantly.

Borromini couldn't work. He cried, and prayed for his cousin's soul, all day and all night for a week straight. *I knew him less than a year but he was my best friend. He treated me with respect.*

—

Riding from the funeral Mass for his cousin—held, appropriately, in Saint Peter's—Borromini took stock of his situation. *Unfortunately, I can't stay in Leone's house; I have to find an apartment of my own. I've also lost my champion at Saint Peter's. These are not good things. I know what I need to do. What I need to do is get that Carlo Maderno to shift his focus from Leone to me. Hmmmmmmmmmmm.*

Chapter XXXIV

Borromini was drinking his third coffee when he saw Carlo Maderno. He'd been sitting in the bar diagonally across from Maderno's home on the narrow Via dei Banchi for twelve straight nights, working up the nerve to approach the master. "It's tonight or never,' he decided. Francesco jumped out of his chair and crossed the street, looking like a jaguar about to pounce on an innocent deer.

"Mister Maderno, hello."

"How nice to see you," Maderno said. "It's Francesco, is it not?"

The excited Borromini recited the lines he'd practiced hundreds of times. "What a break to run into you. I been anxious to return the Vitruvius books and thank you. Let me check. Yes, I have 'em right here in my saddle bags."

The sixty-four year old architectural genius laughed to himself. *Too much coincidence, yet it might be interesting to find out what the young man is up to.*

———

Maderno helped Francesco with the manuscripts. "You say you have read all ten books," he said. "That's quite impressive for a man of your tender age."

"I'm twenty-one—not so young," Borromini replied. "I read every book on architecture I can get my hands on. I don't want to be a stonecutter all my life. I want to be an architect. Like you."

Maderno studied the intense young man and wanted to cry for him. *Every stonemason on earth wants to rise to the position of architect but a precious few achieve that dream. What a dilemma. I don't think it would be fair to discourage him, yet I want to be honest with him.*

"It's not easy, rising from stone-cutter to architect," Maderno said finally, coming down on the side of candor. "Believe me, I know from personal experience."

"I know about that personal experience. I spent the last few months checking—asking around—I wanna learn how to accomplish what you have." *I probably shouldn't have said that. Oh well, too late now.*

Carlo Madero's first impulse was to censure the aggressive youth. On second thought, he was amused. *At his age I was just as ambitious—maybe more so.*

"And what did you learn about me in your research? Anything interesting?"

The question puzzled Borromini. *I dunno if this is interesting. Oh well.* "I know you started cutting stone, just like me. Up in the Lombard region, just like me. Then, about thirty years ago—in 1588, when you were already thirty-two years old—your uncle, Dominico Fontana, sent for you to come to Rome. He was Architect of Saint Peter's cause Pope Sixtus V liked him most."

"Very good, Francesco. Is that it?"

Pumped-up, vigor was oozing from every pore of Borromini's body. "Oh no. After that Pope Sixtus died a few years later, your uncle moved from Rome to Naples and I heard he made lotsa enemies when he was in power, that's why he moved, and I believe when you designed the façade of the church of Santa Susanna it caught the attention of Pope Paul V right away, almost twenty years ago, and he was so impressed with it he made you his architect and the Architect of Saint Peter's and that's how you became a famous architect, just like I want to be." *You're talking too much, Francesco. He might not like it I but I don't care—it's the way I feel.*

Maderno sat down. He had the feeling he was adrift in time. "Francesco, you bring back a pocketful of memories."

"Am I right? I been at the church every day since we met. I studied that façade of Santa Susanna. I know it inch by inch and that. It's what my mentor in Milan called a 'true masterpiece.' I never seen nothing like it, in Milan, Rome or anywhere. That's a dream I have—to do something great like that. You know what? You shown me the future of architecture."

Maderno's face lit up like Saint Peter's at Christmas. *This young man has spirit—not to mention good judgment.* "To be an architect, Francesco, you need more than enthusiasm and analytical thinking—both of which you seem to have in abundance. To be an architect, you also need practical traits. You must know how to draw."

"All I do is read and draw," Borromini said. "I like to do both. Mister Biffi in Milan said that of all of the apprentices in his workshop, I was the best drawer."

Maderno thought about his situation. *I'm getting old and Leone is dead. I can definitely use some help. Besides, Francesco is practically family.* "I'm presently working on designing the façade of Sant' Andrea della Valle, and I could use a copy of my drawings. Come into the house, and I'll give you a set. Let's see how it goes with this first commission. Would you like that?"

Borromini made the Sign of the Cross. "Leone, God rest his soul, told me one time you were the nicest man. He, God rest his soul, was dumb. He left out you were the greatest too."

Chapter XXXV

Young Bernini walked around his brand-new workshop, fondling every piece of marble and furniture in the room. *Something is missing, but I don't know what.*

GianLorenzo heard a faint tapping on the front door. When he pulled the door open, he found his father standing there, hammer in hand, grinning from ear to ear.

"How do you like it," Pietro asked, pointing to the plaque he had just nailed to the door.

STUDIO OF
GIANLORENZO BERNINI
SCULPTOR

GianLorenzo grabbed Pietro and hugged and kissed him on both cheeks. "Now I know what was missing," he said. "Father, it's amazing, but, somehow, you always seem to know what I'm thinking, usually before I even think of it."

—

Because Cardinals Maffeo Barberini and Scipione Borghese both made surprise appearances, the party to celebrate young Bernini's own workshop was even grander than the one held in honor of his first commission.

Cardinal Barberini presented GianLorenzo with a leather-bound set of poems, which he had written, and Cardinal Borghese brought enough fresh fruit and flowers to decorate every workshop in Rome.

"A toast to our young genius," Scipione said. Everyone raised his goblet. "We salute you, GianLorenzo Bernini. In this studio, in your strong little hands, you hold the future of sculpture, and maybe of all art. Salute."

—

After the crowd left, and Angelica and the girls cleared away the debris, Pietro and his son sat down for a talk.

"Father, why do you think Cardinal Borghese wants to see me in his office first thing tomorrow morning?"

"To offer you a major commission, I would guess. Knowing the Cardinal, if it weren't especially important, he would have mentioned it at the party. GianLorenzo, may I make a suggestion? Before you work for anyone else, I think the first piece you carve in your own studio should be for yourself. Make it small—a tabletop piece—and keep it on your workbench. You can enjoy its beauty through the years, and it can serve as a benchmark, so to speak. Incidentally, I think that you are ready to sculpt a multi-figured piece, something more complex than you have ever attempted. After all," he laughed, "you are eighteen now."

—

Pietro examined his son's latest work carefully while GianLorenzo fidgeted, anxiously awaiting his father's valued opinion. *When I suggested he try something complex, I never dreamed he'd make it this complex. Somehow, he has captured the drama of love prevailing over lust in a little over fifty inches. And the way he accomplishes this—it's amazing. The faun straining against the twisted tree trunk trying to reach the tree's forbidden fruit, the scattered, angelic putti, playfully pushing him back, as if to say, 'You know better, or at least you should.' I see serious passion in this piece.*

"What do you call it," Peitro asked, reigning in his enthusiasm, making his usual attempt to help his son keep a perspective on his work, and life.

GianLorenzo was devastated by the cold question. "Faun Teased by Putti, naturally. Looking at the group, I guess that isn't obvious."

Pietro ignored the sarcasm. "Are you satisfied with it?"

"I feel that I have overcome the difficulty of making marble like wax," young Bernini said, still angry.

Pietro also ignored his son's boasting. *I can understand his braggadocio at this point in his life—if I had my own studio at eighteen, and was producing work of this caliber, I would probably be insufferable.*

"Making marble behave like wax—that's a perfect way to describe your extraordinary talent," Pietro said. "But, what I'm wondering is, are you are happy with how the piece turned out?"

The compliment cheered and settled down the emotional youth, who now gave his father's question serious thought. When he finally answered, he answered from the heart.

"I'm happy with the group, but I'm not completely satisfied," he said. Young Bernini stopped and gazed up to the heavens. "I can't seem to produce a work that is as beautiful as the one I see in my mind."

Chapter XXXVI

D awn was breaking when GianLorenzo dismounted at the main entrance to the Quirinal Palace where Cardinal Scipione Borghese was waiting for him. He smiled inwardly—courtesies and accommodations such as this no longer surprised young Bernini. He was comfortable in his newfound celebrity.

"Ah, GianLorenzo, what a pleasant way to start the day," the Cardinal said as he enveloped the youth in one of his patented bear hugs. "Come along, we have important matters to discuss."

—

Patron and prodigy made their way through the sumptuous palace.

"I believe this is the first time I've met you for a business talk without your father being present," the Cardinal said.

"I only hope and pray that I'll make him proud," GianLorenzo replied. His eyes swelled with tears. Real ones.

Cardinal Borghese noticed the outpouring of emotion and slapped the youth on his back. "Don't worry. Any father would be proud to have a son as talented as you."

Young Bernini froze Cardinal Borghese with his gaze that would have stopped a run-away horse. "I meant in every way, sir."

Scipione coughed, trying to remember if he was this smooth at eighteen.

—

The duo reached the Cardinal's elegant office, which was awash in masterpieces of art and sculpture, both contemporary and ancient.

"I have an incredible surprise for you," Scipione said, "but first, do you know the epic poem, the Aeneid? The part where Aeneas is ordered by the gods to escape from Troy?"

"Cardinal Barberini exposed me to Virgil," GianLorenzo said. "I love the mythological tale—I've even committed many parts to memory. Cardinal Barberini said that there are numerous paintings representing the legend, but no sculpture has ever been carved capturing the moment when Aeneas flees Troy, carrying his father, Anchises, his son, Ascanius, and even some household goods. Cardinal Barberini felt the subject was probably too complex for sculpture."

Scipione rubbed his hands together in glee. "That is precisely the reason I commission you to create a life-size piece capturing the event. In marble, of course. I have the perfect place for such a group in my new villa on the Pincio, and you can be sure I will pay you handsomely."

"Your Eminence, until now, my father has been handling my finances, so I must learn how to charge. In the meantime, why don't you pay me for this group based on your level of satisfaction, after you've seen the finished product?"

Cardinal Borghese grabbed young Bernini and gave him another bear hug. "You are amazing, young man. Most artists can't add one and one, and here you are setting me up for a huge fee."

GianLorenzo was surprised that the Cardinal could see right through his tactics, so he tried to change directions. "Sir, if you prefer . . ."

"No, no. Don't misunderstand me, son. As a patron, I prefer an artist who is also an astute businessman, rather than someone like Caravaggio—or even Annibale Carracci. I mention two stupendous artists whose work I hold close to my heart, but men like them inevitably turn out to be nothing but trouble, in one way or another."

—

"Now, let's unwrap the big surprise," Cardinal Scipione Borghese said as he opened the door to the adjoining office. There, sitting behind an enormous desk, was Pope Paul V himself. Young Bernini walked briskly across the room, bowed, and kissed the pontiff's ring.

"I see the young genius with two first names has arrived," the Pope said. "Thank you for coming, GianLorenzo. Please, sit and make yourself comfortable."

Young Bernini sat. He figured something very good was on the horizon, but he didn't know what to say, so he sat with his hands folded in his lap and said nothing.

The Pope continued. "I wish to present you with something unprecedented in the sixteen hundred years of the papacy."

Cardinal Borghese—who loved games of this type and had choreographed this one—added to the suspense. "My aides and I have made a careful check, in the Vatican Library and elsewhere, and, at eighteen years of age, you are the youngest sculptor in history to receive this singular honor."

GianLorenzo jumped out of his chair and kissed the Pope's ring. "The surprise—is it a papal commission? Oh, excuse me, Your Holiness, I didn't mean to be so forward. Father says it's my Neapolitan blood."

"It is a papal commission—and more," the amused pontiff said. "The commission is for you to carve my portrait. A bust of Paul V."

—

Cardinal Borghese walked young Bernini out of the palace. "Why did you tell my uncle that you wanted to sketch him next week as he goes about his normal activities? That's totally different from the normal practice of sittings."

After his behavior with the Pope—which he prayed his mother would not hear about—the young sculptor thought he should chose his words carefully.

"Obviously, I could determine physical likeness with a sitting or two, but I'm more interested in the inner man. His essence, if you will."

"So, what are you saying? That movement . . ."

"I'm saying that when a person is in motion, those qualities which are his alone, and not of a general nature, appear. To me, the trick of producing a great portrait is being able to recognize the unique qualities of individuality, rather than the generality common to all."

"In this manner, you can discern papal qualities?"

GianLorenzo seized the opportunity to impress the Cardinal. "God, himself, has infused the Holy Father with papal qualities." He paused for effect. "My role is to capture and portray these qualities in marble—as perfectly as possible."

Scipione gave young Bernini a last bear hug and sent him on his way.

Walking back to his office, the Cardinal replayed the morning over in his mind. *I definitely was not that suave at his age. I can't think of anyone who was.*

Chapter XXXVII

When young Bernini purchased the immense block of marble for the Borghese commission, the broker informed him that no block small enough was available for the miniature papal bust he was planning. Several days later, when he was informed that several possible blocks had arrived, GianLorenzo dispatched his newly hired assistant to purchase one.

The youthful apprentice returned and triumphantly presented his boss with a small, shiny marble block. GianLorenzo took one look at the stone and stormed out of the studio. The assistant's bragging about having obtained a bargain hung in the air—lost in the drama of departure.

Young Bernini ran all the way to the broker's shop. He shoved the door open.

"Where are you, you no good bastard. Did you sell my assistant this piece of shit?"

As the proprietor came out from his rear workroom, the young sculptor threw the piece of marble at the broker's head. The proprietor ducked, barely avoiding decapitation.

"I didn't know it was for you, it's so small, and . . ."

The young perfectionist had no patience for excuses.

"I want the best piece of marble in Rome in my studio before sundown, or we'll never do business together again. Is that clear? And, I'll see to it that no one else in Rome buys from you either. Is that clear?"

"Yes, son."

"It's sir to you."

"Sorry sir."

GianLorenzo started to leave but stopped and turned. The more he thought about the trick the broker had tried, the more upset he became.

"One more thing," he said. "Don't you ever, ever, ever, think that I skimp because a project is small. I give the same care to every job, regardless of size. Do you understand?"

Without waiting for an answer, young Bernini left, slamming the door, rattling its hinges.

—

The broker retrieved the disgraced piece of marble. "So I tried," he said out loud, laughing.

Chapter XXXVIII

On the way to their son's first major unveiling, Angelica Bernini was worried. Her usually upbeat husband was slumped in the seat of their carriage, with a faraway look in his eyes.

Pietro suddenly spoke. "In every brilliant mind there is a dull spot. That's the problem."

Angelica took Pietro's hand and kissed it. "I assume," she said, "you are referring to GianLorenzo's plan to have his bust of Pope Paul V unveiled in conjunction with Cardinal Borghese's Flight from Troy. You've been saying that is a major problem for some time. Why?"

"Because the Pope's bust is only about twelve inches tall and his nephew's group is huge—life-size. 'It will be a great juxtaposition,' GianLorenzo said to me. 'It will be a great disaster,' I said to him. 'Why,' he asked. 'Because,' I said, 'whether you mean it or not, the Pope will feel insulted because of the immense size differential.' But I got nowhere. In every brilliant mind there is a dull spot."

"The boy has always had a mind of his own. Is that so bad?"

—

GianLorenzo was waiting for his parent's carriage.

"What if the Pope doesn't show up," he asked his father. "I'll be devastated if he doesn't come tonight. What would I do?"

Pietro quickly pasted a smile on his previously gloomy countenance. "I'll tell you what to do. You smile and keep smiling, because tonight will still be an auspicious occasion—the unveiling of a major work of art, for a major patron, by a major artist is always an important event. Now let's go in."

—

The Bernini's made their way through the elegantly coifed crowd of Cardinal Borghese's recently finished, gaily-decorated villa. Angelica had never seen a party like this in Naples. An unending array of delicious food was being passed by a parade of uniformed waiters and a string quartet was performing. Mimes and jugglers amused the guests.

Cardinal Borghese, with GianLorenzo at his side, called for quiet. "I am standing between the two reasons we are here tonight," he said. The Cardinal slowly pulled the silk covering from the sparkling marble group. Oohs and ahs filled the room, followed by thunderous applause. "Beautiful ladies, and gentlemen, I give you the nineteen year-old genius who carved this stunning Flight from Troy, GianLorenzo Bernini."

GianLorenzo stared straight ahead, as if in a trance. He didn't hear the thunderous applause—all he could think of was that the Pope hadn't come. Pietro, instantly sizing up the situation, rushed to his son's side and whispered in his ear, "Forget the Pope for now. This is the most important moment of your life—make the most of it."

Young Bernini looked at Pietro, blinked twice, and broke into a big grin. He wrapped his right arm around his father and signaled for quiet with his left. He spoke in a firm but humble tone of voice.

"Beautiful ladies and gentleman. I am overwhelmed by your kindness and generosity. If you will allow, I would like to acknowledge the five who have made tonight—and my talent, if you will—possible."

The crowd buzzed, five? Who could the five be, they wondered.

"First, I ask my mother to come forward and take a bow. There she is, in the back of the room. Please come ahead mother. GianLorenzo wrapped his free arm around her. "Please recognize Angelica Bernini, my lovely and understanding mother."

The smiling group burst into applause. No one could remember an artist acknowledging his mother at an unveiling.

"Secondly, please acknowledge the man who taught me everything I know about carving. He's a great sculptor in his own right—and my best friend. I give you my father, Pietro Bernini."

The reaction from the crowd was enthusiastic and noisy—a father's acknowledgment was also unprecedented.

"Thirdly, I'd appreciate it if Cardinal Maffeo Barberini would come forward and take a bow. For more than ten years, this sophisticated and patient gentleman has been my mentor and academic teacher, almost daily putting up with my barrage of questions—some good, some stupid. Cardinal Barberini."

The applause, mixed with laughter, was stronger than ever for the popular Cardinal.

"Fourth, the months I spent designing and carving the group you see before you were months of joy because I not only knew that the work was going to be displayed in the most beautiful setting in the world—the villa we're in tonight—but I also knew that it would be appreciated by the most knowledgeable collector in the world. My patron, Cardinal Scipione Borghese."

GianLorenzo put his hand out to shake with the Cardinal, who pushed it aside and gave young Bernini a bear hug to end all bear hugs. The crowd went wild.

The young genius, with an inherent sense of drama, allowed the celebration to abate of its own accord—like the resolution in one of Shakespeare's plays Cardinal Barberini had him study.

"Last, but most importantly, I want to publicly thank God for all that He has bestowed on me."

GianLorenzo struggled to control himself. The crowd was spellbound by the youth's obvious sincerity. Young Bernini finally pulled himself together and continued his most important thought of the evening.

"Frankly," he said, "as far as my talent is concerned, I consider myself a tool of God's Grace . . ."

With that, young Bernini burst into tears.

The guests were stunned. They fell into a deadly silence, and then erupted into the most raucous reaction of the evening.

—

By noon the next day, half of Rome claimed to have been present at the most dramatic unveiling the city had ever experienced.

Chapter XXXIX

The unveiling was pleasant for young Bernini in more ways than one.

Just prior to the presentation, a strikingly beautiful Contessa slipped GianLorenzo a folded note. No one noticed.

The man of the hour waited until the elegant lady's husband, the Count, was otherwise occupied, and then acknowledged the bold invitation with a slight nod of his head.

—

An awe-inspiring pattern of gorgeous ladies seeking to share young Bernini's bed had developed, and, not surprisingly, GianLorenzo was delighted to participate.

The decision was not arrived at easily, however.

Early in his meteoric career, the young sculptor had agonized over the matter of making love with married women. *Am I breaking God's law?*

Eventually, GianLorenzo came to the conclusion that there was nothing wrong with the assignations—even if the women were married—because it was the females themselves who instigated the affairs.

After all, what's the sense of being a celebrity if you don't have the emoluments?

Chapter XL

Beyond Michelangelo

GianLorenzo fretted about his forthcoming meeting with the Pope during the entire ride from his home to the Quirinal Palace. *Can I possibly have ruined my career just because I wanted to have an interesting unveiling?*

—

Young Bernini was ushered into the Pope's office. "Please, GianLorenzo, tell me what you were thinking," Paul V said without any preliminary pleasantries.

The youth decided his only chance was to guide the discussion to his talents. "Your Holiness, I would be devastated if you were displeased with my work."

The pontiff studied the frail youth for some time. When he finally spoke, the Pope softened his tone but avoided young Bernini's trap.

"GianLorenzo, you know it is not a question of your unsurpassed abilities, it is a matter of respect. Who is the Pope?"

"I don't know what you mean, Holy Father."

"The Pope is a direct successor to Saint Peter. He is the Head of the Catholic Church—the spiritual Head; the economic Head; the social Head; the military Head; the political Head . . . need I go on? Your plan would have been insulting not only to me personally, but much more important, to the Head of world-wide Christendom."

"I'm sorry, Your Holiness. Father tried to tell me, but I didn't understand what he was saying until now."

Paul V decided his point had been made. "Fair enough. Now, if you are amenable, I shall forget this episode."

"I apologize. I never should have disregarded my father's advice. I assure you, Holy Father, that will never happen again."

—

The Pope walked to a wall cabinet and returned with the miniature bust Bernini had carved of him. He turned it in his hands, handling it carefully, as if it were a sparrow with a broken wing. GianLorenzo held his breath.

"This is the most incisive portrait I have ever seen in my entire life," the pontiff said.

Young Bernini wanted to hug and kiss the Holy Father, but decided extreme discretion was in order.

"You are most kind, Your Holiness. Thank you for giving me the opportunity to capture your dynamic human qualities in cold, hard marble."

"Yes, they do come through, don't they? Now, to show you how much I admire your unprecedented talent, GianLorenzo, I commission you to sculpt a full-size bust of your Pope."

—

When the happy young sculptor reached the entrance to the palace, Cardinal Borghese was waiting for him. Instead of greeting him with a hug, Scipione put his arm around his prodigy and led him to the guard's office.

"We can talk here," he said, indicating a chair GianLorenzo should sit in. "I hope you enjoyed the party last night. The entire crowd was mesmerized by your wonderful talk as well as your spectacular group."

"Than you for hosting the party, sir. Your kindness is only exceeded by your knowledge and taste in the arts."

"GianLorenzo, you know that I have great affection for you as a person and artist, so you will appreciate what I'm about to tell you is for your own good."

Having a good idea of what was coming, the youngster sat motionless. *I hope I look sufficiently contrite.*

"GianLorenzo, there are very few absolutes in life, but here is one for you to remember. Never, ever, play a joke the Pope or have him think you are ridiculing him—which amounts to the same thing. Enough said? Now let me give you a few observations about the Flight from Troy. First of all, when I told people you carved it out of one block of marble, they were dumbfounded. Second, jealous rivals—and you already have some—harped all last night about the balance of the group. They called the composition precariously unstable."

Young Bernini winced, and Scipione noticed.

"Those are their words, not mine. I explained that you designed the trio that way—precariously unstable—because that is the legend and the whole point of the piece. After all, Aeneas, carrying his father, with his son hanging on, is fleeing the city in fear—fear you miraculously captured in their expressions. 'The point is,' I told the nay Sayers, 'the group is not on its way to Sunday Mass.' I also told them that I think you have created a masterpiece, and I meant it."

"Sir," GianLorenzo said, beaming from ear to ear, "it's truly an honor to be associated with such a perceptive patron." And he meant it.

Chapter XLI

Beyond Michelangelo

On December 7, 1619, GianLorenzo Bernini turned twenty-one. In the next six years, the world was treated to a display of artistic virtuosity by young Bernini never before—nor ever again—witnessed.

Two history-making elections underscored the unprecedented outpouring of sculptural masterpieces. The Sculptor's Guild in Rome elected GianLorenzo into its membership on his twenty-first birthday—the earliest possible date under the Guild's rules that anyone can be elected into the organization. Two years later, in 1621, disregarding his youth and focusing on his astonishing body of work, the Academy of Saint Luke, the prestigious artist's society of Rome, elected young Bernini its President.

Neptune and Triton, young Bernini's first life-sized fountain, was produced for Cardinal Alessandro Peretti, who used it as a centerpiece and focal point for the fishpond in the famous gardens surrounding his villa. The guests at the unveiling were amazed that Bernini was able to get fluidity into his first important fountain group.

"GianLorenzo conceived of the group in sculptural terms," the stately Cardinal Peretti explained to the exclusive crowd of nobles at the unveiling. "Look at the dramatic figure of Neptune as he strides forward—his posture causes almost perceptible movement in the static marble. I will be surprised if future fountains are conceived in any way other than sculpturally."

Monsignor Pedro De Foix Montoya, the Spanish cleric, commissioned two life-size marble busts for San Giacomo degli Spagnuoli, the Spanish church in Rome. He wisely allowed young Bernini to select the themes.

The results were electrifying.

Bernini produced two complimentary, but opposite, marble portraits—Anima Beata (Blessed Soul) and Anima Donnata (Damned Soul). The blessed female soul looks so angelic as she gazes upward the viewer understands that heaven will certainly accept her. On the other hand, the damned male soul looks like the devil himself: This man is living hell, where he is obviously headed.

"Aeneas and his family are lonely at my villa," Cardinal Scipione Borghese said to young Bernini. "I need a major, over life-size group to compliment your incomparable Flight from Troy."

"What a lovely way to put it," GianLorenzo replied. "What subject do you have in mind?"

"Another mythological group," the Cardinal said. "I'm thinking of the Rape of Proserpina."

The sculptor could hardly hide his excitement. "I know the exact moment to be captured. It's when the love-crazed Pluto snatches the voluptuous Proserpina, intending to carry her into his hell. I see it as brutally violent and sensuous at the same time."

"Start as soon as you can," said Cardinal Borghese, the largest collector of pornography in Rome.

When completed, the group became the talk of Rome. Young Bernini's stunning masterpiece put every viewer in the middle of the action—they can not only see, they can actually feel Pluto's coarseness and bestiality as he digs into Proserpina's smooth, velvety skin. The women of Rome particularly loved the group. They cheered the way the young genius portrayed Proserpina's active resistance to the rape—smashing her left arm into the brute's confident face and twisting her body away from him.

"Son," Angelica said, "in my opinion, passive resistance to rape, as it used to be shown, is ancient history. I predict your magnificent group will become the quintessential depiction of rape from this day forward."

The sixteen-year reign of Pope Paul V ended with his death in 1621. The brilliant, highly egotistical pontiff made certain he would be remembered for all time by having his name emblazoned in huge letters on the façade of Saint Peter's—which he had previously commissioned from Carlo Maderno.

Twelve days later, sixty-seven year-old Alessandro Ludovisi was elected Pope by acclamation and chose to serve as Gregory XV. The aged pontiff immediately sent for young Bernini, who had been in a nervous state since the death of his most prominent patron, Paul V.

"I'm sorry I cannot use your services, GianLorenzo," the newly crowned Pope said. "I'm from Bologna, so I'm partial to artists from my hometown. I am certain you understand. In fact, I have asked Domenichino to return to Rome. Are you familiar with his work?"

"Yes, Your Holiness. Domenichino is a most accomplished painter. More importantly, he studied in Bologna under an even greater painter, Annibale Carracci. I idolized Mister Carracci—he was a good friend of mine and one of my inspirations."

Before the meeting was concluded, Bernini's silk tongue carried the day. He was commissioned on the spot by the pontiff to sculpt one papal life-size marble bust, and two papal busts in bronze. Urged to give the busts preferential treatment due to the Pope's advanced age, the prolific genius presented the busts to Gregory XV a short eight months later.

"You are admiring what I call a speaking likeness," the Pope's Cardinal/Nephew, Ludovico Ludovisi, said to the celebrities at the sought-after papal unveiling. "Perhaps my friend GianLorenzo will tell us how he achieved the saintly expression on my uncle."

"There are hundreds of factors that add up to a successful portrait bust, of course," young Bernini replied, always happy to talk about his technique. "How do I create a 'speaking likeness'? Mere resemblance is not sufficient; I must express what goes on in the heads of heroes like the Holy Father. Furthermore, I have found that the expression most characteristic of an individual is just before—or just after—he has spoken. Therefore, the most important, and difficult, decision I must make is to chose a movement, and then follow through."

The Pope was so taken with the busts he bestowed the Cross of the Knight's of Christ on the sculptor. The knighthood is the highest honor a layman may receive from the Church, and at twenty-three years old, GianLorenzo Bernini was the youngest person to ever receive the honor.

—

When young Bernini learned that Cardinal Borghese had given his masterwork, the Rape of Proserpina, to Cardinal Ludovisi, he collapsed into his bed. Angelica assured her son he hadn't had a heart attack—he was merely depressed. GianLorenzo lay in bed writing plays for a week before Cardinal Barberini finally visited him.

Is he against me, too? "Thank you for coming, Your Eminence. But please tell me—what did I do wrong? Cardinal Borghese told me he loved the group, that it was the best thing I'd ever done."

"Sorry I couldn't come by sooner," Cardinal Barberini said. "I have been away from Rome. GianLorenzo, this is your first failing mark, and it is in papal politics. Pay attention now. It is precisely because the work is so extraordinary that Scipione's move was a coup on his part. There is no situation more difficult or more dangerous than that of a Pope's nephew after the death of his uncle."

Stunned, young Bernini shot up in bed. "Are you saying that the Cardinal/Nephew of the last Pope gave my marble group to the Cardinal/Nephew of the present Pope to try to stay in favor with the new papal regime?"

"Close, but there is much more than that involved in this situation. It may sound unbelievable, but the gift of your sculpture forms the basis of a new and closer era in the relationship between the powerful Borghese and Ludovisi families. In fact, the nobility is buzzing about the gift and how Scipione used it to such advantage. You may have noticed that these nobles operate under their own set of rules."

GianLorenzo was feeling better by the minute. "They may have their own set of rules, but, truly, this gift business is something I never contemplated."

Cardinal Barberini looked at young Bernini with a combination of awe and concern. "How could you? Nobody could. Don't you realize art this powerful—your art—is basically unprecedented?"

The inveterate collector, Cardinal Scipione Borghese, met with the newly minted Cavaliere, and informed him that Aeneas and his family are once again lonely at his villa. Young Bernini—who feared that Scipione's gift of his work signaled that his commissions from the Cardinal were over—was ecstatic when he was commissioned to sculpt another mythological group, this time Ovid's legend of Apollo and Daphne.

"I know the moment I must capture," Bernini said, adrenalin flowing. "The precise moment Apollo catches Daphne, causing her to get her wish to turn into a laurel tree."

"I don't know," Scipione said. "That metamorphosis from human flesh to inanimate object has been interpreted by numerous painters but it has never been attempted by a sculptor—much less in a life-size marble piece. Artists and laymen agree it cannot be done . . ."

The Cardinal stopped abruptly; a knowing look flooded his pudgy face. He lit up. "So that's it. You want to carve that moment precisely because it has never been done before. Shame on me—I should have known."

As GianLorenzo finished the roughing stage of Apollo and Daphne, a curious thing happened. Cardinal Borghese had him stop work on that group and commissioned him to sculpt a statute of David, the biblical giant killer. *I assume the decision is strictly a matter of politics so I don't plan on losing one night's sleep over the matter.*

In the statute of David, Bernini easily and quickly captured the intense action of the legend—the moment David is releasing the stone from his sling. But, the young genius had trouble visualizing the menacing look he wanted his hero to have. To solve the problem, young Bernini had his mentor, Cardinal Barberini, hold a mirror, enabling him to sketch his own expression (as he did in his earlier statute of Saint Lawrence). The result is a ferocious David full of fire and passion—complete with penetrating gaze, knitted brows and a clenched jaw. A fascinating, and revealing self-portrait of the Cavaliere.

"I want viewers to feel that they are personally involved in the confrontation," young Bernini said at the lavish unveiling. "I want viewers to feel that the brute Goliath is situated right behind them, and is about to die."

At the festive unveiling, Cardinal Borghese, always looking for ways to entertain his distinguished guests, saw an opportunity. "What is your thought process, Cavaliere? Everyone in this room is talking about how your dynamic statute of David easily overshadows Michelangelo's static statute of David. How do you trump the master?"

Unknown to Scipione, young Bernini actually relished the opportunity to impress the most important citizens of Rome. He stood, waited until the room became quiet, and then spoke slowly and carefully.

"After I receive a commission, my mind initially focuses on all of the antique models that relate to my project. Then, at some point, an idea strikes me—I don't know when this is going to happen, it just happens. Then, somehow, my mind shifts and this idea grows into a set of impulses—like a beautiful flower opening in spring. These impulses are creative impulses, and they are all my own. Then, like the idea before it, my impulses start to grow. I can actually see them grow in my mind, becoming larger and larger, more important, more original. And then my mind shifts again . . ."

The assemblage sat spellbound as they watched Bernini drift into a trance—astounded that they were hearing a certified genius reveal his thought process. Eyes closed, the Cavaliere appeared to start again but then stopped. The crowd held its collective breath, hoping and praying he would continue. Scipione was torn. *I never expected this. I think he's going to cry.* As he was about to call a stop to his little game, young Bernini continued.

"What was I saying? Oh yes, my mind. My mind watches my creative impulses grow, and then it shifts again. And here's the most confusing, but exhilarating, part. As these impulses develop, they eventually take over my mind completely and put me into a state of frenzy."

To the crowd, the Cavaliere looked like he was going to collapse. Nobody had ever experienced anything like this—young Bernini looked like he was more asleep than awake when he continued.

"At that moment, in that state of frenzy, I become a tool of God's Grace . . ."

The Cavaliere, who had been standing, slumped down into his chair. No person in the room moved a muscle—they were frozen in place like the citizens of Pompeii. Bernini continued, speaking so softly, everyone leaned forward, eager to catch every word.

"This frenzy I'm in, it's a frenzy of Grace. And when I'm in this State of Grace I do not work the marble, I devour it. To put it another way, when I'm in this State of Grace, I cannot strike a false blow."

—

The unveiling of the monumental marble group Apollo and Daphne was the most extravagant unveiling in a string of extravagant unveilings.

Young Bernini created an absolutely gorgeous Daphne who is horror-stricken as Apollo grabs her. Daphne is unaware her cries for help are being heeded, however, so her wish is granted and the viewer sees her arms and legs actually begin to turn into branches, roots, and laurel leaves. Apollo is depicted slowing down as he collects his prey. From his expression, we see that he is thrilled to be on the verge of capturing Daphne, but we also understand that Apollo doesn't yet realize his predicament—that he can never possess the ravishing beauty. Bernini had accomplished the impossible. The group is incredibly delicate; yet it is so powerful it rams the heart-wrenching mythological tale into the viewer's gut, going down like a deadly potion in a goblet of smooth brandy.

All this in cold, hard marble.

—

Monsignor Montoya, commissioned a life-size marble portrait for his tomb. Within a year, the bust was completed, but the tomb was not. Consequently, the work was hung in the sacristy of the Spanish Church for the interim period. The room was constantly filled with spectators who wanted to see the Cavaliere's latest work.

One day, Cardinal Barberini and GianLorenzo joined the throng. When the viewers saw young Bernini enter, they respectfully cleared a path to the wall where the portrait bust hung. A friar—head bowed, praying under his breath—followed close behind, lost in his piety. When he inadvertently walked into the wall, the elderly cleric saw the marble bust.

"Oh my God," he exclaimed, "it's Montoya, petrified." The Friar crossed himself three times to atone for his blasphemy. Hearing a commotion, the crowd turned its attention to the front of the room and emitted a collective gasp—Monsignor Montoya himself had entered the sacristy.

Cardinal Barberini called out to Montoya. "Come here, my friend," the Cardinal said. He put his arm around the Monsignor's waist. "Folks, I have known Monsignor Montoya for about twenty years." He then dramatically brushed his hand across the real cleric's face and said, "This is a portrait of Montoya." He then brushed his hand across the face of Bernini's marble bust. "And this," he said, "is Montoya."

—

As the pair was leaving the sacristy Cardinal Barberini paused. "How do you do it," he asked Bernini. "How do you make cold, white marble appear to have warmth and color? I've noticed that you've accomplished that in virtually all of your work, but in this Montoya bust you have taken that principle to new heights."

"It's easy," Bernini replied. "Allow me to explain. If someone were to whiten his hair, beard, eyebrows and, if possible, the pupils of his eyes and his lips, and then showed himself in that state, even those who saw him every day would have difficulty in recognizing him."

"What are you getting at," Cardinal Barberini asked.

"Just this," Bernini said. "When a person falls into a faint, the pallor that spreads over his face is alone sufficient to make him almost unrecognizable, so that we often say 'He no longer looks himself.' For this reason it is very difficult to obtain a likeness in a marble portrait, which is one color."

"Well then, how do you do it? Get the color, I mean."

The spectators had gathered around the young genius and the Cardinal, hanging on every word. Young Bernini noticed this of course. He waited for just the right moment and then continued.

"In a marble portrait it is sometimes necessary, in order to imitate nature well, to do what is not in nature. That is to say, sometimes in a marble bust it is necessary to create effects of color by a number of tricks, and even exaggerations or distortions, drilling more deeply than was natural in places to create accents of shadow, or leaving the marble upstanding to catch the light."

"I think I'm fairly sophisticated in these artistic matters, but, I must confess, at this point, I'm a little lost," the Cardinal said. "Please—be more specific."

"Fair enough. For example, in order to represent the darkish patch that some people have around their eyes, it is necessary to hollow out the marble at the place where this darkish color is, so as to create the effect of the color, and by this artifice, to make up, as it were, for the defect in the art of sculpture, which cannot give color to things. Obviously, nature and imitation are not the same thing."

"If I understand what you are saying," Cardinal Barberini said, "you achieve your dynamic chiaroscuro effects through the use of different textures."

"Exactly. Painters can use different color paints, sculptors have a more difficult time of it. That is why Michelangelo, great as he was, never sculpted portrait busts. Too hard, even for him."

—

After only 2 ½ years as Pope, Gregory XV died in 1623. Cardinal Maffeo Barberini, Bernini's mentor of almost twenty years, was elected Pope and chose to serve as Urban VIII. The evening he was sworn into office, the fifty-five year old pontiff called GianLorenzo into his private quarters. He poured two goblets of wine, handed one to young Bernini and raised his glass. He spoke in a clear, loving voice.

"It is your good luck, Cavaliere, to see Maffeo Barberini Pope; but we are even luckier in that Cavaliere Bernini lives at the time of our pontificate."

"Sir . . . I mean Your Holiness, I am indebted to you for many things. The education you have bestowed upon me—I will cherish that forever. As if that isn't enough, your creative and scholarly intelligence have been an inspiration. When I needed someone to talk to, you were always there for me. My father made me a sculptor, Holy Father, but, along with my parents, you made me a man."

"GianLorenzo," The new Pope said, "I remember a conversation we once had about one of your idols—Michelangelo. I believe you have surpassed him in the art of sculpture, but I fear you need to know more about painting and architecture. Please see that you continue your study of these disciplines. To do my part in expanding your expertise, I hereby appoint you Supervisor of the papal foundries at Castel Sant' Angelo. Also, I appoint you Superintendent for the Aqua Felice Aqueduct, and Commissioner of the Pipes and Fountains of Piazza Navona."

"I am overcome with joy, Holy Father."

"Wait, there are two more matters," the pontiff said, smiling broadly. "At the little church of Saint Bibiana, workmen uncovered the Saint's remains while digging under the main altar. So instead of only minor repairs that were to have been done, I commission you to renovate the entire church, design a new façade, and sculpt a statute of the Saint herself."

"Your Holiness, I feel as if I'm embarking on a new life, so to speak."

"You are. Now we come to the last and most important matter. The massive space under della Porta's dome—the Crossing, at Saint Peter's. I want you to design a structure, a canopy, to encase the High Altar. I want a baldacchino that is in proportion to the great basilica itself."

Memories of his departed friend Annibale Carracci flooded Bernini, but he quickly recovered. "Holy Father, you have made me the happiest twenty-six year old on earth—and wherever else your friend Galileo says exists."

—

Incredibly, Bernini's love life kept pace with his meteoric professional career—in originality as well as in sheer volume.

Chapter XLII

Borromini couldn't sleep. He'd repeated Carlo Maderno's magic words over and over in his head so many times he knew them by heart.

"Francesco, your work is of the highest quality, and I'm happy and proud of what you are doing for me. Next week come for supper and I'll give you a second set of drawings to copy. By then, I should have the drawings for the dome of Sant' Andrea della Valle ready."

Almost methodically, little by little, the kindly master was taking Borromini under his wing. The initial supper invitation grew into weekly invitations, and finally, the pair met at Maderno's house socially two or three times a week. They discussed their work, and their memories of Lake Lugano, in equal measure.

Maderno truly appreciated Francesco's diligence and expanding skills, plus, he was the closest thing he had to a relative in Rome—which would always remain a foreign country to someone from the Lombard Region, regardless of how long the stay in the Eternal City.

On Borromini's part, his initial respect for Maderno grew into genuine love for the gentleman. In fact, since his stepfather raised Francesco, Carlo Maderno became the father Borromini never really had.

—

Francesco felt guilty for harboring one major reservation regarding his mentor. The concern tortured the youth since the first day he saw Saint Peter's, but he couldn't figure out a way to broach the subject with Maderno.

Borromini's problem concerned his idol, Michelangelo.

Next to Maderno, Francesco admired Michelangelo more than any person, dead or alive.

But, Borromini couldn't figure out why Maderno tampered with Michelangelo's plans for Saint Peter's. *It makes no sense. First of all, it's not Maderno's nature to interfere in another artists project. Secondly, how could anyone improve on Michelangelo's work, much less his most significant project—Saint Peter's, the greatest church in Christendom?*

—

"Francesco," Maderno said one night, "I know you want to be an architect more than anything in the world, but I don't want you to lose your carving skills. Take this sketch I've drawn—it's for putti to go over the entrance doors to Saint Peter's. Also, I want you to carve a marble base for Michelangelo's Pieta."

Borromini couldn't believe his ears. *Here's the chance of a lifetime. I can bring up the subject of my idol.*

He pounced.

"Speaking of Michelangelo," Borromini said, "why did you change his Greek-cross plan for Saint Peter's into a Latin-cross design? I hope you don't mind if I ask. I've read everything written about Michelangelo, but nobody has written about your role with his work."

"Michelangelo is your idol, Francesco, I'm aware of that. So maybe you don't want to hear the whole story."

"That's exactly why I wouldn't want to hear anything less," Borromini said.

—

Carlo Maderno drained his wine goblet and took a deep breath. *Here goes—I hope Francesco can handle the truth.*

"In 1546, Michelangelo was seventy-two years old—alert and feisty as ever—when Pope Paul III appointed him Architect of Saint Peter's and instructed him to finish the basilica. Since the previous architect was Sangallo the Younger, one of his bitter rivals, Michelangelo basically demolished or discarded all of Sangallo's work, including his Latin-cross design."

"Why do rivalries like that spring up?" Borromini asked. "I read Michelangelo told a friend that Sangallo's plans, 'provided pasture for dumb oxen and silly sheep who knew nothing about art'."

"I don't know, Francesco, I guess it depends on each person's nature." Maderno reflected for a minute. "Actually, I can't think of one rival that I have. But, back to Michelangelo. In addition to dropping the nave—which Raphael, another of your idol's rivals, had also planned for Saint Peter's—Michelangelo simplified the wall treatment, enlarged the central piers and added pilasters, both inside and out."

"Why's this story so rough on my idol?" Borromini asked, relaxing.

"Michelangelo overlooked several essentials in his planning, which is why I put the nave back in. First of all, we needed room to accommodate the huge crowds that flood the basilica on special holy days. Also, space was needed for a sacristy and a chapel for the canons. And, finally, there was a subtle reason for the nave—the Council of Trent. I assume you've read about how that important body recommended that all future churches should be built in the shape of a Latin-cross, like the one Christ was crucified on."

Relived, Borromini got up from the table. "That it—some bad planning? The way you talked, I thought there was something way worse than that."

"Francesco. I regret to inform you that the dome you see today on Saint Peter's was designed by Giacomo della Porta, not Michelangelo."

—

Borromini was stunned. He didn't know what to think or say. *I know that Carlo Maderno enjoys a reputation for total honesty, yet every book I've read talks about 'Michelangelos' dome.*

"How do you know that?" Borromini asked, in a manner more challenging than he meant it to be.

"If you're saying I never knew Michelangelo personally, you are correct. I was only eight years old when he died in 1564. But Giacomo della Porta and I were extremely close friends. Many of his ideas in the magnificent façade of Il Gesu were inspirational to me when I designed the façade of Santa Susanna."

"You did better than your friend. You took his ideas to a new level, if that's the right way to say it."

"Thank you, but my friend was the premier architect in Rome toward the end of the last century. And he revered Michelangelo as much as you do—he finished most of Michelangelo's Roman projects, including the famous Capital Hill."

"What do those things have to do with the dome?"

Maderno took a slow breath. "I want you to understand that della Porta was not a jealous rival of Michelangelo's. To the contrary, he even called Michelangelo his mentor."

"But, I'm positive Michelangelo designed a dome for Saint Peter's—I seen the model"

"Yes he did. Michelangelo designed a dome for the church, but the only work completed on it before he died was the drum—that's the cylindrical support for the dome, as you know. Giacomo della Porta studied the model Michelangelo had made, and came to the conclusion—reluctantly, he told me—that the dome, as designed, would appear too flat when viewed from the ground."

"A little redesigning, huh?" Borromini said. The thought made him feel better. "So what?"

"Francesco, della Porta's redesigning—as you call it—took place over a period of approximately thirteen years."

Borromini staggered under the weight of the number. He was no architect, but he grasped the significance of the thirteen-year figure instantly. "You're saying Giacomo della Porta's dome was a brand new dome. That's what you're saying, isn't it?"

With his fingers, Maderno made an adjustment to his hair. "As a matter of fact, della Porta's dome was so totally different from Michelangelo's dome, della Porta was required to submit his new design for approval to the Reverenda Fabbrica di San Pietro—the body in charge of all work performed at Saint Peter's, and the organization that has been paying you all these years for your work in the church. The significance here, obviously, is that della Porta's submission was necessary in spite of the fact that Michelangelo's design had been previously approved by that same group."

Borromini made a last feeble attempt in defense of his idol, which was akin to reaching for a toothpick in a storm-tossed sea. "Did you yourself see della Porta's drawings?"

"Giacomo showed me almost every drawing he made for the dome over the years. As I recall, he made the dome about twenty-seven feet higher, made the ribs lighter and closer together, raised the attic, added lunettes and raised the lantern. Yes, it was a new dome."

Borromini put his face in his hands, and then placed them over his ears.

Maderno waited until he could make eye contact and then continued. "One more thing. When della Porta's dome project was approved by the Fabbrica—that was about 1586—my uncle, Domenico Fontana, was Architect of Saint Peter's. He confirmed everything I've told you. Sorry."

"I'm going to throw up," Borromini said, without a trace of embarrassment.

Maderno felt bad but also felt compelled to continue. "That's normal. Whoever hears these facts has that reaction. Or they refuse to accept the facts. Truth is, nobody likes to have a story they believe exposed as false. Especially a story they have believed all their life."

"I'm afraid to ask you about the façade and portico," Borromini said, resigned. "At Saint Peter's. How did they come about?"

Maderno laughed. "Finally an easy part. The nave, façade and portico were all part of the same commission. When Camillo Borghese was elected Pope in 1605—serving as Paul V, of course—he ordered me to finish Saint Peter's. It was immediately clear what needed to be done. First, I convinced the Holy Father to allow me to tear down the portions of the old Saint Peter's that were still standing. After that, it was easy to get him to see that a nave, façade, and portico were crucial."

"No more copying, Francesco." Maderno said one night.

In the early days of their relationship, Borromini would have exploded with grief. Now, however, he realized the master was probably leading up to something important, so he remained quiet.

"I fear that we are wasting your talent," Maderno continued.

Francesco smiled. *I was right, there is something good in the air.*

"You should not be a mere copyist." Maderno handed Borromini a piece of paper. "See if you can produce preliminary drawings from these sketches of mine. If all goes well, as I assume it will, you can then complete the working drawings."

"This practically makes me a real architect," a grateful Borromini said, the buttons on his blouse close to popping. "One more step, that's all that's needed—to make sketches myself and then draw working drawings based on 'em, my own ideas."

"You are almost ready for that last step, Francesco, and I'll be the happiest man in the world when it happens. Notice I said 'when,' not 'if'."

"Working from your sketches," Borromini said, "I'm overwhelmed by this. I don't have the words to thank you. I'm speechless you could say."

"Don't say that," Maderno said. "I enjoy our conversations at our suppers too much. Your theories about melding architecture and mathematics—I enjoy hearing about that more than anything. I think you are on to something. Go now, I'm tiring earlier and earlier. By the way, come to the basilica early tomorrow. I want you to meet someone our Pope proclaimed would be the Michelangelo of our time. He's a true prodigy—the best I've ever seen. He may replace Michelangelo as your idol."

Chapter XLIII

When his father asked to meet in Saint Peter's, at the Crossing under the dome, young Bernini was surprised. Normally, their bi-weekly meetings took place in GianLorenzo's studio.

"Son, I have something important to discuss with you," Pietro said, "and I wanted to meet here to emphasize my point. Your mother says I always take your part. Well, if I do, it's because you've earned my support over the years. But now, I fear I'm crossing that line."

GianLorenzo put his arm around his father's neck and their eyes locked. "It's okay, you have the right. Come out with it—I'm a big boy."

Pietro's face lit up—filled with grateful surprise and thanks. "Okay. GianLorenzo, look at this space—it's so huge, I think half of Rome could fit in here comfortably. And the height under the dome, it's so . . . well, let me get to the point. How in the world do you expect to fulfill the commission to build a canopy here without ruining your reputation? Maybe the Holy Father did you no favor. Maybe Carlo asked to be bypassed."

"Father," GianLorenzo said, "I'm truly surprised at you. Here I am, twenty-six years old, and instead of encouraging me—which you've done since I was old enough to hold a chisel—all of a sudden you're discouraging me. Why the sudden reversal?"

"GianLorenzo, I'm not questioning your abilities—you know better than that. I'm questioning whether anyone . . . anyone, can create a structure that is proportional to the vastness of space under this dome and the gigantic proportions of this basilica, and still make it beautiful. And, important. Remember, the baldacchino will encase the space over Saint Peter's remains—the most sacred shrine in Rome."

"Father, I . . ."

"Please, let me finish. You'll need an army of men. I know there are more talented artists and artisans in this city than anywhere else in the world, but are there enough? And will they work for you? And will you have time to supervise them properly? You have quite a bit on your plate right now you know."

"Father, I . . ."

Pietro put his finger to his lips and placed his arm in his son's. Arm and arm, they walked around the Crossing, each lost in his own thoughts. After what seemed to GianLorenzo like an inordinate amount of time, Pietro finally broke the silence.

"GianLorenzo, I'm certain you know how much you mean to me and your mother. I'm not just talking about your artistic achievements; I'm also talking about your personal achievements. You're a man of honesty and integrity, and you make us proud. You've already had more honors and recognition than most men have in a lifetime. And best of all, you are happy. I hope you get my point—we don't want anything bad to happen to you. Even if it's not your fault, a failure is a failure—pasta for the legion of jealous rivals you've accumulated."

"Yes, father, the commission is one of monumental proportions, with an endless stream of monumental problems to overcome. But it is also the most prestigious commission in the world today, and I know for a fact that Carlo Maderno—or any other artist in Rome—would kill for it."

Bernini paused, afraid that he was being too harsh. He lightened his tone.

"Father, let's analyze what has happened in my life—generalizing, of course. After you taught me how to work the marble, I started carving small, tabletop pieces. From there, I moved on to busts and memorials. Then came the life-size and over life-size groups for Cardinal Borghese. Presently, I'm working on my first architectural commission and first life-size religious statute, and don't forget, along the way I established my own studio. That's steady, serious growth, wouldn't you say?"

"No question," Pietro said, regretting that he had forced his son onto the defensive.

"More importantly," Bernini continued, "in everything I've done, I've tried to accomplish things in marble that have never before been accomplished—and most people feel I've achieved that goal so far."

"Come on son, you've achieved the impossible and more. You know that. Everyone knows that."

"I thank you for that." GianLorenzo's lips tightened involuntarily; he pursed them so they would relax. "What I'm getting at is this. I think the baldacchino commission is a natural progression for me. Don't forget father, you're the one who told me to play the game of life to win, not not to lose."

"GianLorenzo, you argue so well, you could be a lawyer."

—

Bernini cupped his father's face in his two hands and kissed him on both cheeks.

"Father, when you talk, I listen. I know that I couldn't do this job alone, even if I wanted to—that's a luxury I fear is lost to me, probably forever. I must utilize my assistants to help at every stage, except design, of course. I must also supervise the entire crew of workers. Don't worry; I'm organized—after all, you taught me. Are you with me?"

"Am I with you. What does that mean?"

Bernini pinched his father on both cheeks.

"Will you help me on the baldacchino?"

—

Even though the night was cold, Pietro jumped into bed naked and immediately attacked his wife.

"My, my, we're extra frisky tonight," Angelica said. "Something good has happened, hasn't it?"

"Good? Try super, sensational, great," Pietro said, smothering his wife with kisses. "Are you ready for this? GianLorenzo asked me to help him with the baldacchino commission."

Angelica screamed with joy. "After all this time? It's been . . . how long?" She counted on her fingers. "I can't believe how fast time flies—it's been almost exactly five years since you advised him on the Flight from Troy. This, my dear husband, is definitely a date to celebrate."

Pietro loved it when the Neapolitans went on the attack

Chapter XLIV

Beyond Michelangelo

Hundreds of artists and skilled craftsmen milled about the Crossing of Saint Peter's, including gilders, sculptors, carpenters, painters, founders, brass workers, and stonecutters. Pietro called for their attention and the group quieted down. Carlo Maderno and Francesco Borromini watched from the rear of the pack.

"Gentlemen, as you know, my son GianLorenzo has been commissioned to build a baldacchino on this spot where we stand. This will be a monumental undertaking and the total commitment of every trade and discipline is critical if we are to succeed. Each of you has been hired because you are the best in Rome at what you do. Your commitment needs to follow."

The artisans reveled in the compliment.

"Quiet down, please," Pietro continued. "Now, I want all of you to understand my roll. I will handle the administration of the job, including purchasing of materials and getting you paid."

"Hey. What about the important side of the job—the creative and design side," a short, skinny gilder called out.

"Naturally, my son GianLorenzo will handle all artistic matters. That is all artistic matters. Does anyone here have a problem with that?"

A strange quiet engulfed the group of highly talented men, who were, on the whole, advanced in age. The workers had never encountered a situation quite like this. They eyed each other, but said nothing.

Pietro noticed. "Gentlemen, you were told this when you were hired."

"But he's only in his twenties," said one old-timer. "Sure, he can sculpt better than anyone, but what does he know about building," another chimed in.

—

GianLorenzo, who had concealed himself, stepped from behind a curtain. An uneasy silence encased the workers—nobody knew the young genius was in the basilica. Bernini surveyed the room, taking his time, letting the men sweat. Later, no one could remember Saint Peter's being this quiet. When he finally spoke, it was in a loud, firm, authoritative voice.

"My comments will be short. I have gathered you here under della Porta's dome, for a serious reason. I want every one of you to absorb, into your very being, the majesty—and challenge—of this grand undertaking. For the next eight or nine years, we will be engaged in the most important commission in Rome and the Catholic world; building a baldacchino over the sacred place Saint Peter is buried. Let me give you a few highlights. The monument will consist of four twisted columns made out of dark gilded bronze—to contrast with the white, marble walls you see about you—topped by a superstructure with triple scroll-like volutes, which will connect each of the columns with the crown. A tasseled valance will frame the upper structure. The monument will soar almost one hundred feet into the air—as high as the Palazzo Farnese. I have to say that I believe this baldacchino will be so beautiful, so breathtaking, it will stupefy all of Rome—and the world.

The men broke into spontaneous applause, unprecedented in situations such as this.

"Thank you, men. I'm sure you can understand that a project of this magnitude demands men who can work together as a team. Like a hand in a wet leather glove. May I assume that is clear?"

"Yes." "Of course." "Absolutely," could be heard in the enthusiastic assent.

"Excellent," Bernini said. "Now, to that end, will the three gentlemen who raised their objections earlier please see my father. He will pay you to date. You are fired. Meeting adjourned."

Chapter XLV

As he made his way out of Saint Peter's, GianLorenzo saw Carlo Maderno. He hugged him and affectionately kissed the elderly master on each cheek.

"I think of you every time I walk down this magnificent nave," Bernini said. "And that beautiful portico. In my opinion, the design is perfect—as good as anything in Rome."

Maderno was pleased with the obvious sincerity of his young rival.

"Thank you, GianLorenzo, that certainly is a great compliment, coming as it does from the number-one artist in Rome. May I present my assistant, Francesco Borromini. Francesco, say hello to GianLorenzo Bernini—he's the person I was telling you about and you just heard speak."

The two young men shook hands.

"What is it you do," Bernini asked, looking at Borromini's hands. *With rough and callused hands like that, I wager he is a stonemason.*

"I'm a stonecutter from up north," Borromini said, "but I'm gonna become an architect."

"The Lombardy Region, I'll wager," Bernini said, totally disinterested in Francesco's dream. "Most of the good ones come from there."

Borromini shoved his hands into his pockets and didn't say another word.

—

"Francesco, what's the matter? I've never seen you like this," Carlo Maderno said after Bernini excused himself. "You were positively impolite to GianLorenzo."

"Did you hear when he talked?" Borromini said. "I thought you were the Architect of Saint Peter's. You said you were."

"You know I am. What are you getting at? Is something wrong?"

"Is something wrong?" Francesco said, getting more and more worked up. "Why aren't you the architect for the baldacchino?"

Maderno's body shook involuntarily. What Francesco asked had haunted him ever since Pope Urban VIII shocked the artistic world by granting the prestigious baldacchino commission to young Bernini—even though previous Popes had authorized Maderno to work on the identical project. Maderno, of course, was smart enough to hide his disappointment from everyone.

"Simple," Maderno said. "In his infinite wisdom, the Holy Father decided to by-pass me, and my aching body, and grant the commission to the virile, twenty-six year old genius, GianLorenzo Bernini."

"Why would he do that?" Borromini asked. "Bernini's a sculptor. What does he know about architecture, or building? I could help you if you got the commission."

Of course—that's what this is about. "Don't get yourself all riled up Francesco, I understand the Pope's decision."

"You understand what? Why this was done to you?"

Almost by rote, Maderno articulated the reasons he had reluctantly arrived at to satisfy himself. "It's logical. The Crossing is such a gigantic open space, it demands a freestanding work of art of Herculean dimensions. The structure must have more than architectural aspects, it must also be a piece of sculpture—beautiful to look at on its own, but also perfectly integrated into the very fabric of this great basilica. And GianLorenzo has proved that he is the best designer in Rome, probably the world."

"I don't care about that. That Bernini fellow stole the baldacchino commission from you and I resent it. It's not fair."

"Please Francesco, don't get angry with GianLorenzo. If you must get angry with someone, it should be with the Pope who awarded him the commission—but that wouldn't make any sense, would it?"

"It's not fair," Borromini said, his voice starting to attract attention, but he was too upset to notice or care. "Didn't you do some preliminary work on the structure?"

"Please, lower your voice and listen to me. What I did or didn't do is immaterial at this point. I don't mean to preach, but you are young and extremely talented as a stonecutter and architectural draftsman. Fine. You say you want to be an architect. Well, if you want to succeed as an architect, you'll have to learn to compromise."

"I need to be a whore to receive commissions?"

"Please, Francesco, lower your voice. I'm not saying that at all. You need talent to obtain commissions—which you have—and talent will overcome many things. Sometimes, however, in the rarefied, realistic world of patrons, you must . . . adjust. Make concessions. Be smart. Try to think more like GianLorenzo."

"You want me to think like him?" Borromini shouted, but caught himself. He lowered his voice so low, Maderno had to strain to hear him. "I don't like his attitude. Did you see how he looked at my hands?"

"Thank you for settling down, Francesco, now here is the point I wanted to make. GianLorenzo sculpted one of the most powerful pieces in artistic history—the Rape of Proserpina—and do you know what his patron Scipione Borghese did?"

"I don't know and I don't care," Borromini mumbled.

"Francesco, please. Listen. Not only did Cardinal Borghese not pay for the jewel, he gave the group away—to Cardinal Ludovico Ludovisi, the Pope's nephew. And, do you know what GianLorenzo said to his patron? Nothing. He used his head and said nothing. And do you know what happened? Cardinal Borghese almost immediately commissioned two more major groups from him."

"I'm glad he didn't get paid."

"But you see, dear boy, he did. Cardinal Ludovisi paid GianLorenzo more for his masterpiece than his patron would have."

"That's different from your being passed over."

"Maybe it is. Let me try to explain this in a different way. You know the façade of Gesu? Do you remember who designed it?"

"Giacomo della Porta," Borromini said, perking up—happy that he knew the answer.

"Correct. Now, do you know who designed the great church itself? It was Vignola. Jacopo Vignola. He was Cardinal Farnese's architect for some twenty years. Why did della Porta design the façade when Vignola designed the magnificent church? Or, to put it another way, why didn't Vignola design the façade for the church he designed?"

In spite of himself, Borromini was getting impatient with his mentor. "I don't follow you," he said in a tone he immediately regretted.

"I'll tell you why. Vignola didn't design the façade of 'his' church because his patron passed him over for the design of a younger man—Giacomo della Porta. Sound familiar?"

Maderno's logic was too much for Borromini to bear. He examined his hands—as if he was a surgeon about to operate—clinched his hands into fists, and exploded. "Did you see the way that Bernini looked at my hands? Like I was a peasant."

Borromini reached down, picked up a loose fragment of marble, grit his teeth, and hammered it over and over with the side of his hand, karate style. He pounded so hard, blood gushed from his hand, but Francesco didn't notice. "When that Bernini stole from you," he said, "it was the same as stealing from me."

Francesco slung the blood-soaked piece of marble across the floor of the basilica and then ran after it, kicking at it wildly. Completely frustrated, he finally stopped, took a kerchief from his pocket, and wrapped it around his right hand.

Carlo Maderno wanted to cry. He tried to speak but couldn't find the right words.

Borromini continued. "I will never forget what that person did to us. Never."

Maderno watched, still speechless. He was horrified at Francesco's actions, but in a way, he wished he had that kind of raw emotion. *Of course, if I ever acted like that, there is no way I could have held the position of Architect of Saint Peter's for all these years much less received all of the important commissions I have received.*

Maderno studied Borromini, who was now kneeling in a pew, praying. *Besides his explosive temper, Francesco certainly has some strange habits and ideas. When he's not with me, he wants to be alone. And, with all of the beautiful women in Rome, I will never understand his vow of celibacy. But I don't care about those things. Underneath, he has a big heart—I've literally seen him move little dogs out of the way of carriages more than once. He's an intellectual, a good conversationalist, and he has talent. For me, he has been a wonderful companion and an enormous help on my projects over the years. I love him like a son, but he's not easy.*

Maderno watched Borromini make his way to the confessional, a trail of blood marking his path. He sighed and shook his head. *In my heart I know Francesco has the ability to be a great architect and have a successful career. I just hope he doesn't make a mess of his life—I fear he may be his own worse enemy.*

Chapter XLVI

Nick J. Mileti

Giulio Mazzarini was Bernini's best friend. The indefatigable Bernini basically had no time for social friends. But when Cardinal Barberini introduced GianLorenzo to Giulio, the two talented youths hit it off immediately.

The Bernini/Mazzarini social friendship quickly prospered because—as in most close friendships—each saw himself as a mirror image of the other. Both young men were suave, well-read, well-groomed, well-dressed, serious ladies men—who were also highly intelligent and even more ambitious (in no particular order). And they both had talent.

There was one basic difference. Bernini had already arrived at the top of his profession and was the number one celebrity in Rome, while Mazzarini—four years Bernini's junior—was still on his way up the power ladder.

Maffeo Barberini liked and respected Giulio Mazzarini. When he was elected Pope, Mazzarini became one of his inner circle, traveling Europe as the Pope's personal representative. Each successful assignment led to another, and Bernini was confident that stardom was clearly a matter of time for the low-key, but cunning, papal diplomat.

The two young, attractive men in their colorful capes, flowing black hair and penetrating dark eyes, were the talk of the town. It was rumored, and widely believed, that between them, they had been with every noblewoman in Rome, regardless of her marital status.

—

One night, with four beautiful women in tow, Giulio arrived at GianLorenzo's studio to find his friend working, obviously unmindful of the time. Mazzarini indicated to the ladies that they should sit down and be quiet.

"I'm ready for some food and drink," the aggressive Princess said. She remained standing. "He hasn't even had the courtesy to acknowledge us. I don't want to wait. Why should we have to wait for him?"

Having encountered this attitude many times, Giulio knew exactly how to deal with it. "Go then, and be quick about it," Mazzarini said.

The beauty immediately sat down, pouting. Giulio took her hands and stroked the smooth, silky skin.

"You must understand my friend GianLorenzo. He's not a snob, it's his concentration. His concentration. It's so intense, when he's working he doesn't see anyone enter. Once, I came here with the Pope. GianLorenzo was so absorbed in his work, he never greeted the Holy Father."

The Princess was shocked. "My God, what happened?"

"The Pope, who knows Bernini as well as any man alive, silently seated himself. We watched him work for an hour or so and then we left, just as silently. In fact, see that youngster on the scaffolding with GianLorenzo? That assistant is there to prevent him from falling off—my friend pays absolutely no attention to anything but his carving as he moves about. I suppose that's one reason he's the best in the world."

The Princess, now a believer, relaxed and watched Bernini with fascination. She was stupefied; the sculptor seemed to be in ecstasy. The way his eyes glowed as the chips flew—she had never seen anything like that before. It was as if the nearly complete statute was alive, coming out of the marble to greet her creator.

"I recognize the subject," she said, very, very softly. "It's Saint Bibiana, isn't it? I know all about her—Bibiana was my mother's name."

"A papal commission," Giulio said. "The life-size statute is going to adorn the High Altar of the modest church bearing her name—which GianLorenzo has totally remodeled, even the façade."

"I can't believe it. Look at that humble expression on her face. To me, he has captured the exact moment of the Saint's spiritual transformation, just before her martyrdom. On the other hand, the statute has a sensuous quality about it—maybe it's the way he has draped her body. It makes me tingle. Humble and sensuous, at the same time. How can he accomplish such a thing?"

"Princess, GianLorenzo truly considers his talent God-given, and that he himself is merely an Agent of God. To put it another way, last night he told me that he didn't make the statute, that Saint Bibiana herself sculpted and impressed herself in the marble."

"An Agent of God, how nice," the Princess said. She looked at her friends. "Why don't we relax and enjoy the show? An Agent of God is definitely worth waiting for."

Mazzarini laughed out loud and gave the Princess a hug and kiss. *I have a feeling that tonight is going to be more fun than usual.*

Chapter XLVII

Nick J. Mileti

Carlo Maderno tapped his fingers on the arms of his chair, nervously waiting for his first meeting with Urban VIII since the fateful day when the strong-willed Pope, referring to the baldacchino commission, bluntly told him, "You will have to resign yourself to see Bernini do this work."

Maderno was pensive, but realistic. *Almost without exception, every newly elected Pope has his own personal artistic and architectural favorite. Why should Maffeo Barberini be any different?*

Actually, unlike his assistant, Maderno was not bitter about being passed over for the most important commission of the day—he was just thankful that the Pope had retained him as Architect of Saint Peter's. *I just hope it is recognition of more than my age.*

Deep in his heart, Maderno was afraid that today would signal the finale to his long and illustrious career, in which he served several Popes. *In fairness to this new Pope, I must admit illness is taking its toll. This gout is definitely slowing me down.*

Within these conflicting emotions, regardless of what might happen today, the grand old master of Roman architecture was serene. *I take solace in the fact that my highly regarded façade, portico and nave of Saint Peter's—not to mention my facade of Santa Susanna and dome of Sant' Andrea della Valle—will insure my place in history. I do, I really do.*

—

"Carlo," the Pope said as he entered the room, "you look deep in thought. Are you feeling well?"

The pontiff could feel his architect's nervousness. He handed Maderno a goblet.

"Drink up," he said. "The wine will settle your nerves. Now, Carlo, first I want to clear something up. You know that I favor Bernini—everyone knows that. It's nothing negative to your superb abilities—it's just that Bernini is the most talented individual I have ever seen in my entire life. So, you may ask, why didn't I appoint him to replace you as Architect of Saint Peter's when I was elected Pope?"

Maderno studied the bottom of his goblet.

"It's because I respect you too much, Carlo, both as an architect and as a man. Truth is, your talent and kind disposition have earned you the affection of every citizen of Rome. As long as I am the Pope, you will remain Architect of Saint Peter's."

The aging master slowly raised his head. Tears streamed down his face. The pontiff handed him a silk kerchief.

"Now, to get to the business of the day. I have Cavaliere Bernini so busy at Saint Peter's I don't want to divert his attention from that critically important work. That means, for you, I have exciting news. After many years of trying, my family and I have finally secured Palazzo Sforza and the surrounding property. From this day forward it will be known as Palazzo Barberini and will serve as our family residence. What do you think?"

Maderno couldn't believe his ears. *It looks like I am getting a commission instead of a sacking.*

"It is an inspired acquisition, Your Holiness."

"Yes it is, isn't it? Beautiful as the palace is, however, it does demand a significant number of changes to suit the needs of the Barberini clan. Therefore, my friend, if you feel up to it—physically, I mean—I'd like you to plan the rehabilitation and decoration of the structure."

"Holy Father, this is truly one of the most satisfying commissions of my life. I cannot wait to begin. If it suits Your Holiness, I would love to see your ideas of what needs to be accomplished."

"You know me too well, Carlo," Urban said, barely suppressing a laugh. He pulled a pile of sketches from the top drawer of his massive desk. "The family has also contributed suggestions, since they will be living in the palace." The Pope smoothed out the rough plans, which Maderno glanced through.

"You can be certain," Maderno said, "by the time we are finished, Palazzo Barberini will rival any other palace in Rome—including Palazzo Farnese."

Urban VIII smiled. *How did the old man know exactly what I had in mind?*

On his way out of the office, Maderno stopped at the door. "Holy Father, you make me feel thirty-nine, not sixty-nine."

The pontiff laughed. "And to think there are some people, particularly in Germany and England, who dispute the Pope's divine powers."

—

Borromini and Maderno stood in the courtyard of the Barberini Palace, looking intently at the massive structure.

"What are you thinking?" Francesco asked.

"I plan to change the building into an H-shape," the reinvigorated Carlo Maderno said.

Francesco never ceased to be impressed with his mentor's analytical, progressive architectural mind. "So the palazzo becomes more of a country villa than an urban palace. At this semi-remote location, I can see your thinking. I'm correct, am I not?"

Maderno wrapped his aching arm around Borromini's waist. "Francesco, here is the best news. In recognition of the fine creative work you did designing the lantern for the dome of Sant' Andrea della Valle, I am making you my chief assistant on this job."

Borromini was ecstatic. "Does that mean that I can do the redesign of the building? Like a real architect."

Maderno chuckled out loud. "Don't get greedy, Francesco. I said you would be my assistant, not that I'm retiring. Assistant means I tell you what I want, then you draw it to my specifications."

Borromini's face turned to stone. Maderno knew how sensitive Francesco was and immediately regretted his remark and tone. *I hate to hurt him, but the point had to be made. The last thing I need is a misunderstanding in this papal commission I was so lucky to receive.*

"It sounds like I'm to be a mere copyist," a dejected Borromini said. "I'm already twenty-six years old, when do I become an architect, like you?"

—

The pair walked to Maderno's carriage in silence. When they reached it, Borromini, head down, kept walking.

"I guess you didn't hear me," Maderno called out. "I said that in addition to being a stonecutter on this job, you would also be my chief assistant. I can't do any better than that. Please, come with me, we'll have supper together at my house. We can talk about this some more."

Borromini kept walking. He suddenly stopped and turned. "I still love you," he said, and, head down, walked on.

Maderno rode home alone in his carriage. Tears filled his eyes. *I'm not sure if these are tears of despair, due to Francesco's lack of appreciation, or tears of joy, for the affection he feels for me. Probably both.*

Chapter XLVIII

Beyond Michelangelo

The newest member of Bernini's workshop looked around the studio he had joined a day earlier. A stonecutter, the youngster was hired to work on the baldacchino project. He approached the foreman and asked permission to talk, which was granted.

"Please don't take this the wrong way, sir, but there are so many men working here, will I ever see the results of my labors? I'm proud of the work I do."

The boss of the workshop exhaled a deep sigh. *Why is it always the same question?*

"Yes, you will see results, just don't expect any credit." The foreman didn't want to be too harsh on the young man, but had learned over the years to answer that particular query in a straightforward, honest manner. "You'll be working on the baldacchino—the most important project in Rome today—and it is GianLorenzo Bernini's project. The Pope commissioned it to Bernini, Bernini designed it, Bernini is working on it everyday, to the detriment of his health I might add, and Bernini will take credit for it."

"But sir, with all due respect, doesn't a project of this magnitude need hundreds of men to complete it?"

"Of course. But that doesn't mean it isn't Bernini's project, does it? If you have a problem with that, I suggest you put your tools back in your bag and look for other work."

"Honestly? I did that, sir. All I heard was, 'If you want to work in Rome as a stonecutter, you work for Bernini.' I was told that has the largest and busiest studio in Rome."

"Well then, what's your problem? It's pleasant here in his workshop, and in order to attract the best possible talent, he pays better than anyone else in town. And, working here, you will learn from a true genius. If you run into him when he isn't working—which, I admit, is rare—you will find he is very approachable and helpful. But I warn you, never bother him when he is working. Never. Or you won't last long around here."

The youngster returned to his workbench in the rear of the studio. A worker at the next bench walked over. "Welcome. What's wrong, you look like you're going to be ill. Ah ha. I'll wager you were just told that you will receive no credit for the work you will do here."

"How did you know?"

"They told me the same thing—in fact everyone who comes to work here asks the same question when they start. Personally, after I thought about it, I understood the Cavaliere's position. We assistants only contribute details; not that details aren't important—they are. But Bernini's the master, and the master does all of the important work, and always will. That's why he doesn't give credit to others."

"Never?"

"Not so far. And, by the way, I agree with him. Not that everybody does. Why do you think you were lucky enough to be hired to work at that desk? I'll tell you why. One of our best young sculptors left to set up his own studio. He was with us for a number of years and was very good—especially with the drill—but he wanted recognition. What do you think happened when he asked for that recognition? The Cavaliere never put his chisel down. He paused for a few seconds from his work and said, not unkindly, 'Good Luck in your new position Mister Finelli,' and resumed cutting. Pietro Bernini paid him, and Finelli was gone that day."

"That's another thing I don't understand. His father hired me, but I was told I answer to GianLorenzo. Why?"

"Good grief, didn't they teach you anything in Milan? Bernini is the busiest artist in Rome. Pietro is helping his son with the administrative details of the baldacchino job, but the young Cavaliere is the artistic and overall genius. Think about it. If we were only working on a job the size and scope of the baldacchino, an effective organization would be needed, but we're also working on a number of important other projects—several significant portrait busts, the tomb of our beloved Pope Urban VIII, a fountain in the Piazza di Spagna and . . . well, you get the idea.

"Doesn't the man ever sleep?"

"Not really."

Chapter XLIX

Bernini sat on the edge of the fountain he had built in the Piazza di Spagna. His friend Giulio Mazzarini sat next to him. The pair—who had been celebrating all night following the unveiling of the fountain—were the only people in the square on this clear, crisp spring morning. They took their shoes and socks off and playfully splashed their feet in the cold water of the fountain. Giulio munched on a piece of chicken he salvaged from the party, while Bernini ate an apple.

"This is without a doubt the most interesting, unique fountain I've ever seen," Giulio said. "Do you have a name for it?"

"La Barca," Bernini said. "The boat. Unfortunately, last night at the unveiling, everyone called it La Barcaccia, which I take to mean Rotten Old Boat."

Mazzarini kicked water at his friend. "Why aren't you ever satisfied? I heard the comments, and not one person meant it in a pejorative way. When they called this fountain Old Boat, they didn't mean Rotten Old Boat, they meant Old Boat in a humorous way. In any case, in my opinion, you should be pleased Rome took your fountain into its heart and gave it a clever nickname. How do you do it? Get this kind of visceral reaction—to a fountain, I mean?"

Bernini thought a minute while he finished his apple and then dropped the core in the pool of water.

"It's simple. Generally, I start from my sculptor's point of view to get the fountain to flow. Then I give it an architectural analysis, to make certain it relates to its environment—in this case the magnificent Piazza di Spagna."

"And specifically?"

"Specifically, I've found that for a fountain to make sense, one must give it some real significance, or, at least, an illusion to something noble, whether real or imagined. What I did in this case, by placing the boat low in a pool of water and making it appear to be sinking, I created subtle, almost subconscious, dramatic tension."

"And the fact that you've added the Barberini escutcheon makes the drama all the more compelling, doesn't it? Will the papal boat sink? You are so clever my friend."

Bernini raised his arms in pretended surrender. "That's not a cheat. After all, Urban did commission the fountain."

—

"You looked a little sad all night long, GianLorenzo," Giulio said. "Can it be because I'm leaving for an assignment in France and you're going to miss me?"

"That and more," Bernini said. "I'm worried about my father. Did you see how pale he looked last night at the festivities? He hasn't been feeling well lately but I can't get him to stay home and rest. He keeps saying that helping me keep the baldacchino project on track is the most important thing in his life. He won't listen to mother or any of the family either."

"How old is your father?"

"He's sixty-seven, but he is working at the pace of a much younger man. What do you think I should do? Any advice?"

"GianLorenzo, what can you do? Just keep smothering him with love and pray for the best. Your father is old enough to know what is important to him in his life."

Bernini froze. *Little does Giulio know how insightful he is.* He looked his friend in the eye and tried his best to speak without falling apart.

"Giulio, my father has always known what's important to him, and I've been the direct beneficiary of that. The ironic thing is, my father's overriding commitment to me is the only thing in my entire life I have ever felt guilty about."

Giulio studied his friend's sharp, angular face. He had never seen GianLorenzo this shaken-up and decided to remain still. *I doubt that he wants to pursue this—but with GianLorenzo, you never know.*

Young Bernini's gaze drifted away. "Sometimes when I think about my father, I feel like I've eaten a barrel full of the cream my mother occasionally whips up."

Mazzarini burst out laughing and hugged his friend. "Now that's what the Church calls mortal guilt."

Chapter L

Beyond Michelangelo

The year 1629 started out as a banner year for Borromini and Bernini. Tragically, the deaths of the major figures in their respective lives turned the year into one of sadness and heartbreak. Francesco Borromini was thirty years old and GianLorenzo Bernini was thirty-one.

Carlo Maderno and Pietro Bernini died.

—

Borromini was gaining more and more respect from Carlo Maderno, and his percentage of self-generated projects was slowly growing. In addition, even though Borromini's design efforts on the Barberini Palace were limited, the work he performed was received with enthusiasm.

"Francesco, I love the way you have set those windows into recessed arches," Maderno told him in January, the day before he died.

Borromini was not with the seventy-three year old Carlo Maderno on his last day, something he regretted—and fretted about—the rest of his life.

Francesco watched his mentor's body being laid to rest in the church of San Giovanni dei Fiorentini where the Pope himself said funeral Mass.

"I will join you in heaven," a grief stricken Borromini said, crying like a baby who needed to be changed.

—

With Carlo Maderno's death, the prestigious post of Architect of Saint Peter's became vacant.

In the face of all logic, Borromini was optimistic that Pope Urban VIII would appoint him to that position. *After all, I've read every architectural book ever written. Not only that, I've done some work in the basilica.*

A few days after Maderno's death, Pope Urban VIII appointed GianLorenzo Bernini to the post of Architect of Saint Peter's. Borromini became hysterical. *Here I am, practically a full-fledged architect, and what is that Bernini fellow? A mere sculptor, and a poor one at that.*

—

In spite of his grief over Maderno's death, Borromini forced himself to keep regular work hours at the Palazzo Barberini because that commission was now also vacant.

Francesco was absolutely positive that he would receive the Barberini Palace commission from the Pope. *I was Carlo Maderno's chief assistant on the Barberini Palace job, and I even designed numerous features myself. Not only that, lately I carried my mentor to the job, he was so sick and infirm—surely this compassionate Pope will relate to that. Best of all, that Bernini person has never set foot in the palazzo.*

When Borromini learned that Pope Urban VIII also granted Bernini the Barberini Palace commission, he was beyond hysterical, he was crazed—ranting and raving to anyone he could corner on the street. He would grab the unlucky person by the shoulders and shout at the top of his husky voice.

"This Bernini person—he's a menace. First he stole Maderno's commission for the baldacchino and now he's stolen two appointments from me. He's a thief. No, he's worse."

The peasants who were stopped had no idea what Borromini was talking about. The clerics and nobility, on the other hand, understood completely. They didn't agree, but they understood.

—

On a windy, rainy night in August, when Bernini arrived home, all of the lights were on and several unfamiliar carriages were parked in front. GianLorenzo crashed through the front door and ran into his young brother Luigi.

"It's father, isn't it," Bernini said on the dead run.

"The doctors and priest are in his room, and . . ."

Bernini was already on the third floor. His mother was pacing back and forth in the hall outside of the bedroom, and the girls were praying in the adjoining room.

"How bad is it, mother?"

Angelica threw her arms around her son and hung on. She was crying hysterically. "He's had a stroke and can't talk very well. The doctors said he shouldn't be disturbed."

GianLorenzo carefully peeled off his mother's arms and sat her in a nearby chair. He then barged into the bedroom.

"You can't come in here," the older doctor said. "This man is deathly sick, and . . ."

"All of you get out. Now. I want to be alone with my father. Out."

—

Bernini sat on the side of the bed. He took his father's hand and lifted it to his lips. He held it there. Pietro smiled—he seemed to gain strength from his son's expression of affection.

GianLorenzo wiped the sweat off of his father's still imposing forehead. He stared at his hero for a full fifteen minutes, his mind cataloging his wonderful life with his father.

"Father, I have something to confess. Back in Naples, when I was a little boy, I heard you tell nonno you were moving the family to Rome on account of me. I just wanted you to know that I know. Without a doubt, that was the most unselfish act I can imagine and I want to officially say thank you. I've wanted to tell you this for a long time."

Pietro attempted a smile. "You are welcome, my son," he managed. "Believe me, it was the best thing I've ever done in my life—besides marrying your mother and having you, of course."

Pietro tried to sit up but fell back down. Bernini wanted to cry but fought back the tears. He picked up his father's hands again and kissed him on the forehead.

"If you have the strength," GianLorenzo said. "I've always wondered how you arranged that papal commission. Are you up to telling me?"

Pietro tried to laugh but it stuck in his throat. "It was easy," he said. "I bribed Cavaliere d'Arpino. The artist was in great favor in those days and was in charge of Pope Paul's Chapel in Santa Maria Maggiore. No, bribe is too harsh a word—let us just say that I gave him a generous gift which he obviously appreciated."

—

Pietro looked at GianLorenzo through his misty eyes. *Is that the aura of greatness I see around my son or am I just fading fast?*

"Believe it or not, I have something to confess to you," Pietro said, slumping lower in the bed, in spite of himself. "When I would ask you things like, 'Is that the best you can do?' or, 'Are you satisfied with what you have done?' it was calculated. I was trying to get you to be in competition with yourself. Can you forgive me?"

"Forgive you?" This was getting to be more than Bernini could handle. He shook all over. "I thank you. Because of you, father, I've never been completely satisfied with anything I've done. So I keep striving to do better. And I always will. What I'm trying to say is this. You—and God, of course—should get the real credit for my many successes."

Pietro squeezed his son's hand as hard as he could. The effort caused him to wince.

"Shall I call the doctors?" GianLorenzo asked.

"No. No. Tell your mother to come in, please, and bring the priest. I love you, son. And I am proud of you. What I saw almost thirty years ago has come true—you have gone beyond Michelangelo. In sculpture at least. I only wish the baldacchino were finished, so I could see with my own eyes that you have also surpassed the master in architecture—which I'm sure you will. Now you may leave. I'm very tired and want to sleep."

Bernini hugged his father and showered him with kisses. He laid his head against his father's cheek, making no attempt to hide the tears. He spoke between sobs.

"I love you too, father. In my life, I've been fortunate to know many renowned people—Popes, Cardinals, nobility, artists—some of the most esteemed and important individuals anywhere. But, if all of those wonderful people were molded into one, the resultant individual wouldn't add up to one Pietro Bernini. I love you father, you are the best father anyone could ask for. You will live inside me forever."

Sixty-seven year old Pietro Bernini died that night and was buried three days later in Santa Maria Maggiore. Urban VIII said the Mass.

A few days later, the Pope appointed GianLorenzo Bernini Architect of Acqua Vergine, a post previously held by his father.

Bernini's numerous positions were each accompanied by a generous annual stipend, which, when added together, amounted to a tidy sum.

In addition, of course, the fees he received for commissions were substantial income for the Cavaliere—who was notorious for charging what he thought was fair but everyone else considered outrageous.

Bernini's bonuses and gifts from appreciative patrons also added up.

All in all, Bernini was rapidly becoming one of the wealthiest citizens in Rome and the Papal States.

Borromini resented GianLorenzo's wealth as much as he resented his fame. *I'll show that Bernini person—I will never let money be important in my life.*

CHAPTER LI

Beyond Michelangelo

The day after Bernini's appointment, Borromini made it a point to be the first to arrive at the Barberini Palace, only to find Bernini already there, giving the job his first inspection.

"Good afternoon," GianLorenzo said, but Borromini didn't think that was funny. "You are the first to arrive and I commend you for that. Wait a minute—weren't you Carlo Maderno's assistant? Castellano or something."

"It was Castelli but I changed my name to Borromini. I hope you don't mind."

I guess I should expect the sarcasm. From what I've heard, he's been bad-mouthing me all over town. "Very well then," Bernini said. "Let us get a few things straight before the others arrive."

Borromini cringed visibly.

"Don't worry. I want you to continue doing exactly what you were doing under Mister Maderno. The only difference is you will report to me instead of him, and I'll be checking on your work every day."

Francesco was incensed. *I feel like telling him to take this job and stick it up his behind.* "That's not necessary—I'm a good worker."

"I'll be checking on the others, also, so don't think that I'm picking on you. In fact, Mister Maderno told me that you are an excellent craftsman . . ."

"Decorative sculptor."

"So I'd like you to also work on the baldacchino job. That is, if you'd care to."

Maybe I misjudged this man. "That, that, would be wonderful," Francesco said. "When can I start? Not that I care about money, but do I get paid for my work on each job?"

Bernini suppressed a smile. *Money is like a performer at Carnival—it does work its magic.* "Tomorrow," GianLorenzo said. "You can start tomorrow. Alternate between here and Saint Peter's and, of course, I will see that you are paid properly for both jobs. Good day, Borromini."

Chapter LII

Beyond Michelangelo

"I'm so sorry I'm late, Holy Father," Bernini said, gasping for air as he kissed the Pope's ring and bowed. The Cavaliere was out of breath after the swift ride from home to Saint Peter's. It was late, but the two most important men in Rome often met in the basilica after closing, so they could have privacy.

"Think nothing of it, GianLorenzo," the pontiff replied. "I was happy to be here alone for a few minutes—it gave me a chance to study your progress on the baldacchino. I assume you were sketching and lost track of time."

"You know me better than anyone on earth, Your Holiness, except maybe my sweet mother. Sometimes I think she knows me too well."

"Your mother is a fine woman. Now, GianLorenzo, I understand you are rethinking the superstructure."

"As you know, I made a cast of the statute of the Risen Christ, which was to top the canopy. Now that I see the statute, I feel it would be too heavy and out of proportion. I have some alternative ideas that I think you'll be pleased with . . ."

"We can discuss that another time—Sunday night supper would be fine. For now, permit me to tell you why I wanted to meet you here at the Crossing. It is obvious that the baldacchino is going to be a spectacular addition to the basilica. But as I look at the progress—and it's moving along nicely—it is clear to me that the magnificent structure you have designed shames the four bare, gigantic piers. This Crossing obviously needs to be decorated, and I am interested to know how you would do it."

———

Bernini felt like a fortuneteller who guesses the right answer on the first attempt. *For twenty years I've been waiting for this delicious question—since I first stood here with Mister Carracci.*

He spoke excitedly. "First of all, I would move the tomb of Pope Paul III. It's the only sizeable monument in any of the piers so it's out of place here—and it's out of scale. I'd move it to the left of the apse, across from the tomb I'm building for you. The balance will be just right, and the two monuments will make a distinctive frame for the apse."

The Pope grimaced. "I wish I had thought of that."

"You would have, eventually," the suave genius said. "Now, here is what I see as the appropriate decoration for the Crossing. I see four huge statutes in niches, one in each pier, celebrating the four most important relics of the Church. I also see the actual relics displayed in smaller niches, above the statutes."

"Huge? How huge are you thinking?"

"The statutes need to be three or four times life-size to be in scale with the basilica, the Crossing, the baldacchino and these gigantic piers. I see statutes of Longinus and the Lance, Helen and the Cross, Veronica and the Veil and Andrew and his Head. The smaller upper niches should have balconies and be framed by Solomonic, twisted, columns."

The Pope was enthralled. *I can't believe the Cavaliere could come up with a meaningful plan on the spot—yet here it is.* "Will you have time to carve these four great statutes by yourself?"

"Your Holiness, I will design everything down to the smallest detail. Saint Longinus I will sculpt personally because I believe he is the key element in the scheme. The others I will assign to three of the best sculptors in Rome. Needless to say, I will supervise them closely—very closely."

"And models," the pontiff said, becoming more and more excited. "I assume there will be models."

"I will prepare full scale models—probably in stucco—which will be put in place. That way, you can see the full scope and effect of this momentous project."

Bernini waited while the full impact of the oral presentation sunk in. With exquisite timing—at which he was becoming a master—the consummate showman then presented the Pope with his clincher.

"Oh, one more thing, Holy Father. Remember those Solomonic columns that were salvaged from the original basilica of Saint Peter's? Well, I have located them, and those are the columns I will use to flank the upper niches."

Bernini received the prime commission to decorate the Crossing of Saint Peter's at the next meeting of the Fabbrica.

Chapter LIII

For several years in the 1620s, hundreds of workmen scurried about Saint Peter's, creating one of the world's wonders—the baldacchino over the High Altar. On this particular morning, Bernini was giving instructions to a dozen decorative sculptors when he spied Borromini on the edge of the group. *What is that man doing here? Can't he even follow directions?*

"Shouldn't you be at the Barberini Palace working on the stairway?" the exasperated GianLorenzo asked Francesco. The other artisans cleared their throats and intently studied the floor, the ceiling, and the walls of the basilica, as if searching for a minor scratch in the biggest church in the world.

"I need to talk with you," Borromini said. "Now, if you don't mind, Your Highness."

Bernini sent his embarrassed workers—who wagered that Borromini wouldn't last the day—away, and gave Francesco his attention. *He is an imposing fellow, but I wish he would change his work clothes occasionally—they smell exactly like his attitude. I don't care, those things are not that important; I'm going to try to live with him, at least until the baldacchino is finished. I like his work ethic and he has more than a little talent as a decorative sculptor.* "What can I do for you Francesco?"

"I quit the job at the Barberini Palace," Borromini said. "It was that Pietro man."

Bernini couldn't believe his ears. "Pietro da Cortona? He's as good an artist and architect as is living today—and a lovely human being besides."

Borromini was like a bulldog, clinging to his prey. "That's the one. He changed some of Carlo Maderno's drawings on the Barberini Palace, so I quit. This way, I thought you might give me extra work on the baldacchino. I been waiting patiently."

"Pietro didn't 'change any drawings.' What happened was, Urban commissioned him to redesign the east façade of the palace. These things happen all the time. You're waiting? For what?"

"I want to help design the baldacchino."

Bernini was losing his patience and tried his best to control his temper. "Francesco, what are you thinking? Any fool with two eyes can see that the basic structure of the baldacchino has been in place for some time—I've had more than sufficient assistance in that aspect of the job from my brother Luigi. And others. The decorations you're designing are very important to the job, you should know that."

"I want . . . I need more responsibility. Those decorations are minor and you should know that. I could design the superstructure of the canopy. I hear that's not done yet."

I can't control this man anymore. I need to get rid of him. "Sorry, I don't mean to be rude, but I must hurry off to a meeting with the Holy Father. Let me think about this." *On the other hand, why don't I pick his brain for ideas? What is my downside? Nothing. Actually, I know exactly what a man like this needs. A bone. I need to throw Borromini a big, tasty bone to keep him in line.*

—

It was a balmy summer night in Rome—the windows were open all over town, including those in the Pope's residence. The smell from the clinging yellow jasmine vines filled the air.

"I was thinking on my way over here tonight," Bernini said to the pontiff. "The poem you wrote for my Apollo and Daphne group is so good, it should be inscribed on the base. Please, recite it for me once more."

Urban enjoyed reciting his poetry more than almost anything. He took a drink of his after-dinner brandy, cleared his throat, and spoke. "Whoever in love pursues the delights of a fleeting form fills his hand with leaves and plucks bitter berries. Which reminds me, GianLorenzo. Your love life. Is it up to your usual standards?"

Bernini quickly downed his goblet of brandy and almost chocked on it.

—

The Pope poured Bernini another brandy. "Before you go," he said, "I have another commission for you. The Sapienza—the University of Rome—is looking for an architect. Naturally, I would recommend you, but I fear that you are much to busy. I leave it up to you."

Bernini smiled inwardly. *I can't believe it—the Holy Father is handing me the solution to the Borromini problem on a silver platter.*

"Your Holiness, thanks to you, I am much too busy. But, I do have a suggestion. A young man named Francesco Borromini is an up-and-coming architect. He's a very important member of my teams at Saint Peter's and your palace. Perhaps you would care to meet him." *I have never turned down a commission before—I hope His Holiness doesn't see through my stratagem.*

"That is not necessary," the Pope replied. "Your word is good enough for me."

—

The next day Bernini told Borromini he had secured the architectural job at the Sapienza for him. Borromini absorbed the news without a trace of emotion, like a penitent hearing his sentence of Our Fathers and Hail Marys.

"Does that mean," Borromini asked, "I don't get to design the superstructure of the baldacchino?"

"Absolutely not," Bernini lied. *I don't understand an oaf like this—it never entered his mind to say thank you.* "Here are drawings of four volutes for the canopy. Please look them over and give me your opinion on their stability."

Chapter LIV

Saint Peter's was overflowing with decorations and people. The dedication that all of Rome was waiting for—that of the towering baldacchino—was finally at hand.

"Why we standing back here," Borromini said to one of his fellow stonecutters. "We built it."

"Please be quiet, Francesco. It's a fact of life that the nobility and clergy sit up front and we stand in the back. And that is that. Now be quiet and enjoy one of life's greatest moments—the Pope himself saying Mass from the High Altar under the baldacchino."

"Another thing," Borromini said. "Why is that Bernini man sitting in the first row? Who does he think he is?"

"You're impossible," Borromini's fellow worker said. "All you want to do is argue. Okay, I'll tell you who Bernini is. He is the Father, Son and Holy Ghost of the baldacchino. He conceived it, he designed it and he worked on it every day for nine years. Did you hear what I said? Nine years. And, if you think he had fun in that sweltering foundry year after year, then you just don't know anything."

"I don't care if it was ninety years. Conceived it? My mentor conceived it and he should have received he commission."

"Oh, now I see. If Carlo Maderno had received the commission, you would have had a significant role. That's it, isn't it?"

"So? I did most of the work on the structure we're looking at—the one you call Bernini's baldacchino."

"Stop. I was there every day and I know better. Now be quiet or you'll be asked to leave."

―

When Urban VIII finished Mass, he turned and faced the congregation.

"My dearly beloved. All of us here in the year of our Lord 1633 were part of history. I had the honor to be the first Pope to celebrate Mass under this majestic edifice that I was lucky enough to commission from the greatest artist of all time, GianLorenzo Bernini. Will Cavaliere Bernini please come forward?"

The faithful watched in hushed reverence as Bernini slowly walked to the altar. He bowed and kissed the Pope's ring, and then faced the worshipers. He tried to talk but no sound came out.

"I don't think he's going to be able to keep it together," Angelica said to her son Luigi.

The crowd held its breath—it was becoming painfully clear that the Cavaliere was succumbing to the emotion of the moment.

Bernini wiped the tears from his eyes. He spoke haltingly.

"I . . . I . . . I only wish my father could have been here today to see . . ."

Bernini tried, but he couldn't stop the tears. He looked down at his mother and family. He looked at the Pope. He looked at the people. And then he descended from the altar.

Nobody could remember Saint Peter's being this quiet. And no one present ever forgot the exact words of what had to be the shortest speech in history.

—

Borromini was lying in wait in the portico when Bernini and his family, surrounded by well wishers, came out of the church. Francesco pushed himself through the mass of people and lunged at Bernini, trying to choke him.

"You thief," he screamed, "you stole it."

Luigi jumped on Borromini's back and put his head in a hammerlock. The crowd of spectators, dressed in their Sunday best, was aghast.

"Who is this person," Angelica asked GianLorenzo.

"Nobody important, mother. He's a stonecutter who has done a little work for me."

Upon hearing this, Borromini screamed even louder.

"What's your name," Angelica asked her son's assailant.

"Francesco Borromini. What's it to you?"

Angelica nonchalantly kicked Borromini in the balls. "Don't you ever, ever, call my son a thief again."

Borromini collapsed in a heap. The onlookers gasped, then applauded.

"Come along family," the still beautiful, impeccably dressed matriarch said. "We mustn't be late for Sunday dinner."

Chapter LV

Nick J. Mileti

The Spanish Order of the Discalced (shoeless) Trinitarians was a group of poor monks who collected money to free Christians who had been captured by the Moors. Even though their work centered in Spain, the Order felt it needed a presence in Rome, near the Vatican, for religious as well as propaganda purposes.

By Church standards, the Trinitarians were a minor Order when judged against the larger, more powerful arms of the church. The Trinitarians, however, were as ambitious as their grander cousins, and wanted a church of their own. Even though it obviously would be much more modest than Il Gesu of the Jesuits, Chiesa Nuova of the Oratorians, or Sant' Andrea della Valle of the Theatines, the Trinitarians knew having their own church would still send a powerful message.

Fortunately, in addition to regularly performing their good works, the Trinitarians had the foresight to acquire an irregularly shaped, but beautifully located, piece of land near the Barberini Palace. In 1634, the Order decided it was time to build their church and ancillary buildings.

—

"Whom can we get to build our church," Juan San Bonaventura, the Head of the Order asked at the meeting called for that purpose. Slight in stature, Juan was a dark and portly Spaniard who was respected and admired by the other monks. He carried himself well and therefore appeared taller than he really was. Bonaventura was also careful—even suspicious—by nature, which is why he was elected Head of the Order.

The meeting room, which was filled with earnest clerics, was small but sparkling clean. Excited by the thought of their own church and buildings, the brothers all began to talk at once.

"I think Bernini is everyone's first choice, but he's much too expensive for us." "Did anyone hear how much his bonus was for the baldacchino?" "Whatever it was, he earned that and more." "What's the difference, even if we had the money, the Holy Father would never release him." "Who can we get?"

Father Bonaventura continued. "Settle down please. We need an architect, and I intend to interview the best architects in Rome. But, since we have no money—as always—we need God's help. I suggest we all direct our meditation and prayers to this critical matter."

"May I speak?" a freckled-faced brother asked tentatively from the rear of the room. His eyes searched the upturned faces of his fellow clerics, and seeing no objection, the brother, new to the Order, continued in a small voice. "I heard something very interesting a few days ago. I heard that Bernini recommended a man named Francesco Borromini to be Architect of the University, and that our beloved Holy Father spoke in his favor. Needless to say, he was appointed to the post. What I'm wondering is, shouldn't we interview this Borromini first? Thank you for listening."

—

"Welcome, please sit there Mister Borromini," Bonaventura said. "Spread your drawings on the table so that we can evaluate your previous work."

Francesco broke into a cold sweat when confronted with the question he unrealistically hoped wouldn't be asked. He wiped his brow and fought to hide his concern. *How can they do this to me?* "Just Borromini will be fine, and I have no drawings to show you."

The monks were stunned. "We may be a small, humble Order," Bonaventura said, "but this church, cloister, and lodgings are critically important to us. How can we take a chance on an inexperience architect?"

The brothers started to gather their things.

Fortunately, Borromini was prepared for this situation and had spent days rehearsing his speech. "Wait. Wait and hear me out." He spoke rapidly, but earnestly, which impressed the pious monks. "Thank you. I am celibate, like you. I have devoted myself to God, like you. I believe God put me on this earth to be an architect much as He has put you on earth to be monks. Why not consider this your chance to do God's work by granting me this commission."

Collectively the monks stared straight ahead, hating the situation. The interview was supposed to be to consider the quality of this gentleman's work, and instead he had no architectural experience but, rather, he appeared to have a sack full of needs.

"Borromini, our hearts go out to you," Bonaventura said. "But we must be practical. Sorry, but we cannot take a chance on an inexperienced man."

—

Borromini stood. Surprising even himself, he was uncharacteristically calm.

"Let me finish my thought. First of all, I know your work and your financial circumstances. How can you save money when you give everything you collect to the infidels? You can't. Another thing. Even though I hold the prestigious position of Architect of the University of Rome, I haven't started work for them, so my time is available for you."

"We have heard that Bernini recommended you for that position," Bonaventura said.

Borromini stiffened. "That man had nothing to do with it. The Holy Father himself suggested my name. Now, if I may continue. I've labored all my life and saved what I've earned, except for books. So, as you can see, I have time and money for the moment. I've read every book and treatise on architecture ever written. Have you seen the lantern on della Porta's magnificent dome at Sant' Andrea della Valle? Of course you have. Well, I personally designed that lantern, and . . ."

The room was getting restless and Borromini, who was becoming tentative, could sense it. He needed to make his move. He cleared his throat and spoke with a panache that impressed even the careful Bonaventura.

"Gentlemen, I place myself at your dedicated, shoeless feet. I have decided that I will work for your Order for nothing. You heard me right. I will charge you no fee for the entire project—the lodging, the cloister and the church."

The monks made the sign of the Cross in unison.

"Are you talking about everything," an incredulous Bonaventura asked. "Designing? Administration? Supervision?"

"All of the buildings and all of the services. Everything. So what do you say, do I get the job?"

A moist-eyed Bonaventura looked his group over. All he could see was a sea of smiling faces and glistening eyes.

"I know my brothers," he said to Borromini. The elated cleric paused, gasping for breath. "I don't think we need to talk with the other applicants. After all, how can we say no to the opportunity to perform God's work?"

Chapter LVI

The missionary Order, the Collegio di Propaganda Fide, was established to coordinate the many groups dedicated to the important task of propagating the Catholic faith to all parts of the world. It was an important Order, and consequently had sufficient funds to acquire a prime piece of land and building, adjacent to the popular Piazza di Spagna.

Cardinal Antonio Barberini, one of the Pope's nephews, was in charge of the Order. He was showing Bernini around their facilities.

"As you can see, Cavaliere, this façade is crumbling in several places. Look. Here . . . there . . . there . . . there . . . and there. We've owned this building for over ten years—it's time we do something to make certain our people are safe when they come to work here. What do you suggest?"

"I see what you mean," Bernini said, 'but you must not be too harsh. After all, this is a 15th Century building and all 200 year old buildings eventually show their age." Bernini was thinking fast. *I hope I'm not being too obvious. I'm as busy as I want to be, but on the other hand, Antonio is one of Urban's favorite nephews. Plus he's paying me to design the sets for the plays and operas at the Barberini Theatre. Oh well, as father used to say, there are two kinds of decisions in this world—the one's you make, and the ones that are made for you.*

Resigned, Bernini spoke, lacing his tone with the same enthusiasm an inveterate coffee drinker shows when sweetening his espresso with three spoonfuls of sugar. "I see that the greatest damage exists on the side facing the square, what I call the defining side. I recommend a new façade for it. I see brick. Yes, definitely brick."

"Good," the Cardinal said. "Now come inside with me. I want to show you where we want you to build a new chapel. We want to dedicate the chapel to the Three Magi—the three kings who were the first pagan converts to Christianity."

Bernini studied the location. "Excellent. I see a round and petite chapel—it shouldn't take over a year to build."

The Cardinal was overjoyed. "Then you'll do it? Both the church and the façade? Thank you, Cavaliere. You will be paid handsomely, of course."

Chapter LVII

Francesco Borromini was beyond happy—he was ecstatic. *I have done it. At last. I'm an architect with my very own commission. Who can I tell? A pasquinade? No, the little battered statute is covered with political messages.* Borromini remembered Giuseppe, the bookseller. *That short, squinty-eyed man would sell his wife for a fee, but he has some good qualities: Giuseppe is the unofficial town crier and best of all, he deals with all the right people—all potential patrons of mine.*

Francesco rushed to the bookstore. "Do you have any books on monasteries," he asked, trying his best to act dignified. "Hurry, I have important work to do."

"As a matter of fact, I do," Giuseppe said. "Here it is. Monasteries in the Middle Ages."

Borromini barely leafed through the leather-bound volume. "I'll take it. Aren't you going to ask why I want a book on monasteries?"

Giuseppe laughed. "I have a feeling you're going to tell me."

"I been hired by a major religious Order regarding a number of buildings for them. A monastery is the first on the list."

"Hired? You've been hired to do what," Giuseppe asked.

Borromini was thrilled. *He fell right into my trap.* "To design buildings, that's what. You are addressing Borromini the architect, not Borromini the stonecutter."

"My heartiest congratulations, my friend," Giuseppe said. He gave Francesco a hug and pinched him on both cheeks. 'I wish you the best of luck in your new life."

Borromini stopped short, his smile morphed into a thoughtful look. For the first time, the brand-new architect focused on the larger significance of his appointment. *I didn't look at this commission quite that way. Thank you God. It really will be a new life and it's about time.*

—

Giuseppe wrapped the book and collected the money. Borromini was smiling from ear to ear. *I've been selling this man books for years, and that is the first honest-to-goodness smile I've ever seen on him. I guess he needed this appointment.*

He handed Borromini his book and change. "You'll notice that I gave you a little discount—it's my way to say I'm happy for you. I want you to know I never give my other famous architectural customer a discount."

As soon as he said it, Giuseppe realized he had blundered. *I can't believe I said that.*

Borromini slammed the book on the counter and stormed out of the shop. A few seconds later, the door re-opened.

"Giuseppe, pay attention to what I'm going to say because I'm not going to repeat it. Make your choice. Borromini or that Bernini person. Which do you want for a customer?"

"It's you, of course," Giuseppe said without any hesitation. "Without a doubt, it's Borromini."

Giuseppe took the book to Borromini and gave him a warm hug before closing the door. *Naturally I'll keep both—I need the business. Besides, how would he know?*

Chapter LVIII

Beyond Michelangelo

Bernini had never been on the inside of a confessional before. *Funny, it looks exactly like the other side.* At precisely midnight, as planned, he heard footsteps in the dark, small, out-of-the-way church. *Ah, the marble broker.*

"Did you bring it," Bernini asked the man who had just slipped into the confessional. GianLorenzo had covered the square wire mesh opening with a black cloth and held his nose as he spoke, so his voice could not be recognizable. "Did you follow my instructions?"

"Yes sir," the broker said. "I selected the finest piece of white marble available in the city, and it's the size you requested, forty by forty, and . . ."

"Did you bring it?"

"Oh, sorry. I left the marble on the table in the front of the church, just as you ordered. Thank you for the money—it was way too generous but . . ."

"Consider half of the payment for the stone and half for forgetting this ever happened. Do we understand each other?"

"Sir, I couldn't tell anyone if I wanted to. I don't even know your name and you have a funny voice."

Bernini liked that. "Thank you and good night," he said to the most confused man in Rome.

When he could no longer hear the clatter of the horse's hooves, the Cavaliere left the confessional and examined the small block of marble. *Perfect, and well worth the small fortune it cost.*

The Baths of Caracalla were gigantic. In their heyday—which lasted over a period of 300 years, a thousand years earlier—the Terme, as they were called, held over 1,500 citizens. Today, except for the feral cats, the baths were abandoned—no longer useable and some distance from the center of Rome.

Which is precisely why GianLorenzo picked this place to hide.

Dressed entirely in black, Bernini made his way from the nearby church to the temporary studio he had personally set up earlier in the most remote part of the Caracalla ruins—the old Latin Library. Everything appeared to be in place: The canvas was stretched to keep the rain out and the light concealed, the tools were arranged on the workbench, and the large basket of fruit sat next to the cot—which was to be used for cat-naps, if any.

Disregarding the time of night, the most renowned sculptor in the world slipped on his smock in the darkness, and, strictly from memory, started to rough out a bust of Cardinal Scipione Borghese.

Bernini worked day and night—basically non-stop for three days. In that period, he ate a piece of fresh fruit every hour and napped for two hours each night. At the end of the physical ordeal he felt much too exhilarated to be tired. The Cavaliere performed a jig around the over-life-size bust and then kissed the marble.

"Scipione," he shouted, the words ricocheting against the gigantic stones of Caracalla, "in the last three days you and I have made history. A marble bust in three days."

—

Since he was not feeling too well, Cardinal Borghese requested a private unveiling of the bust he had commissioned—which fit perfectly into Bernini's plan. After the requisite bear hug, the Cardinal poured his prodigy a goblet of wine and settled into his favorite overstuffed chair.

"Why don't you do the honors," Scipione said, barely able to contain his excitement.

Bernini lifted the silk cloth from the bust. "What do you think," he asked, "do you like it?"

A smile froze on Cardinal Borghese's face. He was unable to speak.

The Number One patron of the arts starred at the bust, but all he could see was the flaw—a severe crack in the marble—across the forehead. His forehead.

I've seen flaws in finished marble pieces before, but this flaw is certainly the ugliest flaw I have seen in my fifty-five years on this earth. From an ordinary sculptor I could expect something like this. From Bernini, it is beyond my comprehension.*

GianLorenzo couldn't remember when he'd had more fun. He could see that Cardinal Borghese was shocked and disappointed, but too much a gentleman—and friend—to mention the flaw.

"It's overwhelming," Cardinal Borghese said carefully. "You certainly are the best sculptor in Rome."

Borromini laughed to himself. *I remember when father asked me what I would say if I hated a piece of art but didn't want to offend the artist, and I told him I would say, "Great isn't the word." Scipione has obviously perfected the same strategy.*

"Thank you," Bernini said, pretending not to notice the discomfort of his patron. "By the way, this wine is excellent. May I have another?"

The Cardinal poured GianLorenzo another wine, but he spilled almost as much wine as he poured into the goblet.

"Excuse my shaking hand," Scipione said. "It's a hereditary thing. I hope the wine didn't get all over you. I think I need to sit down."

"It's probably the heat in the room," Bernini said. *I think I've taken this joke far enough. This man is so emotional about art, the flaw—in his own forehead, no less—might cause a real heart attack.* "Please excuse me, I forgot something in my carriage. I'll be back in a minute, and in the meantime, do enjoy your bust."

As soon as GianLorenzo left the room, Cardinal Borghese grabbed a bottle of brandy and took a long, hard drink straight from the bottle.

—

"What's that you're carrying," Scipione asked when Bernini returned.

"You may peek under the cloth," the Cavaliere said as he placed the object next to the flawed bust. "It's something that may possibly interest you." He couldn't resist. "Then again, maybe not."

Cardinal Borghese gingerly, apprehensively, lifted the cloth and exposed a bust of . . .

Himself.

"Is it my eyesight causing me to see double? What in the world is going on, I . . ."

And then the reality hit the Cardinal with the force of a chariot crossing the finish line at full speed. *I can't believe it—when the flaw in the original occurred, this genius carved a second bust of me.* Scipione hugged Bernini so hard, the sculptor was afraid his bones would break.

"The busts are perfect. Putting the flaw aside, I have never seen two portrait busts that were so realistic and yet so flattering. GianLorenzo, my friend, you have out Berninied Bernini, if I may put it that way."

"Then I assume you're not angry with me for my little joke? Remember, you once said I shouldn't ever play a joke on the Pope, but on you it would be okay."

"Angry? On the contrary." Cardinal Borghese gave Bernini his strongest bear hug ever. "I will be eternally grateful to you, Cavaliere, for being so thoughtful."

—

GianLorenzo couldn't resist one more piece of showmanship.

"Please," he said to Scipione, "can you sit for another moment?"

Bernini picked up his scratch pad and made a few bold strokes. He handed the sketch to the puzzled Cardinal, who glanced at the sheet and burst out laughing.

"This is the most devastatingly accurate drawing in history," Cardinal Borghese said. "I can't wait until my friends see it—they will all love it. I repeat what my uncle, the Pope, said when you were ten years old, 'Is there anything you can't do?' Remember when he said that?"

"How could I forget? By the way, you'll be interested to know that I call sketches like this, caricatures, in honor of the great Annibale Carracci, who taught me—I draw them all the time and I think they will become popular with people."

GianLorenzo started to sway, back and forth. "May I have a goblet of water, please? I'm feeling . . ."

Cardinal Borghese tried to catch his friend, but he was too late. Bernini had collapsed.

Chapter LIX

Borromini and Bonaventura walked arm in arm. The pair was making the last inspection of Francesco's very own commission—the Trinitarian project—and they both felt good about it.

"Any success I had here," Borromini said to his patron, "I owe to you. You didn't tell me what to do or how to do it. Believe me, putting three buildings on this little, irregular site was not easy—even for me."

"Francesco," the Head of the Order said, "you didn't charge us. Remember? We felt any interference on our part would have been wrong in God's eyes."

—

First the duo examined the monastery Borromini had built at the rear of the site. It was a simple design—the building went straight, with the rooms set in a single row.

"This part wasn't hard," Borromini said. "The cloister and church, they were a different matter. Placing them on this site—that was some challenge."

The cloister had been placed to the right side of the church, and occupied a small rectangular space.

"I'm lucky to find a place to walk in," the Head of the Order said as they entered the peaceful area. The cleric wrapped his arm around his architect. "This cloister is so pleasant, my brothers spend most of their time here, walking and meditating. The only time they want to leave is to eat or sleep."

"What do they like best?" Borromini asked, trying not to appear too anxious for the accolades.

Bonaventura smiled. In the course of construction, he had noticed that Francesco needed a great deal of support, and he was happy to continue providing it.

"Honestly, everyone loves the way you alternated the width, height and style of the arches. But its your method of cutting off the corners, using both a convex and straight line treatment, that seems to be the key to the cloister's character, personality and strength—traits I hope we all possess."

—

The pair walked into the church, which had the official name of San Carlo alle Quattro Fontane, reflecting its location. The aging artist, Cavaliere d' Arpino was seated in the front row, alternately praying for salvation and analyzing the little masterpiece for its secrets. The three exchanged greetings.

"Congratulations, Francesco," d' Arpino said. "With this complex, you have joined the ranks of the major architects in Rome. And congratulations to you, brother Bonaventura, for having the foresight and ingenuity to find and engage a talent of this magnitude."

Borromini was too amazed to speak. *What a hypocrite this small waxen-faced creature is. I've seen him around town hundreds of times, without a hint of recognition.*

"The brothers and I call it San Carlino, due to its small size," Bonaventura said, oblivious to the drama. "I hope you don't mind, Francesco—that name is a term of endearment. We all feel Borromini came up with an ingenious plan; notice how the dome seems to be floating? Francesco, tell Cavaliere d' Arpino what you told me, how you did it."

Borromini lit up, happy to discuss his baby. "I used a geometric approach—it's something I've wanted to try all my life. First I placed two equilateral triangles of the same size next to each other. Then I drew circles within them. Then I drew an oval around the circles. That gave me the shape of the dome."

D'Arpino was struck dumb. "That's absolutely amazing. An old man like me would never have thought of something like that. And the curves—I don't think there is a straight line in the church—they give such movement."

"Do you like the decorations?" Borromini asked brightly, forgetting his initial resentment and anxious for even more praise.

D' Arpino was taken aback. He looked around—there was white stucco everywhere. "It's decorated?"

"Yes it's decorated. Of course it's decorated. Do you think my patrons have money to burn, like the Pope? You know that baldacchino? I heard it cost ten percent of the papal income for the nine years it was under construction."

Bonaventura tried to disappear into the woodwork.

D' Arpino decided to change the subject. "I have heard that this entire church could fit into one of the pillars of Saint Peter's? You know the pillars I mean. The ones at the Crossing holding up della Porta's magnificent dome—the dome I frescoed. The pillars Bernini is decorating."

Borromini turned red in the face. "Don't mention that name to me again. I must go now."

A Brother rushed up. "Borromini, Borromini. We have received three more letters, two from Germany and one from Flanders. Everyone wants a copy of the plans for San Carlino. Please have them engraved—we can both use the money."

Borromini cringed. *Never. I have no intention of giving my baby away.* "I will think about it some more," he called over his shoulder.

—

The confused Cavaliere d' Arpino watched Borromini depart.

"What's this business with Bernini," d' Arpino asked. "I have never heard GianLorenzo speak ill of Borromini."

Bonaventura shrugged. "Rumors have come to me from here and there, but I have no intention of pursuing the matter with Francesco."

D' Arpino laughed. "I don't blame you. One last question. How was Borromini in the day-to-day supervision of construction?"

Bonaventura was pleased to be back on solid ground. "Outstanding. Francesco was outstanding. He guided the builder's shovel, the plasterer's darby, the carpenter's saw, the stonemason's chisel, the bricklayers trowel and the ironworker's file, with the result that the quality of work is high but not the cost, as his detractors claim, and all this springs from his intelligence and his industry."

"Good, good, that's very good," d' Arpino said. *Amazing. This Borromini seems a bit off-center to me.*

Chapter LX

B̲ernini awoke in bed two days after he collapsed.

"He's suffering from total exhaustion," the doctor said. "Your son must, I repeat must, remain in bed for a minimum of one month, and I'm counting on you to keep him there, Mrs. Bernini. His life depends on it."

—

As soon as the doctor left, Angelica confronted her son, repeatedly hitting him over the head with a towel.

"Where were you for three days?" Pow. "With another one of your fancy lady friends?" Bam. "One of these days, those creatures are going to be the death of you." Bang. "And you're going to be the death of me." Boom.

GianLorenzo pulled the towel out of his mother's hand and lifted himself from the bed. He gave Angelica as strong a hug as he could muster, and then fell back, exhausted by the effort. Like all Italian mothers, Angelica softened when her son turned on the charm.

"Please, mother, bring me a large bowl of your famous pastina. I am starving. With olive oil and lots of cheese."

"Finally," she said gazing up to the heavens, addressing God directly, "he's going to eat some real food."

Angelica left the room humming her favorite Neapolitan love song, the one she used to sing to GianLorenzo when she held him in her arms and rocked him to sleep.

Bernini laughed to himself. *That gets her every time.*

"And bring me a pen and some paper," he called after his mother. "I've had several more plays in my mind for some time."

Chapter LXI

Beyond Michelangelo

The Barberini Theatre was located in the Barberini Palace and was the only theatrical venue of its kind in Rome. One by one the candles were snuffed in the showplace.

As the hall grew dark, a hush fell over the 3,000 patrons who had filled the theatre in anticipation of a new Bernini play. The sophisticated crowd knew that Bernini had never failed to surprise and entertain, but they were especially excited tonight, having heard that the Cavaliere had developed some amazing new tricks of illusion for this new comedy.

—

The play ended and the curtain came down to thunderous applause. GianLorenzo rose from his front row seat—which was adjacent to the Pope and the Barberini clan—to acknowledge the standing ovation.

"Stand up, mother," the playwright said, "the ovation belongs to you as much as it belongs to me." When Angelica stood, the crowd became even more vocal. "See," GianLorenzo said, "the Romans know where the real power lies."

An elegant dowager, bedecked in gold jewelry and diamonds, approached Bernini and his mother. "Hello, Angelica. GianLorenzo. Congratulations, Cavaliere, it is your best play yet—certainly the most exciting. May I introduce my daughter, Sarafina, and her son, Andrea?"

Bernini shook hands. *Here we go again. I don't care if she is the matriarch of one of the most important families in Rome—I'm not interested in marrying her daughter.*

"Loved your play," the daughter said, batting her eyes in the most seductive way she knew. "Especially the part where that actor kept brushing the curtain with his torch, and when . . ."

". . . When the whole stage caught fire," the six year-old boy cried, "that was the best part. I knew that was gonna happen."

"Please don't interrupt, Andrea," Sarafina said, gently pushing her son aside. "As I was saying, half of the crowd didn't realize it was a trick and started running for the exits, but I knew . . ."

". . . And then when the fire stopped and a garden took its place; that was the best part. It was a really pretty garden, remember mom?"

Bernini felt sorry for the attractive daughter. *This child isn't giving his mother a chance to impress me.* GianLorenzo saw a way out of the situation. He picked up the little boy and swung him around. "You have quite a few favorite parts, old man. I'm glad you liked the play so much." He put the child down and addressed the women. "You both must be very proud of Andrea—he's so bright."

As usual, a crowd had gathered around Rome's number one celebrity. The crush of well wishers made Bernini and his mother late for the party in his honor, which was hosted by the Barberini. The Cavaliere was able to avoid the dowager at the party, but her daughter managed to get a note of invitation into his hands.

—

"That's the kind of woman you should keep company with and eventually marry," Angelica said on the ride home in the carriage. "You are getting up in years, GianLorenzo, you're almost forty you know, with no marriage prospect in sight."

Bernini loved this conversation, which he had with his mother every other day. At least it seemed that way. *She'll never give up, but I love her persistence. She's like the Church: Never-ending.*

"What kind of woman is that," GianLorenzo said, teasing his mother, which never seemed to amuse her.

"You know perfectly well—I've told you enough times."

"Tell me again,"

"Good breeding, sophisticated . . ."

"Rich, phony and boring. No thanks. I'm not interested in getting married—I'd rather live at home with you, Luigi, and the girls. You all understand me. Besides, I have no need to get married—if you know what I mean."

"Oh, you. You're incorrigible," Angelica laughed, as she gave her famous son a Neapolitan-size hug.

Chapter LXII

Cardinal Virgilio Spada was a member of a powerful family, an able administrator and a leader of the Oratorian Order, which valued his judgment, particularly in architectural matters.

The Order of San Filippo Neri—the Oratorians—was formed in 1561. Saint Neri, who was one of the Church's great reformers, believed that religion could, and should, effectively be spread through the use of the arts, particularly music (hence the musical term Oratorio).

Integrating the demands of art with those of religion, however, created several architectural challenges for the Order. Plus, there were other problems. For one thing, although it was well located in the city, the Oratorian's site had an unusual shape. Additionally, any new facilities would have to be coordinated with the existing mother church, the Chiesa Nuova.

Always on the lookout for fresh architectural talent, Cardinal Spada visited the cloister of San Carlino as soon as it was completed and immediately sensed the significance of the beautiful, but revolutionary design. The ingenious placement of the building on the tiny, odd shaped site particularly impressed him.

The architectural dilettante sought out the Trinitarian's Juan San Bonaventura, from whom the Cardinal received a glowing recommendation. He promptly met with the Order's architect, one Francesco Borromini.

—

At the next meeting of the Oratorians, Cardinal Spada was the first to ask the Order's president, Padre Angelo Saluzzi, for permission to speak.

Looking left and right, smiling a practiced smile, the Cardinal slowly and deliberately made his way to the front of the room. He was a short man with a plain, almost square face, dominated by dark eyes. One sweep of the room told him he had their attention and it was time to begin. When he talked, he held his head at a distinct angle—looking like a musician cradling his violin under his chin.

"I have discovered an extraordinary man—an architect new to Rome—whom I predict will someday be as well known as anyone working today in our city."

The members of the Order were shocked. They knew the Cardinal well. They admired his ability to be alternately pious and clever, modest and ambitious, but in the past they knew him to always exhibit patience and caution. He certainly was not prone to exaggeration.

"Even Bernini?" Saluzzi asked.

"Except Bernini, of course," Cardinal Spada quickly added. *I hope I didn't show my prejudice against the Cavaliere.* "I recommend that we hire this man as second architect—I'm confident he can help our friend Paolo Maruscelli solve our design problems."

The members of the Order all spoke at once: "Who is this latter-day savior?" "Do we know him?" "Can't we get Bernini?"

The president called for order and turned the meeting back to Cardinal Spada.

"I also like Paolo," the Cardinal said. "But, and that is a large but, he hasn't been able to solve our design problems, has he? As for Bernini, there is absolutely no chance the Holy Father would release him—I have already checked with His Holiness. The architect I refer to is named Francesco Borromini. Has anyone here heard of him?" The fathers indicated they had not.

Cardinal Spada flashed his famous smile. *It's so pleasant to have the upper hand. Especially in architectural matters.*

Borromini spread his drawings on the large table in Padre Saluzzi's office. Cardinal Spada and Paolo Maruscelli read the plans from across the table, in the upside-down position. Borromini spun the drawings around to accommodate Cardinal Spada.

"Paolo, what do you think of Francesco's solution," Saluzzi asked.

"I think," Maruscelli replied, "that it is no better than any of the ideas I have submitted in the seven years I have worked for you."

"And you, Virgilio," the unruffled Saluzzi asked. "What do you think?"

Cardinal Spada cleared his throat. *After all I have done for him over the last seven years, I think Paolo is trying to undercut me as well as Francesco. We'll see about that.* "I agree with Paolo. May I suggest that Francesco try again? May I also suggest that he give me a chance to study his drawings before he officially submits them next time?"

"Thank you, Virgilio—you make sense. Now, Francesco, you haven't said a word. Would you care to comment?"

Borromini scooped-up his plans and stormed out of the room. The three men remaining in the room watched in horror.

Paolo Maruscelli: *I'm glad you all got to see the kind of madman I've had to work with.* "I look forward to seeing his second attempt."

Virgilio Spada: *Do I really need this?* "Let me talk with him. I've heard that Francesco can be temperamental, but I remain confident that he can help us."

Angelo Saluzzi: *I'm not sure what's going on here, but whatever it is, I don't like it.* "Virgilio, as usual we're counting on you."

Chapter LXIII

B̲orromini shuffled into Giuseppe's bookstore, studying the floor of the shop with his downcast eyes. *What is wrong with me? Why can't I solve the problems at the Oratory? There has to be a logical reason. I know I'm smarter than that Maruscelli. To be stymied in my second commission as an architect would be a disaster for me.*

The bookseller watched with deep concern as his best customer picked his way through the shop. "What in the world is wrong, Francesco? You look like your winning horse dropped dead just before he reached the finish line."

Borromini pawed the books lining the shelves. "Nothing is wrong. What makes you think anything is wrong? Nothing is wrong with me, maybe something is wrong with you."

"Looking for anything in particular this evening?" Giuseppe asked. *He's even worse than usual tonight. Without a doubt, this is the unhappiest man in Rome, yet I like him. Maybe he's just lonely. It can't be his work—I hear he did an outstanding job on San Carlino and is the architect of the future. I don't know; he's hard to figure.*

"Maybe. Anything new? In architecture," Borromini asked without interrupting his search.

"Let me think," Giuseppe said, examining the books stacked on the counter. "No. You bought the newest architecture volume last week. But here's something that might interest you. He picked out a slim treatise on philosophy, written in Latin. "It's called Back to Basics."

———

Cardinal Spada was waiting for his architectural find. *If he doesn't deliver this time I'll have to dump him.* "Welcome, Francesco. What have you brought?"

"Before I show the drawings," Borromini said, 'I want you to understand something. My first solution was no good because as second Architect I had to collaborate with Chief Architect Maruscelli, and . . ."

"Don't, Francesco. I'll take your word for it," Cardinal Spada said. "Anything else? I hope not, because I'm dying to see your plans—you sounded so excited."

"You will be too when you see what I designed. Before you examine the plans, I'll tell you the situation I see here. First, your Order needs to bring together all of their activities into the building next to the church. And you started to do that by building the sacristy and a foundation for a small courtyard—following Maruscelli's drawings. Correct?"

"Correct," Spada said. "And that's where the design problem lies—coordinating the windows of the new Oratory with those of the pre-existing pillars."

"You haven't thought your situation through. For example, have you thought about who will use these facilities. It's the public and the clerics—two totally different groups, with totally different needs. Am I correct?"

"Correct."

Borromini was on a roll; his voice and stare bordered on the hypnotic. "And then there is the façade. It must be harmonious with, but subservient to the Chiesa Nuova. So you have more than a design problem between the Oratory and the small cloister. You also have usage problems and practical problems. I solved all of your problems—by going back to basics. Let me show you."

—

As Borromini unrolled the drawings, Cardinal Spada studied his newly discovered architect. *He is a smart one, that's for sure, but he is a trifle strange. Like the way he always wears those old-fashioned Spanish clothes, which are always black. I wonder what the point of that is. He's a good-looking enough man—tall and muscular—but those clothes make his bronzish-colored face appear even darker. If he were from Naples or Sicily I could understand his dress, but he's a northerner. He's probably bonding with his first real client, those Spaniards.* "What do you mean, going back to basics?"

Francesco smoothed out the plans and placed a goblet on each corner to hold the sheets down. "I was stymied, and then I asked myself, 'What is a façade?' The answer struck me like a bolt of lightning. A façade is merely a false front, decorated as nicely as possible."

Virgilio, the architectural dilettante, laughed. "That certainly is basic."

Borromini gave the Cardinal a stare that would wilt a nobleman. "I haven't made my point yet. What that means to us is that we can plan the uses of the building totally separate from the design of the façade."

Spada appeared confused, which cheered Borromini.

"Look at this drawing of the façade of the Oratory," Francesco continued. "See where I've placed the main front door? That is not the main axis of the building—the main axis of the building is over on the right. In other words, I've made the real side entrance look like the main entrance, and the real main entrance look like the side entrance. The result is that the side entrance—what appears to be the main entrance to the building—will serve as the entrance to the oratory for the general public, and the side entrance—the real main entrance—will serve as the entrance to the building for the clerics in their every day use. Are you with me?"

"Yes . . . yes . . . yes."

"One more point about the façade. In order to maintain the dominance of the church's marble façade, as well as to provide a pleasant contrast, I will use a delicate brick on its veneer."

"Perfect."

"That solves the problems of access and flow." Borromini flipped several pages. "Now I will show you how I solved your internal design problem of coordinating the walls and windows of the planned oratory and the small cloister. Your problem is, the corner pier of the courtyard is larger than the others. Solution? Simple for me. I merely changed the rhythm of the spaces between the piers in the oratory."

Spada was ecstatic. "Simple to you maybe, but not to us or Maruscelli."

Francesco flashed a smile Giuseppe the bookseller would have loved. "Finally, at least for now, if you look at this drawing, you will see that I added a second level and steps to reach it. I don't know if you noticed, but the sacristy and church are on different levels, so I needed to add some sham windows, and . . ."

—

Cardinal Spada again spoke first at the following meeting of the Oratorians. He walked to the front of the room and dramatically dropped a set of drawings on a table.

"Borromini has got it," the Cardinal said. "No need to look further. If an angel had descended from heaven, he could do no drawings with fewer errors..."

"Virgilio," Padre Saluzzi said, "aren't you exaggerating about this Borromini again?"

"Absolutely not. There is no error in this design, no license, no offense against good architecture. Gather around everybody, allow me to show you how this genius solved all of our problems."

—

"Did Paolo have anything to do with these brilliant plans?" Padre Saluzzi asked Cardinal Spada at the end of the meeting.

"No, no he did not, "Spada replied. "Sadly, I fear Paolo Maruscelli's days as Chief Architect of the Oratorians are numbered. I think Francesco Borromini should be appointed to that position. What do you think, Mister President?"

—

Borromini bounced into Giuseppe's bookstore. He whistled while he made himself an espresso. He skipped the sugar and downed the coffee in one gulp.

"Giuseppe, my friend, do you have any new writings on Saint Filippo Neri or his followers?"

At this point, Giuseppe was totally confused. *Look at this—the last time Borromini was in my shop, I was afraid I was going to have to call the undertaker.*

"No disrespect, Borromini," the bookseller said, "but I'm thrilled to see you so happy. I don't know what happened, but when I see you happy, that makes me happy. As for a book on Neri, are you taking a break from reading about buildings—and philosophy?"

"As the Oratorian's new Chief Architect," Borromini said, not trying to conceal a smirk, "don't you think I should know more about their Order?"

Chapter LXIV

The young girl tripped and fell as she hurried up the stairs to Saint Peter's—the food she was carrying splattered all over Bernini, who was on his way out of the basilica. He extended his hand and lifted the beauty up.

Matteo Bonarelli, who was waiting for his dinner, watched the drama from the portico. *Oh my God, it's Costanza.* He rushed to the scene, pushed his wife aside and started brushing the food off of Bernini's smock.

"Please, don't be angry sir. She was bringing my dinner. I like to eat here on the job so I can get more work done and . . ."

Bernini focused on the thin little man who was hiding his wife behind him. *I wonder if he can handle her. I doubt it. He doesn't look like he can handle much of anything.* "Didn't you start to work for me last month? It's Bonarelli, isn't it? Matteo Bonarelli."

"Yes sir. I'm doing some finishing work on the tomb of Countess Matilda. I'm carving an angel."

"And who is the angel performing this heavenly duty, bringing you food?"

"That's my wife, sir. As I was saying, I like to eat on the job so that I can work straight through the day." *I hope he gets the point—I've mentioned it twice now.* "Costanza, come around here and say hello to Mister Bernini."

———

Costanza decided a strategic retreat was in order. *Jesus Christ, I've run into my husband's employer.* Back straight, she started to slink out of the group.

"Come back here, Costanza," Bernini said, failing to control the teasing tone in his order. "You forgot something."

Costanza turned and approached the Cavaliere. With her head slightly bowed and a contrite look on her face, she could have passed for a nun approaching the confessional. Matteo was confused but Costanza had no trouble reading the situation. *Well, well, well. Mister big shot wants to fuck me. I'll make the bastard pay for the privilege.*

"You forgot to say good-by," Bernini continued.

"Good afternoon Mister Bernini," Costanza said softly, fluttering her big brown eyes. She turned to leave once more.

Bernini fixed the sensuous beauty with his renowned penetrating gaze. *She's complex, this one. She looks like a saint—a sensuous one, but a saint nevertheless—but moves like a whore.*

"Come to my studio tomorrow without the spaghetti," the Cavaliere said. "You can model and earn enough so your husband can buy a hot dinner. Would you like to do that?"

"What time," Matteo asked. Bernini smiled to himself. Costanza performed a perfect semi-curtsy, turned and fled.

"She's a shy little thing, isn't she?" Bernini said.

"Not that I noticed," Matteo replied.

―

It was almost midnight when Matteo arrived home for supper. Through glazed eyes he made out the plate of spaghetti sitting on the kitchen table. It looked as cold as his wife's expression.

"Where have you been, you drunken slob? Eat. I'm not cooking twice in one night."

"I stopped in a tavern," Matteo said, trying not to slur his words. "I was trying to forget today's fiasco."

"It was an accident. So what? Who is this Bernini anyway? Some kind of God? And while we're complaining, I've got a complaint of my own. Why did you say I would sit for him?"

"You just don't understand, do you? Bernini is my boss. He's putting food on this table and we're eating very well, aren't we? You'll sit for him because it will be good for my career, which is taking off now that I'm working for the most prominent artist in Rome. Now warm up that meal before I kick you in your beautiful ass."

―

Costanza strode into Bernini's workshop without knocking. All work stopped. She was wearing a loose, straight hanging dress that hinted at the fullness of her ample breasts and the slimness of her hips. A straw hat sat jauntily on her short, perfectly coiffed hair. The workmen stared—they couldn't take their eyes off of her full, sensuous lips.

"Sit here," said the foreman, who was expecting her. Costanza ignored him, keeping her eyes on Bernini who was working on scaffolding. "You better sit madam," the foreman said, "the Cavaliere might work for hours without noticing you are here. I could tell you stories . . ."

Bernini hit the floor with a bang. "How nice of you to come, Costanza. Please make yourself at home—I'll sketch you for a short time."

The amazed workforce immediately went back to work but surreptitiously glanced up when they thought it was safe.

—

"Go home Costanza," the Cavaliere said after five hours of sketching. "Unless you would care to join me for dinner. I know a delightful trattoria I think you will like."

"I'm famished."

As soon as the couple left the workshop, the buzzing started.

"Eat in the middle of the day? Never seen that before." "Barely stops to nibble a piece of fruit and now a trattoria? Something's going on." "Did you see how fast he stopped working? What happened to his usual concentration? He must have been watching for her."

—

"Ah, Cavaliere, come in, come in," said the owner of the tavern. "Everything is ready for you. This way please."

"I thought we going to a trattoria," Costanza said. "This looks more like the rear of a tavern."

"It is the rear of a tavern," Bernini said as they reached the top of the steep stairs. The owner opened the first door revealing a surprisingly large, beautifully decorated room.

"I'll be along in a couple of hours with food and more wine," the proprietor said as he hurried out of the room.

Before the door was closed, the couple was wrestling on the bed—tearing off clothes, kissing, searching, and finally making love. Rough, carnal, animal love. Not a word was spoken.

—

Bernini tried to pour Costanza a goblet of wine but his shaking hand spilled most of it on the bed. Costanza howled. She grabbed the bottle and poured the rest of it over her smooth, lily-white body. "If you want more wine, you'll have to lick it off."

"I don't do that," the Cavaliere said. "We'll see," she said, pretending to laugh.

—

The lovers lay arm in arm in the oversized bathtub.

"Mister Bernini. The notorious Mister Bernini. Everyone in Rome knows you hardly ever eat—nibbling on fruit all day."

"So?"

Costanza pulled GianLorenzo's hands under the water, placing them strategically at two erogenous zones. Bernini rubbed her gently in both areas as he licked the inside of her left ear.

"I can sort of understand how you can work without eating, but when you make love? Where do you get your super energy? Owwwwwwwww that feels heavenly."

"I have super energy?"

"Do you realize we've made love seven times today? Seven. I know, because I started to count after five, which used to be my personal record."

"Is there a question I'm missing?"

Costanza jumped out of the tub onto the bed. "There certainly is. Why are you wasting time licking my ear when there is so much more Costanza available? Right where your hands were."

Bernini shook his head. "I told you, I don't do that."

"You'll do what I tell you or you can kiss Costanza one last time—and you'd better make it a long one because it will be a good-bye kiss."

The Cavaliere never hesitated. He started licking her perfect breasts and worked his way down.

"That is nice. Now, I want you to put your finger in my ass and move it in rhythm with your tongue. After that, I'll tell you what else I like. Understand?"

The most famous and talented artist in the world nodded meekly.

The Bonarelli apartment was dark when Costanza arrived home.

"Is that you sweetheart?" Matteo called from the bed. "Come to bed, I'm cold. How did things go with my boss?"

Costanza tore off her clothes and jumped into bed naked. She started to kiss her husband all over. "I'll warm you up," she said. "And if I had to guess, I'd say your career is in pretty good shape."

Chapter LXV

Beyond Michelangelo

Although the Bernini family normally attended Sunday Mass at Santa Maria Maggiore across the road from their home, today GianLorenzo insisted his mother join him for a second service—the last Mass at Saint Peter's.

Knowing her son as well as she did, Angelica was certain that he harbored a hidden agenda; she just didn't know what it was. *His surprises are always interesting and often thought provoking—like the time he showed me The Rape of Proserpina.*

After the Mass, the basilica was empty except for a few clergy from out of town who wandered about. Bernini led his mother to a small tomb. "Do you know anything about her? Countess Matilda, I mean."

"GianLorenzo, everyone knows that the Holy Father is partial to her and had her remains brought to Rome from Mantua. I've always wondered why he did that."

Bernini laughed out loud; invoking stern looks from the visiting clerics. He acknowledged their disapproval and continued in a softer, more respectful tone of voice.

"Partial to her? He venerates her. So would you if she willed all of her land to you—technically I should say the Church. Her holdings were most of Tuscany by the way. That's why Urban commissioned me to design this tomb to honor her in Saint Peter's."

Angelica remained quiet while she studied the tomb. *The niche is beautifully designed and the columns hold the tomb together nicely. But the Countess's face—it is not very expressive, so I doubt GianLorenzo carved it.* She noticed that her son kept looking about. *He wants me to meet someone—that must be it.*

"Son, I think Countess Matilda had to be an extremely moral woman. I like that. What do you think?"

The comment stung, like a schoolmaster's cane disciplining a naughty pupil. "Let's go mother," Bernini said. "I just remembered a very important meeting."

"GianLorenzo, what is it?"

"I brought you here to meet someone, but the more I focus on you and the saintly Matilda, and the pious life of each of you, the more I realize it may have been the stupidest idea in the history of mankind. Let's go. Right now."

A confused Angelica followed her son, who was walking briskly out of the basilica. When they reached the portico, she noticed a pretty young girl rushing up the outside stairs. When GianLorenzo glimpsed Costanza, he quickly turned and led his mother down the opposite side of the stairs.

Chapter LXVI

Giulio Mazzarini was tired. His trip from Paris was exhausting, and it was late. Nevertheless, he went directly to see his friend.

"How nice to see you, Giulio," Angelica said. "GianLorenzo's in the studio putting the finishing touches on a bust. I see you've brought some wine. Good. I'll put some fruit in a basket and we'll go to the workshop."

"But, Mrs. Bernini," Giulio said. "I don't want to interrupt him if he's working."

"Giulio, you've been in France too long. GianLorenzo's power of concentration is only exceeded by his carving skill. Remember? He won't even know we're in the room, and he'll only see us if we want him to."

Angelica was correct, of course. She and Mazzarini sat and enjoyed each other's company over goblets of French wine—which they agreed was vastly inferior to their Italian vintages.

"GianLorenzo hasn't changed one bit since you've seen him," Angelica said. "It's still impossible to get him to stop working and eat supper, so I often come to the studio late at night and force him to pause and eat a piece or two of fruit."

Giulio watched the chips fly. "What intensity—he looks like an alchemist trying to melt gold using only his gaze. I don't see how you can get him to pause."

"Watch," Angelica said. She pressed her finger and thumb into the apples until she was satisfied that she had picked the hardest one in the basket. "GianLorenzo," she called out three times at the top of her voice. Nothing. Undaunted, the petite matron wound-up and threw the apple at her son's head, scoring a direct hit.

GianLorenzo stopped. He rubbed his head where the projectile hit and burst out laughing. Giulio laughed so hard he fell off of his chair. Bernini jumped off of the scaffolding and grabbed his best friend. They exchanged hugs Scipione Borghese would have envied. GianLorenzo gave Angelica a hug and kiss.

"Does she ever miss," Giulio asked Bernini.

"Not really," GianLorenzo replied. He was proud, and happy to admit it. "She has a natural gift for being a mother."

—

"Giulio, I can't believe it's really you," Bernini said. "Now that we're alone, tell me everything. What are the French women like? When did you arrive? Do you like France? What sort of man is the King—Louis XIII isn't it? How about this Cardinal Richelieu I've heard so much about? Tell me everything. Giulio, it's you. I can't believe you're really here."

"Things are going well in Paris. Cardinal Richelieu likes me and I think he's grooming me to be his successor as Prime Minister. That's the highest position in the French court, but of course it's up to the King. The Queen, by the way, is a lovely lady. In the meantime, I'm receiving more important assignments every day. But enough about me. I see terracotta models in the corner—there must be over twenty—are they of Saint Longinus? For the Crossing?"

"There are exactly twenty-two. As you can see, I had a devil of a time capturing the Roman soldier's inner feelings right after he stabbed Christ and converted—that's the moment I chose to capture. Believe me, conveying what must have been extremely complex feelings, in a stature over fourteen feet high, was not easy, even for me. Would you like to see the results?"

"Could I? But it's late, I'm sure Saint Peter's is closed."

Bernini put his arm around Giulio and led him out of the workshop. "Saint Peter's," he said, "is never closed to me, my friend."

—

The streets of Rome were bustling with merrymakers celebrating yet another religious holiday. Bernini's carriage slowly made its way through the throngs of intoxicated revelers.

"I knew you were famous," Mazzarini said, "but this is ridiculous. Every person we passed waved. Sober or drunk, they all waved at you. Do they know you or just want to?"

"What's the difference? Either way, it's not painful—I'm sure you will find out some day."

When they arrived at Saint Peter's, a Swiss guard—with a great flourish—escorted the master and his guest through a side entrance into the great basilica, lighting enough candles to allow easy viewing. The pair made their way to the Crossing.

"Stand in the middle, next to the baldacchino," Bernini said. "I want you to get the overall picture of what took eleven years of my life—parts of it anyway."

Mazzarini was overwhelmed. "This Crossing—it's magnificent now. Michelangelo's piers were drab and ordinary; but you have transformed them into things of enormous beauty. And they complement your incredible baldacchino perfectly. Nobody will believe this entire Crossing wasn't planned at exactly the same time."

"What do you think of the four statutes?"

"I love the gigantic niches you carved into the piers to show them off. To me, though, only Saint Longinus appears to be by your hand."

"My, my," Bernini said. "Aren't you turning into the connoisseur? I guess your art collecting is paying dividends. Anyway, it broke my heart to turn the work away, but this one time I was just too busy. Care to guess who carved the other three?"

Giulio laughed. "I may be getting sophisticated in artistic matters, but I still have a long way to go. Help me out."

"Let's start with Saint Helen. I gave her to Andrea Bolgi—he's done an excellent job for me in my workshop. Saint Andrew I gave to Francois Duquesnoy, the Flemish sculptor. He's also been a valuable assistant, especially on the baldacchino. Saint Veronica was carved by Mochi, and . . ."

"Wait. Did you say Mochi? Francesco Mochi? Why would you choose that has-been?"

Bernini shrugged. "I didn't. For reasons known only to the Holy Father, Urban personally selected Mochi. I agree with you—at one time, he was an excellent sculptor, but he never grew. And he's insanely jealous of me. On this job he was impossible to supervise; he wielded his direct papal commission like a blunderbuss."

Mazzarini studied Saint Veronica more closely. "What a shame," he said. "She's the only one who doesn't relate to the baldacchino in particular, or the Crossing in general. The pose—it's all wrong. Veronica looks like she's rushing to market, or is about to smother a foe, instead of carrying a kerchief to wipe the brow of Christ."

"Mochi is a petty rival, that's all he is," Bernini said. "How petty? First he complained that his precious Veronica was going to fall off of the pedestal I designed. Then, he prevented the workers from dusting Veronica every week—as they do all of the statutes in Saint Peter's—because, in his words, 'it was completely finished and there was no place for the dust to lodge'."

"What's the point of a remark like that?"

"He thinks he's clever; he's relating to the rough texture I gave Longinus's skin. He can't—or doesn't want to—understand that I did that on purpose, with a clawed chisel, so his skin would resonate with changing light. Besides, Longinus stands nearly triple the size of the average worshiper and will always be viewed from a great distance."

"Don't get overly excited, my friend," Giulio said. "Everyone in Rome knows Mochi has become vexatious in his advancing years. Now, let's discuss the real thing—your Longinus. To me, the way you posed and detailed him creates as much drama as your David did; I feel as if I'm directly involved in the action. I can (almost) hear your Longinus saying, 'Truly, this man was the Son of God'."

"Or," Bernini said, "maybe his gesture and expression are saying, 'don't get mad at me, I didn't know he was the Son of God when I speared him'."

Mazzarini and Bernini shared the kind of laugh only long time friends understand.

—

"Speaking of the Pope," Bernini said, "his tomb is coming right along."

Mazzarini gave his friend a double take. "Who was speaking of the Pope? You seem distracted. Are you okay?"

Bernini appeared not to hear Giulio. "I've been working on his tomb for about ten years, but I fear it will be another ten before it's finished. Are you too tired to come home with me? I want you to meet her."

"Meet who? Who is her? Are you sure you're okay?"

"My mistress."

—

"What's wrong, GianLorenzo," Giulio asked as they rode through the deserted streets of Rome. "The sun is coming up—perhaps that will cheer you up."

"Her husband worked on the tomb of Countess Matilda. Two of the angels."

"She's married? Your mistress is married? I guess you don't see her that often then."

"Almost every night."

Mazzarini was incredulous. "She's married and you see her almost every night? How is that possible? What about her husband?"

"Maybe he knows," Bernini said. "I'm not sure."

"GianLorenzo, listen to me. Of course he knows."

"Do you really think so? Then why hasn't he done anything about it?"

Giulio thought about that for quite some time. "Didn't you say he works for you? Maybe he needs the job."

—

"As I recall," Mazzarini said, "you never wanted to see any woman more than once—two times at the most—so why would you want to see this one every night? What about all of the other beautiful women in Rome?"

"Not every night. I have supper with Urban on Sunday evenings. Look, Giulio, how can you understand this if I can't? She has some sort of strange power over me."

Giulio nodded his head. "I get it. It must be strictly sexual. She must be sensational in bed for you to act like this."

"Sensational? That's much too mild a word. She's better than all of the other women I've had—combined."

Giulio—knowing his friend's romantic history—drooled at the thought.

—

The carriage arrived at the Bernini home and the two friends entered GianLorenzo's room. Giulio stopped abruptly. "That's a beautiful painting of the two of you. Her name, what's her name. Did you paint it?"

"Costanza Bonarelli. Of course I painted it. I painted everything in this room. I know you're going to ask me why I don't paint more—everyone does."

"You're right. I think as a painter you rival Guercino or Claude, maybe even Michelangelo, although your style is totally different from his. Why don't you paint more?"

"Actually, if you spent more time in Rome, you'd realize that I paint quite a bit. I just can't get excited about painting—maybe it's too easy for me. Look at this, you'll see one of the reasons I prefer sculpture."

Bernini uncovered a portrait bust that was sitting on the table next to his bed. Mazzarini gasped. He stared at the thirty-inch marble bust of Costanza Bonarelli for a full five minutes before he could speak.

"This bust makes your point about sculpture, that's for sure. You've hit another high point with this portrait, my friend. It probably has more naturalism and passion than anything you've ever done."

"So what should I do," Bernini cried. "I'm out of my mind."

"I'm not sure what you should do," Giulio said, as he ran his hands over the smooth, white marble, "but I'll tell you what I want to do. The way you've cut her chemise—open like that—I want to run my hand inside it. I want to feel her breast, the one you show the smallest part of. And I'm your best friend. And this is cold, hard marble. Imagine."

"What the hell are you talking about?"

"What I'm trying to say is, my emotional reaction not only shows the power of your bust, but maybe, just maybe, that's why her husband hasn't said anything. Maybe he's so satisfied sexually—satiated might be a better word—he doesn't care who else sleeps with her."

"You think she's sleeping with her husband too?"

"And probably half the city of Rome," Giulio said, "judging by the sensuousness you captured in her bust."

—

"Do you really think she's sleeping around," Bernini asked. "Once, when she showed up at our hideaway all disheveled, I made her swear to God that she was faithful to me. She immediately placed her right hand on her heart, gazed toward heaven, and said, 'God, if I am unfaithful to GianLorenzo Bernini, strike me dead.' That's exactly what she said, so I can't believe she is unfaithful to me."

Mazzarini stared at his friend. *He's rich. He's the most famous artist in the world. Beautiful women fall over each other trying to seduce him. And he allows himself to be bamboozled by what is obviously a trollop. This is pathetic.* Giulio decided to try to reason with his friend, although he wasn't sure anybody, or anything, could help in this situation.

"Think about what you're saying, GianLorenzo. You are saying that you're worried that Costanza is being unfaithful to you while being unfaithful to her husband. In other words, you are concerned that she is being unfaithful in her unfaithfulness. Now isn't that ridiculous?"

Bernini didn't answer; he just stared straight ahead. The orderly Florentine half of his mind understood perfectly what Giulio was saying. Unfortunately, the tempestuous Neapolitan half couldn't compute the logic. He felt sad and lonely.

Chapter LXVII

Bernini and Mazzarini were sitting on the Pincio, in the gardens of the Villa Borghese. They were surrounded by lush foliage and groves of trees. There were lakes, broad stone walks, fountains and innumerable busts and statutes. Rabbits, squirrels and even white deer scampered about. Thousands of flowers were artfully arranged and every color in the rainbow was represented. A good place to rest and think.

"How many portrait busts would you say you've done," Giulio asked, getting right into the business at hand.

"Let me think a minute. Over twenty. Why?"

"That's incredible. You're not even forty years old, and you've carved over twenty busts, and Michelangelo carved none in his eighty-nine years. At least that's what I read. Why is that?"

"Portrait busts are probably the most difficult things in the world to carve." Bernini said. He stared into space and shrugged. "I guess that means that Michelangelo was smarter than I am."

"Ha. I'm sure it means that you are more courageous than your idol. Are you aware that since you carved the bust of King Charles I of England, every ruler in Europe wants you to sculpt his portrait? That bust made you the most famous sculptor in the world and the rulers—Kings, Emperors, all of them—want to bask in your reflected glory. Which is why I bring up portrait busts."

"I'll take a wild guess," Bernini said. "Your mentor, Cardinal Richelieu, wants me to carve his portrait."

Perhaps this will not be as difficult as I feared. "You are not only courageous, my friend, you are smart. The Cardinal has been personally badgering the Pope's nephew for some time now, trying to obtain your services, but he's not getting anywhere."

Bernini laughed to himself. *Francesco Barberini told me about this over a year ago. Funny how good information always makes one appear smart.* "That's because I no longer have time for portrait busts," GianLorenzo said. "Even if I did, I won't carve one unless the sitter is present and I can observe him personally."

Mazzarini's eyes locked on the magnificent view across the city, which extended clear to Saint Peter's. His mood turned as gray as the overcast sky.

"I'm afraid there is no way Cardinal Richelieu will leave France. Are you saying that the King of England came to Italy and sat for you personally? I have trouble believing that."

"Actually, I did suggest to the King that he come here, but he had some sort of trouble at home and couldn't leave. Then Urban urged me to try to accommodate the King. It seems His Holiness had a political agenda."

"Only that he was trying to get England back into the Church," the political genius said, "and you were the vehicle of choice."

"Whatever. In any case, I requested a painting." Bernini said. "I told his envoy that if the painting was of sufficiently high quality, I would reconsider."

"So that's how the great Sir Anthony Van Dyke got involved. I hear he painted three views of the monarch from life—full face, left and right profile—which the King sent to you by personal envoy."

Bernini thought about the first time he saw the painting. As he spoke, tears filled his eyes. "When I unwrapped the triptych, I was overcome with emotion. Van Dyke had created a masterpiece in its own right, and it stirred in me a searing desire to carve the King's bust. Van Dyke is truly the greatest portrait painter of our age."

"I fear," a thoroughly dejected Mazzarini said, "there is no artist in France comparable to Van Dyke." He continued so softly, Bernini had to strain to hear him. "It really would have helped me with Richelieu, though. That's life, I guess."

—

GianLorenzo looked at his best friend—who appeared on the verge of tears—and relented. "You win, Giulio, but I have two conditions. First, commission the best artist in France to paint a triptych of your Cardinal Richelieu. That should be easy. The second one, I don't know. You must convince Urban to release me for the commission."

Mazzarini perked up—his stratagem worked and now GianLorenzo was talking his language. "That will be relatively easy. I know Urban would prefer remaining neutral in world events, but I don't think he can escape the fact that Catholic France is of tremendous importance to the papacy."

"Then it's settled. If you can accomplish those two things, you may tell your patron that I will carve his portrait. But I insist you stress that I only agreed because of our life-long friendship."

Giulio hugged his friend and kissed him on both cheeks. "GianLorenzo," he said, "you are a jewel."

"By the way," Bernini said, "since Richelieu wants a portrait bust comparable to that of the King of England, the fee—which was double my usual amount—will also have to be comparable."

Chapter LXVIII

T he poetry was sublime and the Pope's pleasant voice was lulling Bernini to sleep.

"Don't doze off, GianLorenzo," the cultivated pontiff said as he closed the book of poetry he had written and Bernini had illustrated.

"I wasn't sleeping, Your Holiness," the Cavaliere said honestly. "I close my eyes to concentrate on your beautiful lyrics. I enjoy your poetry almost as much as I cherish these suppers in your home on Sunday nights."

GianLorenzo and Urban adjourned to the sitting room to drink an after-supper brandy. It was in this setting that the artist's commissions were normally discussed, so this was, not surprisingly, Bernini's favorite part of the evening.

"If I may say, Holy Father, you seem pre-occupied."

"GianLorenzo," the Pope said, "you were an incredibly perceptive child when we met oh so many years ago, and you have only refined your complex mind. When my other guest arrives you will understand my melancholia."

—

Bernini was shocked to see Galileo Galilei escorted into the room by the pontiff's secretary. *Do my eyes deceive me? How can Galileo be here in Urban's private sitting room after their falling out?*

"Hello young man," Galileo said, shaking GianLorenzo's hand. "At last we meet. I'm a great admirer of you and your work."

"That is a real compliment, coming from a man of your stature," Bernini replied. He glanced at Urban surreptitiously, to see if he had offended the Pope. The pontiff was stoic. *To me, it's obvious from looking at Galileo that he's a nice gentleman as well as an intellectual genius. People say I have a penetrating gaze, but his piercing eyes remind me more of father's. I think he's trying to temper his long face with that bushy, white beard, mustache and hair down the side.*

"When I look at your work," Galileo said to Bernini, "an unusual thought occurs to me. I think that your art—all of it—is the forerunner of what some of us scientists and so-called thinkers are trying to say. You are bold and natural, yet everything you create appears to be based on the classical, which is as it should be."

"Perhaps," Bernini said, "perhaps . . . perhaps all revolutions, whether they be scientific, artistic or otherwise, are essentially alike."

"That is very perceptive, young man. You could say that all of us who have a new method of reasoning, which is not as absolute as the Church, are . . ."

"Enough," Urban said, startling both Galileo and Bernini into silence. "Galileo, do you know why I sent for you?"

The great man did not flinch. Bernini could see that he was weary, despondent and resigned. "No, Holy Father, I do not."

The pontiff paused purposely, giving his guests time to speculate on his forthcoming pronouncement. When neither displayed any visible emotion, the Pope spoke, not in the singsong manner he used when saying Mass, but rather in a heavy voice rife with fatalism.

"Galileo," Urban said, "I am releasing you from your confinement here in Rome. You are free to return to your home outside of Florence, which you may not leave, of course."

The words rolled from the Pope's proud lips as if he were granting Galileo the favor of the century.

—

As GianLorenzo watched the two strong-willed men, his mind drifted back to the unforgettable day in 1633 he had been invited to the home of Cassiano dal Pozzo. Bernini had been shown into the salon of the collector's beautifully appointed villa. The room was filled with paintings by Rubens, Vouet and, especially Poussin. *I'm happy some of my paintings are hanging with these.*

"Welcome to my humble abode," Cassiano had said. The severely arched eyebrows and look of sadness on his host's sharply lined face told Bernini there was a major problem in the air. "Join me in an aperitif and I'll tell you what is on my mind, the importance of which I cannot overstate."

The Cavaliere watched his host with interest. *I've always liked Cassiano and not only because he's learned and cultivated and a great patron of the arts. He's come a long way from his early employment in the Barberini household—I don't think anyone knows more about Leonardo than he does, and his scientific knowledge is legendary. But what does he want from me?*

"I need a favor GianLorenzo," Cassiano said, as if reading his guest's mind. "As you may know, Galileo is a close friend of mine. He is to appear before the Inquisition today for his final hearing. While he could be sentenced to death by burning at the stake, to avoid that fate he tells me that he plans to recant and admit publicly that he's wrong about the earth revolving around the sun—even though he isn't, of course. The thought of seeing that great man grovel sickens me."

"Indeed," Bernini said. "But where do I fit in?"

"You are my last hope. I didn't want to bother a man as busy as you, but I've approached all of my other contacts to no avail. No one, not even the ambassador, could get Urban to change his mind. Because of your unique relationship with the Pope, I believe that one word from you would surely cause the Holy Father to dismiss all of the charges and set Galileo free."

"Cassiano, you flatter me. If I believed I could help Galileo, I would do so with no hesitation. Unfortunately, my relationship with the Pope—and it is truly unique—does not extend to religious matters. My father, rest his soul, taught me that I should keep my religious opinions to myself."

"But I knew your father and he was a compassionate man."

"Nothing could be more accurate," Bernini said as he recalled his father crying while telling him about the Giordano Bruno burning. "But in addition to his soft heart, father was also a brilliant man. He taught me that clergy, regardless of rank, do not appreciate the intervention of laymen in their business. For me to get into the middle of this controversy—much as I'd like to—it would probably hurt Galileo's chances rather than help him. Urban is a very, very, very strong-willed man."

—

Bernini snapped out of his daydreaming. With mind and body back in the Pope's sitting room, GianLorenzo took a long drink of brandy and gradually focused on what Urban was saying to Galileo.

Beyond Michelangelo

" . . . And I did everything for you. I even allowed you to stay in the Tuscan Embassy here in Rome instead of jail, with your own servants no less. Now, by permitting you to return to your own home in Arcetri—which, as I said, you may not leave—I'm satisfied that I've done everything in my power for you."

"You are a true friend," Galileo said to the Pope. Bernini couldn't tell if Galileo was being sarcastic.

—

After Galileo left, neither Urban nor Bernini made eye contact nor spoke for a full ten minutes, each awash in his own thoughts about the great scientist.

"You know what Galileo did, don't you?" Urban finally asked,

The Cavaliere studied the Pope's face as he sipped on his brandy. *He doesn't know where to start with this story which obviously distresses him. I'd better play it safe.*

"Some of it, I guess. I'm not sure."

Urban finally spoke—his resigned tone reminded Bernini of his mother trying to get him to eat meat.

"Our beloved Holy Father, Paul V, forgave Galileo for advocating that the sun is the center of the universe and the earth travels around it. In fact, he was so gracious, the Holy Father dismissed his transgression against the teachings of the Church with a mere rebuke. That was some thirty years ago. One would think the world-renowned scientist, and my friend, would learn his lesson. But no, Galileo took it to the next level and recently wrote a book, entitled 'Dialogue on the Two Major Systems of the World.' He put all of the stupid objections to the Copernican system in the mouth of an ignorant character named Simplico."

"Forgive my ignorance, Holy Father, but I don't see the problem."

"The problem, as you put it, is that many of the things Simplico says in the book sound exactly like things I have said in the past. For example, Galileo, through Simplico, paraphrases and mocks my statement, 'It may be that God, for all His own unfathomable reasons, made it appear that the earth revolves around the sun—without its actually doing so.'"

Bernini almost fell off his chair. *That is brilliant. It's from the same school as my "Great isn't the word," but better. Father would be proud of his friend the Pope.*

Urban continued, becoming more agitated by the minute. "Here's the madness of the situation. I have always treated Galileo like a friend—his access to my papal chambers has been almost unlimited. In fact, we were so close, some years ago I wrote a paper and dedicated it to him."

The pontiff stopped abruptly. He sipped his brandy and gazed out the window, shuddering as he contemplated the heinous crime committed against his person by the most famous astronomer alive.

The pontiff's tone was now one of anger. "What treatment did I receive in return? Galileo made fun of me. He mocked me. He embarrassed me, for the entire world to see. Why he did it, I do not know. He said he was just playing a joke on me. Perhaps he was, but even if it was only meant as a joke, it was impossible for me to overlook or excuse his actions. I am sure you understand."

Bernini nodded vigorously. *I understand more than you know.*

—

Bernini was as depressed and disconsolate as an artist who has lost his muse. The only thing he could think about on the ride home was Cardinal Scipione Borghese's admonishment, delivered to him so many years ago.

"Listen to me and listen good," Scipione had said. "You don't play jokes on the Pope. On me, fine. On your mentor, Cardinal Barberini, fine. On the nobility, fine. On your friends and family, fine. On the Pope—and it doesn't matter one whit who is Pope—never. GianLorenzo, the Pope is my uncle, but I would never play a joke on him. There are very few absolutes in life, but I'm giving you one now. Never, ever, embarrass the Pope."

Bernini screamed out loud to Galileo's planets, wishing he could open the heavens and turn back the clock.

"Galileo, why couldn't you have been present that day so long ago? If only you had been there you would never have committed your blunder—or was it merely a miscalculation? You drove a chilling spike into the heart of your brilliant career. For what? My heart goes out to you. If only I could have helped."

Beyond Michelangelo

The Cavaliere pulled his scarf tighter around his neck. *Is that a cold wind from the north I feel, or is it my imagination playing a contemptible trick on me?*

Chapter LXIX

Borromini strolled into Giuseppe's bookshop, whistling off-key. Once Giuseppe got over the shock of seeing Francesco happy, he immediately made his best customer his usual espresso. "Another new commission I assume" Giuseppe said while he mentally tallied the potential sale. *Happy customers invariably buy more.*

Borromini's laugh echoed throughout the store. "Better than that," he replied. "Much better. I found out that Bernini fellow has a mistress. One of his assistants told one of my workers."

"What's so good about that?"

"It gets better," Borromini said. "The woman is not only married, the cuckold works for that man."

"His mistress is married and her husband works for Bernini? That is something. What I don't understand is why all this makes you so happy."

Borromini gulped down another espresso and rubbed his callused hands together in glee.

"Giuseppe, I would think a sophisticated man like you could figure it out. When the people of Rome find out that Bernini man has a mistress who is married—and I'm going to make sure they all know—they will vilify him. Then, when they find out that the soiled woman is married to one of his assistants, everybody will turn their back on him. Especially the clergy. I predict that even the Pope—his darling Pope—will turn away from that Bernini man. His reputation will be sullied beyond repair. He will be eternally sorry that he ever took credit for my work and stole my jobs and money. That's why I'm happy. Wouldn't you be?"

"Let me make you another espresso," Giuseppe said.

—

Cardinal Virgilio Spada made a call at the project for the Oratorians to inspect the progress. The Cardinal found Borromini perusing plans with a carpenter in a corner of the monumental hall of the Order's Vallicelliana Library.

When Francesco saw Spada, he rushed over to him. "It's coming beautifully, isn't it?"

"You have designed a masterpiece, Francesco," the Cardinal said, and he was sincere. "I don't think I've ever seen wood used to such a spectacular effect as on these library shelves."

Borromini's chest puffed. "This library just goes to show you what I'm capable of doing if the patron leaves me alone and doesn't harass me. I don't know why but your brethren seem to thrive on meetings. They've been driving me crazy with all of their demands and conditions."

"Don't let the Father's bother you," Spada said. "They mean well—they only want everything to be perfect."

"Virgilio, you are extremely knowledgeable in architectural matters. Can't you explain to them that if they leave me alone, they will get a much better building?"

"Believe me Francesco, I try. But unfortunately they won't listen to me anymore than they listen to you."

"Here is the most frustrating thing of all. They worry about every little detail in relatively unimportant places like the cloister, and give me a free hand in the library—the most important room in the complex. Excuse me now, I'm busy."

Cardinal Spada smiled as he left the room. *Social graces are definitely not this genius's forte.*

—

When he reached the door, Virgilio stopped and walked back. "I almost forgot. Bernini sends his thanks to you."

Borromini dropped his pad and pencil, his mind whirling. "I don't have time for stupid jokes."

"Francesco, I'm serious. I was at the Barberini Theatre last night and saw a Bernini play. It was wonderful. And guess what. Bernini was there and introduced his mistress to me. Just like that. And do you know what he said? He said, 'If I'm not mistaken, your friend Borromini has spread the word around town about my affair. Please thank him for me because he did me a big favor. Now that the affair has been exposed, I can take my darling Costanza with me everywhere. Be sure you tell him.' Those were his exact words."

"Why that . . ."

Cardinal Spada picked up Borromini's pencil and pad and handed them to the architect.

"Don't be upset, Francesco. How were you to know that your whispering campaign would backfire? Schemes of this nature are sensitive—they don't always work out the way one hopes."

Borromini scoffed. "How would you know about schemes? You are like my hero, Carlo Maderno. You love everybody."

Cardinal Spada smiled broadly, running his hand through his thinning black hair. *Perfect. Exactly what I want people to think.*

Chapter LXX

GianLorenzo scaled the stairs to his hideaway, three at a time, pealing off his clothes as he climbed.

"Darling," he said, pulling open the door and tossing his clothes on the floor. "I can't wait to . . ." Bernini's heart sank—the room was empty. He checked under the covers and in the bathroom. Nothing.

GianLorenzo took the rest of his clothes off and slipped into bed. *She must be late again.* He took the bottle of brandy—which was always waiting for him on the side table—and drank straight from the bottle.

—

Dawn started to break, although it was still dark. Bernini's carriage was positioned behind a large shrub, so that he was hidden, but he could see Costanza's apartment. *I swore to my darling that I would never spy on her, but this isn't spying, I just happen to be in the neighborhood.*

The sky was slowly getting lighter. Suddenly, the front door flew open and three people stumbled out. They were disheveled—laughing, drinking and wrestling with one another. In the poor light, Bernini had trouble recognizing the merrymakers, but they were certainly having fun, there was no doubt about that. The woman took both men in her mouth at the same time. The drunken men were whooping and hollering as they both mounted her simultaneously, one from the front and one from the rear. GianLorenzo was getting hot all over watching the three bodies undulate in rhythm.

The sun finally broke through. Bernini was stunned. He rubbed his eyes—not believing what he was seeing. It was Costanza and her husband. *That's strange, the third person looks exactly like my brother Luigi. Oh my God, it is my brother Luigi.*

—

Bernini jumped out of his carriage and raced toward the pile of naked bodies. Costanza saw him coming and ran into the building, pulling her husband along. Luigi took off in the opposite direction, with GianLorenzo in close pursuit.

The chase zigzagged through the streets and alleys of Rome until the younger Luigi, who was pulling away, tripped. GianLorenzo found an old, rusty iron bar and began beating his brother with it. He delivered blow after blow after blow to Luigi's body until his brother's calls for mercy became fainter and fainter and finally stopped.

—

Angelica held Luigi's hand while the doctor examined him. GianLorenzo watched from the corner of the room. The doctor finished and put his instruments away.

"Your son is lucky, Mrs. Bernini. He only sustained a few broken ribs. From what I can see, it could have been much worse."

"Luigi's lucky? You are wrong Doctor. GianLorenzo is the lucky one. If the injuries had been any worse, Mister Genius would have had to deal with me."

The doctor laughed as he departed. *An angry Neapolitan mother—now we're talking injuries.*

Angelica noticed that Luigi had dozed off. She motioned for GianLorenzo to come to the side of the bed. "I kept telling your father that some day you'd get into serious trouble with that temper of yours," she said. "I hope you've learned your lesson. When Luigi wakes up I want you to apologize to him."

GianLorenzo stared at the floor, contriteness dripping from every pore. The line came easily: "Mother, you don't know how sorry I am."

—

Bernini went into his bathroom and removed a long, sharp razor. After he tested the edge for sharpness he sent for his faithful servant.

"Claudio, in the thirteen years you have been with me, have I ever asked you to do anything that wasn't proper?"

"Of course not, sir. Why do you ask?"

"I need your help. Do you know about my friend Costanza?"

"With all due respect, sir, everyone in Rome knows about her."

'Then you know where she lives."

"Yes, sir."

"Excellent. Excellent. Now, I want you to take this razor and carve a star on Costanza's face. Or a circle or a triangle. Get my point? I don't care what the design is, nor the quality of the carving, I merely want to be certain that she will never again make a fool out of me or anyone else."

Claudio hesitated when Bernini handed him the razor. "Are you sure you want me to do this sir?"

"Claudio, that lady disgraced me publicly and needs to be punished. When will you do it?"

"Immediately, sir."

"Good. After you have disfigured her, I want you to ride to Siena and look after my interests there. I don't expect to see you for at least six months. Actually, a year would be better. Take this pouch—the gold coins will supplement your regular wages nicely."

"Yes, sir. I understand everything perfectly."

———

When Luigi was healed, Angelica accompanied GianLorenzo into Luigi's bedroom. "I wanted mother to hear this," GianLorenzo said. "Please forgive me, Luigi. What I did was stupid and I apologize. Can you return to work? I need your help at Saint Peter's"

———

Luigi was so happy to be working again that he lost track of time; it was pitch black when he left the great basilica after his first day back on the job. Luigi wrapped his scarf around his neck as he bounced down the stairs of the church. He heard a twig snap and spun around to see GianLorenzo, with his sword drawn.

Bernini lunged at his brother. "I hope you didn't think you'd get away with only a few broken ribs."

Luigi sidestepped the sword, jumped on his horse and rode as fast as he could across town to their house. He pounded on the front door, which

Angelica opened for him. "Quick, mother. Close the door. GianLorenzo is trying to kill me again."

Bernini arrived several minutes later. "Open up, it's me," he shouted as he pounded on the door.

Angelica opened the door a crack, blocking the entrance with her body. "Stop this. That is your brother—your flesh and blood. Stay out there until you calm down." She closed and latched the door.

Adrenaline flowing, GianLorenzo broke the wooden door down. He grabbed his mother by the upper arms and shook her. "Where is he hiding?" The back door slammed shut. GianLorenzo released his mother and picked-up the chase.

Luigi dashed across the road and into Santa Maria Maggiore. He relaxed in a pew. *Surely I'll be safe here.*

Luigi was being logical, but unfortunately for him, his half-crazed brother was not.

GianLorenzo followed him into the church, brandishing his sword and spewing epithets as he chased Luigi through the church. It took four priests—actually two monsignors and two priests—to finally subdue the kicking and screaming hot-blooded genius.

The police led the great GianLorenzo Bernini away.

Chapter LXXI

As soon as Borromini walked into his shop, Giuseppe the bookseller knew that his normally dour customer was happy. *Twice in one month, I'm not sure I can handle this.*

"You obviously haven't heard what happened to Bernini," Giuseppe said.

"Of course I have, Borromini answered. "He was arrested, tried and convicted of attempted murder."

"No, I mean . . ."

"And he was fined 3,000 scudi. As far as I'm concerned, it should have been 300,000."

The reality hit Giuseppe like an unexpected kick to the stomach. *Borromini obviously hasn't heard that the Pope not only sent an absolution of the charges to Bernini—written on excellent parchment, no less—he also waived his fine and, incredibly, included a eulogy of his virtue, which said, "You are a rare man, sublime genius and born by divine intervention and for the glory of Rome, to bring light to the century."*

"Here's a new treatise on geometry that I think you'll enjoy," Giuseppe said, attempting to sound excited. "Have an espresso while you look it over." *No way I'm going to deliver the bad news to my best customer. I've learned my lesson.*

Bernini wrote in his latest letter to Mazzarini, who was back in France,

> And in conclusion, after the trial, I went straight home and chopped her head off. Don't panic, I don't mean literally. Remember that painting of Costanza and me that you admired—the one that hung in my room—it's now a painting of me, period. And remember the bust of her that you lusted over? I gave it to a friend in Florence. You may think that's the end of Costanza, but it's not. I'm sculpting a bust of Medusa with Costanza's face and snakes for hair. You can figure out why, I'm sure.

G.L.

PS: I'm embarrassed to tell you that this entire Costanza episode laid me up for some time. You were right all along, my friend—if I'd listened to you, all of this grief could have been avoided. Oh well, life goes on. I do take solace in the fact that even though I tried to kill Luigi in a fit of temper, the entire population of Rome sided with me. I heard more than one person say, "You can't blame Bernini, after all, he is half-Neapolitan."

Chapter LXXII

Beyond Michelangelo

Angelica pondered her alternatives on her way to the Quirinal Palace. *Should I go through with this? I hate what I'm about to do but I'm afraid of what might happen to GianLorenzo if I don't take action. Please God, give me the wisdom to do the right thing.*

—

"Come in Mrs. Bernini, it is always a pleasure to see you." Cardinal Francesco Barberini said. He led Angelica into his large, ornately decorated office and gave her a coffee. She presented the Cardinal a tin of her homemade biscotti. Like always, half were made with lemon frosting and half with orange frosting. They were famous throughout Rome.

"Sweets by the sweet," the Cardinal said. "A slight alteration of the words of a writer from England named William Shakespeare. I recently acquired a set of his plays. Not bad, for an Englishman."

Angelica knew that the Pope was extremely strong willed and secretive and therefore preferred handling most matters himself. But she also knew that Cardinal Barberini was technically Urban's Secretary of State, and it was protocol to go through channels in matters such as this. She gathered her courage.

"It's GianLorenzo," she said. "I'm afraid he is out of control."

Cardinal Barberini grimaced. "That was a most unfortunate incident."

"It's more than an unfortunate incident that I'm worried about. He showed a total lack of respect for me. His own mother."

"Lack of respect? The Cavaliere? That's hard to believe—from what I've seen over the years, he respects everyone, even his enemies."

"Yes, and that's one of the reasons his father and I were always so proud of GianLorenzo. It's this Bonarelli girl who did it. She changed him. She must have given my son the evil eye. I think she's a witch."

"Mrs. Bernini," the startled cleric said, "don't tell me you believe in witches."

"Cardinal Barberini, in Naples, everyone believes in witches. In any case, whether she's a witch or just a horrible creature, she has turned my son into a monster. He's not himself. He's out of control."

"Out of control? You've said that twice. Why do you say he is out of control?"

"Someone needs to reason with him. Someone he respects."

"I understand. But, why do you say he is out of control?"

Angelica finished her coffee and took another cookie. She looked around the room while she munched on it. Cardinal Barberini waited patiently. *The lady is obviously trying to decide whether she should say what is on her mind.*

Angelica finally spoke in a small, halting, but determined voice.

"GianLorenzo thinks . . . he thinks . . . GianLorenzo thinks he is King Of The World."

Cardinal Barberini jumped out of his chair, knocking over the remaining biscotti in his haste. He picked them up, wiped them off, and put them back on his desk. He then took Angelica by the hand.

"You and I," he said, "need to talk with the Holy Father. Now."

Chapter LXXIII

After tucking Urban into bed, Bernini began to lower the shades in the Pope's bedroom. While GianLorenzo performed this task every Sunday night after supper and after-meal discussions, tonight the vibrations in this very personal room felt different to him.

"Please come here and sit next to me, Cavaliere," the pontiff said, patting the edge of the bed.

Bernini shuttered inwardly. Normally the Holy Father falls asleep as soon as his head hits the pillow. Worse, I've never sat on the edge of his bed before. Something is definitely amiss. This informality scares me.

"GianLorenzo, how old are you," Urban asked. "About forty?"

Bernini relaxed. *Happily, it appears this conversation is headed in the usual direction of my marital status.*

"Forty is correct, Your Holiness. Exactly."

The pontiff wasted no time getting to his point—which he made to GianLorenzo a minimum of once a year. "It's time you marry. It's time you settle down and have a family."

Bernini smiled inwardly. *This I can handle—I've dodged this one for years.* "The statutes I carve will be my children," GianLorenzo said. "They will keep my memory alive in the world for many centuries."

"... For many centuries," the Pope said in tandem with Bernini. "Cavaliere," Urban continued, "I know that answer by heart. In the past, I was happy to accept it. No longer. Sorry."

Bernini felt like he was tumbling down an abandoned mineshaft. *Damn. I expected a certain amount of fallout from that business with Luigi, but it looks like things are going to be worse than I imagined. Much worse.*

"GianLorenzo," Urban said. "Since that fateful day thirty years ago when our beloved Pope Paul V charged me with your future, I have tried to be your mentor, your patron, your protector and your friend. And I must admit, it has truly been my pleasure."

"Holy Father, you've been even more, you've . . ."

Urban raised his hand, silencing Bernini.

The Cavaliere gulped. *Oh, oh. Urban never schusses me. I sense disaster.*

"GianLorenzo, I am speaking to you in all five of my capacities—yes, I've added my position as Your Pope. Listen carefully; this is the last time I am ever going to say this. I want you to settle down and get married. Goodnight, Cavaliere. Don't forget to pull down that last shade."

Chapter LXXIV

Beyond Michelangelo

The ten uniformed servants stood at attention in the courtyard of one of the most impressive country villas in Italy. Nestled in the foothills east of Rome, the marble mansion was scrubbed clean, the fallen flaming red leaves were swept off of the gravel driveway, and the uniforms were all starched double strength.

"Who is this Bernini fellow," the cook whispered to the head housekeeper standing next to her. "The mistress, she ordered me to prepare a lavish banquet for every meal this weekend—she even gave me the menus. I've never seen her like this."

"You truly are a dolt, and you will never be more than a cook if you don't keep track of the upper-classes. GianLorenzo Bernini is a very famous man."

"So that's why our masters have been so nervous lately—snapping at me and such."

"That's the least of it. I heard there was some unpleasantness in Rome and the Holy Father ordered Mister Bernini to take a wife. Now pay attention, I hear the carriage."

"I get it," the cook said, pleased with herself. She straightened her highly uncomfortable white uniform. "This Bernini is looking for a wife and the Duke and Duchess are proposing Marietta . . ."

"Subtly, one would hope," the head housekeeper said.

—

"Marietta, remember to pretend you are interested in everything the Cavaliere says," the Duchess advised her daughter as they awaited the arrival of their distinguished guest. She moved around the study, straightening pictures, arranging and rearranging knick-knacks, generally making Marietta more nervous by the minute.

"We've been over this a thousand times, mother. I know what to . . ."

"How about timing? It's important for you say the right thing at the right time. If he says he likes our garden—and who wouldn't?—you say his Neptune and Triton would look perfect over the pond."

"And how much I love his barcaccia fountain."

"No, no. He named it La Barca and doesn't like it when it's called La Barcaccia. I know, I checked. Now relax, I hear them coming."

—

The carriage, pulled by four princely black stallions, thundered up the long, winding driveway, creating a blur of the perfectly groomed cypress tress lining each side. When the ornately decorated carriage stopped, the uniformed driver's assistant jumped down. He opened the door on Bernini's side first.

The Duchess glided across the courtyard. *At least he got that right.*

"Welcome to our humble abode, Cavaliere," the Duchess said as she inexplicably curtsied. "We are pleased and honored to have such a distinguished guest on this sunny afternoon."

"Not as pleased and honored as I am to be in the company of such a youthful and beautiful hostess," Bernini said, bowing and kissing her extended hand.

GianLorenzo's penetrating gaze locked on his hostess. *Nice. Very nice. Young and sensuous—must be a second marriage.* "Your gown—it's exquisite, and the green in the bustle matches the color of your lovely, and if I may say, expressive eyes."

"Please don't hesitate to say whatever is on your mind—as long as it's complimentary," the Duchess replied. *How could I say that? Why am I so flustered?*

—

The Duchess took Bernini's arm and led him toward the villa. "Did you have a pleasant ride from the city?"

"The Duke and I had a delightful time chatting—the hours virtually flew by. I must say, your husband is exceptionally knowledgeable about artist matters."

So far, so good. I'm glad I made the old fool read all of those books.

—

Bernini took a quick glance around the study and concluded there was old, old money in this household. "This is a magnificent room," he said. "Did you decorate it or did you employ an artist?" *I'll wager a year's income she says her daughter decorated the room—they all do.*

"No . . . yes I did. I'm so pleased you approve." *There I go again. I was supposed to say that Marietta decorated it.* "Why, look who is sitting here. Cavaliere, this is my daughter, Marietta. Marietta, say hello to Cavaliere Bernini."

"Charmed," Marietta said in the throaty voice she and her mother had agreed upon.

—

The remainder of Bernini's weekend was a blur of lavish meals and trysts with Marietta, who was more inventive than most.

—

"So what do you think of my holdings," the Duke asked as they dismounted in front of the spic-and-span stables. "Come into the casino, Cavaliere, we'll have a taste of my vin santo—from my own vineyards."

Bernini sighed. *Here it comes and it's about time. This has been fun but I must get back to work.*

"Cavaliere, I'm not good at pretending. May I be frank with you?"

Bernini nodded. "I'd be most appreciative."

The Duke emptied his goblet and poured himself another vin santo, which he also drank.

"Everyone in Rome, and the countryside for that matter, knows that you have decided to take a wife, and in the past year you have been offered—and turned down—extensive dowries, vast tracts of land and even significant titles from other noble and wealthy families. True?"

"Alas, it is true, and flattering," Bernini said.

"I don't think you should consider it flattering. You are, after all, the most prominent artist in the world today, wealthy in your own right, connected at the highest levels of society, handsome and interesting besides. The Duchess says you are the best conversationalist she has ever met, and you have a highly defined sense of humor. Hell, you're lucky I'm married or I'd propose to you myself."

The Duke and Bernini shared a hearty laugh.

"Cavaliere, Marietta is my only child. My wife and I love her dearly and we will do anything to make her happy. She's thirty-five years old—the perfect age for you, if I may say—smart, sensitive and beautiful. At least we think so,"

Bernini sipped his drink and remained quiet.

"Here is my proposal, but I want you to consider it negotiable: Half of this 8,000-acre estate, with a villa built to your specifications; a palazzo in Rome on the Corso, also built to your specifications; one hundred thousand scudi; and your choice of several family titles. There are incidental benefits, of course, such as the most lavish wedding Rome has ever seen, and so on. What do you say?"

GianLorenzo sipped on his drink. *I get the feeling they want their daughter to marry the thought of Bernini, not Bernini the person.*

—

The Duke slipped into bed, where the Duchess was awaiting him. "What did he say," she demanded. The Duke, accustomed to his wife's aggressiveness, paid no attention to her tone of voice.

"He said something like, 'If I were going to get married, I'd marry your daughter—but I'm just not ready. Marietta is sweet and you and the Duchess are lovely people. Very lovely. Anyone would be proud to be a part of your family.' That's what he said, isn't that nice? What's wrong? Why are you so quiet?"

"Just thinking. Good night dear, go to sleep."

As soon as the Duchess heard her husband snoring, she slipped out of her bed and into Bernini's.

—

"I was expecting you," the Cavaliere said as his lovely hostess cuddled up. "I knew that once you heard that I wouldn't be your son-in-law, you would come."

"That's not very flattering, now is it?"

Bernini laughed and gave the Duchess a serious kiss. "On the contrary. I told Marietta not to come tonight. That's a compliment to you."

The Duchess propped herself on one elbow. "What went wrong? Didn't she satisfy you? I heard that you have an insatiable thirst for the good life—including an inordinate number of women—so I told Marietta her best chance was to be a tiger in bed."

"Marietta is a wonderful lady in every sense of the word, and I assure you, she totally satisfied me. I'm just not ready to get married—I'm not sure why, but I'm just not."

"If you change your mind, you know where we live."

Bernini kissed the Duchess's eyes, slowly, one at a time. "Inordinate, you say. Would two be an inordinate number of women tonight?"

The Dutchess smiled and pulled herself against GianLorenzo. "Why am I not surprised? One condition. Before I call Marietta, I'd like to be with you alone for a while—I've thought about nothing else since you arrived. Don't worry, we have plenty of time to satisfy your insatiable appetite."

Bernini ran his forefingers over his hostess's perfectly shaped nipples. "What time does your husband rise? Not too early I hope."

"The Duke never rises before mid-morning. Just to be safe, though, last night I put a large measure of sleeping powder in his brandy—he always drinks at least two big goblets before retiring. Oohhhhh. Don't stop there."

Chapter LXXV

Beyond Michelangelo

Francesco Borromini and Cardinal Virgilio Spada stood in the pleasant square that fronted the Chiesa Nuova. They were studying the recently completed façade of the Oratory designed by Francesco. The bright sun shimmered overhead, casting shadows of various shapes and intensities across it.

"It's staggeringly beautiful," Spada said. "In some ways, your design of this façade has accomplished the impossible. You've made me proud I recommended you."

A smile spread across Borromini's face, like the sun breaking through on a cloudy day. "Impossible? I accomplished the impossible? Tell me more."

The Cardinal smiled to himself. He recognized his architect's on-going need for positive reinforcement. "The façade—it's dramatic and subtle at the same time, which is not an easy combination. The way you blended the lateral and vertical elements together into a continuous, gentle curve—it's amazing. The eye gets forced across the building."

Borromini's mind drifted into the rarified air reserved for creative geniuses. "How wonderful it would be if one could construct a whole façade out of a single piece of terracotta."

"Actually," Cardinal Spada said, "you have come close to doing exactly that. I think the way you used the brick is the key. One seldom sees brick that thin. Plus, it's laid with so little mortar; you've made the surface appear smooth. Brilliant. I predict this structure will inspire architects for generations to come, and bring great honor to the Filippini."

"They get the honor? The Filippini should go to jail for the grief they caused me. I think I've aged twenty years working with these men. From what I can see, they have drastically changed since Filippo Neri died. They have desecrated the great Saint's memory."

Cardinal Spada, who was now the Head of the Order, was shocked and deeply offended by Borromini's comment but managed to maintain his composure. "What do you mean by that?"

"Today's members have focused on their nobility and forgotten the humbleness Neri preached and lived by. They are so busy telling me what to do—playing architect—when do they have time for the good works their Order was built upon?"

Cardinal Spada was speechless. Francesco had a point, but he wasn't about to admit it to him. Besides, the problems were not all one sided—he had to intercede with his brothers a number of times to save the hardheaded, opinionated architect his job. *Working with Borromini is seldom pleasurable, but fortunately it is always worth the effort. Thank God for that.*

Chapter LXXVI

Nick J. Mileti

The façade of Saint Peter's troubled Pope Urban VIII all of his life. The esthetically sensitive pontiff felt that the otherwise beautiful structure appeared squat—and most people agreed with him.

Carlo Maderno designed the façade of the basilica—for Pope Paul V—but the fault with the proportions of the façade did not lie with him. Maderno had built massive foundations on each end of the façade, which were designed to hold large bell towers. The façade's appearance was compromised because the bell towers Maderno designed were considered extravagant and therefore never built.

When Maffeo Barberini became Pope Urban VIII, he moved to correct the aesthetic problem by commissioning Bernini to design bell towers to give the needed lift to the façade.

Bernini designed two beautiful, multi-columned bell towers. Each tower had three levels, with each level forty or fifty feet tall—substantial towers to harmonize with the vastness of the church and its façade.

Bernini decided to erect the tower on the south end of the façade first—away from the Vatican—so as not to inconvenience the workers in the papal offices. After the first section of this south tower was erected, the Romans were lavish in their praise. After the second section was added, the citizens could barely contain their enthusiasm for the tower's beauty. The genius Bernini had done it again—he was correcting the proportion problem of the façade, and at the same time presenting spectacularly attractive bell towers to the city.

And then, cracks began to appear in the base of the façade of Saint Peter's.

—

The Fabbrica adjourned to the meeting room in the Vatican after personally viewing the fissures in the facade. The Cardinals sat at a large table, intently studying the architectural and engineering drawings that had been placed in front of them.

The question was whether Bernini's bell tower caused the cracks.

The Pope entered the room briskly and immediately began to speak.

"As you can see from the documents and drawings of the studies I authorized, the ground under the south bell tower shifted. We all knew the soil in that area was unstable and a certain amount of natural settling was inevitable. After considerable study, the experts and I have concluded that the tower is sound. Therefore, I have authorized Cavaliere Bernini to complete his wooden scale model of the third section, which he will paint so that it will replicate the real thing. And just to be safe, the Cavaliere has agreed to reduce the size of the final section. We shall see the results in situ shortly."

—

The festive crowd in front of Saint Peter's was enormous. Word had spread throughout Rome that Bernini was going to unveil his new scale model of the redesigned upper portion of the south tower, and the Pope, himself, was going to be present. Of course, any Bernini unveiling was an event, even if only of a wooden model.

Cardinal Spada and Borromini stood at the rear of the eager group of spectators. "Look,' Francesco said, "that Bernini fellow is about to pull the cord. I hope he slips and falls and breaks his neck."

—

The covering fell from the wooden model. The crowd, consumed with anticipation, gasped.

Followed by deafening silence.

"Look," Cardinal Spada said to Borromini, "Urban and his entourage were here less than five minutes and they're leaving. I have never seen anything like this. Everyone hates the Cavaliere's design." *Perhaps Bernini's coveted standing with the Holy Father will finally be available to me— where it rightfully belongs.*

Borromini smacked his patron on the back. He was smiling ear to ear. "These are the ruinous results visited on Rome by those Popes who are pleased to give all the work to one man alone, although there are an abundance of meritorious men in the city."

"And you are certainly one of them," Spada said. "I predict you will now receive the papal commissions your talent demands."

Borromini was too wound-up to hear the Cardinal. "You know the problem, I assume."

With great self-control, Cardinal Spada spoke to Francesco in an even tone. "I may only be a dilettante when it comes to architecture, but even an amateur can see that the third section is too small. It's totally and completely out of proportion. Clearly, Bernini overcompensated—that's what he did."

"I can't wait to spread the word," Borromini said, rubbing his hands together in glee.

"Don't waste your time, Francesco, the Holy Father will save you the trouble. Based on what I saw here today, I am sure Urban will immediately order the model torn down. At that point, everyone in Rome will know about Bernini's blunder."

Chapter LXXVII

For the rest of his life, even though he tried, Bernini could never explain why he attended Mass that Sunday at Chiesa Nuova, instead of at one of the churches closer to home as he usually did.

"Over here," the young priest called out over the worshippers streaming out of the church. "Over here, GianLorenzo. I have something to tell you."

The Cavaliere made his way to one of his favorite clerics. The two friends embraced. "I loved your sermon, Father. It had something for everyone."

"You always say the right thing, Cavaliere. What a surprise to see you in my church this morning. We are honored to have you for Sunday Mass, although, I must say, everyone was so busy looking at you, I don't think they heard a word of my sermon. No matter. What I wanted to tell you was I have someone I want you to meet."

Bernini instinctively frowned, a look he was usually able to suppress in public. "Father, with all due respect, I'm not interested in meeting any prospective brides. I'm just not ready to get married."

The priest greeted several parishioners while he gathered his thoughts. He turned his attention back to his famous friend.

"GianLorenzo, please listen to me. I know you have been bombarded with marriage proposals but this is truly different. It's not the girl's idea. It's not her family's idea. It's not even her father's idea. This is strictly my idea—they don't even know I'm talking with you."

The Cavaliere fixed the priest with his patented penetrating gaze, but the padre never flinched. Slowly, Bernini's gloomy face lit up as his mind shifted from automatic rejection to understanding. He wrapped his arm around his clerical friend.

"Padre, what you say is not only different, it's refreshing. Truthfully, it never entered my mind that such a thing was possible. Of course I'll be happy to accommodate you."

Bernini and the young priest sat outdoors at a small café in the Piazza Navona.

"This is a delightful spring day, the kind poets love," GianLorenzo said, hating the need for small talk but appreciating his friend's motives. *What a mistake I made coming here.*

"You did the right thing by coming this morning," he priest said, as if he could read Bernini's mind. "The worse that happens is you will meet two nice people."

The pair, each lost in his private thoughts, sipped their cappuccini in silence and waited no more than five minutes.

"Here they come," the Father said, pointing out a couple approaching from across the piazza.

—

Not wanting to disturb her working son, Angelica crept into the library carrying a silver tray overflowing with fresh fruit. She was so surprised when she found GianLorenzo staring into space she dropped the tray, which clanged when it hit the floor. Fruit flew in all directions.

Oblivious to his mother's presence and the noise, Bernini continued to stare into space.

"What's the matter, son?" Silence. More staring. "GianLorenzo, can you hear me? I asked you what was the matter." More silence. More staring.

Angelica walked around the table. "Maybe you can hear me better from this side. I've never seen you like this. Are you feeling okay?" More silence. More staring. She took her son by the shoulders and shook him.

Bernini glanced at his mother.

"You're alive—thank God for that. GianLorenzo, in the forty-one years since I delivered you, I've never seen you waste one minute. Until today. Why are you staring into space with a glazed look in your eyes that can't even focus on your own mother?" More silence. More staring.

"Sweetheart, you are worrying me. Should I call the doctor?"

The word 'doctor' somehow penetrated the Cavaliere's clouded mind.

Gradually he focused on the speaker—his still beautiful mother—which triggered:

"I'm in love."

—

Angelica burst out laughing. She prepared herself for a violent reaction from her son—which occurred whenever anyone laughed at him, regardless of the reason—but this time he merely stared blankly into space.

"Does she have a name, this person you love?"

"Caterina. Tezio. Caterina Tezio. Caterina. Notice how it flows off the lips? Caterina. You say it."

"Caterina. It's a lovely name. Have you known her long? This is the first time you've mentioned her."

"I met her this morning at a café in the Piazza Navona."

"This morning? That explains everything. You've been hit by a fulmine."

"A fulmine?"

"That's the thunderbolt, son. You've been hit by a bolt from the blue. Un colpo di fulmine. The thunderbolt."

—

"Are you up to talking about it," Angelica asked her highly charged son.

"I guess so. The padre saw them coming across the square. I stood for the introduction.

'Paolo Tezio, Caterina, say hello to GianLorenzo Bernini. Cavaliere, meet Mister Tezio and his daughter, Caterina.' Those were his exact words."

Angelica waited. *I haven't seen a case this bad since I left Naples.*

"Mother, I took one look at her and quickly sat down before I fell down. I tried to talk, to make conversation, but no words came out. I started shaking all over. It was weird."

"A fulmine of major proportions, no doubt about that. What happened then?"

"It was embarrassing. I just sat there and stared at her. Finally her father said they had to leave, and they did. I just sat there."

"The priest, what did he do?"

"It's blurry. I think he bought me another cappuccino, I don't really remember. I don't even remember how I got home."

—

Angelica picked up an orange from the floor, pealed it and gave it to her son. She sat next to him and waited for him to finish the fruit, which he did in record time. She repeated the process. *Poor baby, he's obviously famished—another sure sign.*

"Here's what I think," she said, half-a-dozen oranges later. "Along with your remarkable talent, God has given you incredible instincts. I see it in all of your work. Your father used to say that your talent and your instincts were intimately intertwined—that you couldn't have your extraordinary talent unless you also had extraordinary instincts."

Bernini was having trouble thing straight. *What do instincts have to do with a thunderbolt?* "What are you saying mother?"

"What I'm saying is, if your father was alive, I'm certain he would say, 'Trust his instincts.' So I will. You have my blessings, my darling son, whether you need them or not. As your father used to say, 'If this wasn't so much fun, it would be hard work'."

GianLorenzo jumped up and grabbed his mother. He twirled her in the air.

"Put me down, you rascal," she cried, loving every minute of it. "You're messing up my hair."

Chapter LXXVIII

GianLorenzo kept peeking at Caterina as his carriage made its way through Rome. He tried to make conversation several times but couldn't. *This fulmine is getting on my nerves. On the other hand, I love looking at my darling and listening to her melodic voice.* "Your family, tell me about it," he managed.

"My father is a lawyer—in the curia," Caterina said. "My beautiful mother died giving birth to my baby sister, so my father raised the two of us all by himself."

"I wager that you helped," Bernini managed once more.

GianLorenzo continued to peek at his intended. *When the padre told me Caterina was the most beautiful girl in Rome, I thought he was exaggerating to pique my interest. Truth is, he was understating the case. I couldn't make her more beautiful if I had to model her out of wax.*

"Of course I helped as much as I could—cleaning, cooking and looking after my baby sister. Things like that. You're probably going to ask why my father didn't remarry; everyone does. When I asked him that some years ago, he said he loved my mother too much to think of another woman that way. He's a perfect father, and I'm the luckiest twenty-two year old in Italy. Why are we stopping here?"

The Cavaliere jumped out of the carriage and raced around to the other side. He opened the door and took Caterina in his arms. "It's our house—this is where you and I are going to live."

—

Caterina struggled free. "Please take me home," she said. "Please. Right now, if you don't mind. What kind of girl do you think I am?" She held out her hand for the driver to help her up.

"Please don't go, Caterina. I bought the house for the two of us. Isn't it big enough or in the right section of Rome? I'll put a studio in—and a theatre. I love the theatre. If you don't like this house, I'll buy you another."

The young beauty gasped audibly. *Can this world-famous artist be talking marriage to someone like me? No, I don't think so. No, I have no titles. No dowry. I can't think of anything I have that would interest him except my beauty—I've heard the stories about his womanizing all over Rome and they are not flattering. What have I got to lose if I confront the issue?*

"GianLorenzo, this isn't a house, it's a palace. And the location, here next to the Piazza di Spagna, it's perfect. But, unless I'm terribly mistaken, something is missing here. A critically important something."

Bernini turned the situation over in his mind and smacked his forehead so hard it turned red and welted up.

"Did you hurt yourself? Are you okay?" Caterina ran her ivory-white hand over the deep red blotch, causing the Cavaliere to swoon. He leaned against the carriage to avoid falling down.

"Caterina, darling, this is the single most embarrassing thing that has ever happened to me in my life. Here I am going on and on and I forgot the most important thing. I forgot to ask you to marry me."

Caterina threw her arms around GianLorenzo. She ran her hands through his luxurious head of hair. "If you ask me," she said, "I might say yes."

Bernini fell to one knee. "Caterina. Miss Tezio. Miss Caterina Tezio. Darling. Will you marry me?"

"I might say yes. On the other hand, I hardly know you, GianLorenzo, and some of the things I've heard about you and the women of Rome are less than flattering and I have no dowry and . . ."

"Stop. Stop right there. When I saw you for the first time, I was hit by the thunderbolt. It was love at first sight and that is that. As for those other women, forget about them. They are ancient history. I'm like your father in that regard—you are the only woman for me for the rest of my life. And forget about a dowry. If I don't care about a dowry, why should you? I love you, I want you to marry me, and I'm not getting up off my knee—which is killing me by the way—until you say yes."

Caterina burst out laughing. "You are one of a kind, GianLorenzo. A sense of humor to go with your talent—just like I heard." She threw her arms around her prize and gave him a tantalizing kiss, her first. "Father says he liked you from the first time we met—although you didn't say much."

Beyond Michelangelo

"I love your father almost as much as I love you," Bernini said with a smile. "I only wish you could have met my father—you would have loved him. Now hurry, my sweet, let's walk through the palazzo, as you call it. Then we will immediately visit your father and my mother. And then the Pope. And then, right away, we'll get married. I'm not sure I can wait."

"You'll wait," Caterina said, planting her second historic kiss on his anxious lips. "You have no choice."

Chapter LXXIX

Beyond Michelangelo

The Pope's aide poured anisette, passed the biscotti and closed the door quietly on his way out of the pontiff's lavish study.

"Anisette this evening," Bernini said. "That's quite a surprise. After twenty years of brandy following our delightful Sunday night suppers, you have switched to anisette. May I ask why?"

The pontiff starred at the liquid in his cut-glass goblet and frowned. He took a small sip of the anisette and frowned again. "Ugh. Definitely a drink for the women of the realm. To answer your question, I haven't been feeling well lately and the brandy is too strong for me at this point in my life. To be truthful, Cavaliere, I fear the end is near."

Bernini was stunned by the pontiff's words. *Clearly, the Holy Father is failing, but why would he be this pessimistic? Can it be his direct line to the Good Lord?*

Urban took another small sip of anisette. "Enough of that kind of talk. Speaking of women, tell me about your Caterina. I don't mean how pretty she is—I saw that for myself—I mean Caterina the person. The wife."

"My favorite subject, Your Holiness. Caterina is faultlessly docile, prudent and not at all tricky. You are correct, she is beautiful, but she is beautiful without affectation. She is such a perfect mixture of seriousness, pleasantness, generosity and hard work, she might be a gift stored up in heaven. My father used to say that the greatest thing that ever happened to him was having me as a son. Well, Holy Father, you have been my mentor, patron, protector and friend—for over thirty-five years—and you have been the person most responsible for me becoming rich and famous beyond my wildest dreams. But, for all of your largesse and advice, you have never done me a greater favor than insisting that I marry and settle down. My Caterina is your greatest legacy."

Urban's eyes closed and his head slowly fell forward. When his chin hit his breast, the Pope caught himself. He snatched his anisette and took a long sip. "GianLorenzo, you've earned everything you have. In fact, I believe you are easily the most consistent artist who has ever lived."

Urban has never dozed off in front of me. His condition is worse than I thought. "With all due respect, Your Holiness. While you were gracious enough to never mention it to me, I know that you hated the third level of the bell tower at Saint Peter's."

"Cavaliere, that was only a wooden model. The problem, as I see it, was that you felt pressured to place it in situ prematurely. I venture to say that most—if not all—of your models, regardless of the material they are made of, changed from creative inception to actual completion. Am I right?"

Bernini smiled and nodded but remained silent. *He sounds exactly like my father teaching me the rudiments of sculpture when I was a little boy.*

"I also never mentioned that all of my advisors wanted me to not only tear down the wooden model, but they also wanted me to tear down the first two sections of your stunning south bell tower. I refused to do that, of course. Not out of friendship, but because I know that eventually you will get it right. You always do."

—

The mere mention of the bell tower depressed Bernini. Urban, who knew GianLorenzo better than anyone alive, observed the Cavaliere's sadness. He quickly changed the subject.

"Tell me what you call your recently completed fountain that compliments my family's palazzo so perfectly," the Pope asked. "I plan to open the piazza to the public so that the entire population may enjoy your latest triumph—I consider it a whimsical masterpiece. I particularly like the fact that the fountain is so spectacular from any viewpoint, the citizens can drive their carriages—or walk—around all four sides, without any fall off of its beauty. Piazza Barberini; that has a nice ring to it."

"I call it the Triton Fountain, Your Holiness. I think little girls will like the playful dolphins, and big girls will like the Triton's rippling muscles."

Urban started to object to Bernini's comment—which he felt was immoral—but he wasn't feeling up to it. "Now, to talk a bit of business. I want you to build a small fountain near your Triton Fountain. When the public is about, I want a place where thirsty people may quench their thirst from a spout."

Bernini sparked. "With maybe an open shell where horses could drink from a little pool of water. In fact, maybe even puppies and kittens . . ."

"Good night, Cavaliere."

Chapter LXXX

Nick J. Mileti

The courier from Paris arrived at the Bernini home with a triple portrait of Cardinal Richelieu and a letter from someone named Cardinal Jules Mazarin. Caterina summoned GianLorenzo from his studio. For the break in his hectic work schedule, she brought her husband some fresh fruit and sparkling white wine. Bernini eagerly ripped open the letter, which he read aloud.

'Dear GianLorenzo:

Yes, I changed my name. I believe the Gallic Jules Mazarin will serve me better here than the original Giulio Mazzarini. Looking ahead, I'm confident the French would never want to admit that an Italian of less than noble birth is in control of their country—which, between you and I, is where I feel I'm headed; the great and generous Cardinal Richelieu is pushing me forward as if I am his own son. In that regard, thanks to you and Richelieu, I finally wear the Cardinals cap. How could Urban say no to the two most important men in Europe? Obviously, he couldn't. And speaking of the Holy Father, I'm sure you know by now that he has graciously agreed to allow you to carve Richelieu's bust. Why would His Holiness deny you the Thomas Baker commission and endorse that of my patron and protector?

Bernini put the letter down. *How does Giulio know about the Baker situation? I guess the world is getting smaller every day.*

"Sweetheart," Caterina said, "what is the situation with this Thomas Baker?"

"Nothing important. Thomas Baker, a young fop from England—a nobleman, actually—saw my bust of King Charles I and liked it so much he came to Rome and paid me double my usual fee to carve his portrait. When I was more than halfway through the job, the Holy Father leaned what I was doing and sent word for me to stop. Naturally, I agreed, but I had my assistant Andrea Bolgi finish the bust in total secrecy."

Bernini watched his wife carefully to see if she disapproved of his actions. *I might as well learn early in our marriage if I can be totally honest with her.*

"What a shame the Pope found out about the Baker bust," she said. "How do you think he found out?"

Bernini heaved a sigh of relief. "I heard that Cardinal Spada told the Holy Father. Apparently Virgilio heard about it from the architect Francesco Borromini—who seems to be making a career out of trying to hurt me. I never did learn why Urban objected to the commission. Oh well, let me continue reading Giulio's letter."

> 'The answer my friend is papal politics. Urban didn't want you to carve a bust of any other Englishman because, in his judgment, that would diminish the impact of his ordering you to carve the King's portrait. You see, the Holy Father is still hoping King Charles I will lead England back into the fold of the Catholic Church, and with his wife being Catholic, that is more than a remote possibility. On the other hand, Urban felt that your carving a bust of Richelieu would not anger the King of England, but, rather, would please the King of France immensely, and help cement the relations between France and the papal states (By the way, in this regard, Urban differs from Paul V, who was always courting favor with Spain). As you can see, balancing the equities between the French and Spanish super powers is uppermost in the Holy Father's mind. Must run, but before I do, accept my congratulations on your recent nuptials. I hear your bride is gorgeous. As Ever, Giulio (to you and you only).'

Bernini unwrapped the portrait and held it up for Caterina to see. The couple studied the painting carefully.

"Philippe de Campaigne is no Van Dyke, is he darling," Caterina said. "But then again, who is?"

GianLorenzo looked at his wife in disbelief. *Not too many people in Rome would recognize the French painter of this triptych. I have a feeling that everything new I learn about my Caterina is going to be good.*

Chapter LXXXI

B orromini's gaze swept the courtyard. He was standing with the Rector—a crusty middle-aged man who nevertheless had gray hair—in the center of the Sapienza, the University of Rome. "Beautiful, isn't it," the Rector said. "I think Giacomo della Porta was one of the most underrated architects in history."

Borromini nodded. "The pillars, pilasters and arches create a serene setting for your students and faculty—which is exactly what you need at a university to foster study and learning." Francesco looked around the courtyard, as if he were a bank robber casing the neighborhood. His mood darkened. "May I ask why I was appointed your architect over ten years ago and you are only now commissioning me to design and build the church?"

The Rector was jolted by Borromini's directness. He felt like one of his professors who had underestimated his most serious student. "I'll be happy to explain. Over the years, we have had many problems—and concerns— here at the University. We wanted them all resolved before embarking on this phase of construction. Frankly, some of these matters concerned you, Francesco."

Borromini winced. *They must have heard about the situation with the Oratorians.* "Since I am standing here, I gather you have resolved your concerns about me."

"Francesco, we all love what you did at San Carlino. The Trinitarian monks praised you to the heavens. They raved about every aspect of your work and we were ready to commission you to design Saint Ivo—as we plan to call our church. But then, some of my compatriots heard rumors about your subsequent work—specifically for the Oratorians. We talked with many in the Order. They said you were a difficult man to work with."

"Have you seen any of my work there? I'm proud of what I accomplished—in spite of those people." Borromini walked to the short end of the courtyard and examined the bricks.

The Rector sighed. *Here comes his notorious temper I fear. And yet, weren't some of our best students just as intemperate? Look at Galileo.* He rejoined Borromini.

"I formed several committees. We examined your work for the Oratorians very carefully and are not displeased with what you accomplished for them. We eventually talked with Cardinal Spada. He said that it was the Oratorians and not you who caused the arguments and delays. The Cardinal also said that you would have done much better with less interference from the Fathers."

Borromini continued to study the brick wall of the courtyard. He finally grunted, "Everyone knows that."

"Francesco, listen. We are not architects, we are educators, and education is a difficult enterprise at best. We know that we have an ideal setting for our university with this courtyard. Do you know how it was accomplished?"

Borromini scratched his head. *This is the stupidest situation I've ever been in.* "I don't know what you mean."

"It was accomplished by telling della Porta our needs, and then getting out of his way, so to speak. As I said, we are educators, not architects."

Borromini stopped pretending to study the brick wall and focused on the Rector. *Am I dreaming? Is this man saying what I think he is saying?*

"Tell me your needs for the church," Francesco said, not attempting to hide his excitement.

—

The Rector chuckled to himself. *Finally—we're getting someplace.*

"The overall plan for the university is in place. You are to use this semicircular end of the courtyard as the façade for the church. It must blend in with the remainder of the complex, and we expect you to make the most of the site. Keep in mind the basic purpose of the church is to serve the religious needs of our students and faculty, although—and this is important—the facility will also serve as a meeting place for the students to hear lectures."

Borromini felt like he had just won the lottery at Carnival. "That's . . . that is it?"

"Naturally, there will be details along the way, but, basically, that is it. Francesco, we are thrilled that you are our architect. I am glad . . . in our collective opinion, you are the future of architecture, just as we hope we are in the world of education. Everyone here at the Sapienza is excited to see what you can do for us. If the church you design is dramatic, or even revolutionary, so much the better. To a man, we want the church to symbolize our mission. After all, we may study the past, but as a university we must apply the knowledge of the past to look forward, to serve the future needs of mankind. Otherwise, what's the point of our existence?"

The Rector watched the smiling architect leave the courtyard. *That was close. I almost said I was glad that Bernini recommended him and that I wanted his church design to be as forward looking as Bernini's sculpture and architecture. Lucky for us, Virgilio warned me that any mention of the Cavaliere would set Francesco off and undermine our relationship. We want our Saint Ivo to be a church for the ages, and the happier Borromini is, the better our chance for greatness. I'm sure of it.*

Chapter LXXXII

Beyond Michelangelo

'Dear GianLorenzo:

I'm writing in the name of Louis XIII, King of France. Said King appointed me Prime Minister of France when my mentor, Cardinal Richelieu, recently died. His Majesty is aware of our close relationship and therefore felt a letter from me would be the best and most persuasive way to proceed. Here's the point—the King wants you to move to France to live and work. He told me to offer you a considerable stipend, but I responded that he had a better chance for success if he gave you whatever you asked, and he agreed. So there you have it—an invitation from the King and an open purse.

Must run, but before I close, please know that I was devastated when I learned of your dear mother's demise.

I have many fond memories of her and I think she liked me—although not so much when we caroused around Rome together. I cried, literally, when you told me that when you went through her belongings, the only thing you found were self-portraits you had painted. You knew she loved you, of course, but I doubt that you ever knew how much.

When she was hard on you—as you often complained—it was only to make you a better man. She did a pretty good job, wouldn't you say? I'm just glad she lived long enough to see you settle down with Caterina; I only wish your father could have met your remarkable wife.

Really must close. GianLorenzo, all of the courtiers tell me I am now the most important man in France. I immodestly mention this to help you understand the enormity of the King's most generous offer. As Ever, Giulio (to you only).'

Urban read the letter twice and then it slipped from his shaking hand. He sipped on his anisette and a few drops trickled down his chin. Bernini sat frozen in his chair. The ailing pontiff, weak and frail, retrieved the letter, fingered it, and then re-read it several more times.

Bernini watched in horror. *This great man is failing before my eyes—I'm not sure I can handle this.* "Holy Father," he said, "Caterina suggested that we leave this decision to you and I agree with her completely."

The Pope was moved—tears filled his eyes. "Are you certain? Cavaliere, this judgment carries with it significant ramifications for you and your lovely family."

"Your Holiness," GianLorenzo said, "you know that I have sought and treasured your advice all my life."

"I am tired, my son, so I will speak bluntly and then retire. Over the years I have observed that projects in France are begun in heat but end in nothing. So, to rely on the French is a dicey matter at best."

The pontiff picked up his goblet and drained the remaining liquor. Bernini reached for the bottle of anisette, but Urban waived him off.

'My limit is one these days. Now, please, I've never felt this tired."

Bernini held back his tears as he helped the Pope into his bedroom. He tucked the pontiff in and drew the blinds. As GianLorenzo began to close the door, Urban raised himself on his elbows.

"Cavaliere, allow me to complete my thought as succinctly as possible. In my opinion, you are made for Rome and Rome is made for you. Good night and goodbye."

―

Maffeo Barberini, Pope Urban VIII, died that night—July 29, 1644—one week before the 22nd year of his pontificate. When the people of Rome learned of his death, they cheered.

Chapter LXXXIII

The Bernini carriage rumbled through the streets of Rome. The Cavaliere and his wife sat quietly as they made their way home from the funeral Mass for Pope Urban VIII. Caterina broke the oppressive silence.

"Sweetheart, I understand the people cheered when they heard about the death of the Holy Father. Why would they do such a barbaric thing?"

GianLorenzo sat quietly for some time considering his wife's question. "My guess is the average person feels Urban gave too much of the Church's money to his family. That, and they resent the fact that the Church's treasury is basically empty. Although the disastrous Castro War was the primary cause, I receive some of the blame for that."

Caterina was taken aback. "That makes no sense to me."

"They have a point. Do you have any idea how many artistic commissions I received from Maffeo after he became Pope? Take a guess."

"I can't guess. We've only been married five years and I'm not sure what occurred prior to that time. In fact, most of it—those personal things—I definitely don't want to know."

"Come on—this is a serious matter we're discussing. The answer is over thirty—and depending on how you count, closer to forty. Add to that the numerous paying positions he appointed me to and you can see why my rivals are screaming that I depleted the papal treasury. Now do you understand why I'm so worried about who will be the next Pope?"

—

Caterina gave her husband a tender kiss and straightened his collar.

"Darling, I want you to stop being nervous and remember something. Your name is Bernini, not Barberini. Maffeo may have had the God-given title, but you have the God-given talent. And when Urban's successor is elected—and I don't care who it is—that state of affairs will not change. What I'm saying is, yes, there will be a new Pope, but you will still be the most talented artist in the world. And after the next Pope dies, there will be another Pope and you will still be the most talented artist in the world. And so on, and so on, and so on. Some of those Popes, by the way, will be strong, some will be weak, some will be clever and some will not. But you—you will always be the most talented artist in the world.

"So you see, sweetheart, God has clearly given my GianLorenzo the better of the deal."

Chapter LXXXIV

Beyond Michelangelo

Cardinal Virgilio Spada never felt better in his life. He had been instrumental in getting Cardinal Giambattista Pamphili elected Pope.

The conclave had been unusually lengthy and contentious, primarily because the French contingent was awaiting word on how to vote from their leader in Paris, Cardinal Jules Mazarin. *I knew that I had to get my man elected before Mazarin's instructions arrived.*

As a close advisor, Cardinal Spada was confident that his knowledge in all matters, particularly architectural, would finally be appreciated, and rewarded, by a Pope.

—

"Welcome Francesco," Cardinal Spada said. "Take a last look at my sparse surroundings here with the Oratorians. Tomorrow I move into the Quirinal Palace."

"That's why you sent for me," Borromini said. "To tell me that? I was working on my drawings for Saint Ivo and need to get back to them if you will excuse me."

Virgilio winced. *If there is a more difficult genius in Rome, I don't want to meet him. I have my hands full dealing with one Borromini—I could never handle two of them, no matter how talented.*

"Sit down Francesco," Spada said. "Have you heard of Cardinal Pamphili?" A sulking Borromini shook his head. "Most people haven't. He is pious, honest, straightforward, and loves the poor. He is Innocent X, the newly elected Pope who hates the Barberini. Do you have any idea what that means?" Borromini again shook his head. "There is good news and good/good news. The good news is, if I have any say in architectural matters—and I will—for the first time in your life, you will receive the majority of papal commissions."

"Maybe I will have a cappuccino," Borromini said. "Are you positive that's not the good/good news?"

"Definitely not. The good/good news is that besides hating the Barberini, the new pontiff also hates the Barberini coterie. Do you know who was the closest person to Urban outside of his family? Bernini. GianLorenzo Bernini, that's who."

Borromini jumped out of his chair and circled the room, deep in thought. "I can't focus."

"I'll spell it out for you," Cardinal Virgilio Spada said. "If I have anything to do with it, Bernini won't be receiving any more papal commissions. Equally important—maybe more important—I wouldn't be surprised if the Holy Father finds a way to harm your rival."

Chapter LXXXV

Nick J. Mileti

Dear GianLorenzo:

I tried my best to stop the election of Giambattista Pamphili, Innocent X, but I was too late. I opposed Cardinal Pamphili because I feared he would be much too oriented to the Spanish. But I had another reason to veto him. You and the Barberini. Yes, I believe this taciturn, nasty, mean—did I leave anything out?—seventy year old man will do everything in his power to hurt the Barberini and anyone who was on intimate terms with them. In other words, you.

I'm sure you know by now that the Pope's first act was to establish a Commission (which was stacked) to investigate the riches of the Barberini. You'll be happy to know that I'm going to petition Innocent to obtain pardons for them all. I swear to you, I will do everything in my power to bring justice to this situation.

I'm sure you also know that the Barberini clan is on its way to Paris to work with me, and you should be too. Sorry, GianLorenzo, but this is a vindictive old man. Not only that, his relatives and advisors worry me as much as he does—especially that sister-in-law. Hope all is well with you—considering. As Ever, Jules (strictly Jules from now on, even to you. Who's bitter?)

Chapter LXXXVI

Donna Olimpia Maidalchini walked like a man, talked like a man, was built like a man, and even looked a little like a man. Her looks and manners held no handicap for her however, because Donna Olimpia was the widow of the elder brother of Giambattista Pamphili, the newly elected Pope.

Luckily—most say brilliantly—whenever her brother-in-law needed assistance over the years, Donna Olimpia supported him financially, without ever seeking the return of any of the money. Giambattista was so appreciative and indebted to her, when he was elected Pope in 1644 he made Donna Olimpia the most powerful woman in the Papal States. Instead of following the usual procedure of appointing a Cardinal/Nephew as key advisor, what Innocent did was make his sister-in-law his key advisor and placed her in an office next to him—a highly unconventional move that had all of Rome buzzing.

Donna Olimpia was well known—even notorious—in the city long before her brother-in-law was elected Pope. Consequently, the question on everyone's lips was, "How will that domineering, scheming, ill-mannered Donna Olimpia use her newly acquired power?"

They found out almost immediately.

—

Donna Olimpia strode into the Pope's office the day after his election.

"What do you mean there will be no possesso? I don't care if the papal treasury is almost empty, we must have a papal procession and it must be spectacular. Think about it. No one will take you seriously if you slide into your exalted office and don't herald your pontificate in the proper fashion. Worse, you might be considered merely an extension of the Barberini term, and the last thing you want is to be associated with those criminals. Your job is to borrow the money. I'll make the arrangements. Don't worry about borrowing money—Popes do it all the time."

"What you say makes sense, Donna Olimpia."

—

The most lavish papal procession anyone could remember proceeded from the Vatican to the Capitoline Hill. Every official of the Church participated, resplendent in his most extravagant garment. A triumphant arch, built for the parade, greeted the marchers after they climbed Michelangelo's stairs and passed between the two lions—which, in a masterstroke of papal political creativity, gushed wine, instead of water. The peasants, who thought they'd died and gone to heaven, stayed up all night, drinking wine and toasting their new savior, Innocent X.

Meanwhile, Donna Olimpia watched her perfectly planned extravaganza with two-dozen handpicked ladies of the nobility. Each husband paid a small fortune, in cash, to Donna Olimpia for the privilege.

That night, specially made fireworks filled the Roman sky, complimenting the numerous parties that raged until dawn. The most sought-after gala, of course, was the ball Donna Olimpia hosted at the family's palace in Piazza Navona. At her insistence, the servants strictly enforced a sliding scale: A buffet in a relatively obscure room commanded the smallest donation, while the most ambitious persons—those who wanted to be seated in the same room as Donna Olimpia—paid the most. To maximize profits, the elite group that paid top dollar was given the opportunity to bid for the most coveted invitation of all; the chance to sit at the supper table with the new power in town. The auction was secret, and only Donna Olimpia handled the non-refundable cash bids, which grew daily, then hourly, then minute-to-minute.

The word quickly spread throughout Rome—and indeed all of Europe—that using subtlety in Innocent's papal court was like putting salt in your cappuccino.

Chapter LXXXVII

Cardinal Spada was relaxed waiting for Innocent to finish his business with an aide and meet with him.

"Virgilio," the pontiff finally said, turning his attention to his most trusted aide," no one must know that you are my Secret Almoner—you report to me and me only. You may announce to the world, however, that I have appointed you my Official Advisor on matters relating to the Arts."

"No advisor will work more diligently in your behalf, Your Holiness."

"As it should be. Now, I have an architectural matter to discuss with you—your greatest area of expertise I understand. What do you make of the various reports on the south bell tower at my beloved Saint Peter's? They all indicate that the cracks are normal settling and not dangerous to the basilica."

Finally. I was afraid he would close the matter without conferring with me. "I have studied the reports carefully, Holy Father. They are impressive, and yet they are only opinions."

"True," the Pope said. "What is your considered opinion?"

"In my opinion, the cracks are there, endangering the entire structure—and Bernini caused the cracks. To be safe, I think you should tear Bernini's bell tower down."

"Unfortunately, it's not that simple. The detailed reports are public knowledge, I've heard that the Cavaliere has an extremely strong case, and, worse of all, the people of Rome love the two sections built to date."

The Cardinal thought for a few minutes. "Here is my suggestion Your Holiness. I suggest that you convene a Special Committee. Hold a series of hearings—I assure you there are numerous architects and artisans, other than the ones who have written these reports, who will testify against Bernini. Deliberate for an appropriate amount of time and then rule the entire bell tower must be torn down—both sections."

—

Donna Olimpia dismissed her son Camillo from the supper table and addressed her brother-in-law.

"What are your plans for my son," she demanded.

The Pope exhaled carefully. "Donna Olimpia, I have appointed him a Cardinal and made him Commander-in-Chief of the papal army. Isn't that enough?"

"Are you aware, my dear brother-in-law, that you are the only Pope in recent memory who doesn't have a Cardinal/Nephew he can count on? There are many in your entourage, but whom can you count on besides me? Having more family at your side administering your affairs will be reassuring, don't you think."

"What you say makes sense, Donna Olimpia. Now, I have a matter to discuss. Are you aware of the bell tower Cavaliere Bernini built on Saint Peter's? On the south end of the facade."

"Didn't that Barberini Pope, Urban VIII, commission the bell towers? And wasn't Bernini his pet? And aren't there cracks in the façade where everyone can see them?"

Innocent nodded vaguely after each rhetorical question.

"That Barberini clan has fled to France to avoid your justice, but if you punish Bernini, don't you realize that you punish them?"

The Pope nodded, this time more enthusiastically.

"So what are you waiting for? Tear the bell tower down."

As Bernini walked through the Quirinal Palace on the way to Innocent's office, he saw all new faces. *They all recognize me, but I don't know one of them. After twenty-one years of Maffeo Barberini as Pope, I forgot that the staffs change every time a new Pope is elected.*

After a considerable wait in the anteroom, the Cavaliere made his way across Innocent's large office. He studied the elderly pontiff sitting at his desk. *He's thin, with small eyes, eyes that tell me he doesn't trust people. His beard is not attractive—it looks like a mouse nibbled on it. He looks his age, but is not as ugly as his detractors claim.*

Beyond Michelangelo

When GianLorenzo reached the Pope he bowed and kissed his ring. With a slight motion, Innocent indicated he should be seated.

"Congratulations on your election, Your Holiness. If there is anything I..."

"Cavaliere, I have granted you the privilege of this private meeting to tell you that I intend to give you the opportunity to refute those who maintain that the weight of your bell tower is ruining my beloved Saint Peter's."

"Holy Father, I am grateful beyond..."

"We will be holding a series of hearings soon—you will be notified. Good day, Cavaliere. Thank you for coming."

Chapter LXXXVIII

B orromini was surprised to see Cardinal Spada arrive at Saint Ivo where he was hard at work. *He looks serious, like something's wrong. I hope it's not going to be another lecture—I don't have the time or the interest.*

"What is it, Virgilio?"

"You worry me, Francesco," the Cardinal said. "The bell tower hearings are set to start this Friday, and I'm afraid you will lose control when it's your turn to testify. Please. I beg you. Stay calm—we want to keep everything under control."

"We," Borromini said. "Who is we?"

Cardinal Spada stopped cold. *All I need is for Francesco to find out that Donna Olimpia and I are planning this entire debacle. With his lack of control about anything relating to Bernini, it would remain secret for about five minutes.* "Don't worry about that. I stopped by to tell you one more thing. I'm going to testify in Bernini's behalf and I don't want you to lose your head when I do."

Borromini was flabbergasted. "What are you talking about? Why would you do that?"

Cardinal Spada sighed. "Isn't it obvious? So the Cavaliere will continue to trust me. I swear, Francesco, you are a gifted architect, but when it comes to political matters, you leave a great deal to be desired. Just trust me and maintain your composure."

"Anything else?"

"Yes. How is the restructuring of the Collegio di Propaganda Fide progressing? I need to be kept abreast of that job because the Holy Father was reluctant to intrude into the Order's affairs until I told him your appointment would oust Bernini as their architect."

"To answer your question, the designs for the long facades are underway and..."

"Bernini's little church inside—the Chapel of the Magi—where does that stand? That's what I want to know."

The sly look on Borromini's face told Virgilio what he wanted to know, before his architect said even one word.

"I told my patrons," Francesco said, "that Bernini's chapel could not be incorporated into my new scheme, and even if it could, it has serious structural deficiencies. I presented a thorough and exacting case, complete with architectural and engineering drawings and data. My conclusion, of course, was that Bernini's church has to be demolished. The sooner the better." Borromini smiled. "I hope you don't mind."

Chapter LXXXIX

Nick J. Mileti

The Hearing Officer gaveled the proceedings to order. "I am pleased to see all of Rome's architects, engineers, masons and other artisans present for this historic occasion. This is the first of five planned hearings to determine if the two sections of the bell tower atop the façade of the basilica of Saint Peter's, built on the south end over the last six years and designed by Cavaliere GianLorenzo Bernini, are endangering the entire church and should therefore be torn down."

The standing-room-only crowd murmured audibly. Suddenly, the room fell silent as Innocent X entered the hearing room. After the pontiff and his entourage were seated, Bernini was escorted into the room and was seated at a table directly in front of the Pope and the members of the Committee.

GianLorenzo started to sweat as Mazzarini's words bounced around his head. *This man is vindictive. I never expected this much ceremony, and what is the Pope doing here? I better not mention the Barberini or Urban.*

"I have come here this morning," the pontiff said, "to insure these hearings are fair to our distinguished brother with the formidable reputation, GianLorenzo Bernini. With that in mind Cavaliere, you will be given the first opportunity to tell this Committee, and me, your side to this sorry state of affairs. You may proceed."

Bernini stood and examined the crowd. *They're all smiling. Is that because they are on my side or because they are happy I'm about to be skewered? And there's that Borromini fellow in the back of the room. He's the only one frowning—what does that mean?*

"Your Holiness, distinguished members of the Committee, I am happy to have the opportunity to give you the facts. After receiving the commission . . . I designed what I consider an attractive set of bell towers to be erected on the massive foundations Carlo Maderno designed for that purpose. As is usual in an important commission, I constructed a scale model of the towers, and after a careful review, the Fabbrica enthusiastically approved my plans. Prior to commencing construction, however, a report was requested from two master builders regarding the condition of the soil. As I'm sure every man in this room knows, that is the custom where other foundations may exist, or there is a question about the stability of the land."

Bernini studied the crowded room as he sipped from a goblet of water. *Bringing all of these experts into the mix was a good idea. I just wish I could read the Pope—the man is inscrutable.*

"The two experts attested in writing to the complete soundness of the foundations and soil, so I was officially ordered to proceed. The first section was begun in 1638 and finished a year later. The second section was then begun; it was completed in 1641, two years later. As you can imagine, Holy Father, under the circumstances every safeguard was taken during construction. In spite of all of the careful planning and execution, when the second section of the south tower was erected, cracks began to appear, and it is no coincidence where they materialized. These cracks—they showed up in exactly those places where the vault of the portico built by Maderno was added to the front of the basilica. So you see, this is normal settling, and the situation goes back to the time of Paul V."

Innocent shot up in his ornately upholstered chair. "Are you saying the cracks are the Pope's fault?"

Bernini was taken aback. *I should have said that more smoothly. Oh well, deep in my heart I have a feeling it doesn't matter one whit.*

"Of course not, Your Holiness. What I meant was normal settling always appears when new sections are added to old ones. To continue, to be safe I then redesigned the third level—I made it smaller—and built a wooden model to scale. I then had it erected in situ so everyone could assess its impact."

The room rang with laughter.

I guess I should have left that part out. Bernini took a large sheaf of papers from the table and handed them to the pontiff's aide. "Please study these reports, Holy Father—and also have your advisors review them. These reports confirm that the bell tower is plumb on all four sides."

Innocent flipped through the pages and put them aside. "Anything else, Cavaliere?"

"As a matter of fact, there is, Bernini said. "I have a suggestion that will resolve this issue once and for all. I will personally pay experts to sink two shafts in appropriate places, so that you will see with your own eyes whether I have created any cause for the movement. To be more than fair, if you prefer, you and your advisors may pick the experts and the exact spots you want the shafts sunk. In any case, I will assume the entire cost of the plan. Is that not more than fair?"

The crowd held it's collective breath awaiting the Pope's reaction to Bernini's audacious proposal.

Innocent started to speak but stopped. *This Bernini is one clever fellow—I best be careful.* He looked at Cardinal Spada who nodded his head ever so slightly. The pontiff smiled inwardly.

"You may proceed with your plan, Cavaliere. These hearings are adjourned until the test results are available."

Chapter XC

"**G**ood luck, darling," Caterina said as she placed her husband's cloak around his shoulders and wrapped a long, woolen scarf around his neck. "You must feel good with the positive test results in your pocket."

Bernini gave his wife an extra-long hug. "I wasn't going to tell you, but you might as well be prepared. We're facing a disaster of monumental proportions—the hearings are rigged."

Caterina took a step back and studied her husband. *I've never seen that expression before—he looks like he's headed to the guillotine.* "GianLorenzo, please sit down and tell me what is going on."

The Cavaliere slumped into a chair. "It's rigged. I had a feeling something was amiss, but it was only a feeling. Now I have proof and there is not a thing I can do about it."

"Sweetheart, I've never seen you this depressed. If you don't care to discuss it, I will understand."

"It's okay. That man who just left—he's a friend of mine who owns an out-of-the-way tavern I used to frequent on a regular basis, so we're good friends."

Bernini stole a glance at Caterina to see if she put two and two together. *With all of this grief, all I need is a fight with my wife about an ex-mistress.* Not seeing any change in his wife's expression, the Cavaliere continued, relieved by his good luck.

"He said that he noticed two men whispering in the corner. When he heard my name mentioned he slid into an adjoining booth to listen. One man said to the other, 'When you testify that Bernini's plans were flawed, do so with the utmost sincerity. Show respect—my people want the hearings to appear totally above board. Don't bother about his procedures, or schedules or similar matters, just his plans. We have witnesses lined up to condemn every aspect of his bell tower'."

"That is atrocious. Did your friend recognize either of the men?"

"No, but listen to this. This is unbelievable. My friend heard the other man say, 'To testify against this malicious and wily man—meaning me—I will gladly pay you the money you request, even though you ask for a princely sum'."

"Hold it right there," Caterina said. "Are you sure you heard correctly? That sounds backward to me. Doesn't the man arranging for false testimony usually pay the bribe?"

Bernini laughed in spite of himself. "Now do you see why I'm so depressed?"

"Sorry darling, you get no sympathy from me. You should be proud that you are so successful and important people will pay real money to kick you off the top of the mountain. And when those pathetic, ordinarily-talented souls lie through their teeth, keep in mind that your name is GianLorenzo Bernini and you are the one with the God-Given talent—not them."

Bernini studied Caterina's face. *She's serious—not just trying to cheer me up. How can I be so lucky? First the world's best parents, then the world's best mentors and patrons, then the world's best career, and now the world's best wife. Father was right—I obviously have an aura of greatness about me.*

"Oh, and honey," she called as GianLorenzo climbed into his carriage. "your mother told me all about that particular tavern."

Chapter XCI

Beyond Michelangelo

The hearing proceeded as choreographed. Bernini presented his positive test results. Cardinal Spada testified that the cracks were normal settling and not dangerous to the edifice. A plethora of architects, engineers, masons, stonecutters, and contractors floated negative remarks in a sea of respect—praising the character of Bernini the man, as well as lauding his various other works.

Bernini suffered in silence.

Borromini enjoyed the parade of anti-Bernini witnesses immensely, so he didn't mind waiting. When he was called to testify, Virgilio knew immediately he had wasted his time admonishing his prodigy to maintain his composure.

—

"The man has no training as an architect," Borromini said, standing erect and speaking in a somber tone in an attempt to add verisimilitude to his testimony. "He exhibits no understanding of the ancients. He doesn't even have experience as a stonemason. What his bell tower does to Carlo Maderno's magnificent façade is criminal."

Cardinal Spada tried to close down his frenetic friend. "Excuse me, Mister Borromini, have you seen the Cavaliere's other works?"

"I think his sculpture is unbalanced and his plays aren't funny. He has no experience as an architect—I designed the baldacchino and Saint Bibiana is too small to count. That man caused the cracks and they are going to cause Saint Peter's to collapse. Look here. I've made these drawings to show exactly where each crack is, and the precise damage each one has caused."

Borromini's precise drawings were passed from hand to hand. Bernini refused to look at them.

Spada rolled his eyes. *He's upsetting the pace and structure and I don't know how to stop him.* "Thank you for your thoughts, Mister Borromini," he said. "Now, if there is nothing else . . ."

"Did I mention that Bernini is incompetent? He is. His towers have six times as much weight as Maderno's foundations were designed to hold. To prove it, I have produced another set of drawings I'd like to show you. As you can see, my design is for lighter towers that will enhance Maderno's façade, instead of threatening the existence of the church they sit on."

Cardinal Spada watched the Pope carefully during Borromini's tirade. *What am I worried about? Innocent is obviously enthralled with Francesco. I don't know whether it's for Borromini or against Bernini, but what's the difference?*

Bernini again refused to examine Borromini's drawings. *The bastard—he's obviously using this hearing as a platform to showcase his talents and demonstrate to Innocent that he should replace me as the Architect of Saint Peter's. It's not a bad trick I must admit. This madman is smarter than I thought.*

—

When Innocent issued his pre-ordained ruling to tear down Bernini's bell tower, the citizens of Rome staged a lengthy sit-down on the grass in front of Saint Peter's in protest. Naturally, this tactic, and all of the other expressions of support to save Bernini's sublime bell tower, had as much impact on the Pope as a fly has on an obelisk.

Chapter XCII

Cardinal Spada made the short trip from Saint Peter's to the Quirinal Palace in record time. He rushed to Donna Olimpia's office and requested an immediate meeting.

"What's so important that it can't wait until tomorrow for our weekly session," Donna Olimpia asked. Her tone was as cold as the December morning air.

Virgilio put on his most serious face, although he was happy to have an advantage over this obnoxious woman—no matter how slight. "Bernini has struck back," he announced with a hint of arrogance he meant to hide.

Donna Olimpia studied the man standing before her. *This man is such a bother. I wish my brother-in-law wouldn't rely on him as much as he does—he's not family and I don't trust him.*

"Struck back? I don't see how he can hurt us—we're in control."

Always the politician, the Cardinal immediately backed down. "Perhaps my words were too strong. As soon as the Holy Father ruled that his bell tower had to be dismantled, the Cavaliere began working furiously—sculpting a statute he calls 'Truth Unveiled'."

"Virgilio, I'm very busy today. I have a private dinner with the Spanish Ambassador and there is a large sum of money at stake."

"Please allow me to finish. I'm certain the piece is an indirect attack on His Holiness and the rest of us. It will take years to finish, however, and by then the unpleasant business of the bell towers will be forgotten. No, I'm talking about the tomb of your nemesis, Urban VIII, Maffeo Barberini."

Donna Olimpia stopped signing papers and looked up.

"Go on," she said.

Cardinal Spada relished the small victory. "Twenty years have elapsed since Bernini received the commission from Urban, and he has been working on the tomb sporadically at best. But, immediately following the bell tower debacle, this shrewd genius rushed to complete the group. In fact, the Cavaliere pulled the cover off the work less than an hour ago. As soon as I heard, I hurried to see it, and believe it or not, a crowd had already gathered in front of the monument."

Donna Olimpia immediately grasped the enormity of the problem. "What you are saying, I gather, is that Bernini has stolen the spotlight from our papacy and placed it back on Maffeo Barberini. Is that what you are saying?"

"Worse. Much worse. The tomb is a true masterpiece—so spectacular, it not only glorifies the subject, it glorifies the artist as well. The monument is that good."

Donna Olimpia's devious mind was churning. *We need an antidote. It must be dramatic and we need it fast. But I need time to think.* "Meet my brother-in-law and me at Saint Peter's tonight after closing time—make it nine o'clock. I want him to see the tomb, but I don't want people to see this Pope studying the previous Pope's memorial. Good day Virgilio."

—

The Pope, his sister-in-law, and his Artistic Advisor gazed in awe at the tomb of Urban VIII. A bronze statute of the Barberini Pope stared back at them, giving benediction from a stark white marble plinth. Below the pontiff they observed a highly decorated bronze sarcophagus, flanked by gleaming white marble statutes of the pontiff's two virtues—Justice and Divine Love.

Not surprisingly, the tomb sparked a different emotion and reaction in each of the spectators.

Cardinal Spada: *Bernini's use of contrasting textures and colors gives the group a life-like movement. Surely, this style of tomb will be copied for generations. I must stay on the side of this genius, no matter what that Borromini says.*

Donna Olimpia: *Fighting this kind of talent will take every bit of ingenuity we possess.*

Pope Innocent X: *Wishful thinking, on my part. This is not the disgraced Pope I'd hoped to see, this is a deified Pope. Perhaps I cannot avoid working with the Cavaliere after all.*

—

Donna Olimpia broke the awkward silence. "We need a major announcement to deflect attention from this tomb and to force people to focus on our pontificate. Not surprisingly, I have come up with the answer."

Cardinal Spada turned his head and rolled his eyes. *Not surprisingly, I'm sure you have.*

"Tell us what you are thinking," the Pope said, eager for an idea—any idea.

"What is coming in 1650, three years from now? The Holy Year, of course. And where do the pilgrims who come from all over the world go? To the great basilicas, of course. And what is the greatest basilica after Saint Peter's? San Giovanni in Laterano, of course. Why? Because it is the Cathedral of Rome and the Pope's Church." *Let me test this so-called Artistic Advisor.* "What do you think, Virgilio?"

Cardinal Spada smiled broadly and bowed slightly at the waist. *Two can play this game.* "Brilliant, Donna Olimpia. Positively brilliant. Since the Cathedral is practically falling down, our far-sighted leader, Pope Innocent X, has commissioned the restoration of the once-great basilica."

"For the glory of God," Donna Olimpia said.

"And for the benefit of the millions of pilgrims who will be coming to Rome," the Cardinal added.

—

Donna Olimpia took the Pope's elbow. "I will announce this news immediately and give it reinforcement throughout the coming years. I assure you, my dear brother-in-law, your brilliant decision will reverberate throughout the city and surpass everything else happening in Rome. Including this tomb."

"Then it's settled," Innocent said, flashing a rare grin. "Virgilio, you supervise the restoration. I have only two conditions. Finish before Christmas Eve, in the year of Our Lord 1649, and retain the ancient form of the basilica."

Cardinal Spada also grinned. *At last, a major project worthy of my talents.* "The restoration," he said, "will present a delicate structural challenge. I recommend that we commission Francesco Borromini for the job—he is the most technically competent architect working in Rome today. What do you think, Holy Father?"

The pontiff glanced at his sister-in-law, who nodded without a bit of subtleness.

"Excellent suggestion," the Pope said. "That Borromini fellow was the only person who made sense at those bell tower hearings."

Chapter XCIII

Beyond Michelangelo

The aged pontiff intermittently dozed on and off. His Artistic Advisor had placed a thick set of architectural drawings before him and Innocent X absolutely, positively could not make sense out of any of the pages. *How I hate these weekly artistic-type meetings. Theology? Yes. The Church? Yes. My family? Yes. The arts? Not interested. Those artists are dirty and scrubby and not reverential enough. At least Virgilio keeps those men away from me.*

Cardinal Spada, familiar with the routine, sat quietly by. The pontiff awoke suddenly and looked around, confused.

"You are looking at Borromini's plans, Your Holiness," Spada said. "They are for a completely new basilica."

The Pope rubbed his eyes. "Oh? Where is it to be located?"

The Cardinal sighed. "I guess I'm not making myself clear. Instead of submitting plans for the restoration of Saint John Lateran, Borromini has submitted drawings for a completely new church."

"For the last time, Virgilio, I ask you where he proposes locating the new church."

"Holy Father, Borromini is proposing that you tear down the crumbling church of San Giovanni in Laterano and build this new one in its place."

"Tear down the Lateran basilica? Is he mad?"

Cardinal Spada hesitated. *I'd better be careful; I'm on shaky ground.* "I asked him the same thing, Your Holiness, and his answer was that Pope Julius II allowed Bramante to tear down the original Saint Peter's and built a new church from scratch."

Innocent X was now wide-awake. "You tell your friend that his name is Borromini, not Bramante. Tell him times have changed. Tell him anything you want. His commission is to restore and renovate the Lateran. Under no circumstance will I allow the Cathedral to be torn down or altered drastically. That church was ordered by Constantine the Great and has been an important basilica for over one thousand years. It truly is the House of God, and I will not permit some architect—whatever his name may be—to defile it."

With one mighty swing of his arm, the Pope swept the plans off of his desk. Cardinal Spada scrambled to retrieve them.

"Virgilio, why did you bring me these plans," Innocent asked, softening as he saw the humiliated Cardinal scrambling to retrieve the scattered sheets. "You should have known better."

Cardinal Spada gulped hard. *If he finds out I supported Borromini's idea, my days are numbered.* "I apologize, I was merely trying to keep the architect happy."

"In the future," Innocent said, "I suggest you concentrate on keeping your Pope happy."

—

Cardinal Spada paced back and forth in his office, hands clasped behind his back. He felt like a schoolmaster about to deliver a lecture to an unruly freshman. Borromini arrived carrying a set of drawings and was waved into a hard-backed chair. The Cardinal got right to the point.

"Francesco, I checked my journal. Do you have any idea how many times you badgered me about knocking down the Lateran since my ill-fated meeting with the Pope?"

"Six?"

"Try forty-five," Spada said. *How can I get mad at this man? He's like a big teddy bear.* "Francesco, this must stop. You are sitting on the most prestigious commission of Innocent's pontificate. I know you are the best man for the job but you are trying the Pope's patience as well as mine. Make up your mind. Right now. I've committed us to a very tight schedule so every day counts. If you will work within the existing structure of the church, fine. If not . . ."

"I only want what is best for the Church, and that basilica is in terrible shape."

"Which is why you were commissioned to renovate it. Francesco, I need your answer and I need it now. Renovate or lose the commission."

"Will you give me permission to see Innocent to try to convince him?"

Cardinal Spada fought to maintain his composure. *Why do I always have to resort to verbal blackmail with him?* "Let me put it another way Francesco.

If Urban were still Pope, who do you think would have received the commission to renovate the Lateran, the second most important church in Christendom?"

Borromini slumped in his chair. "Do I have to say his name?"

"That's right. Cavaliere GianLorenzo Bernini. Let me tell you something else, Francesco. I have heard any number of men say that by receiving this prestigious papal commission—your first of this magnitude—you have surpassed your rival and avenged the wrongs he has piled upon you over the years. Are you prepared to abandon that victory?"

Borromini pointed to his set of drawings. "Take another look, my plans for a new basilica are stupendous, and . . ."

"One last thing, Francesco, and I mean last. Think about what might happen if you walk away from this job. Anything is possible. For example, Bernini might get the commission."

Borromini grabbed his set of drawings for the new basilica.

Cardinal Spada assumed the short-tempered artistic genius was going to storm out of his office. *Oh well, it was either him or me.* The Cardinal was wrong.

Borromini studied the first page carefully and folded it neatly in half. He then folded the page in half again. He repeated the procedure, page by page, until the pile overflowed Spada's desk.

Borromini scooped up the plans and cradled them in his arms, as one would hold a young child.

"Where is the nearest fireplace?"

CHAPTER XCIV

Beyond Michelangelo

Dear Jules:

Thank you for your most recent invitation to join you in France—you've obviously heard about the bell tower fiasco. I discussed the matter with Caterina and we decided I should stay put, even though things are at a low point for me. I am the object of ridicule since that fiasco. No one says anything to my face, but I can feel it. Caterina says not to worry—Rome sometimes sees dimly, but never loses its sight. Not bad, eh? I've used the line many times since. Actually, my darling wife has been my salvation. She says my talent will prevail over petty rivals, vindictive Popes or whomever.

Thanks to Caterina, I've thrown myself into my work instead of my bed—as you remember I used to. She insists that work is much better for me than lying in bed feeling sorry for myself. She's right, of course. Interestingly, it's strange not being bombarded with papal commissions. That snake who vilified me, and my work, at the bell tower hearings, Francesco Borromini, seems to be getting most of them. I wish I knew why he hates me. I really do. Oh well, as Caterina says, I can't worry about petty rivals.

Truthfully (and I'm not rationalizing here) the situation is a liberating one. It has given me a chance to do some independent work and clean up some loose ends. In that connection, after almost exactly twenty years, I have finally finished Maffeo's tomb—can you believe it? It's the talk of the town. Also, I have started a large group which features an over life-size Truth looking up at Father Time. I plan to bequeath the group to my first born heirs in perpetuity—I want my descendents to be reminded to always work with Truth, since in the end, she is always discovered by Time. (Am I over-reacting to the injustice of the bell tower demolition?)

Also, after working on it for some seven years, I'm just finishing a chapel for the Raimondi family in San Pietro in Montorio on the Janiculum Hill. It's a smallish chapel in the out-of-the-way church so I was able to try something I've been thinking about since I first saw Caravaggio's paintings when I was a little boy and became fascinated by what can be accomplished with hidden light.

Also, I have finished a memorial to Maria Raggi, which is hanging in Santa Maria Sopra Minerva. I used different materials (gilt bronze and marble) and colors (black and yellow) to achieve visual drama without sacrificing the religious impact. Everyone seems to like it.

Today I met with Cardinal Federigo Cornaro. You may know him—he is from a storied family in Venice. In any case, he heard I was available and wants me to build a family chapel in Santa Maria della Vittoria. I'm excited beyond words because the chapel is to be dedicated to Saint Teresa of Avila. (You will recall we went to the never-ending celebrations when she, along with Ignatius, Francis Xavier and Philip Neri were canonized. Twenty-five years ago—where has the time gone?). Anyhow, I know Saint Teresa's writings intimately. In fact, now that I'm married and religion is a major factor in my life (did you know that?) I've read her complete works, as well as those of Saint Thomas Aquinas and others. What excites me is Saint Teresa wrote dramatically—some say sensuously—which basically gives me a blueprint for the work. I plan to capture the moment of ecstasy when the seventy year-old meets God and is transformed into a beautiful young woman. In other words, in the Cornaro Chapel, I hope to present Saint Teresa's experience to the faithful.

That's enough for now—this is undoubtedly the longest letter I have ever written (it's hard to sit still). I write you all of this detail at my wife's request. She's worried that since Maffeo died, I don't have anyone one to confide in. Besides, I don't want to keep you. Running a country and baby-sitting an infant—even if he is a King—must be time consuming, and then some. I wish you would come home to visit, but I understand. Sort of.

Love, GianLorenzo

Chapter XCV

G iuseppe the bookseller was feeling blue. *My sales are down at least 20% without my best customer's business. Where is that Borromini—has he left town?* Suddenly, just as Giuseppe was blowing out the candles to close for the night, Francesco arrived.

"Come in, come in," the bookseller cried as he quickly re-lit the candles. *Supper is on the table but I don't care. This man has bought hundreds of books from me—still, that wife of mine will complain that I'm late for supper.* "You look awful—like you can use a piping-hot espresso." *There I go again, always saying the wrong thing.*

To Giuseppe's delight, Borromini didn't appear to hear his gaff. "And a cornetto," Borromini said. "Any more in the back room? I don't care if they're stale, I'm famished."

"Look around while I see what I have left over. Since I've seen you, a number of new volumes have come in. Where have you been by the way? That Lateran commission keeping you busy? It certainly is a feather in your cap."

Borromini gulped the coffee and stuffed the roll down his throat. "If you have more, I'll take them." Again, the architect ate like he was going to the guillotine. "Renovation is infinitely more difficult than starting from scratch," he said, "which I wanted to do but they wouldn't let me."

"Who are they?"

"That Pope Innocent X, and, for all I know, probably that Cardinal Spada."

"I thought they were your patrons."

"Imagine if they were my enemies. Listen to what my beloved patrons have caused me to do at the church all day. I pace and measure distances. I crawl up and down ladders. I poke in every opening in the great basilica. To see in the dark crevices I take a candle and force my body into them . . ."

"Isn't that dangerous?"

"Of course it is, so what? I've got to. I slide my body everywhere, and believe me, some of those places are precarious and dangerous. It's one dirty, filthy job. I'm covered with dust and dirt and chalk all day. I look and I sketch—I sketch and I look. I have one week to go until I have to submit my plans to my beloved patrons."

"If you are at the basilica all day, when do you make your drawings?"

"At home at night, after they close the church. Usually I draw straight through the night and then go right back. I told Virgilio I'd have the complete set of plans for the renovation ready by next Friday and I will, even if it kills me. Giving me that line about that Bernini possibly getting this job—well, if he thought that would motivate me, he was right."

—

Cardinal Spada fingered the thick set of drawings spread across his desk.

"Borromini, my friend, you truly make me proud that I recommended you to the Holy Father." He leafed through the sheets, one by one. "You have done it. On first impression, it appears that you have analyzed the needs perfectly. With these plans in hand, I believe we can meet the Pope's deadlines."

"Of course we can. Isn't that why I was hired? Aren't you going to study the drawings more carefully—I'm proud of them."

Virgilio sighed. "Tonight. I'll study them thoroughly tonight. For now, I suggest you go home and rest—you look exhausted. *I might as well get it over with. Maybe he won't have the energy to argue.* "I really do love your concepts, Francesco. I believe your ideas will raise the beauty—and efficiency—of the church to an unprecedented level. There is one thing, however."

The weary Borromini stopped in his tracks and slowly turned until he was face to face with his patron. *What now? Can't he see how tired I am?* "What one thing?"

"The present magnificent wooden ceiling. I don't think Innocent is going to permit you to tear it down and built the vault you planned in these drawings. Don't worry, I will discuss the entire matter with His Holiness."

Borromini tried to speak but no words came out. He turned to leave but stumbled and fell.

Cardinal Spada hurried to his friend. *Good grief, he's fainted. Maybe I should have waited.*

—

Cardinal Spada's aide admired Borromini's talent but was seldom happy to see him—his boss was always grumpy after meeting with the temperamental architect. "What are you doing here Francesco? Your meeting with the Cardinal isn't for three hours."

"I'll wait."

"Wouldn't you rather come back? His Eminence is with the Holy Father." *This has all of the markings of a major disaster.*

"I'll wait."

—

Cardinal Spada burst into the waiting room. "Great news, Francesco. Come into my office. The Pope loves your ideas and we are to start the renovation process according to your plans immediately"

"What about the vault of the nave?"

"My instructions are to commence with the stucco and marble but not to touch the ceiling at this time."

Borromini got up to leave. "That is unacceptable."

Virgilio immediately began his well-rehearsed speech. "Think for a minute, Francesco. Your brilliant mind has produced a sophisticated plan for the second most important church in the world. Those plans have been approved. We have permission to begin work—not next year or some other time, but tomorrow. This is a notable commission that will bring you, and the Church, great honor."

Borromini sat back down and turned the Cardinal's argument over in his mind. He finally spoke. "That is all well and good, but first I was prevented from erecting a new basilica, and now I'm not being allowed to renovate it properly."

At least this is going the way I thought it would. "But, Francesco, you are going to renovate it properly. If I understand your plans, we'll start with the outer aisles—which will take some time to rebuild—and proceed from there. Eventually, we'll get to the columns of the nave. Obviously, before we can do anything with the ceiling, the columns will have to be integrated into the new structure. Don't you see? By that time, anything is possible. Now, please, go home and get some sleep. Tomorrow, we begin."

"We better be able to build that vault I designed, that's all I know."

—

"Before you go," Cardinal Spada said, "I have more good news for you. Innocent liked your plans for the Lateran so much, he authorized me to commission you to enlarge the conduit for the Acqua Vergine. He wants you to extend it to the Piazza Navona."

"Is this a device to placate me? If it is, it won't work."

"Francesco, this is an important papal commission. After the water is available, the Pope is going to ask Rome's leading architects to prepare designs for a fountain in the center of the square, using the obelisk that is lying broken in the Circus Maximus."

"Interesting. Will I be asked? Will that Bernini be asked? If he is, I'm not interested."

"I will see that you are at the top of the list. Remember, you will be bringing the water to the piazza—that will certainly give you an advantage over the other submissions. As for Bernini, I assure you the Holy Father will not ask the Cavaliere to submit a design. His anti-Barberini bias is much, much too strong."

Chapter XCVI

Beyond Michelangelo

P rince Nicolo Ludovisi—the thin and gaunt noble with large doe-like eyes nestled under a tiny forehead and slicked-back black hair—had to wait approximately one minute until Bernini showed up. "Cavaliere, you aren't usually this late," the Prince laughed, hugging and air-kissing his favorite friend.

"Nicolo," GianLorenzo asked, "why are we meeting in Giordano's palace here in the country when Paolo and his wife aren't even here. Of course, I know your proclivity for intrigue so that's it, isn't it? You must have a diabolical-type plan, otherwise, why meet like this—at a mutual friend's castle miles from Rome."

Prince Ludovisi laughed again. *If I had to wager—and I love to gamble—I would bet the Cavaliere has a pretty good idea of what I'm up to. I don't know anyone smarter than he is.* "When you hear me out, GianLorenzo, you'll see how right you are. Now, I know how you hate to waste time so I'll get right to the point. I want you to submit a design for the fountain Innocent wants to have built in Piazza Navona."

It was Bernini's turn to burst out laughing. "No disrespect Nicolo. You know the love I have for you, but what's the point? I've heard that every architect in Rome of any stature—and even some pathetic amateurs—has been asked to submit a design. Except me. That's fine. As far as I'm concerned, the Pope can . . ."

"Hold on, GianLorenzo. Hold it right there. Don't get temperamental on me; it's not your style. You are the best architect in Rome. You know that, I know that, and the Pope and his sister-in-law know that. The problem is, stubbornness is about to commit armed robbery on Rome and history."

"Nicolo, you are a true friend with a poet's mind. Tell me what you are thinking—specifically, why are we here?"

"Simple. I want you to design a fountain for Piazza Navona, and then build a model of your design. Then, I will make certain the Holy Father sees it. All in utmost secrecy, of course."

"Nicolo, you are a marvel. That is a simple, bold and brilliant plan—so good it's worthy of that other Nicolo, Niccolo Machiavelli. I have only one question, which, knowing you, you have undoubtedly thought through. How would you know when to make your move?"

"Easy. The Holy Father is planning to have dinner with his family in the Pamphili Palace on the Feast of the Annunciation. I'll secretly place the model in a room of the palace he is certain to pass through."

Bernini's mind was churning. *This is exactly what I thought the Prince was up to. Being married to the Pope's niece means he will be at the dinner. The feast of the Annunciation is next week. After the fun I had with Scipione's second bust, a week feels like a lifetime.*

"Nicolo, I've thought there should be a fountain in the center of Piazza Navona since the first time my father showed me the magnificent square when I was a mere child. In my mind, I know exactly what the fountain should look like—sketching it and making the model are details."

"Then you'll do it? In time?"

"Nicolo, my friend, you can pick up the model in five days. For now, I'm off. Please convey my regrets to Paolo and his wife when you see them. By the way, before you leave, be sure to see the busts I carved of the two of them—especially Paolo's. It's like a Carracci caricature, only in marble. He is a real sport, that man."

—

The dinner in the Pamphili Palace was as sumptuous as the Pietro da Cortona frescoes lining the walls. When the costumed waiters began to clear the fourth course of skewered chicken and rabbit, Prince Ludovisi walked slowly out of the room. He then ran to the back entrance to the palazzo and waived for his co-conspirator—a workman incongruously dressed as a nobleman—to enter.

"Take the package and follow me. Hurry, but be quiet," the Prince ordered. He led the man through the palace. "Put it there, on that table in the middle of the room. Good. Thank you. Here, take this money—half for the task and half for dressing in that ridiculous disguise. Can you find your way out?"

The worker nodded, signaled thanks and left.

The Prince removed the silk covering—the beauty of the model stunned him. *That Bernini—he isn't human.* He slipped back into the dinner. "Did everything go according to plan?" his wife asked. The Prince nodded. No one else at the animated table even noticed that he had left the room.

Beyond Michelangelo

Donna Olimpia was getting more and more impatient. *That brother-in-law of mine knows we have business to discuss, where the hell is he?* The most important—and obnoxious—woman in the country called out to her young servant. "Anna, the Pope was to meet me in my office after dinner before going back to the Quirinal Palace. See if you can locate him."

The nervous girl returned and curtsied. "The Holy Father is in the room next to where you had dinner."

Donna Olimpia frowned. *He's going to be the death of me yet.* "What in the world is he doing there? Could you tell?"

"I don't know. There are lots of men around the Holy Father and he's saying things to them. He's walking around the room and the men, they are following him."

"Could you hear what he is saying?"

"No mam."

"Go back and see what he's doing. I have work to do here."

Anna returned, out of breath. She stood at attention, waiting to be acknowledged. Donna Olimpia looked up from her work. "Well?"

The young servant curtsied once more. "From the best I seen, the Holy Father is looking at something."

"Looking at something? Could you tell what that something is?"

"No mam."

"Then why do you say he is looking at something?"

"Because of what I heard him saying."

"Well? Come on, child, I have work to do. What did you hear him say?"

"I heard the Holy Father say, 'I've been looking for a half-hour and it doesn't matter at what angle, I have yet to find a flaw'."

What could he be talking about? "Is that all he said?"

"No mam. I heard him say many nice things, like, 'I can't believe it's so beautiful,' and, 'It's amazing,' and, 'It's perfect.' Is there anything else, mam, I have to pee."

"Oh, go away." *With all of this work on my desk, I have to go look for him.*

—

Donna Olimpia stood at the door—when the entourage saw her they scattered, as usual. Innocent waved his sister-in-law into the room.

"Can you believe this?" he said, pointing to Bernini's model.

Donna Olimpia didn't bother hiding her displeasure—she never did with her brother-in-law. "You've kept me waiting while you looked at a . . . model?"

In a shocking reversal of form, Innocent X ignored Donna Olimpia's remark. "This is a trick of Prince Ludovisi," he said, and then added pointedly, "but it will be necessary to make use of Bernini despite those who do not wish it."

Donna Olimpia appeared thoughtful for one of the few times in her life. *What has gotten into the old fool?* She spoke carefully, picking out every word like a jeweler examining a batch of recently submitted precious stones. "But Bernini was the closest confident of the decadent Barberini clan," she said. "You can't grant him the commission. Have you forgotten, the fountain will be outside, in our very own front yard?"

The elderly pontiff, energized by Bernini's work, ignored his sister-in-law. He continued speaking, with a far-away look in his eyes. "Those who do not wish to have Bernini's works executed had better not get a look at them."

In spite of herself, the disgusted Donna Olimpia took a long, hard look at the model and then stormed back to her office. *This damn Bernini is undercutting me and I don't like it.*

A malicious grin forced its way onto Innocent's usually dour face. *That felt good—maybe I should do it more often.*

Chapter XCVII

Bernini walked through the Quirinal Palace, acknowledging the greetings of staff members who recognized him, but he didn't know. *This feels a little strange. When I think about it, I haven't been here in four years. That's the longest since I was ten.*

When he reached the Pope's office, Innocent waved GianLorenzo into a chair. To the Cavaliere's amazement, the pontiff then walked around his desk and sat next to him.

"Naturally," Innocent said, "as soon as I saw your model of the fountain for the Piazza Navona, I sent for you. What do you call it?"

"I call it Fountain of the Four Rivers, Your Holiness, but heaven only knows what the people of Rome will call it."

The Pope laughed, but wasn't sure why. "I am an admirer of all of your fountains, especially the Triton. I love the way the water spills from the open shell. You seem to have a special knack with water."

Bernini sat quietly, with a big smile pasted on his face. *Unbelievable. He loves the Triton Fountain at the Barberini's.*

Innocent continued, oozing sincerity. "Cavaliere, I will be frank with you. The reality is, even though I admire all of your work, there has been almost no activity in the arts in my pontificate. San Giovanni in Laterano was nothing more than a slight renovation—certainly not important enough for you to be interested in. And the work in my family's palace was insignificant. That is why I awarded both of those minor commissions to Francesco Borromini. In other words, it's not that your towering talent was being overlooked; it's just that the papal treasury has been low. You will be happy to know that due to my frugality, we are now on firmer ground and I am able to offer you a commission to carve a papal bust. In addition to the Four Rivers Fountain, of course."

Bernini kept up the smile. *If he lays it on any thicker, I'll need hip boots to wade out of here.* "Three or four days of observing you as you go about your business should be sufficient."

Innocent rose and shook Bernini's hand. "Just tell my secretary what you need. One more small thing before you leave, Cavaliere. Have you stayed in touch with the three Barberini in Paris?"

Bernini's on-going smile disguised his surprise. *Is this a trap? This has been the most unusual meeting of my life—perhaps the entire matter has been a trick after all.* "No, Your Holiness, although I do correspond regularly with my friend Cardinal Mazarin."

"Excellent. The next time you write Cardinal Mazarin, ask him if he thinks the Barberini would be interest in returning to Rome with no fear of retribution." The pontiff stroked his chin and gazed into space. "Now that you and I understand each other, there seems little reason to perpetuate the hostility against the Barberini, regardless of what others might think." *Besides, I can think of many ways they can assist my papacy.*

"I will see to it, Your Holiness."

"Good-by, Cavaliere. When you speak to my secretary, make an appointment for supper in my chambers. I look forward to breaking bread and talking with you privately."

An elated GianLorenzo walked briskly through the palace. *As usual, Father and Caterina were both right. Don't ever bad-mouth, and talent will out.*

—

Giuseppe the bookseller went to Borromini's modest home—he'd heard his best customer was in bed. *Maybe he'll buy these two books I've brought along.* Francesco's servant-lady answered the knocking. "Come in, Giuseppe. Cardinal Spada is with him."

The servant escorted Giuseppe to Borromini's bedside. Giuseppe recoiled at what he saw—the sleeping, normally robust and strapping architect looked pale as a ghost. Giuseppe went to Borromini's side and took his hand. Francesco didn't stir.

"The doctor assures me there is nothing physically wrong with Francesco," Cardinal Spada said. "He says his fit must have been caused by something mental."

Giuseppe frowned. *I heard Innocent awarded Bernini the commission for the fountain in Piazza Navona, which Borromini was positive he was going to get. Knowing Francesco, he's more upset that Bernini got the commission than he is that he didn't.* "I have no idea what could have triggered his attack," Giuseppe said. "Do you?"

"I've been concerned about Francesco for some time," Cardinal Spada said. "He was very upset when Innocent wouldn't allow him to tear down the old ceiling in the Lateran and build a new one to his own design. Then, when I told him the Pope awarded the fountain project to Bernini—which I wish I hadn't done—that's when he snapped."

Giuseppe frowned. *Here's my chance to pick up some juicy information—this Cardinal is well connected.* "Why do you think His Holiness commissioned Bernini? All of my customers—actually, all of Rome—were dumbfounded."

Cardinal Spada eyed Giuseppe. *Here's my chance to spread some serious gossip—this bookseller is notorious.* He pretended to give the question deep thought. "The only thing I can figure," Virgilio said, "is that Bernini bribed someone close to the Holy Father—perhaps his sister-in-law. The one they call La Dominanta. Naturally, I would appreciate it if you kept that information to yourself."

Chapter XCVIII

The Englishman took the only vacant seat in Bernini's theatre. *This chap next to me is dressed in an odd fashion—he must be from the continent. Portugal or Spain I'd guess. I think he's an artist but, no, he has an aristocratic look about him. Hold on. I recognize that straight hair, high forehead, upturned mustache and stern countenance.*

"Aren't you Diego Valazquez, the Spanish painter? In my travels I've seen many of your paintings, and they are superb."

Like all celebrities over the ages, Velazquez hated being bothered by adoring fans. "Have we met, sir?"

"Please excuse by bloody-poor manners. My name is John Evelyn, and I'm from England. It's a pleasure to meet a famous artist such as yourself."

Valazquez studied the ebullient Englishman with interest. *I don't meet many Englishmen, although his pursed lips on his clean-shaven face, and his curly light brown hair give him away.* "English you say. That is amazing. I'm Spanish, you are English and we meet in Italy. The world is getting smaller every day."

"Indeed," Evelyn said. "And I can tell you one of the reasons. Every artist in Europe wants to come to Rome these days. It's that Bernini chap—they all want to work for him, be inspired by him, or just meet him. I interviewed Nicolas Poussin and Claude Lorrain. For my diary. They told me they were working in Rome instead of France because of Bernini. And Nicholas Stone the Younger. The carver was sent here to study under Bernini and to purchase casts and drawings for his father's workshop back home in England. And you, sir. Why are you in this heavenly city?"

"I'm traveling extensively on behalf of my King—buying paintings, mostly by Italian artists. I met the Cavaliere on my last trip here and we became friends. In fact, I'm staying in this magnificent palazzo as his guest, and the lovely Caterina of course. Needless to say, I value our relationship."

"Excuse me while I make a note of that in my diary. I envy you, knowing this remarkable man so intimately. He is much too busy to spend time with just anybody—like me. Permit me to give you an example."

Evelyn hastily thumbed through his diary.

"Here it is. Dated Fall of 1644. I'll read it to you. 'Tonight I attended a public opera wherein Bernini painted the scenes, cut the statues, invented the engines, composed the music, writ the comedy and built the theatre all himself'."

Velazquez continued his examination of the Englishman. *He seems like a nice enough man, but strange. What kind of man keeps a diary? That sounds like woman's work to me.* "You left a few things out. Did you know the Cavaliere also produces, directs and acts in most of his own plays? He obviously loves all things theatrical. Think about it—in all your world travels, how many people have you met who have a full-scale, fully equipped theatre in their home?"

"Hold on, dear man, I want to make a note of that."

"Here is something else you may want to make a note of. Last night at supper, we were discussing the theatre, and Bernini said, 'Ingenuity in design is the magic art by means of which one so deceives the eye as to create amazement, and to make appear true what is in substance false.' Knowing GianLorenzo as well as I do, I'm sure he was also talking about his body of work."

"Just a minute—I want to make a note of that, too."

"Don't you get tired doing all that writing?" Velazquez asked.

Evelyn shrugged as he madly scribbled.

"Okay," Velazquez continued, "I'll give you one more item of interest. Not too long ago, I saw Bernini's play 'Two Theatres.' There was a second audience facing us, on the other side of the stage, and . . ."

"Hold on, I don't get it. Was the second audience watching the same play as you? Was it a play within a play? Was it an illusion, or was it reality?"

Velazquez burst out laughing and stomped his foot, causing the nearby spectators to stare. When they realized it was the famous painter, Velazquez, they stared all the more.

"It was all of the above and none of the above. In other words, it was quintessential Bernini."

"Mister Velazquez, should we be worried?" John Evelyn said as he glanced furtively about the theatre. *What a lousy time to be seated in the front row—those dikes on stage look like they're going to burst any minute.*

"You may call me Diego. Why should we be worried?"

"No reason, Diego." *I can be just as macho as any Spaniard.* "It's just that if those dikes break, we're going to see a flood. Wrong. We're going to be starring in the bloody flood. But if you don't mind, I don't mind." *That should show him.*

"Don't be such a baby," Velazquez said, trumping the Englishman.

Suddenly, a great quantity of real water poured onto the stage and rushed down toward the audience.

Inspired by the competition, Evelyn maintained a stiff upper lip. "It's probably not important, Diego, but why is everyone scrambling toward the exits?"

"Relax, John, if I may call you John."

Evelyn nodded while holding his breath.

Velazquez continued. "I must admit it does appear that the few of us remaining in our seats are going to drown." *I'll give the English wimp credit—he's scared to death, but is trying his best not to show it.*

In a flash, a sluice gate opened and the great flow of water was swallowed up. The audience returned and burst into a fifteen minute standing ovation.

—

The Englishman, John Evelyn, made a written comment on the play, which he labeled 'Inondazione del Tevere.'

Interestingly, Evelyn's diary is one of the few records of GianLorenzo Bernini's extensive, and extraordinary, theatrical career. Unlike England, which began establishing a literary tradition over a hundred years earlier, theatrical accomplishments were not considered important in 17th Century Rome.

Chapter XCIX

Bernini spoke sincerely to the Pope. "It was gracious of you to include my friend Diego Velazquez in this delightful supper. Actually, I love our private weekly meals—where we can discuss matters beyond trivialities which one is forced to do in large groups—but when we adjourn for our brandy, you will see why I suggested Diego join us."

In the salon, the servant served the drinks and then retrieved a large painting Bernini had smuggled into the palace. For dramatic effect, GianLorenzo took his time lifting the silk cloth covering the portrait Velazquez had painted.

"Troppo vero, troppo vero (too true, too true)," the Pope murmured, obviously focusing on his expression in the painting—a cross between meanness and authority.

Velazquez was devastated. *Good God, Innocent hates it. How could he? It's perfect.*

Bernini immediately sensed the problem. *I remember Giulio telling me this Pope had no artistic taste. I see what he means.*

"If I may be so bold, Your Holiness, don't be so hard on yourself. The look Diego has captured is one of deep thought. In my opinion, the painting is a masterpiece, as good or better than anything Van Dyke or Titian ever painted—and I say that knowing Titian's masterpiece, the portrait of the Farnese Pope, Paul III."

Innocent started to lighten up. "I have seen that painting, Cavaliere. Do you really think my portrait is that good?"

"I think this painting is so spectacular," Bernini said, "I'm going to recommend Diego's admission into the Accademia di San Luca based on it."

"Yes, Cavaliere," the pontiff said, "now that you mention it, I see what you mean. Thank you, Velazquez, I will cherish the portrait, and will see that you are appropriately compensated."

Bernini stole a glance at his friend who sat stiffly, with a smile pasted on his face. *I can't wait to write Giulio. Innocent is actually going to pay Diego? He'll never believe this story.*

"You honor me, Holy Father," the relieved Velazquez said. "This is a moment I will cherish forever. Now, we must not forget the portrait Bernini has carved. We felt you would enjoy seeing them side-by-side for the first time."

Velazquez removed the cloth from the life-size marble bust. The Pope broke into a big smile.

"Thank you, Cavaliere. You make me look positively handsome."

—

The Pope had trouble taking his eyes off the Bernini bust, but finally managed. "Before you leave, Cavaliere, I want to discuss with you the decoration of the nave of Saint Peter's. That is, if you have time for another major commission."

"I'll wait outside," Velazquez said.

"That is not necessary, Diego, there is nothing secret about this commission. Cavaliere, I ask whether you have the time, because redecorating the longest nave in the Christian world is obviously a gargantuan task, and, the work must be completed before the next Holy Year of 1650. I am aware that you are working on numerous private projects."

Bernini had difficulty ignoring the stupefied look on Velazquez's face. *Diego is as astounded by this commission as I am. But I'm a better actor.*

"Rest assured," the Cavaliere said, "your fountain in Piazza Navona is at the top of the list. But to answer your question, I will make the time. As a matter of fact, since I designed the baldacchino and decorated the Crossing I have been anxious to see the nave coordinated with them. I have designs in my mind and will bring you sketches shortly."

—

Velazquez jumped into Bernini's carriage. "Thanks for your help, my friend. You are as good a politician as I've seen anywhere in Europe. Tonight, as I observed the high esteem Innocent holds you in, I couldn't help thinking it was only a few short years ago that he ordered your bell tower torn down. The turnaround is a remarkable accomplishment—more like a coup—on your part."

Bernini slumped back in the carriage, his eyes closed, savoring the moment.

Diego continued. "And another thing. Have you noticed since the Barberini are back in Rome—and in the patronage business—the artistic community is considerably less hostile to GianLorenzo Bernini?"

"It is only fair," the Cavaliere said, sitting up, brandishing an exceptionally broad smile. Bernini felt good—like he did every time Caterina found a sore muscle on his body while giving him a massage and then rubbed it away with tantalizing, sensuous, provocative, suggestive, arousing and, best of all, demanding strokes.

—

The pair rode through the streets of Rome in silence, each reflecting on the events of the unusual evening, and how they applied to him.

"Tell the driver to stop," Velazquez shouted. He pointed to a tavern overflowing with drunken revelers. "Wasn't that one of our old haunts."

"Diego, the last time you were in Rome, every tavern in town was one of our old haunts. Shall I leave you off here?"

"Leave me off? What's wrong with you—aren't you feeling well?"

"I'm feeling fine," Bernini said. "Extra-fine. Super-fine. It's just that those whoring days are behind me."

Velazquez studied his friend. *I know he loves his wife, but why would he do something this drastic?* "You're serious, aren't you? Yes, I will get off here. Don't worry about me, I'll eventually find my way home. Good night, old man. I guess, in certain ways at least, the Italians can't keep up with the Spaniards."

"See you in church," GianLorenzo called out. *I hope Caterina is waiting up for me.*

Chapter C

Cardinal Spada expertly picked his way through the debris of San Giovanni in Laterano. *The progress since we started two years ago is startling. I give Francesco credit; he has been everything I hoped for—and more.*

Borromini was examining the fresco of Cavaliere d'Arpino over the altar of Pope Clement VIII when he spotted his patron. He scrambled down the ladder and hurried over to the Cardinal.

"Virgilio," the architect said, "if we're going to stay on schedule, we must start work on my vaulted ceiling immediately."

Cardinal Spada put his arm around Borromini's shoulder and walked to the center of the nave. *This is going to be one horrific morning.* "Francesco, I'm proud of you. Not only are we on schedule, the work so far has turned out even better than I dreamed."

"Virgilio, I . . ."

"The fluting on those giant floor to ceiling pilasters, the Corinthian capitals, the wide openings between the pilasters—all of it. Inspired. And . . ."

"Virgilio, replacing the columns with these pilasters was in the plans from the start. So were the wide openings between the pilasters. Yes, we now have a feeling of dynamic rhythm and a much more beautiful church. What I've done is inspired. Fine. But there is nothing new here. I think you're avoiding the issue—I want to talk about my barrel vault. It's going to bring the windows, niches—all of the diverse elements in the basilica, together. You want a harmonious whole? My barrel vault will give it to you and the Pope. When can I start on it?"

Cardinal Spada took a deep breath, exhaled and did it again. *Nobody will ever know what I have to go through for the glory of God.* "Francesco, I just spent four hours of the Pope's precious time trying to convince him to allow us to tear down this wooden ceiling. His Holiness is intractable. Sorry, but the answer is no. Sorry. Look at it this way, Francesco. While your beautiful barrel vault would be perfect, bringing everything together, retaining the flat wooden ceiling is not the worse thing that can happen. Look at it—you must admit it is beautiful in its own right. And, it is replete with Church history. Can't we just move on and finish the job? That's what Bernini would do."

Borromini counted the pilasters. Then he counted the arches. Then he counted the windows. Then he counted the niches. *That bastard—comparing me to that thief Bernini is a disgraceful maneuver. Still, he does know how to reach me.* "I'm taking off the rest of the day—if you don't mind, Your Royal Highness. I have something important to do."

Cardinal Spada shrugged. *That wasn't nearly as tough as I thought it would be. Something is going on in that complex mind.*

—

Borromini entered the church of San Giovanni dei Fiorentini, crossed himself, and knelt in front of Carlo Maderno's resting place.

"It's me again, Carlo, and you would have been proud of me this morning. Remember when I laid in bed for three months because that Bernini fellow received what should have been my papal commission for the fountain in Piazza Navona? Anyhow, out of the mouths of babes and all that, my little nephew, Bernardo, said something one day when he came to visit me in bed. He said, 'Why did that bad man do this to you, uncle?' After he left, I couldn't read or do anything—all I could think about was what the little boy said. It wasn't easy, but eventually I concluded the child was right. That thief not only received my commission, he got me in bed as a bonus—not that I'm certain he cares whether I'm dead or alive. In any case, what I was saying was, when Virgilio said today that I couldn't renovate the Lateran the way I wanted to—properly in other words—I remained calm, just like you would have. You would have been proud. And that's the way it's going to be from now on. Do you know what I'm going to do now? Instead of falling into bed sick like I used to do, I'm going to buy a book and read it tonight. Goodnight, Carlo. You are still the only man who never turned against me. I love you and I always will."

—

Giuseppe the bookseller watched his best customer dismount from his horse and enter his shop. *Borromini has a strange look about him tonight. He's walking like he's in sort of a trance.* "Borromini, how nice to see you. Look at this architecture book over while I make you a cappuccino."

"An espresso will be fine. Notice how calm I am tonight?"

Giuseppe took a second look at Borromini. "Calm is the perfect word. Frankly, I was certain you'd be ranting and raving. Frankly, even I was shocked when I heard Bernini received the commission and you didn't. After all, your mentor Carlo Maderno did design the nave and Innocent X has been your patron since he's been in office—except for the fountain, of course. I'm glad you're taking it so well."

Francesco looked halfway up from the book he was considering. "What commission is that? Oh, you must mean that Innocent and Spada wouldn't let me tear down the old wooden ceiling at the Lateran."

"Nothing about the Lateran, Francesco. I'm talking about the nave of Saint Peter's—it's finally going to be decorated and Bernini has the commission. The pilasters, the floor—everything. The entire nave. In colored marble. I hear Bernini is going to employ hundreds of workers to finish the job before the Holy Year. No question, it's a major papal commission and it's going to make a huge difference."

Borromini fell to the ground gasping for air. He didn't faint, exactly, it was more like an arrow stunned him and he collapsed from the shock of the impact. Giuseppe ran for a goblet of water and forced Francesco to drink it.

"Are you okay, my friend? What happened? You're white as a piece of marble. Can you speak?"

The traumatized architect wobbled to his feet. Without warning, he grabbed Giuseppe by the front of his blouse and lifted him off the ground. No more than two inches separated their faces.

Borromini tried to speak but no words came out.

Giuseppe prayed silently, and then whispered in Borromini's face. "I am so sorry. I assumed you knew. If you release me, I promise not to mention that name again. Please. It's just a bad habit, always spreading gossip. Forgive me, Francesco, I meant no harm. Please."

Giuseppe the bookseller bounced when he hit the floor. Borromini stepped over the shaking body and stormed into the starless night.

Chapter CI

Borromini tried to mount his horse but kept falling off. He decided to walk home and lurched through the narrow, twisted streets of Rome, bumping into all sort of people as he made his unsteady way through the city.

"Hey, watch where you're going you peasant." "What's your problem—are you drunk?" "Bump into my wife one more time and you're a dead man."

Borromini heard faint voices but couldn't focus. *What do all these people want from me? I know. They're probably part of the conspiracy.* He staggered on, walking into the rear wheels of a carriage carrying two noble ladies.

The elderly matron addressed her friend: "Did you see that? We did nothing wrong—he walked into us." To her driver: "Move on, Maurizio. Quickly." To her friend: "He didn't look drunk. He looked bewildered." The friend to the matron: "Stupefied would be a more descriptive word. My husband had that look on his face when I told him I was pregnant after eleven years."

Borromini picked himself up from the cobblestones and staggered away. He crossed the Piazza di Spagna and tried to drink from the fountain in the middle of La Baraccacia. The architect fell into the water face first, shaking from head to toe.

Four youths, out for a stroll after supper, pulled Borromini to safety.

"You almost drowned in Bernini's fountain," said the oldest one.

He stared at the youngsters for several minutes with no comprehension, and then half-crawled, half-walked away. *Did I hear that Bernini's name? The devil must have done it—he must be near.*

Borromini's saviors looked at each other quizzically. "And our parents say we young people are strange."

Borromini blundered along, searching for his home. When he reached the Piazza Navona he made his way to the steps in front of Sant' Agnese in

Agone and sat next to a pretty nun who was wearing a light blue habit and cap.

"What's behind those boards?" Francesco asked, his words barely discernible to the apprehensive nun. She immediately stood, feeling guilty about abandoning a fellow human obviously in need, but too afraid to remain and help.

"Bernini is building a fountain for the Holy Father. God bless you, my son, but I must be in the convent before curfew."

Borromini attempted to follow her but fell down the steps. *What was that? A female devil sent by that man? I can't remember—is there such a thing as a female devil?*

—

Borromini staggered around aimlessly. *Can this be the Piazza Barberini? I don't live near here.* He stumbled past Bernini's soaring Triton Fountain to his little Fountain of the Bees. Francesco waited—lying on the ground until two horses had their fill from the open shell—and then started to drink from it.

"Move on, mister," a burly workman said. "Cavaliere Bernini built this fountain mainly for our animals. Go drink from his other fountain—right over there."

Francesco crawled to the Triton Fountain and fell in. The cold water tasted good. He climbed out and, once again, headed for home. *Definitely a conspiracy. Bernini, Bernini, Bernini. I can't constantly be hearing his name. What's happening to me? I know, I'm dreaming? I need to find a church.*

—

Borromini found himself sitting on the steps in front of Saint John Lateran, the very church he was renovating. *I'm so tired. I ache all over.* He started to doze off. *Did I see Giuseppe the bookseller recently? I think I did. The nave, something about the nave . . .*

A wagon delivering milk drove by awakening the architect. He stood and looked around. *What am I doing here? Don't I work at this basilica?*

Out of the corner of his eye Borromini noticed a man running. *Who is that? Is he part of the conspiracy? Where did he go? I can't see him. Must be more dreaming.*

Suddenly, Francesco heard a banging sound. He rushed to the side of the basilica and found a door partly ajar—he slipped in and followed the noise. He observed a short man looking through the construction debris, picking up a large piece of marble and striking it with a mallet.

Startled into reality, Borromini shouted, "Hey you, what are you doing there?"

The man tried to escape but Borromini tackled him and grabbed him by the neck.

The middle-aged intruder, weighing about ninety pounds, was no match for the burly architect. "Let me go, you're choking me. Who are you?"

"This happens to be my church," Borromini said, "and if you don't tell me what you're doing here, you'll be sorry."

"Stop choking me. Please. I meant no harm." Borromini eased his grip. The man continued, "My house. I'm renovating my house and I want to do it right—so I came here looking for some marble."

Borromini shook his head in disbelief. "Marble, you were stealing my marble? Why? Are you part of the conspiracy?"

"Please let me go. Put yourself in my position. I wanted a little marble so I could renovate my house in a proper manner. Can you understand what that means to someone like me? I'm a stonecutter and I want my house to look nice. Wouldn't you? Wait, aren't you the famous architect, Francesco Borromini? You, of all people, know what it means to renovate properly. Please let me go."

Borromini snapped. *Renovate properly. Renovate properly. Renovate properly.*

He grabbed a hammer lying on the ground next to him and pounded the skinny man until he heard no more pleading.

—

Beyond Michelangelo

When the workmen arrived a few hours later, they found their boss Borromini draped over a mutilated body, clutching a hammer covered with blood. Out of loyalty to their leader, the workmen tried to cover-up the crime, but a disgruntled worker—fired for stealing and working his last day—had already called the police.

CHAPTER CII

"His name is Bussone and I'm afraid Francesco murdered him," Cardinal Spada said to the Pope.

"I have heard," Innocent replied. "Do you have any idea why Borromini would do such a thing?"

Careful here, Virgilio. This Pope is a very pious man. "Francesco believed the man was damaging the renovation work on the basilica, Your Holiness. He was afraid that would cause us to miss your deadline. To me, Francesco's motives were noble."

"Everyone of my advisors, except you, Virgilio, recommends that I punish Borromini severely and banish him from the papal court. Why do you, in essence, plead for leniency for the murderer?"

"He is not a murderer, Holy Father. He is a great, albeit temperamental, artist who has been under enormous stress lately. Finishing your rehabilitation of the Lateran in record time—in time for the Jubilee Year—has extended even my patience. I think he finally collapsed under the pressure."

"Is it normal for artists to act this way? Does Bernini?"

Cardinal Spada paused long enough to marshal his thoughts. *He must have an ulterior motive here. Since Bernini has been back in papal favor, I notice the pontiff is favoring him more and more. He even questioned me recently about whether he should have torn down the Cavaliere's bell tower. I better be careful—and truthful.*

"Yes and No, Your Holiness. By that I mean many artists act the same way. You are familiar with Michelangelo and Caravaggio—they are classic examples of what I call 'artistic temperament.' Bernini, on the other hand, is unique. His talent is second to none, of course, and yet he is civil, organized, educated and brilliant. Frankly, a combination I have never seen before and don't expect to see again. The Cavaliere avers all of his talents are God-given, and I believe him."

Innocent, who had been listening intently, lost interest. "I must leave, Virgilio. As my Artistic Advisor, what do you recommend I do with your temperamental genius?"

"Exile him for a short time. To Orvieto or Virterbo perhaps. Holy Father, Francesco is an emotional man who strives for excellence. That is his only crime. I am sure you will agree that he has achieved excellence for us. If I may say, with all due respect, Francesco Borromini has earned your compassion."

The Pope flashed a rare smile. "Virgilio, when I appointed you Artistic Advisor, who would have dreamed you would be advising me on murder."

As the Cardinal left the pontiff's office, he heard Innocent send for Donna Olimpia. *I may be Artistic Advisor but she is still sister-in-law. Oh well. I don't take it personally. This Pope has always had trouble making decisions.*

Cardinal Spada found Borromini in the custody of the papal guards. "Francesco, I have wonderful news. Innocent has exiled you to Orvieto instead of putting you in jail."

The guards released their prisoner. "It was just too much," Borromini said. "There were too many things. I was . . . overwhelmed."

"I understand only too well," the Cardinal said. "Go now and have a safe trip. The time will pass quickly."

"Good-bye Virgilio."

"Wait, didn't you forget something?"

Borromini paused. "No, I don't think so."

"I didn't hear you say 'Thank You, Virgilio'."

"Why should I thank you? You wouldn't let me tear down the old, flat, wooden ceiling in the Lateran. You didn't get me the fountain or the nave commission. You couldn't even get me rehired by those Oratorians—your own Order."

The Cardinal smiled and made the Sign of the Cross in the air. *You are the luckiest man I know—without your extraordinary talent, I shudder to contemplate what might befall you in this life.* "Have a safe trip, Francesco. I will miss you terribly."

Chapter CIII

Cardinal Spada led his Pope on an inspection tour of the seven hundred plus feet of the nave of Saint Peter's.

"Now that I see the spectacular job Bernini did on this nave," the pontiff said, "it is hard for me to remember what it looked like before."

Cardinal Spada nodded vigorously. "It's a tribute to you, Your Holiness, that you allowed Bernini to create his own designs without having to follow the old simple geometric patterns. You will notice that each pillar has a different feel, and yet they all have the same elements—oval medallions, putti holding up marble portraits of Popes, putti holding different items, such as tiaras, keys and books, and so on. In fact, believe it or not, there are 56 busts of Popes, 192 cherubs, each about four feet high, and 104 over life-size Pamphili doves."

The astonished Pope walked on, barely able to contain his excitement—which for him was one of life's rarities. *That's the part I like best—the family doves.*

The Cardinal continued, careful to keep telling the Pope the truth about Bernini. *It's my only safe course.* "And, you will notice that the Cavaliere's use of color is nothing short of astonishing. Somehow, through his placement of variegated marble, the overall feel of the nave is subtle and dramatic at the time. As your Artistic Advisor, I assure you that kind of conflicting impact borders on the miraculous."

Innocent made his way to the Crossing. "I can see that this nave blends in perfectly with his other work. Truly, the Cavaliere's decoration of this nave has transformed our beloved basilica as surely as his baldacchino and Crossing decorations did. Virgilio, what is Bernini's secret?"

"He has monster talent and is an organizational genius, Your Holiness. He personally designed each and every pilaster, every arch, and every inch of the floor. And then, he supervised every aspect of the job. He usually had a team of over forty men working here—I know because I counted them one day. The only artist I know with comparable organizational skills is Peter Paul Rubens."

"Rubens?"

I can't believe this man. "You know, the artist from up north who painted the main altar in the Chiesa Nuova, for my Order of Oratorians."

"Of course," the Pope said. "I heard the Oratorians fired Borromini as their architect after thirteen years. Why would they do that? He does so well for us."

Cardinal Spada wanted to tell Innocent the truth—*Because that sneaky, no talent young architect, Camillo Arcucci, poisoned their minds so he could confiscate Francesco's commission*—but thought better of it.

"A minor misunderstanding, Your Holiness. I tried to arbitrate, but to no avail. The Order was as intransigent as a donkey ready to sleep for the evening"

Chapter CIV

Beyond Michelangelo

Sister Maria Alaleone was shaking. She was nervous about meeting with the great man but even more nervous about what she needed to tell him. Bernini entered his library.

"Thank you, Cavaliere, for receiving me in the privacy of your home. As you have probably guessed, I have a delicate matter to discuss. I am told you are of exemplary character so I need not worry about confiding in you. Before I begin, if you don't mind, I believe I need a bit of fortification—if God will forgive me."

Bernini poured his guest a goblet of wine and watched in silence as she downed the drink in one steady gulp. Her coughing signaled she was not accustomed to drinking alcoholic beverages. *This must be a confidence of major proportions.*

The nun carefully placed the empty goblet on the table, daintily dried her lips with a silk kerchief, which was lined in lace, folded her hands in her lap, and began.

"Our family is a proud family, sir, but an unfortunate incident has occurred that has tarnished our reputation." She stopped abruptly, but continued in a lower voice. "Not too long ago, an eighteen-year-old cousin of mine, who is also a nun, did a dastardly thing."

I can't believe this sweet lady used a word like that—it flew off her lips like a rabbit being chased by a fox. "That is a strong word, sister."

"So was her act," she said sternly. "It seems she was in love with a young man of noble birth and the devil entered her body." Bernini made a face—he couldn't help himself. The sister noticed. "I know what you are thinking, Cavaliere, but it is not that simple. What happened was, the two of them hatched a plan, using a servant as a go-between." She paused, took a deep breath and glanced around the library.

"Allow me to refortify you, sister," GianLorenzo said as he refilled her goblet. "The Good Lord will understand."

The sister allowed herself one more major gulp. The coughing was more subdued and GianLorenzo thought he detected a slight grin around her straight lips.

"The plan was simple. The servant locked the young man in a trunk and dispatched it to the convent. Have you guessed? The delivery was delayed."

"Oh my God . . ."

"No, the devil did it. He delayed the shipment and the young potential lover suffocated to death. Unfortunately there were witnesses when the trunk was opened so everyone in the convent is aware of what happened."

—

It was Bernini's turn for fortification. Definitely no coughing here. "I'm so sorry, sister. What can I do to help?"

"You are familiar with the church of Santi Domenico e Sisto of course." Bernini nodded. "I would like you to design our family chapel. I investigated your progress on the Cornaro Chapel in Santa Maria Vittoria, so I know what you design for the Alaleone family would be spectacular. And Cavaliere, we need something spectacular to atone for my cousin's sins."

"Sister, I'm flattered, of course, but the Cornaro Chapel is a very expensive monument."

"We will pay you whatever you request. My family knows that you are the premier architect in Rome, but we are told you are a fair and honest man who will not take advantage of us. Will you honor my family, the entire convent, and me by accepting the commission? We would be eternally grateful."

"The space, how large is it?"

"Not large. In fact, it's really not a chapel, it's more of an indentation, or niche."

"And the subject? What do you have in mind? I would suggest Christ healing a woman of evil spirits—'Noli Me Tangere'."

"I have heard amazing stories about you, Cavaliere, but I had trouble believing some of them. Now that I see you guess exactly what the family was thinking, I'm prepared to believe anything and everything I hear about your various talents."

"Christ before the Magdalen is perfect under the circumstances, isn't it? If the niche of your chapel is as small as you indicate, I will frame it in such a way to make it appear larger. The major figures will be marble, life-size, and . . ."

"Then you will do it?"

"Sister, if I were to refuse you, my darling wife—if she heard the story—would put me in a trunk and delay delivery. I will give you the best chapel I am capable of designing. You and your family can count on it."

"God bless you, and your wife. We in the convent will pray every day for you both. As for the fee, please remember that my family does not have the papal treasury at its disposal. Oh my. Mister Bernini, forgive me if I appear to be negotiating for a lower fee, because I am not. I have heard, however, that you do charge—how shall I say it—aggressively."

Bernini laughed a hearty laugh. *I like this lady, but I must be realistic.*

"Sister, when I was a little boy, a great artist and friend told me I must charge according to my talent and according to the value of my work to the patron. He often pointed out that to reduce the fee for a good cause made no sense because most people consider their personal cause exemplary. He added that if an artist doesn't charge a high enough fee, he demeans his work—meaning that if he himself doesn't respect his own talent, why should anyone else? I swore to him on his deathbed that I would never forget his advice and have lived my life accordingly. Now, I know I have rambled, but in spite of the rambling, have I made myself clear?"

"Perfectly."

"Good. I will set the fee at the end of the job. Good day, sister. Be alert on your way home—that was strong fortification you drank."

Chapter CV

Beyond Michelangelo

Innocent finished saying Mass and the faithful began filing out of San Giovanni in Laterano into the blazing Roman sunshine. Cardinal Spada was anxious to join his family for their usual Sunday dinner, but the pontiff had scheduled a meeting with him for after the crowd dispersed. *I love to stand here in the back and listen to the comments of the worshipers as they leave. I spent so much time in this church, I feel a special affinity—even more than with Saint Peter's.*

"It doesn't look like the same church. Whoever the architect was is a genius." "Thank God they saved that beautiful wooden ceiling." "Now it needs a façade—I hope Borromini gets the commission. He deserves it." "I used to be afraid the church was going to collapse around me—not any more." "What a treat it is to attend Mass here."

—

The church emptied and Spada joined Innocent, who had shed his vestments, in the sacristy.

"Virgilio," the pontiff said, "I thought it would be appropriate to meet here in the Lateran and tell you my idea. I won't keep you."

"Holy Father, your time is my time. You know that."

"First, I want to commend you for your work on this basilica. Also, you were correct about Borromini—he did an outstanding job, and my thought is to reward him by terminating his exile and bringing him back to Rome. I assume you like the idea."

"An inspired thought, Your Holiness." *This man continues to surprise me.* "I will make all of the arrangements. May I make a suggestion?" *I better strike while he's in this mood.*

"Proceed."

"I share your enthusiasm for the work Francesco did restoring the basilica, and I wonder if a further reward is not in order. I was thinking you might want to commission Borromini a Knight in the Order of Christ." As soon as he spoke, the Cardinal had second thoughts. *I hope the Holy Father doesn't think I'm being too presumptuous.*

"Yes, yes," Innocent said as he analyzed the suggestion. "Francesco has definitely earned the honor. One condition, however. You make the presentation of the Chain and Cross. I don't have the patience, or inclination, to deal with your friend at this point in my life."

—

Borromini was escorted into Cardinal Spada's study. "How was the trip, Francesco? I know you must be extremely tired, so I appreciate your stopping to see me before riding to your own home."

Borromini slumped into an overstuffed chair. "Let me put it this way. I was almost as happy to see the Porta del Popolo today as I was the day I came to Rome some thirty years ago."

"Are you saying you didn't like Orvieto?"

"It's a nice little town. I appreciated the peace and quiet, but they don't have any bookshops the caliber of Giuseppe's. I miss his store, even though the man used to drive me crazy."

"Francesco, my friend, I have exciting news. In addition to pardoning you, the Holy Father has decided to make you a Knight of the Order of Christ."

"For what? Killing that man?"

The Cardinal winced. *In the year Francesco was gone, I almost forgot how difficult he could be. Almost.* "For the outstanding work you did in restoring the Lateran."

"That was a ridiculous job," Borromini said. "That church should have a new ceiling."

Don't take it personally, Virgilio. Remember, artistic temperament and all that. "The Knighthood carries an annual stipend. And you can be addressed as Cavaliere—just like Bernini is."

"It does carry a stipend, doesn't it? When is the ceremony?" *I hope he noticed that I ignored his reference to that Bernini person.*

Beyond Michelangelo

Cardinal Spada put on his most political smile. *I notice Francesco ignored my reference to Bernini—hopefully the small town settled him down a bit.* "More good news, Francesco. You don't have to get all dressed up and waste your time. I know you have a lot of catching up to do having been out of Rome for a year so I arranged to personally give you the Chain and Cross."

Virgilio opened a velvet-lined box, extracted the Chain and Cross, and placed it around Borromini's neck.

The architect recoiled. "What are you doing? Where's the Pope—I thought he made the presentation. This should be a major event with me as the center of attraction. This isn't fair. I'm being treated like a distant cousin at a family reunion."

For the first time in his life, Cardinal Spada felt sorry for Borromini instead of for himself.

CHAPTER CVI

Beyond Michelangelo

Bernini named his papal fountain project Fountain of the Four Rivers because he designed the four giant river Gods to represent the four continents of the known world: the Ganges (representing Asia), the Nile (Africa), the Danube (Europe) and the Rio de la Plata (the New World).

After three years of construction, the piping and engineering work were completed; the last major task was raising the enormous obelisk. Bernini designed an intricate set of winches and pulleys, and thousands of Romans from all walks of life watched the intricate operation in a circus-like atmosphere. Adding to the fun, every citizen in the city had a wager as to whether the realistic-looking grotto of faux rocks (made of travertine marble)—which had gaping holes in it so viewers would be able to look through it from every side—could possible support the gigantic, impossibly heavy obelisk.

The obelisk raising proceeded without a hitch. As soon as it was completed, and the various figures and symbols were placed in position, Innocent's curiosity got the better of him and he decided to surprise the Cavaliere with a visit to the construction site.

—

When Bernini—who had been alerted—told his foreman to expect the Pope the next morning, the dutiful worker rebelled. "But the scaffolding and cloth-covered framework are still up," he said. "We've got lots of work to do. Besides, the water hasn't been turned on yet."

I love my foreman's conscientiousness, but like most workers, he can use some social skills. He makes me money, though, so I shouldn't complain. "Slow down for a minute and listen. I have a plan. First of all . . ."

"Boss, have you considered working the streets during carnival time? You'd make a fortune in tips playing magician."

—

At ten o'clock the next morning, Rome was startled to see their Pope, and fifty of his closest advisors, walk from the Quirinal Palace to the Piazza Navona.

Bernini greeted the pontiff. "What a pleasant surprise, Holy Father. The fountain, I regret to inform you, it is not ready. But of course you make look in."

"How long they going to stay?" the foreman asked Bernini. "They been here almost two hours—how can we get anything done with all those people milling about?"

"I've made it a point to stay out of Innocent's way while he looked around," Bernini replied. "But to placate you, I'll try to move things along."

The foreman laughed as Bernini approached Innocent. *Placate? What the hell does that mean. That boss of mine is some dandy.*

"Does it live up to the model?" Bernini asked the Pope.

"Magnificently, and then some. It dominates, but still unifies, my front yard—I should say the piazza. You will notice, Cavaliere, I have learned that conflicting attributes are rare in art and architecture. I would like to see the fountain with the water turned on. Is that possible?"

"That is impossible, Holy Father. I'm certain you can understand that time is required to put everything in order."

"Pity," said the Pope as he gave his blessing and turned to leave. When the pontiff reached the door of the enclosure, Bernini signaled the foreman. When Innocent heard the water gush forth, he quickly returned to enjoy the spectacle.

Smiling from ear to ear, Innocent soaked his hands in the swirling water. "In giving us the unexpected joy of this masterwork," he said, "you have added ten years to our life."

For one of the few times in his life, Bernini was speechless.

The Pope continued. "Virgilio, send one of the men to see Donna Olimpia. Tell him to ask her for one hundred doubloons. When he returns, distribute the money equally among these men who have labored all these years on this masterpiece."

Cardinal Spada had to steady himself. *What sort of strange power does Bernini have over my Pope?*

Borromini was shocked to see Cardinal Spada on the Saint Ivo job. *I've been working on this project for eight years and I've never seen him in this workplace.*

"Virgilio, what are you doing here—is something wrong?"

"I have an important matter to discuss with you, Francesco. But first, let me look around." The Cardinal made a cursory examination of the church under construction. "It's coming along beautifully. What do your patrons say?"

"Virgilio, I'm in heaven on this job. The university people never bother me—not like your friends the Oratorians."

"How long until you finish?"

"Probably another seven or eight years."

"And the patrons aren't haranguing you to finish? Unbelievable."

"Virgilio, these are the best patrons I've had since I designed San Carlino and the other buildings for the Trinitarians. Why is that important? That's important because that trust will get them the best I have in me. I must return to work—do you want to tell me why you came?"

"Francesco, have you seen Bernini's Four Rivers Fountain?"

Borromini wanted to throw up. *I can't believe it. Virgilio hasn't been on this job in the eight years I've been working on it, and when he finally comes he torments me.* "How can I avoid seeing it? Did you forget I'm working in the Pamphili Palace? I thought you arranged that minor commission. Why do you ask?"

"I think Bernini is vulnerable."

Borromini put down his tools and waved the Cardinal onto a bench.

"How exactly do you mean?"

"You've seen the fountain—that obelisk is massive and there are large holes in the supporting faux grotto . . ."

"I thought the same thing at first, but then I studied the fountain carefully—at night, of course. Unfortunately, the way he designed those phony rocks that obelisk will stand forever. I hate to admit it, but for once that man did something right."

"Francesco, slow down. Bernini has many rivals and critics. I believe they can be convinced the obelisk is unstable and therefore dangerous. Especially..."

Borromini's eyes widened as he grasped the point. *And would have to be torn down. Like his bell tower.*

"Especially," Virgilio continued, "if a respected architect who is grounded in the basics of structure were to spread the word throughout the city."

"I'm not sure I..."

"Don't say anything, Francesco, just think about it."

Chapter CVII

Bernini watched his wife darn his favorite smock. *This woman is as mystifying to me as life itself. She is as comfortable dining with the Pope and his court as she is with our children. She entertains royalty in our house and finds time to cook everyday for the family. She is a mother and yet maintains the allure of a teen-age harlot. And she mends my clothes.*

The Cavaliere smacked himself on the forehead. "Sweetheart," Bernini said, "may I please have your sewing kit for a moment? I have an idea, so simple, it's brilliant—if I say so myself."

Caterina looked up, startled. "What are you up to, GianLorenzo?"

The Cavaliere took Caterina in his arms and showered her with kisses. "I love you more every day, darling. You are everything to me."

"And you to me, dear. But why the sewing kit? We've been married almost ten years and you've never expressed the slightest interest in my sewing kit."

Bernini took a spool of black thread from the box. He carefully measured a strand of the silk and cut it. He repeated the procedure until he had four identical lengths of thread. The Cavaliere took his wife by the elbow and led her to their carriage.

"I'm sure," Bernini said, "you have heard the silly gossip being spread by that Borromini fellow—about how the obelisk is going to fall off my Fountain of the Four Rivers. Well, my precious one, when we get to the Piazza Navona, you will see what I'm up to."

—

One of Bernini's workmen was waiting for him when he arrived at the fountain. "Gigi," the Cavaliere asked, "can you make your way to the top of the obelisk?"

"No problem, sir. I'll just . . ."

"Spare me the details. Take these four strands of thread and wrap them securely around the top of the obelisk. Then come down for further instructions."

Beyond Michelangelo

As Caterina watched the workman shimmy up the obelisk, using the rope and pull method, she immediately grasped the plan. She squealed with delight and hugged and kissed her husband. "So that's it—I should have guessed. You truly are a rascal, Mister Bernini."

—

A couple eating gelato in a café recognized the Cavaliere. They ran to the fountain for a better look. A crowd gathered. "Quick," a lady said to her child. "Run home and call your father. The master is here." "Who?" the youngster asked. "Bernini. The Cavaliere. The man who built the fountain. Hurry." Word spread like the mist on a humid evening. The square began to fill. People appeared at the windows of the houses framing the piazza. Diners at the restaurants and trattorias stood on their tables to get a better view. Policemen formed a cordon to keep the crowd a safe distance from the fountain.

Gigi finished his work and effortlessly—actually showing off a little—returned to the ground. The crowd cheered.

"Good work," Bernini told the grinning worker. "Now I want you to go to the four houses I've marked—there are two on each side of the piazza—and attach a strand of thread to each one. Make each strand as taunt as you can."

One by one, the workman began attaching the four strands of thread. When he had the first one in place, the puzzled crowd—which now filled the piazza—applauded politely. For the second, catching on, they cheered. For the third, they screamed and hollered. When Gigi finished, the crowd went wild, shouting at the top of their voices.

"That'll show 'em, Cavaliere." "What a move—Bernini, you're a genius in more ways than one." "The fools are all jealous." "We love you and your fountain, maestro." And the one Bernini liked the best, which was obviously from a knowledgeable fan. "Forget pasta, let Borromini eat those strands of thread for supper."

—

The happy couple got into their carriage, which was quickly surrounded by the adoring crowd. "I think," she said with a twinkle in her eyes, "the people of Rome would appreciate a response from you—your fountain has obviously touched a nerve. Why don't we take a spin around the square before heading home? Would you mind?"

"You talked me into it," the Cavaliere replied as he waived to the loving crowd on the first of fifty—Caterina counted them—snail-like trips around the Piazza Navona.

Chapter CVIII

A dejected Borromini met Cardinal Spada at the cleric's stately hundred-year-old family palazzo.

"I want to better visualize your plan," the Cardinal said. "That's why I asked you here. Come, join me in the courtyard."

Head down, Borromini trailed behind. He looked like a child being led behind the woodshed for a serious beating.

"I know you are disappointed, Francesco," Spada said, "but don't blame yourself. Sometimes our efforts are rewarded—like the demolition of the bell tower—and sometimes they are not. I wish you would learn to relax and take the bad with the good in life, even when it involves Bernini."

"Borromini shook his head. "Why do things always turn out bad when that Bernini person is involved? How could he turn my accusations to his advantage with that cheap trick?"

Spada couldn't resist. "Frankly, I thought it was a brilliant move—diffusing the criticism with a witticism."

Borromini didn't think the rhyme was funny at all. *I hate being here with this man.*

—

The pair faced the small space between the Spada's garden and the palazzo next door. Borromini unraveled the drawings and set them on the ground. He picked up the top sheet.

"Virgilio, when you asked me to look at this little dead-end alley, I was sure you were wasting my time. But the more I thought about it, I saw it as a challenge—how do you transform a tiny nothing into a big something?" He handed the top sheet to his patron. "As you can see from the perspective and cross-section, I've done it."

Beyond Michelangelo

Cardinal Spada studied the plans carefully, one sheet at a time. "Francesco, you are a genius. *I see what he did. He diminished the height of the double Tuscan columns on each side of the colonnade as they recede and finally almost converge.* Build it, Francesco."

"You left out the best part," Borromini said. "My efforts will give you a galleria that appears four times longer than it really is. It's a perfect illusion for the paltry space available to me."

Chapter CIX

Beyond Michelangelo

As the sun tried to break through the early morning mist, the Monsignor escorted Bernini and his patron, Cardinal Federigo Cornaro, into his parish church, Santa Maria della Vittoria. The small, highly popular, highly decorated church was designed by the great Carlo Maderno for the Borghese, and is up the road, diagonally, from San Carlino.

"Welcome," the elderly cleric said as he locked the door behind his distinguished guests. The Monsignor was cheerful in spite of the early hour. "Come in, come in—you have almost two hours before our first Mass and the arrival of the crush of worshipers who line-up all day to see your masterpiece. Cavaliere, I have never seen anything like this in my fifty years in the cloth—not even when we first opened the doors to our jewel of a church."

—

Bernini stared at the Cornaro Chapel as if seeing it for the first time. "This was the most difficult commission I have ever attempted," he said to Cardinal Cornaro. "I don't mean only artistically, I mean emotionally as well. In fact, I was so emotionally involved, I had to force myself to keep going for the five years of construction."

The silver headed Cardinal with the kindly face was confused. *Artists. I'll never understand them.* "Cavaliere, your talent was obviously fed by your emotion because the chapel is perfection itself. Every aspect of it seems logical; so fit together, so to speak. I'd be interested to know the source of the intense emotion that made you so sensitive?"

Bernini thought a long time. *That is a very good question.* He searched for the answer. "I have read all of Saint Teresa's writings, and therein lies the problem. Her words are so emotionally charged, the challenge was to translate her moving words into a shrine worshipers could relate to, and at the same time, translate those sensuous words into a fitting monument to your illustrious family. I needed to capture the saint in what she described as, 'that state midway between heaven and earth, when spirit and matter meet.' In other words, in her state of ecstasy. It was critical for me to capture her delicious words in cold hard marble as honestly as possible because her words have special importance to me: I heard them read at her canonization thirty years ago."

Cardinal Cornaro lit up. "March 12, 1622. The most memorable day of my life as a cleric. Saint Peter's was covered with tapestries depicting the lives and miracles of all five of the persons being canonized. Remember? But, getting back to my family's chapel, what you have accomplished is stunning. You have captured Saint Teresa's ecstasy in both obvious and subtle ways: On the one hand, there is her physical abandon—head thrown back, mouth open and moaning, eyes closed, hand and bare foot hanging loose—which is accented by your skillful use of rippling drapery to conceal but define her body."

"I..."

"Please allow me to continue, Cavaliere. Then there is the smiling, cherubic angel. Is he about to strike Teresa with the arrow of divine love or has he just removed it? And placing her on a cloud—symbolizing her many levitations—that was a stroke of genius. To me, the marble group floats like a white jewel."

"That is very poetic, Your Eminence."

"Cavaliere, your altarpiece is very poetic. I am particularly fond of the lighting; real—from the hidden source, and symbolic—in the form of gilt bronze golden rays."

"That is all flattering, but as you can see, I felt more was needed. Remember, Teresa is experiencing a mystical experience—a transverberation—which is not only the most celebrated of her mystical experiences, you will remember it was cited in the Bull at her canonization."

"I'm not certain what you are saying."

"I'm saying I needed a visual device in the chapel to underscore the importance of this incomparable event. That is where your prestigious family came in. How many families can claim six- or was it seven?—Cardinals and a Doge of Venice? I don't know of any, do you?"

"Not really," the modest Cardinal replied.

"In any case, the family's placement was just as important as using them. That is, I wanted your family present, but I didn't want to detract from the emotional center of the chapel. That's why I seated the two centuries of your family on both sides of the chapel, discussing, meditating, reading and just looking around, but—and this is a major but—they cannot see the mystical experience."

"Because?"

"Because," Bernini said, "ordinary people—no matter how pious or gifted—cannot comprehend an apparition such as was occurring at that moment to Teresa. Your ancestors may have been God-Fearing, Holy Men of the Cloth, but Teresa was the Saint."

"I hate to break up this meeting gentlemen," the still good-looking Monsignor said, "but we shall be opening the church for Mass in a few minutes. "On behalf of all of us mere mortals who labor here, allow me to thank you both for bring something so beautiful and so moving into our daily lives."

The Cavaliere and the Cardinal tore themselves away from the chapel.

"I can tell you this, Monsignor," Cardinal Cornaro said as they walked down the aisle, "if the Good Lord hadn't presented a certain string of events, there would be no Cornaro chapel. I must be the luckiest, most blessed Cardinal alive."

"Lucky?" the Monsignor said. "What do you mean lucky?"

The Cardinal's expression showed he thought what he meant was obvious—he was, of course, too much of a gentleman to comment on that. Instead he said, "A brief window of opportunity opened between the time Innocent dismantled the Cavaliere's bell tower, and the time Innocent granted him the commission to design the Fountain in the Piazza Navona. I was lucky enough to slip into that open window."

The trio stood on the sidewalk and watch the faithful stream into the church. "Tell me," Cardinal Cornaro said, "what reactions have you had to my family's chapel?"

The Monsignor took his time responding; he was happy to have his parishioners see him talking with a Cardinal and a renowned artist. "It depends," he said. "The children and young people love the overall beauty of the chapel—especially the richly colored marbles. Their parents love the religiousness of the chapel. They tell their children how Teresa reformed the Carmelite Order of nuns, went barefoot to stress their poverty and founded 16 convents. What the young like best is when they hear that Teresa said 'God walks among the pots and pans'."

The trio shared a hearty laugh as the astonished faithful whispered to each other about their good luck in seeing two celebrities so early in the morning.

"The nobility and the clergy?" the Cardinal asked. "What do they say?"

"The nobility say they would die contented if they could have a chapel like this, designed by you, Cavaliere. A Prince said he thought you conceived the chapel as one huge painting in which you brought together all of the visual arts—they all use the term 'bel composto,' or beautiful whole. The clergy, they have flocked to see the chapel—as I said, everyone has—and they are the most overwhelmed. Since they all know Saint Teresa's writings intimately, they are in the best position to relate to the enormity of what you have accomplished here. Most of them say the chapel is exactly the kind of experience we are asked to summon up by Saint Ignatius in his Spiritual Exercises. Actually, overall, when any of the faithful gaze at the chapel, I sense they are having a religious experience of their own."

Bernini, who was content to listen to the raves about his latest project, couldn't help speaking up.

"I practice the principles of Saint Ignatius every day. I try to do what he proposed—that is, I try to picture each religious event in its setting and then see the image of the Holy Person, so I can confer with him or her."

"Cavaliere, you would have made a great clergyman," Cardinal Cornaro said, "although our gain would have been the artistic world's loss. I must say I am astounded, but delighted, the chapel I commissioned is having such a positive impact on all of the citizens of Rome. The 12,000 scudi it cost are surely the best monies I have ever spent."

—

Borromini felt he finally had the cause he was waiting for—the cost of Bernini's Cornaro Chapel in Santa Maria della Vittoria. He learned that the cost of the one chapel exceeded the cost of his entire church of San Carlino.

Happily, Francesco trumpeted the numbers all over the city. Sadly, he received absolutely no satisfaction—only apathy.

"So?" "Forget it." "Francesco, don't bother" "You're making a fool of yourself." "Stick to your work—you're a great architect." "You're comparing peaches and figs."

Chapter CX

Beyond Michelangelo

Bernini joined Cardinal Fabio Chigi in the Renaissance church of Santa Maria del Popolo. The Cavaliere and his friend were inspecting the Chigi family chapel and the Cardinal was disgusted by what he saw.

"When my ancestors commissioned this chapel from the great Raphael over 100 years ago, think of how proud everyone in the family must have been. In its present state I'm embarrassed to have my family's name attached to it."

GianLorenzo studied the Cardinal. *I like his looks—his upturned mustache and stripe of beard force one to look deep into his eyes, which always seem to be searching for something beautiful to look at. As a person he reminds me of Maffeo Barberini—he is sensitive and loves the arts, especially my work. I'm sure he's going to want me to remodel this chapel. I'm much too busy but I don't know how I can refuse.*

"Don't be so hard on yourself," Bernini said. "In all fairness to your prestigious ancestors, they have been living in Siena, and Siena is a long way from Rome."

"Well, I live in Rome now and something must be done. Compared to the Cerasi Chapel with its two marvelous paintings by Caravaggio, our chapel is a disaster. Will you help me? Please. Accept the commission to remodel the chapel."

Bernini had drifted off. *How often father would bring me to this lovely church. 'This was the first stained glass in Rome,' he told me once. God, I miss him.* "Father said his technique is called chiaroscuro. Or maybe it was my mentor, Maffeo Barberini, who first explained his use of hidden light. In any case, Caravaggio is definitely one of my idols. I regret that he died when I was so little—before I could meet him."

The Cardinal was incredulous. "Urban VIII? The Pope? He was your mentor? I understand he was an exceptional man. No wonder you are so well-mannered, not to mention learned and articulate."

"Your Eminence, you remind me of him. You are highly intelligent and educated and love scholars, writers and artists as much as he did. No wonder we have been such good friends for so long."

"This is quite a mutual admiration society," Cardinal Chigi said laughing. "What do you say, Cavaliere? Will you do it?"

"I don't know," Bernini said, pretending to be thinking about it. "Let me take stock of the situation. Raphael—he is one of my idols; Santa Maria del Popolo—this church is one of my favorites; and Fabio Chigi—you are one of my best friends."

The Cavaliere paused for effect.

"Not a very difficult decision, is it? For the moment I'm thinking of two major statutes or sculptural groups to compliment what we have here. Plus we'll need to rework the floor and . . ."

"GianLorenzo," Cardinal Chigi said, "you have made me very happy. I won't forget it."

Chapter CXI

Cardinal d'Este arrived at Bernini's workshop where GianLorenzo awaited him.

"Welcome, Your Eminence," Bernini said. "It's a pleasure and honor to meet you." *He's a distinguished looking man with that shock of white hair. I understand he's from a noble family and yet he arrived on time for our meeting. This man bears watching.* "Please join me in the library where you will be much more comfortable."

"The pleasure is mine," the Cardinal said. He sipped on the vin santo and nibbled politely on one of Caterina's biscotti. "I love your studio, Cavaliere. Frankly, it's nothing like I thought it would be."

"Dare I ask what you expected?" Bernini replied. *I'll wager he assumed the place would be a madhouse—the common perception of artist's workshops, especially among the upper classes.*

"I thought I'd find total chaos there. Instead, everything, and everybody, seemed to be completely organized. I thought the sculptors would be screaming at each other. Instead, they were all hard at work."

"People say we are the busiest studio in Rome, and, of course, we all take our work seriously. Now, sir, what can I do for you?"

"Cavaliere, I am here on behalf of my brother, Francesco I, Duke of Modena. He has authorized me to commission you to sculpt his portrait bust. I've brought a triptych you can work from."

—

"Cardinal d'Este, I'm flattered that you are interested in my work. However, unless the Duke is prepared to come to Rome—which he apparently is not—I fear I must regretfully decline. I've made it a policy not to carve a bust unless I can see the subject in person, and, also regretfully, I am much too busy to go to Modena. I hope you understand."

"I am prepared to offer you 3,000 scudi, all in advance. You probably know that Algardi receives only 150 scudi for his portrait busts—not that I would use him."

If this gentleman thinks a cheap reference to my rival will goad me into agreeing, he's dead wrong. "That is most generous, but money is not the issue." Bernini said this in a tone that indicated the conference was over.

The Cardinal, who loved to gamble, was enjoying this high-stakes game with the greatest artist alive. *Just as I suspected, this Bernini is a real competitor. Time to play my trump card.* "Cavaliere, I realize my brother is only a Duke, not a King or Prime Minister."

Bernini blushed. *How did he know about the busts of Charles I and Cardinal Richelieu?*

"Urban was instrumental in those commissions," the Cavaliere said lamely.

"Yes, indeed," the shrewd Cardinal replied. "And I understand your newly-minted patron, Innocent X, is anxious to have the goodwill of the Dukedom of Modena. Perhaps you would care to check with the Holy Father. We can ride to the palace together."

Jockeying for time to think, Bernini pretended he was studying the triple portrait Cardinal d'Este had brought with him. The Cardinal, who knew he had won, fought back a smile.

"That won't be necessary," Bernini finally said. *My relationship with Innocent is fragile enough without this. Besides, what's the point of fighting a losing battle?* "I have an idea. You live in Rome. If you are willing to work closely with me as I carve your brother's bust, advising me regularly on the likeness, I will accept the commission. We can start with the triptych, which, after all, was my only source in the other two busts you mentioned."

"Cavaliere," the Cardinal said without a hint of bravado, "you are most gracious."

—

Caterina studied the bust of Francesco I, Duke of Modena, while her husband waited anxiously for her verdict. "I can't believe one year has passed so quickly," she said. "It seems like Cardinal d' Este was here only yesterday."

"Fourteen months," GianLorenzo laughed, "but who's counting. So what do you think?"

"Why are you worried about my opinion? All of your friends in the nobility have been raving about the bust, and sending their friends to see it before you ship it to Modena. They all absolutely love it and you know it."

"I know, I know," Bernini said. "The nobility love the bust because the Duke appears so noble. I did that on purpose—meaning, when I sculpt a portrait, I look for the nobility in the subject; the details and human flaws don't interest me. Why? Because no one is perfect—except you, of course, my dear."

Caterina blew her husband a kiss. "Of course. Here's what's interesting to me. More than one of the visitors has said the real Francesco d'Este is a weak, irresponsible man and you did the Duke a major favor by investing him with the essence of nobility in your bust."

"Good," the Cavaliere said. "Think about it. The Duke of Modena is in total control of his life and his subjects, so why wouldn't I want to convey that in the cold, hard marble? That is why I placed his head in that decisive pose and added that mass of hair and that billowing drapery. And now that you know my tricks, sweetheart, tell me what you think. You know how highly I value your opinion."

Caterina threw her arms around her husband and squeezed him as hard as she possibly could. *I heard all great artists have a certain amount of insecurity in them, and the greater the artist, the greater the insecurity. I guess it's true.* "Oh stop, darling," she said. "The bust is spectacular and you know it. In fact, it is probably the best portrait you have ever carved—of course I've never seen that bust of Costanza you gave your friend in Florence."

Bernini was astounded. *I cannot believe Caterina said that without any rancor. She is one remarkable woman and I am the world's luckiest man to have married her.* "I love you, Caterina," GianLorenzo said. He smothered his wife with kisses. "Now let's go to Mass and thank God for his blessings."

Chapter CXII

"Virgilio," Borromini said, "where you been? I'm going to explode if I don't hear the answer. Why are you so late?"

Cardinal Spada sat at the table and ordered a coffee from the waiter. He glanced around the Piazza del Popolo—the square was filled with people, but the large terrace of the trattoria was almost deserted. *Why does everything with this man have to be a project?*

"As I calculate it," the Cardinal said, "I am no more than five minutes late."

"It seemed like an hour. Don't keep me in suspense, what did the Holy Father say?"

Spada sighed. *I feel like a nagging wife—sometimes it seems like all I ever do is bring him bad news.* "Sorry, Francesco. His Holiness said no. I tried, but the answer is no. He will not commission a church across from the Quirinal Palace. I truly am sorry."

Borromini slumped in his chair. "Did he say why? It can't be the design. I designed a perfect church."

"The Holy Father had no quarrel with your design. What he said was your proposed church was too large for the site."

"I don't believe that for a minute. My church sits on that site like it was made for it. Virgilio, you know I have the ability to work in crowded urban spaces and still have the project make sense. Look at San Carlino."

"I know that, Francesco, and I told Innocent that. I also told him how much time and effort you put into this project. I even said you would modify the design to make it pleasing to him. But none of it made a difference. Truthfully, I doubt any size church on that site would be acceptable to him."

Borromini sat up in his chair. "It must be something else—something stupid like he doesn't want the view from his bedroom disturbed. Something stupid like that."

Spada winced. *Francesco may be the most unstable artist I've ever worked with, but besides being talented, he is smart—I wonder how he figured this one out. Maybe it was just a lucky guess.*

"No, no, I'm positive it's nothing like that."

Borromini pushed the table back and got up. *This is a disaster. I've got to get out of here before I do something foolish.* "I thought you said Innocent X was my patron and he favored me."

"I did and he does."

"I shudder to think what he might do if he hated me. I'm going."

―

"Francesco, hold on. The Holy Father doesn't hate you, and to prove it he sends his warm regards and an extremely prestigious commission."

"I'm sure."

"No really," the Cardinal replied. "Now sit down and listen to me. Innocent has fired the Rainaldi's, father and son, from the Sant' Agnese in Agone job. That's the Pope's family church, you know."

"Why did he fire them? Do you know?"

"Francesco, sometimes you tax me to the limit. Of course I know; I'm the Pope's Artistic Advisor. If you don't mind, I'd prefer not discussing our disagreements with the Rainaldi's—let's just say there were serious artistic differences."

"Will wonders never cease? You mean I'm not the only artist in Rome to have artistic differences with his patron? Well, well, well. Who is His Holiness commissioning to finish the job?"

"You, Francesco. That's the good news I saved until last."

Borromini jumped out of his chair. "Thanks but no thanks. Not interested."

―

Incensed, Cardinal Spada pushed the much larger and stronger Borromini back into his chair.

"You can't say that," he said, using every ounce of energy to keep from raising his voice in public. "I fought to have you hired and now you're not interested. Are you out of your mind? What are you thinking?"

Borromini sank in his chair. *I might as well tell him the truth—what's the difference?* "I can't bear the thought of looking at that fountain every day. When I worked on the Pamphili Palace I could sneak in the side entrance. That fountain should have been my commission—I brought the water to Piazza Navona. That Bernini fellow always takes advantage of me. Now, are you satisfied?"

"Francesco," Spada said, "sometimes I want to kiss you and sometimes I want to kill you. Today I could kill you. First of all, you were paid handsomely for bringing the water in. Secondly, even you have to admit Bernini's Fountain of the Four Rivers is a brilliant piece of architecture."

"I absolutely do not admit that. Besides, if I'm working so near it, I'm afraid the obelisk will fall and crush me to death some day when I'm not looking."

"Come on, my friend. You yourself admitted the obelisk seems to defy gravity but is firmly secured—cleverly, but firmly secured."

"Anything else?"

"Yes there is," Virgilio said. "Francesco, I say this with complete confidence. If I am forced to tell the Holy Father you rejected the commission to take charge of building his family's personal church, you will never, ever, receive another papal commission. Never. Ever."

"Maybe some other Pope will grant me one."

"Francesco, how old are you?"

"Fifty-four. Why?"

"In those fifty-four years, how many Popes have granted you papal commissions?"

Borromini gulped and mumbled, almost inaudibly, "One"

"Whose name is?"

"Innocent X."

Cardinal Spada smiled broadly. "Any questions? I must be going. Meet me at Sant' Agnese tomorrow morning, about ten. We need to make some critical decisions."

—

Cardinal Spada and Borromini stood in front of the partially built church of Sant' Agnese in Agone.

"Now that I've looked their work over closely," Borromini said, "I can see why there were artistic differences with the Rainaldi's. What a mess."

"Would you care to be more specific or do you want to analyze the situation further before you decide what you want to recommend?"

"Yes and no. Yes, I want more time to think through the interior, but no, I can tell you right now what needs to be done with the façade and the entire exterior."

The Cardinal could barely contain his excitement. "Tell me, tell me. I'm dying to hear."

At this point, Borromini was all business. "Start with these stairs jutting into the piazza. I can't imagine what they were thinking, but the stairs are totally inappropriate and must be torn down. As soon as possible."

"Yes, yes. We are in total agreement with that. What about the façade?"

"The façade is all wrong—for the church and for the piazza. It is too square. The entire façade must be town down. As soon as possible."

"You see, Francesco, there are times I want to kiss you,"

Chapter CXIII

Beyond Michelangelo

Caterina and GianLorenzo stood in the Piazza Navona, looking at the fountain directly in front of the Pamphili family palace.

"What are you planning to do to della Porta's fountain?" she asked.

The Cavaliere looked at his wife with eyes filled with love. "I almost said I'm surprised you know Giacomo della Porta originally designed this fountain, but the longer I'm married to you my dear, the more I realize you are not only the most beautiful woman and mother in Rome, you are also the smartest. To answer your question, I plan to make small changes to what he originally did, but my main idea, which Innocent has approved, is a centerpiece of a Triton . . ."

"Hold it. Stop right there. Did you say Triton, as in the Triton Fountain in the Piazza Barberini? Is this the same Pope who drove the Barberini out of Rome and tore down your beautiful bell tower at Saint Peter's because you were an intimate of the Barberini?"

"What's your point, sweetheart?"

"Isn't it obvious? Innocent has approved a Triton for a centerpiece of the fountain in front of his family's palace while a Triton is the centerpiece of a fountain honoring the Barberini in front of their palace. How do you account for this incredible switch in the Holy Father's attitude?"

"Simple," Bernini said. "For the same reason you married me—I'm loveable."

"Stop that, I'm serious."

"You have maintained it consistently—sooner or later my talent will overcome everybody and everything you said. Well, Innocent may have many faults—he's parsimonious, cranky and mistrustful—but he's no fool. He wanted the most talented artist in Rome to design the fountains in front of his church and palace. Wouldn't you?"

Caterina gave her husband a big hug and kiss. *It sounds better when I say it, but I guess when you tell the truth, it's not bragging.* "What is this Triton going to look like?"

"He will be in the center of the pool, of course. He'll be over life-size, contra-posed, straddling a fish's open mouth. The fish's open mouth will spurt water."

"Sounds good, but what will the Triton look like?"

I might as well admit it. "A Moor. Don't look so surprised—when you talk, my precious one, I listen. Fortunately, the sketches I showed the Holy Father showed no detail. Yes, this Triton is going to look like a Moor and nothing like the other Triton. The people of Rome call the Barberini fountain the Triton Fountain. I hope they will call this one the Fountain of the Moor."

—

"Darling," Caterina said as they climbed into their carriage. "If you are so loveable, why did Innocent commission Francesco Borromini to replace the Rainaldi's and finish his church? You know, Sant' Agnese in Agone, the church we're looking at. The church facing your Fountain of the Four Rivers. That church, right there."

"Sweetheart, I only said the Pope was no fool, I didn't say he was perfect."

Chapter CXIV

Bernini sat with Innocent in the Pope's study. Much to his surprise, he was enjoying his weekly suppers with this Pope, although they were not nearly as stimulating or educational as those with the previous Popes. He studied the Holy Father who had momentarily dozed off. *He looks frail, and every bit his eighty years. I guess the problems with the Turks have taken their toll.*

The pontiff woke up, looked around, and spoke, slowly and cautiously. "Cavaliere, Donna Olimpia brought up something last night I want to get your opinion on. She thought it would be good for my image if there were a statute of the Emperor Constantine in my beloved Saint Peter's. She felt symbolically tying the Pamphili to the man who built the original basilica some 1,300 years ago would be a strong political move. What do you think?"

"A brilliant idea, Your Holiness. Have you discussed it with Cardinal Spada?"

"Not yet, but Virgilio always agrees with whatever Donna Olimpia says. He's not dumb. *Spada also always agrees with what I say, but I trust him as much as I trust a coiled rattlesnake.* What say you, Cavaliere? How would you present Constantine?"

"That's easy, Holy Father. I would capture Constantine at the beginning of the crucial battle for control of Rome, at the moment he sees the apparition—the Cross, and the words In Hoc Signo Vinces (With This Sign You Shall Conquer)—in the sky above him."

"Excellent. What else?"

"Constantine should be astride his horse, ready for battle. I would portray the Emperor mute, awe-struck by the apparition, but his horse should be neighing wildly, rearing on his hind legs. The juxtaposition would be spectacular."

"Isn't that the reverse of equestrian monuments one sees?"

Maybe this Pope isn't as ignorant regarding artistic matters as most people think. "That is correct, Holy Father. As I said, the juxtaposition would be spectacular. Remember, this is a key moment in history—the dramatic moment Christianity was allowed to be practiced throughout the land. After all, that is the essence of what happened when Constantine saw the apparition."

Chapter CXV

Beyond Michelangelo

Cardinal Spada was worried as he approached the Quirinal Palace. *Only two nights to Christmas. We're all so busy at this time of the year it's an unusual night for a private dinner.*

"Virgilio," Innocent said, "what I have to say will only take a few minutes and then I must get some rest. I'm getting on, but before I am called, I must say to you what I have lately been saying to myself. I have already discussed this matter with my confessor."

Cardinal Spada smiled weakly, achieving only limited success in fighting off the panic he felt. *Never has Innocent talked to me like this. What can he be talking about?*

The Pope continued. "You have served me well, Virgilio, but in reviewing my pontificate in my mind, I calculate that you hurried me into making three decisions that I regret. Of the three, the decision I regret the most is the one I made to tear down Bernini's magnificent bell tower at Saint Peter's."

Spada relaxed. *I should be able to talk my way out of this.* "Holy Father, I..."

"No need for you to speak. Don't worry, except for my confessor, I have not discussed this matter with the Cavaliere or anyone else. Nor will I. I mention it to you because I fear the end is near and I want to unburden myself of this terrible guilt."

"But, Your Holiness, what do you feel guilty about?"

"I feel guilty because Bernini convinced me with hard evidence that his south bell tower was not unduly causing the cracks in the basilica, that the cracks which did occur were merely normal settling."

"Exactly," Cardinal Spada said with élan, "that's exactly what I testified at the hearings."

"Don't insult me, Virgilio. I may be old but I still have my faculties. Do you think I have forgotten that you privately urged me to tear down the bell tower? I assumed at the time you testified as you did because you were anxious to maintain the good graces of the Cavaliere for your own purposes."

"You are an astute leader, Your Holiness."

"But, I am being too harsh on you. I must accept full blame. Even though I secretly admired the design of the towers—plus I thought they were going to put Maderno's façade into proper proportion—I ordered the demolition for one reason and one reason only. Hatred. I committed the sin of hatred. Hatred of the Barberini and their coterie. Yes, I allowed hate to control me for quite some time. I believe I redeemed myself eventually, but I fear future generations will be harsh on the Pamphili Pope for dismantling Bernini's bell towers out of sheer hatred. Goodnight, Virgilio, I am tired."

Cardinal Spada was thinking fast. *This idea is so sensational, it may become a standard.* "May I make a suggestion, Holy Father?"

"Make it fast."

"Why don't we destroy everything and anything that relates to Bernini's bell towers? That way, history will never know about your decision."

"Virgilio," Innocent said, as he slowly arose from the table, "you are a brilliant man and an astute politician. But in this case, I am going to assume you are joking. Goodnight."

—

Nine days later, on January 1st, 1655, after serving eleven years as Pope Innocent X, Gianbattista Pamphili died."

—

When Bernini heard the news, he was ambivalent about the matter. Caterina understood.

—

Borromini was shocked to see Cardinal Spada standing at the front door of his house. *Close as we have been, Virgilio has never come to my home.* "Virgilio, what's wrong? Are you sick?"

"Innocent died earlier today, Francesco. My friend and protector and your patron is dead."

Borromini stared at his shoes. *Some patron. He could have done so much more for me.*

"Why are you so quiet," Spada asked.

"I was thinking how lucky I was to receive his papal commission to finish Sant' Agnese in Agone before he died. And, how smart I was to listen to you and accept the commission."

"Francesco, sit down. Please. I have some bad news. Innocent's nephew, Prince Camillo Pamphili, has been put in charge of the project."

"So what? Why should I care who is in charge? I don't."

"You should, because the Prince has ordered an immediate halt to all work on Sant' Agnese."

Borromini slumped in his chair, then jumped up and grabbed one of his swords. He threw it out a window, shattering it. Then he threw his chair out an adjoining window. Then he sat on the floor, took stock of the situation, and cried.

"I hope you realize the progress I've made on the church," the heart broken architect said. "The façade is almost complete and so is the dome—except for the lantern. In the interior, I've made the four main piers more important, and I'm up to the capitals on the columns and pilasters. But nobody cares, do they? Prince Camillo. I haven't met him, what's he like?"

Cardinal Virgilio Spada's sigh could be heard all the way on the other side of the Tiber River—at least, that's what it sounded like to Borromini.

"I'll put it this way, Francesco. The Prince is presently arguing with Donna Olimpia about who should pay for Innocent's casket."

Chapter CXVI

Beyond Michelangelo

Dear Jules (that was not easy to write):

Extremely busy, including the restoration of the Chigi Chapel in Santa Maria del Popolo for my dear friend Cardinal Fabio Chigi. I'm not sure if you've met him but he is a wonderful man who reminds me of Maffeo Barberini. I hear he's one of the serious contenders at the conclave presently underway. In my opinion, Cardinal Chigi would make an outstanding Pope and here's why. He is a modest man of keen intellect and humanist learning but he also has profound piety. Needless to say, I like the fact that he is a friend of cultured persons and possesses boundless moral integrity. On the secular side, he has considerable diplomatic experience. I remember you told me you were upset with him because of his anti-French stance at the time of the Treaty of Westphalia, but in fairness to him, you must remember he was merely following Innocent's orders, who, as you well know, favored the Spanish. Enough about that—papal politics is your forte, not mine. Caterina and the children are all fine. Must run. In usual hurry. GianLorenzo.

P.S. In my rush, I almost forgot why I was writing. Thank you for your latest invitation to live in France on the usual lavish terms—actually, I expected your letter when Innocent died. Your point about not knowing who will be the next Pope is well taken, but at this stage in my life (can you believe I'm 57 years young?) Caterina has convinced me not to worry about details like that. Not that she's saying who will be Pope is a detail. She's just saying my reputation is so strong at this point, even if I don't receive papal commissions, I'll receive all the private ones I can handle. As you can see, my darling wife has given me a much healthier outlook on life. So, my friend, as you have guessed, much as I'd like to see you, my answer is no. Why don't you come home to Rome and eat some decent food? Are they using knives and forks in France yet? GL

Chapter CXVII

The Sistine Chapel was hot, humid and crowded, and the sixty-six Cardinals who were gathered to elect the successor to Innocent X were getting edgier by the day.

"Being locked-up in this small room is one thing," a French Cardinal said, "but the air is so foul I fear we're going to lose more and more of our colleagues. If you Spaniards hadn't blocked Cardinal Sacchetti, we could be home by now—and our three deceased colleagues would undoubtedly still be with us."

The Spanish contingent rose as one and glared at the French, who were already standing and glaring.

"It's your fault—you and your fellow Frenchmen," one of the Spanish Cardinals said in emotional reply. "If you French had any backbones, you would vote your conscience instead of waiting for Cardinal Mazarin's instructions from Paris."

"Gentlemen, gentlemen," the chairman said. "Please. We must keep this most important work on a civilized basis. Now, since the death of Cardinal Carafa, it seems most of you favor either Cardinal Giulio Sacchetti or Cardinal Fabio Chigi. Let us take one more ballot before supper to see if we can break the deadlock."

Some days later, the conclave heard a most unusual announcement from the chair.

"Gentlemen, please settle down and be quiet. Our esteemed brother, Cardinal Sacchetti, wishes to address the conclave."

The weary group quickly fell silent, trying, to no avail, to read their colleague's face and demeanor.

"Friends," Cardinal Sacchetti said, "and you all are my friends, I was pleased to learn that a number of you have received letters from Cardinal Mazarin."

Everyone in the room glowered at the French Cardinals, who were, to a man, studiously examining the figures on Michelangelo's ceiling, as if they'd never seen them before.

Sacchetti continued. "I have seen the contents of the letter and consequently I inform you, with every ounce of humility I can muster, that I am no longer willing to stand for the exalted position of Pontifex Maximus."

What the Cardinal didn't say was that he wrote Mazarin and urged him to deliver the French vote to his rival, Fabio Chigi—which Mazarin did. Bernini's recommendation, of course, was also a major factor in Mazarin's decision.

The Cardinals sat in stunned silence, overcome by this unexpected turn of events. After taking several seconds to absorb the dramatic news, the Cardinals all began talking at once. Cardinal Sacchetti raised his hands, signaling he was not finished speaking.

"I wish to thank all of you who believed in me sufficiently to cast your votes in my behalf. Now, however, I urge you to join me as I cast my vote for Cardinal Chigi. In addition, I strongly recommend a unanimous ballot as a sign of love and respect for our Most Holy Colleague."

The Cardinals burst into applause and surrounded the newly elected Pope, shaking his hand and hitting him on the back.

The vote was unanimous, except for the one cast by Cardinal Chigi, who voted for Cardinal Sacchetti. Everyone later agreed that the unpretentious Fabio Chigi—who would serve as Alexander VII—would never have voted for himself, even if the rules had allowed it.

Chapter CXVIII

Bernini walked through the papal palace, and although every man who worked in the building recognized him, he didn't recognize one person. *Ah, the vicissitudes of life.*

"Welcome, Cavaliere," the papal secretary said. "Go right in. The Holy Father is looking forward to meeting with you." GianLorenzo walked briskly across the papal office, bowed and kissed the new Pope's ring. *It's amazing—I never noticed how much he looks like Maffeo, except his nose is sharper and his ears are slightly bigger.*

"Cavaliere," Alexander VII said, "you were very gracious to put aside your work and come here today. I couldn't permit my first day as Pope to pass without meeting with you because we have much work to do and I don't want to waste a moment. First, Saint Peter's. I'd like you to think about two areas—the vast area in front of the basilica, and the apse. Those two commissions will be forthcoming, but for now, tell me how my family's chapel is coming along."

"I have started carving two groups to fill two of the empty niches. David in the Lion's Den, and Habbakuk with an Angel."

"Excellent. Now that I am in a position to do it, I wish to extend your commission to restore our chapel to include the entire church. Both the inside and the façade."

"A real honor, Your Holiness. I have always loved that ancient church; it's a trove of artistic treasures." *If only father could witness this commission—he loved Santa Maria del Popolo almost as much as I do.*

—

The Pope continued. "On another subject, Her Royal Majesty, Queen Christina of Sweden, is moving to Rome toward the end of the year. Before she arrives, I wish you to renovate the gate through which she will enter the city—the Porta del Popolo. Also, I'd like you to design a ceremonial carriage for her. It's important that the Queen make a triumphant entrance because the world will be watching to see how we treat this famous convert. If you analyze the matter, you will realize her importance to the Church cannot be overstated: Not only did she lose her throne when she converted to Catholicism, her father, King

Gustavus Adolphus, was the Protestant leader who ravaged much of Europe in the Thirty Years War."

Bernini smiled. *Obviously, the Queen's conversion is a valuable propaganda tool for the Catholic Church.* "Holy Father, you can be sure I will do my part to make the Queen's entry into Rome spectacular."

Chapter CXIX

"I'm afraid I'm late," the friar said to the sergeant-at-arms. "Getting through that crowd at the parade wasn't easy. Is this the right place? Where the Commission is considering the charges against Francesco Borromini?"

"Yes it's the right place and no, you're not late," the official replied. "The Commission is expected to bring forth its ruling shortly. Take any chair you choose."

The friar sat and looked around the small, highly decorated room. *I'm surprised there aren't more people here—I think that Cardinal and I are the only visitors. Hold on, that gentleman looks familiar.* The friar walked over to the other spectator.

"Aren't you the famous Cardinal Spada?" he asked.

The Cardinal beamed from ear to ear: Nobody liked being called famous more than Virgilio Spada. "Yes. Yes, indeed. May I help you?"

"I thought I recognized you, Your Eminence. Please don't think me bold but I'm a friend of Borromini's, as I know you are. I'm not really a friend, as such, but merely an ex-patron."

"Of course," the embarrassed Cardinal said. "I recognize you now—Juan San Bonaventura, Head of the Order of Trinitarians. Francesco designed your San Carlino and its cloister. I hold them close to my heart because they were my introduction to Francesco's extraordinary, revolutionary talent. Please, sit and tell me why you are here."

"Our Order is so pleased with the work Borromini performed for us," the padre replied, "we want to help him in any way we can. When the brothers heard about his problems with Prince Pamphili, we met, and I was authorized to come here to see if there was anything the Order could do to help him."

"I don't think so," Cardinal Spada replied. He was touched by the obvious sincerity of the Spanish cleric. "Even if you had been here earlier they would not have allowed you to testify—unfortunately this inquiry relates only to the situation at Sant' Agnese, not to what he did at your marvelous little church so many years ago."

—

The sergeant-at-arms pounded his staff signaling all should rise. A solemn-looking, elderly gentleman entered the room.

"That's the Hearing Officer," Spada explained.

"Where is Borromini? Is he here?"

As if on cue, two men entered the room from a side door. One was an eager young soldier who was trying his best, but failing, to look official. The man he was escorting into the room was an older man who was clearly doing his best to maintain his dignity—he was also hardly succeeding.

Father Bonaventura crossed himself. "I can't believe my eyes."

Cardinal Spada looked away. "Yes, Francesco has slipped a little."

"A little? I didn't recognize our Borromini. Those clothes, that beard—he looks like a bum, although I've heard he has plenty of money. And his demeanor. What has happened to him? He looks like a defeated man, not like one of Rome's best architects, which our Order considers him to be."

Virgilio was pleased that Francesco showed a flicker of recognition to him, but was distressed that the architect looked right past the padre. *His favorite patron and he didn't even recognize him. How sad.*

"A good part of the problem," Cardinal Spada said, "is Francesco's basic disposition. He has always bit a bit moody and irascible—actually, more than a bit—but those of us who are his ardent supporters have always overlooked his faults and concentrated on his awesome talent. After all, everyone has faults but few have his abilities. Unfortunately, however, the man has changed considerably over the years."

"In ways other than his appearance?"

"Tragically, yes." *No use trying to hide the truth—it is common knowledge in my circles.* "It's becoming impossible to even discuss projects with him much less get him to pay attention to his work."

That makes no sense to me. Can we be talking about the same man? "But, Your Eminence, for us Borromini could not have been more alert. He cared about the job, he related to the workmen, and he paid attention to every detail."

"I know—you told me so at the time. Remember when I asked for a recommendation? He has drifted from those heights to his present depths—that's what makes his near total disintegration so sad. How did this calamity occur? As his principle patron, I know Francesco better than anyone, so naturally, I am fully aware of the cause of Francesco's decline before our very eyes—but the truth is so absurd, it's painful for me to discuss."

"Absurd? The truth is absurd? Your Eminence, that is a heavy word."

"Heavy or light, absurd is the correct word." *I've gone this far; I might as well keep going.* "It's Bernini."

Disbelief slowly spread over the padre's face as the Cardinal's remark sunk in.

"You heard correctly," Virgilio continued. "The cause of his downward spiral is none other than Cavaliere GianLorenzo Bernini."

Father Bonaventura was totally confused. "How could Bernini cause this disaster? I don't understand."

Cardinal Spada studied Borromini across the room. The architect was staring straight ahead, his face expressionless. "The jealousy started, I believe, years ago when Bernini receive the baldacchino commission instead of Carlo Maderno."

"Stop there. Why would that make any difference to Borromini?"

"Good question. This occurred before I met Francesco, so I need to guess. As Maderno's prodigy, perhaps he felt he would play a major role in the construction of the baldacchino if Carlo received the commission. Or, perhaps, since Francesco is so principled, he rebelled at the young Bernini taking the work away from the elderly Maderno—who, after all, was Architect of Saint Peter's at the time. On the other hand, maybe it started when Maderno died and Bernini, not Francesco, was appointed Architect of the Barberini Palace and Saint Peter's."

"Did Borromini think he should have been appointed to those positions?"

"Absolutely—he has brought that up to me numerous times. In any case, apparently things went from bad to worse. Francesco told me he was forced to work for Bernini on the baldacchino and Barberini Palace jobs and he resented that. Worse, he said his contributions were not appreciated and, in fact, his work was co-opted by Bernini. Plus, he saw Bernini getting rich and Francesco felt the Cavaliere was underpaying him and even stealing what should have been his money. Of course, I'm not certain of all this because these things happened before I met him."

"But, Your Eminence, what I don't understand is, if all of these things are true, why didn't he fall apart sooner? Excuse me, I should phrase that another way. Why was Borromini's work and attitude so outstanding when he worked for us? After all, everything you just described occurred prior to his coming to work for us."

This Spaniard isn't as dumb as I thought. "Good point. I would guess he was so thrilled and overcome with joy by the way you and your brothers treated him—he talked about it all the time—he pushed those evil thoughts about Bernini to the back of his mind. The point is, since creating your masterpiece, Francesco has slowly fallen apart, bit by bit. Oh, he has done some marvelous work, but nothing has come easy. Over the years, I watched in horror as he attacked Bernini every chance he could. Unfortunately for Francesco, his attacks all failed and, naturally, that added to his frustration. With the exception of the bell towers, of course, where he, almost single handedly, convinced Innocent X to tear down Bernini's masterpiece. I tried to convince His Holiness that the minor settling was normal—I even testified in that regard—but Borromini, and subsequently Innocent, were determined. It seemed like the more Francesco thought about Bernini, the more argumentative he became—it was as if he transferred his attitude and mind-set about Bernini to his patrons. In fact, Francesco's ultimate act of absurdity was when he killed that man at the Lateran. I truly believe Francesco was so frustrated, he had delusions it was Bernini he was beating to death. If that isn't an absurd rivalry, I don't know what is."

Father Bonaventura was stunned. "Where have I been? I swear to you, I didn't know anything about this. I have been in the Cavaliere's company many, many times over the years and I never heard one negative word from Bernini's mouth—about Borromini or anyone else."

"I think that was also a major problem—Francesco resents the fact that Bernini has ignored him over the years. Worse of all, he just hasn't been able to handle Bernini's incredible fame and good fortune. Lord knows I tried to help Francesco keep Bernini in perspective, but it was like talking to a brick wall. I ask you, is anything more pathetic—or absurd—than a one sided rivalry? You see the results before you."

—

The Hearing Officer finished reading from a report and called for quiet.

"Please stand, Borromini. This Inquiry has been held regarding your work for the past several years at Sant' Agnese in Agone. To summarize, you have been charged with not paying the workers, seldom visiting the workplace, and committing numerous architectural faults and mistakes. Prince Camillo Pamphili has brought the charges. The commission has weighed the evidence, both for and against you, and is ready to sentence you. Do you wish to make a final plea in your own behalf?"

Borromini shrugged.

"Does that mean yes or no?"

"No."

"Very well. As head of this Commission, I have been instructed to dismiss you as Architect of the church of Sant' Agnese in Agone."

"You can't dismiss me," Borromini said.

"Don't make this any more difficult than it is," the Hearing Officer said. "This is hurting us as much as it hurts you."

"Isn't that a shame?" Borromini flashed a smile, which surprised everyone. "Allow me to ease your pain. You can't dismiss me because I quit. I resign the commission. I disavow it. I relinquish it. I leave it. In other words, I abdicate. Feel better now?"

—

Borromini sat slumped in a chair. When he saw Cardinal Spada he smiled. "Nice party, eh Virgilio?"

"I have one of your patrons with me. Remember Father Bonaventura? You told me how much you liked those people—the Trinitarians."

Borromini studied the padre for several minutes. As recognition set in, he tried to jump out of his chair to shake the hand of his ex-patron. Too weak, he fell back and smiled.

"Padre—it's you. You, and now the men at the university, you are my favorites. You had the good sense to stay away from me while I was working for you."

Borromini pointed to his clothes. "Do you like my Spanish outfit, padre? Black's a fitting color for today, don't you think?"

Chapter CXX

Nick J. Mileti

TO: Mister Angelo Morisini
        Stockholm, Sweden

Dear Angelo:

I hope you haven't been worried about me but my schedule has been hectic. I arrived safe and sound in Rome on December 20. That's December 20 of this year—1655. When you bid me your secret good-by in Sweden, summer before last, did you ever dream the trip would take over 1 ½ years? Naturally, there were good reasons for extending my trip.

Since I arrived several days before the ceremonies planned for my official entrance, I was escorted by papal representatives (who met me at the border) to the Vatican palace. Believe it or not, I remained in the Vatican as a guest—in a special apartment prepared for my use—for three days, waiting for the scheduled procession. I say believe it or not because I'm told it is unprecedented for a woman to be so honored. The newish Pope, Alexander VII, has extended every courtesy to me. He is also a friend of artists and scholars so we had instant rapport.

I have been presented with numerous gifts, all of which are beautiful, but the most impressive gift was a spectacular carriage and six white horses. The carriage is covered in silver and has finely carved decorations—including my family's arms and other heraldic motifs—and silver statuettes. Inside, it is lined with sky-blue velvet and silver braid. It is the most beautiful carriage I have ever seen.

Cavaliere GianLorenzo Bernini designed the carriage. We studied drawings and sketches of his works—remember? Well, they don't do justice to the real thing. You should come to Rome. I grant you the trip is arduous, but it's worth it if only to see Bernini's sculptural pieces in the Villa Borghese and his baldacchino (canopy to you) in Saint Peter's basilica (church). I don't know if the baldacchino is sculpture or architecture, but it's an incredible work of art. Only the Pope may say Mass at the High Altar it covers.

This Bernini is quite a fellow. I knew of his artistic talents, of course, everyone does, but I had no idea how sophisticated and charming he is. He is a gracious and learned man who can speak on any subject, but, thankfully, is not a snob. He also has a wonderful sense of humor. Example: I was taken to meet the Cavaliere (as he is often called) at his workshop in his palazzo (palace). He greeted me dressed in the heavy rough garment he wears when cutting marble, and he said, "Because I know you to be a serious student of artistic matters, I consider this the most worthy garment in which to receive you." Naturally I understood exactly what he meant so I reached out and touched the garment. Angelo, I wish you could have been here to observe the moment. It was electric. I don't mean sexually, I mean on a higher level. At that moment, it was as if we were one—and the feeling has existed ever since. Another example: When I told Bernini I thought the carriage was beautiful, he coyly replied, "I claim only credit for its faults." I laughed and said, "Then none of it is yours." That gives you an idea of the civilized repartee we enjoy.

I rode in the carriage in my entry procession. The Pope declared the day a public holiday and I believe every citizen of Rome turned out to see what the ex-Queen of Sweden looks like. These Italians love parades, spectacles and the like, and what a procession it was. I was told later that my procession was grander than any possesso (a parade commemorating a Pope's election), which is an astounding fact considering the importance of those cavalcades.

I love my life here in Rome. It's the center of the art world, of course, but even the scientists are starting to move here from Northern Italy, particularly Tuscany. I'm in the process of gathering the most important men of letters and artists into my circle, and am in the process of establishing a literary and scientific society.

I was going to tell you about the time I dined publicly with the Pope and his court but my housekeeper has just informed me my visitor has arrived. It's Bernini's wife, Caterina, who is a delight. She is considerably younger than the Cavaliere but she is wise beyond her years. She and GianLorenzo (as she calls him) are very much in love and have a large and beautiful family. By the way, not surprisingly, Caterina is also a cultivated lady. I don't want to keep her waiting, plus I don't want the biscotti (Italian cookies) to get cold. Caterina is a wonderful cook and baker; in fact, from what I can see, all women in Italy cook well—the food is much tastier than what we get in Sweden.

A few quick facts about the banquet. A man important in the Jesuit Order—a Father Oliva, who is a close friend of Bernini's—preached a sermon, and sacred music was performed. I sat in a special chair the Cavaliere designed, and tried to eat one of the miniature sculptures called 'trionfi' that adorned the tables. They are made out of sugar and then painted and gilded—they are inedible and are only for decoration, but who knew? You probably won't believe this but Bernini also designed the 'trionfi.' Is there anything this gentleman can't do? I don't think so.

The Cavaliere made a special mirror for me, which I proudly show every visitor to my palace (I live in a beautiful palace near Saint Peter's). He also presented me with a self-portrait, which is as good as anything Anthony Van Dyke ever painted. As you can deduce from my rambling, I have such a high opinion of said Bernini that I take every opportunity to do him a good turn, for he has proven himself the greatest and most outstanding man in his craft who has ever lived.

Do come and visit me. Best to my friends—or are they ex-friends now?

Love from sunny Rome. C.

Chapter CXXI

F riar Juan San Bonaventura sat on his horse in the early morning dew waiting for Borromini to arrive at his Sant' Ivo job. *What I saw at that Hearing was a completely broken man—but I refuse to believe my eyes. My heart tells me Borromini is still capable of producing great work. I must see for myself. The Order is counting on me.*

Francesco arrived well before the sun came up. When he saw his old patron, this time he recognized him immediately and ran to him. He gave the padre a serious bear hug.

"That's only the second time I've done that in my life," Borromini said, "and if I'm not mistaken, you were the lucky recipient both times."

I was right—at least regarding his person. Not only does he look better, he's moving with his old grace. I have a feeling he even has his sense of humor back—minimal as it may have been.

"Francesco, may I see what you have done for the university? You said this patron was your favorite along with our Order because neither of us told you what to do—which I interpret to mean neither of us forced you to compromise. Show me how that translates. Do you mind giving me a tour? Or are you too busy?"

"Padre, nothing I can think of would make me happier than to show you Sant' Ivo—my greatest accomplishment."

"You mean after San Carlino, of course."

"Of course."

The pair entered Giacomo della Porta's courtyard.

"For me," Borromini said, "this place is heaven on earth. Look at those porticoes that run down both sides of the courtyard; putting them on two levels was nothing less than inspirational by the master. This entire courtyard was here, including those first two levels under my church. My commission was to add Sant' Ivo at the end, so my building begins at the third level."

As they walked toward the church, Father Bonaventura noticed

Borromini walking taller and holding his head higher. *That's it. Now I've got it. It's pride that moves him and resonates in his soul. I wager pride was what was lacking in the Sant' Agnese job. I wonder why.*

"Yes, I can readily see where your work begins, Francesco, and yet it's remarkable how you blended your structure into della Porta's magnificent courtyard. Honestly, I have never seen anything like this. Tell me your thinking. If you don't mind."

"Well, I worked on this project on and off for almost twenty years—so I have to think a little. The drum, I made it hexagonal, and I added the pilasters to strengthen the meeting points of the convex sections, as well as for beauty. Notice how the buttresses carry the line of the pilasters to the lantern, which I made of double columns. That way they separate the concave recesses, and again, add to the beauty. I was going for a strong upward movement. That's why I added the twisting spiral ramp—made of stone, incidentally—and topped the pyramid with an iron crown, ball and cross."

Father Bonaventura stared in awe. "I am privileged to be looking at the most inventive church exterior in Rome and probably the world. Thank you, Francesco."

"Wait until you see the inside," Borromini said. He was so excited he started to trot. "Just wait until you see the inside. Follow me."

—

The duo entered the small church. Father Bonaventura took one look and collapsed into one of the half dozen sets of pews.

"Are you okay?" Borromini asked. "Did I run too fast?"

"It's . . . it's . . . it's . . . breathtaking," the padre managed. "Don't speak. Please. Allow me the joy of absorbing this masterpiece into my pores."

Borromini sat next to the padre. When he saw the glow on the friar's face, he laid his head on the cleric's shoulder. *I hope he doesn't misinterpret this, but I haven't felt this close to anyone since Carlo Maderno died.*

"Thank you for helping me," Francesco said, sotto voce.

Friar Bonaventura sat still. *I wish I had spent time with Borromini and his patrons since he worked for us. I know I could have helped him be a happier person.*

Borromini finally continued. "The church itself is based on basic geometry. I've been interested in mathematics—at least how it relates to architecture—all my life. What I did here was intersect equilateral triangles to form the hexagon central space you are sitting in. Unusual, isn't it?"

"You must add dramatic, and strikingly beautiful. Then, add to that, the impact of the unique juxtaposition of the cupola to the rest of the church. I must admit I cannot believe what you have accomplished here. The way the walls continue upward and inwards, through the drum, to meet at the lantern is beyond inspired—it's positively . . . exalted. What a concept. And this stucco interior. Tell me why it's painted strictly white and off-white."

Borromini couldn't believe his good luck. This was his favorite question and he answered exactly as he rehearsed every time he dreamed someone would ask him about decorating his projects.

"I want the architecture to speak for itself—to make its own statement—not have the decorations speak for the architecture."

"Just like in our San Carlino and cloister?"

"Exactly like that."

The padre nodded, indicating he understood exactly what Francesco was talking about. *Dare I? Why not, he knows I'm his friend.*

"Not like Bernini. I assume that's what you mean."

Borromini shot up like a firecracker. He looked at the friar and saw Carlo Maderno. *Am I going crazy?* He sat back down.

"I'm tired, padre. Thank you for coming."

Father Bonaventura wiggled in his pew. *I guess I better not ask Francesco about Bernini obtaining the commission for him.*

He spoke, this time more circumspect. "If I may take a few more minutes of your time, I'd like to discuss San Carlino. The Order has authorized me to grant you the commission to build a façade for our little church. About time, wouldn't you say? And, incidentally, I agree with you. This is your greatest accomplishment. Don't get me wrong, Francesco—we all love our San Carlino, but that was obviously merely practice for you. This Sant' Ivo is a dazzling, understated treasure that marks the climax of your career—to date at least. I'm proud to be your patron."

Borromini had trouble focusing on the friar through the tears in his eyes.

Chapter CXXII

Beyond Michelangelo

"What's wrong, darling? Caterina asked her husband. "Pacing back and forth like that, you look like a caged animal."

Bernini stopped. He loved it when his wife fussed over him.

"It's the area in front of Saint Peter's," he said. "I have tried my best to please them but I'm getting nowhere. In fact, I've been to the Fabbrica three times now, and I'm stalled. First I submitted a trapezoidal plan. They rejected it. Then I submitted a circular plan. They rejected it. Then I submitted a square plan . . ."

"Let me guess. They rejected it. Sweetheart, don't take it personally. You yourself said that vast open space in front of the basilica was a monumental challenge. Because of its shape and the uses demanded of it. You explained once, but I forget."

Bernini loved the fact his wife was truly interested in his work "First of all," he explained, "the practical consideration is critical. The Pope makes numerous pronouncements throughout the year from balconies in two different buildings. One balcony is on the façade and the other is on the building to the north side. Obviously, the faithful must be able to see him when he speaks from either place."

Caterina fluttered her eyes. "That certainly is easy to understand. And the other?"

"My old friend Carlo Maderno's façade. Because my bell towers were never built—I still cry over that insane decision—the façade is out of proportion. Somehow, whatever I design has to have the effect, or at least the illusion, of correcting that problem. To the degree that is possible."

Caterina laughed and tossed the Cavaliere an apple.

"Plus, knowing you, GianLorenzo Bernini, whatever you design has to be imposing, dramatic, stunning, beautiful, magnificent, important and practical."

—

Bernini resumed pacing while munching on the apple. "I just don't understand it."

Caterina poured GianLorenzo a goblet of wine and sat in his lap. *This is going to take some finesse.*

"You haven't discussed the matter with the Holy Father, have you?"

"How did you know? Bernini asked.

"Lucky guess," she said as she kissed him and poured them both a wine. "Remember the story you told me about the time your father took you to the Pantheon and there were all those beggars in the piazza outside the building? Remember the lesson you told me you learned?"

"I remember every lesson my father taught me. You are obviously referring to the time I asked him why there were so many beggars outside the Pantheon—no, it was Santa Maria Maggiore—and he said because when the faithful leave it, they feel charitable, and I asked him—God, was I a little snot?—if the visitors were feeling so charitable, why were they so pushy, and he said, 'There are certain situations when a little pressure in the right place is critical,' and you are correct, this is one of them."

Caterina jumped off her husband's lap, straightened her floor-length skirt and cleared her throat.

"I have a suggestion and it has three parts. Number One Part: Some time back, I heard you describe your dream for the piazza. You said you wanted to design a structure that will (I remember your words exactly), 'Embrace Catholics, so as to confirm them in their faith; heretics, to reunite them with the Church; and infidels, to enlighten them in the true faith'."

Bernini's smile was devilish. "Poetic, isn't it? Please continue."

"My suggestion, Part One, is this. Design your dream—as you've done all your life—instead of something you think will please the Fabbrica. Why you got shy on this commission is a mystery to me."

The Cavaliere gnashed his teeth. *This hurts, but it's probably the truth.* "Age. I would guess age." *I can't believe this young wife of mine isn't smirking. She is truly remarkable.* "Now that you've pointed my stupid mistake out," he continued, "I assure you it will never happen again. Never. Now, Part Number Two?"

This man is remarkable—I really thought he'd lash out at me. "Part Two: Take your drawings to the Holy Father and have him approve them."

"Putting pressure in the right place?"

"Not yet. That's Part Three, which is this. After Alexander approves your plans—as he must—present your scheme to the Fabbrica. Now here is where the pressure comes in. When you present your concept to the Fabbrica, you present the plans as the Pope's concept. What do you think?"

Bernini gathered his wife in his arms and showered her with a record number of kisses. He pushed her away, held her perfect face in his hands, and fixed her with a loving gaze.

"My answer to you has Four Parts: Your. Plan. Is. Brilliant."

—

"Distinguished members of the Fabbrica of Saint Peter's," Bernini said. "We have been here all day and I am sure you have heard more about the proposed colonnade than you want to hear."

The chairman of the prestigious assemblage of Cardinals that controlled all constructions and modifications to the basilica knew his group was bored and anxious to return their respective abodes. More importantly, based on the numerous, but subtle, questions raised by its most important member, Cardinal Virgilio Spada, the Fabbrica was ready—indeed, anxious—to exercise its veto a fourth time. *Unfortunately I can't just adjourn the meeting, Bernini is too important to dismiss lightly.*

"Take your time, Cavaliere, this is a matter of critical importance to the Church as well as to Saint Peter's."

"Why don't I summarize?" Bernini said. *This is so enjoyable, I can hardly stand it.* "The transverse oval plan you have before you creates a piazza in front of the basilica. The semicircular arms establishing the square are extended from the basilica by straight arms, which begin at the front end of each side of the façade, and are angled inward. This design has several advantages. It conceals the irregular shape of the site as well as stretching Maderno's bulky façade. In addition, this design also allows the faithful to see the Holy Father from whichever balcony he is addressing them."

"Fine, fine, Cavaliere. Anything else?"

You should only know. "This colonnade will consist of 284 free-standing travertine columns. They will be placed four deep—and will be crowned by 90 large statutes. The columns will be placed so that the faithful can approach the basilica under cover, while the center aisle will be wider to accommodate those riding on horses and in carriages. In spite of that, the columns will be so perfectly situated, there will be two spots—one on each side of the piazza, which I will mark—from which one will receive the illusion that the four deep columns are only one deep."

"Excellent. I assume that covers everything."

Why do I think my bombshell will wipe that smirk off his face? "Despite the project's enormity and complexity, I am scheduling the work to be completed in ten years. In conclusion, I believe this colonnade will be the perfect setting for the papal blessing that the Holy Father gives annually from the Benediction Loggia, Urbi et Orbi (To the city and world). Thank you for your time."

"Cavaliere, you have made a fine presentation, and . . ."

"Dear me," Bernini said, "I almost forgot the most important part of my presentation."

The Cardinals, who had begun to file out of the room, grumbled as they returned to their seats.

Bernini waited until every Cardinal was seated and the room was quiet. He fought to keep from smiling, and continued.

"While I have had the honor of making the presentation to you today, actually these plans are the concept of our beloved Holy Father."

All eyes swung to Cardinal Spada, who sat rigidly, staring straight ahead.

Bernini continued. "His Holiness calls this structure, 'The Sacred Overture to Saint Peter's.' He compares it to the maternal arms of the Church, which, in his own words, 'Embraces Catholics, so as to confirm them in their faith; heretics, to re-unite them to the Church; and infidels, to enlighten them to the true faith.' Thank you again for your time, gentlemen. Good-bye."

"Don't rush off, Cavaliere," the chairman said, thinking fast. "Have a coffee in the next room while we analyze the situation."

—

Bernini was still stirring the sugar into his coffee when the chairman knocked on the door and approached Bernini. Gingerly.

"Cavaliere, please come back when you have finished your coffee. The Fabbrica has voted to approve your plans. Unanimously, I might add. Incidentally, I want you to know it was a distinct honor for me to make the motion for approval—a motion Cardinal Spada instantly seconded."

Chapter CXXIII

Beyond Michelangelo

Cardinal Spada, who had reluctantly agreed to allow Borromini to join him at his favorite restaurant in the Campo de' Fiori, looked across at his temperamental artist and shrugged visibly.

"Why are you shrugging?" Borromini asked. "Don't tell me I did something wrong again."

"It's only that knowing you as well as I do, Francesco, I can guess exactly what you want to ask me. Moreover, my answer to your inquiry should be obvious to you."

I have to admit, occasionally Virgilio impresses me. "Nobody can read my mind. It's insulting. Why do you think you are able to?"

"It's simple, Francesco. You heard about Bernini's success with the Fabbrica and you wonder why I allowed it to happen. Answer. I don't control the Fabbrica, only the reigning Pope does. Why then, you would ask next, why was the vote unanimous? Answer: Of course I voted for Bernini's plan. What's the point of showing my hand? The Cavaliere still trusts me—at least I think he does—so it's to our advantage to keep things that way."

"Virgilio, I wish you could read the pontiff's mind as well as you read mine."

"Francesco, I'm having more and more trouble understanding you. You concentrate on the negative although I bring you the startling news that Alexander himself is going to consecrate your Sant' Ivo this Sunday. As a good Catholic and practicing architect—you should realize how significant that is."

"I can't wait."

Chapter CXXIV

Beyond Michelangelo

Bernini and Alexander stood in the vast space in front of Saint Peter's. The area was filled with a large group of buildings. Some were commercial, others were residential, all were old and in disrepair for one reason or another.

"These structures," the pontiff said to his aide who was furiously taking notes, "will all have to go. See that we reimburse every landowner fairly when we condemn his property. Now, Cavaliere, let's go into the church. Since the commission is underway for this area in front of the basilica, it's time to talk about the other end. The apse."

"Look through your baldacchino toward the apse," the Pope said to Bernini. "What do you see?"

"I see the tomb of Paul III on the left, and the tomb of Urban VIII on the right. Straight ahead I see an ill-placed window, but nothing else."

"My point exactly," Alexander said. "Here is the situation as I see it. You have created the most beautiful church in Christendom with your decorations. Each facet is magnificent in its own right, but taken together, the floor, the arches, the piers, the statutes, the tombs and your towering baldacchino make a perfect whole. But the job is not finished. I have decided it is time for you to decorate the apse, so when the worshipers enter, the basilica is all of one piece."

Bernini beamed from ear to ear. "What do you have in mind, Your Holiness?"

"I want you to move the Throne (Chair) of Saint Peter from the Baptismal Chapel . . ."

"To the apse. Brilliant."

The Pope continued, not at all bothered by Bernini's interruption. "As I see it, the columns and canopy of your baldacchino are the perfect religious frame for the Throne of Saint Peter. After all, your baldacchino soars over the High Altar and the Tomb of Saint Peter."

"Holy Father, not to diminish the fact that the baldacchino would be the perfect religious frame for the Chair of Saint Peter—as you so adroitly point out—I believe the baldacchino would also be a perfect artistic frame for it."

"Then we're in agreement. I look forward to seeing your preliminary sketches, which, knowing you, will be forthcoming imminently. By the way, I am consecrating Sant' Ivo for the Sapienza this Sunday. I would like you to be there."

"But..."

"Cavaliere, I said I would like you to be there."

—

The tiny church if Sant' Ivo was overflowing with clergy, nobility, university personnel, artists and assorted hangers-on. The invited guests took every seat, while the walls and side-chapels were occupied by standees, many of whom spilled into the courtyard.

Bernardo, Borromini's nephew who was developing into an imposing young man, led his uncle into the church.

"You look positively handsome this morning, uncle," Bernardo said. "I've never seen those breeches and that blouse before. Oh, look, Cardinal Spada is waving us over."

"Shall we join him?" Borromini asked.

"No," Bernardo said. "I was told you are to sit in the front row, on the aisle. You are the most important person here, you know. Follow me."

The pair walked up the short center aisle, to the acclaim and comments of the seated participants.

"A wonderful job, Borromini." "It's a masterpiece." "The envy of ever artist in Rome." "Revolutionary and refreshing."

Bernardo and his uncle reached the front row but all the seats were occupied. Bernardo tapped the man sitting in the first seat. The church fell silent as the transgressor turned in his seat.

It was GianLorenzo Bernini.

Before Bernardo could stop him, Borromini grabbed Bernini by the throat and started to choke him. Caught off guard, Bernini could only speak between gasps.

"Stop it you fool. The Pope's secretary seated me here." The Cavaliere's face was turning the color of his hair—a sort of off-color gray. "How was I to know this was your seat?"

Borromini pounded Bernini's head on the marble floor.

"I don't care if the Pope himself sat you there. It's my seat and I want it. I'm the guest of honor, not you."

The horrified guests, who had been frozen in their seats, converged on Borromini and pulled him off the Cavaliere. It took four strong men to hold the struggling Borromini down.

"This man is always taking advantage of me," Francesco cried. "That's all he ever does. That's all he cares about."

"What shall we do with him?" one of the on-lookers asked.

"Nothing," Bernini replied. "Not a thing." He brushed off his clothes, found his hat, and headed for the door. "Help the poor man into his chair before the Holy Father arrives."

As Bernini exited the church, the crowd stood and showered the Cavaliere with polite, appropriate applause.

—

"You kept your cool?" Caterina said when her husband arrived home. "I'm proud of you. Putting the poor soul's madness aside, what did you think of the church?"

Bernini answered without missing a beat. "Great isn't the word," he said.

"Come on, sweetheart, really. I'm serious. I heard down at the market that Sant' Ivo is spectacular. 'A masterpiece in its own time' one lady said. Did you like it?"

"In my opinion," the Cavaliere sniffed, "that man—that Borromini person—was sent to destroy architecture."

"Don't beat around the bush. Did you like his church or not?"

"Ha, ha."

Chapter CXXV

Caterina was worried. Her husband had been home for over an hour and, for the first time in their marriage, hadn't spoken a word to her for the entire time. *I've never seen GianLorenzo like this, not even in the bell tower fiasco. My instincts tell me to let his mood play out.*

Bernini smelled bread baking and heard the oven door slam. *How long have I been sitting here? How embarrassing.* "Caterina. Where are you honey? I'm here, in the library." Caterina brought warm fresh bread, cheese and wine to her husband. The Cavaliere ripped off a piece of bread, inhaled its aroma, and slathered a prodigious amount of cheese on it. He finished the goblet of wine and indicated he was ready for more. "After the day I had today," Bernini said, "if these things had happened before we were married, I'd go to bed for a week. Maybe a month. I thank God everyday that he sent you to me—but today I am especially grateful."

A wave of panic swept over Caterina. *He's starting to scare me.* "These things? What are 'these things' that happened today?"

"Sweetheart, I refuse to burden you with my problems. You have your hands full caring for our eleven darlings."

Caterina, while searching her mind for the best response poured her husband another goblet of wine and joined him. She raised her glass in a toast.

"To our children."

GianLorenzo drank and laughed. "Okay," he said, "point well taken. Here's the situation. First, Alexander caught a design problem in the apse project—we're calling it the Cathedra Petri. The Holy Father questioned whether the shrine I designed to hold the Sacred Chair was large enough, considering the size of the apse. He pointed out it was not in proportion to my huge bronze figures of the Church's Fathers."

Caterina was afraid to relax. *All patrons like to be involved in the artistic end of their commissions. There must be something much more serious afoot.*

"Do you agree with him?"

Bernini grimaced. "Unfortunately, he was one hundred percent correct. That was embarrassing, but that wasn't the disaster. The disaster is this: For the first time in my entire professional life, I am distressed by a papal commission and I don't know how to handle the situation."

Caterina's mind was whirring. *Disaster? This sounds more like a calamity.* "I'll heat some water. Take those clothes off and take a good soak. I'll put out a crispy clean robe and then grill you a nice piece of mutton—it sounds like you can use an extra dose of energy."

"GianLorenzo, my love," Caterina said, "you look like a new man, ready to take on the world once more. Now tell me, what did Alexander commission you to do that has you so distressed?"

The words tumbled out of the recharged maestro. "The commission is to redecorate the stark interior of the Pantheon. Stark interior are his words. Me? I think the building is perfect and, papal commission or no papal commission, I don't intend to change a thing. How perfect do I think the Pantheon is? You know how much I love Saint Peter's. Well, to me, there are a hundred errors in Saint Peter's but none in the Pantheon."

The strong example stunned Caterina but didn't deter her from concentrating on the problem at hand. "I honestly don't see the problem. Here's my suggestion. Part One: Make a few sketches—but take your time in submitting them. Part Two: Keep suggesting changes to the sketches. Be careful here. As you know, Alexander is sophisticated artistically. My guess is other matters will occupy you both and this Pantheon project will fade away."

"But what if His Holiness persists?"

"Then you swing into Part Three. Which is to divert the Pope's attention from the inside of the Pantheon to the outside of the building—the Piazza Rotunda and surrounding streets. As you know, there are squatters, vendors, beggars occupying every inch of the area, so it's no stretch to say it needs a lot of help."

The Cavaliere couldn't resist. "And if that doesn't do it? Let me guess—I kill myself."

"Not funny," Caterina said, not allowing herself to be deterred. "If the commission is still standing, it's time for Part Four. Part Four: Meet the problem head on. Tell the Holy Father how much you respect, admire, and love him, but you are both facing a question of artistic integrity. Explain that you don't want him, or you, to go down in history as a defiler of a perfect structure. Remind the pontiff about what happened when Urban ordered the bronze stripped from the Pantheon to build cannons—and allocated a pittance for your baldacchino. Point out the public reaction would undoubtedly be even worse in this case."

"Ah, yes, the dreaded messages on my little Roman friend, Pasquino. Pasquinades. After all these years, I still remember the most brutal one, word for word, 'What the Barbarians didn't do, the Barberini did.' Thanks for your help, Sweetheart. Everyone says I'm a genius, and I'm proud of that, but the truth of the matter is, you are the real genius in the household of GianLorenzo Bernini—who will forever be your greatest admirer and slave."

Chapter CXXVI

Bernini met his patron, Alexander VII, in the Renaissance church of Santa Maria del Popolo. The pair stood in front of the Chigi Chapel that Bernini had restored.

"Thank you, Cavaliere, the Pope said. "You have basically created a new chapel for my family without destroying the spirit of what Raphael did a hundred years ago. I particularly love the clever touches in your sculptured groups—the angel carrying the prophet Habbakuk, and the lion licking David's foot."

The pair walked to the front door. The smiling pontiff couldn't contain himself as he looked around. The angels seated over the redesigned arches seemed to be smiling at him, and he was confident that integrating the branches of oak leaves into the organ pipes—on either side of the main altar—was an idea only a master such as Bernini could envision and then execute.

"This church has always held a special place in my heart," the pontiff said, his eyes sweeping the edifice, "especially since I was made titular head. Now that you have restored the entire facility, as well as my family's chapel, I love it all the more."

—

Alexander and GianLorenzo stood outside, on the top step of the church, and studied the wall Bernini had decorated for Queen Christina's arrival in the city.

"Cavaliere," the Pope said, breaking the spell, "please come to my office tomorrow morning so we can discuss the details of another commission. You are familiar with the small, irregular site across the road from the Quirinal Palace, of course. Well, I want you to build a church for the Jesuit novices on that land."

Bernini couldn't believe his good fortune. *Spada told me Borromini proposed a church for that very site to Innocent, but the Pope turned him down because the church Borromini proffered would block his view. This is delicious.* "Aren't you worried about your view, Holy Father?"

"Not at all. My plan is to convince Prince Pamphili to be the principal financial patron. I want the church to be dedicated to Sant' Andrea (Saint Andrew) and I think the Prince will agree. You are entitled to know my thinking. Having just seen what you accomplished remodeling a church—the basilica—that is over 100 years old, I said to myself, 'Imagine what the Cavaliere could do if he designed a church from the ground up.' You never have, have you? A Bernini Church—the thought fills me with joy."

"I'm overwhelmed, Your Holiness. Truly."

"You've earned that and more. Good day, my friend, I must go. Oh, by the way, you have convinced me. Forget about redecorating the Pantheon and placing my family's stars on the roof. It took me some time to reach that conclusion, but I confess, your arguments were compelling—especially the one about defiling a classic structure."

—

Giuseppe, the bookseller, was so excited when he saw Borromini approaching he ran through the shop and opened the door for him.

"Borromini," Giuseppe said, "I cannot tell you how excited I am. It took forever, but I finally found you a copy of Vignola's 'Rule of the Five Orders in Architecture.'"

"I'll take it," Francesco said without even glancing at the book.

If I had ten like him I could retire in a year. But then I'd have to be with my wife all day and I wouldn't know the latest gossip. I'd better leave well enough alone. "You have a pleased look on your face," Giuseppe said. "Unfortunately, if I may say, that is a rare occurrence these days."

"It's coming along beautifully—the façade to San Carlino. The patron is still cooperating which is good. The bad news is the cramped location causes innumerable sight line problems. Naturally, I expect to make it work."

"I don't doubt that. The real question is how do you think your design for the façade relates to the church—that's what counts, it seems to me."

"Perfectly, of course. Actually, I wager in the future no one will guess there was an interval of some twenty years between my design of the church and my design of the façade."

Borromini finished his espresso and browsed the shelves on his way out of the bookstore.

Giuseppe called out as his favorite customer reached the door. "Borromini, I almost forgot to tell you what I heard earlier today. Bernini has been commissioned to design a church for the Jesuits, and . . ."

"What possible interest does that have for me?"

"The location. That's what I thought you'd be interested in. It's on the same piece of land I heard you tried to convince Innocent X to build a church on, but he turned you down—something about losing his view. Remember? Just up the street from your San Carlino."

Borromini stared at Giuseppe in disbelief. His eyes glazed over. He started to breathe heavily. Then he fainted.

Giuseppe fanned Francesco with a pamphlet, trying to revive him. *Will I never learn?*

Chapter CXXVII

S tanding on the site across from the Quirinal Palace, Pope Alexander VII glowed as he listened to Bernini describe his plans for Sant' Andrea al Quirinale. He felt smug. *If only my results in foreign matters could be this satisfying.*

"Cavaliere," the pontiff said, "I was certain placing the long axis of your transverse oval plan along the road here—to compensate for the site being wide and narrow—was a brilliant idea, but I never dreamed you could turn the land's deficiency into such an advantage."

Alexander leafed through the drawings and continued. "Here is what I like the best—the High Altar. It will obviously be the first thing to capture the eye of the faithful when they enter. With those two huge Corinthian columns on each side; with that pediment stretching across its width; and by jutting it out from the back wall, you have made the High Altar the dramatic highlight of the church. I venture the worshipers will feel like the altar is reaching out and welcoming them."

Bernini beamed. *How can I be so lucky to have had such knowledgeable patrons over the years?*

"The columns will be variegated, pink marble," the Cavaliere quickly added, keeping the momentum going, "and the altar will have its own dome and lantern—hidden from the worshipers. This will provide natural light, and I plan to augment the natural light with gilded rays and colored glass in order to bathe the altar with a warm, heavenly glow. On the back wall, there will be a large painting held aloft by two angels. The Saint in the painting will be gazing upward at a large statute of Saint Andrew, who will be sitting on a cloud in the broken pediment beginning his ascent into the cupola—that is, heaven. The cupola, which will basically cover the entire church, will be highly decorated and will have eight large windows at its base. The windows are important, because they will provide constantly changing light for the entire interior."

"Everything appropriate will be gilded, correct?

"Your Holiness, when Prince Pamphili told me to design a jewel—ricca e bella (rich and beautiful)—I planned accordingly. Sumptuous is the word that will best describe the church when it is completed—which should be in about seven years, if we can maintain the schedule I have drawn up."

—

"Cavaliere," Alexander said before bidding Bernini goodbye, "Can you spare the time to ride with me to the Castelli Romani in the next day or two? Now that I've seen the spectacular confirmation that you can design a church from scratch, I want you to design two more churches for me. In Castel Gandolfo and Ariccia. That is, if you are interested."

Bernini just barely suppressed the urge to hug and kiss the Pope.

Chapter CXXVIII

Beyond Michelangelo

"Why meet here in Sant' Andrea delle Fratte?" Borromini asked Cardinal Spada. "This church is just a stone's throw from that Bernini's palace and the last thing on earth I want to do is encounter him. As if that isn't bad enough, I hate the interior of this church. Absolutely hate it. I thought you knew that."

"That's one of the things I wanted to talk with you about. Your patron, the Marquis Paolo del Buffalo, came to see me yesterday. He's canceling your commission. He said he's tired of arguing with you."

"There won't be any more arguments. I threw him off the job yesterday and forbade him to return until it was completed. The dome needs a second level—its critical—and then I planned a crowning lantern. It needs a large one."

So that's what triggered his action—he threw his patron off the job. "How long have you been working on this project for the Marquis?"

Fifteen years or so, on and off. Why?"

Good grief. I'll wager they've been arguing for fifteen years, on and off. "What have you been fighting about?"

Borromini pounded his two fists on the back of the pew. "Look around. Should I be proud of this church? Look at it. It's ordinary. If there is anything I dread, it's being ordinary. There are plenty of ordinary architects in Rome but I refuse to be one. I've been trying to give him a church we can all be proud of but he just doesn't care."

Exhausted at the thought of fifteen years of discord, Borromini slumped in the pew. A light went on in his head and he jumped up and ran outside. A confused Cardinal Spada followed the architect a short way up the Via Capo le Case.

"Remember my mentor, Carlo Maderno?" Francesco said. "He told me I had to respect my patrons and work with them. That's a noble thought, but how can you respect a man who drove me crazy about every facet of the interior? He forced me to bend to him in every detail inside the church. But, here's the maddening part, he gave me free reign on this exterior? Does that make sense to you?"

Cardinal Spada put his arm around the temperamental architect's shoulder. *He's right, of course.* "Believe it or not I asked the Marquis that very question yesterday. Brace yourself for his answer. He said, 'The interior of the church is God's temple, but the outside is a detail, a necessary evil that I don't care about.' He compared it to a piece of fruit. 'The substance is inside and the skin can be pealed off with no damage to the fruit'."

"Do you agree with that?" an incredulous Borromini asked.

"Of course not," Spada replied. "And nobody I know agrees with that, either. But he was the patron, wasn't he?"

Borromini started to scream, but when he looked in the Cardinal's face, he saw that Virgilio said it matter-of-factly and was not mocking him. He melted. "Virgilio, the man is only a Marquis. What is royalty compared to the Catholic Church? Nothing, that's what. I thought the Church wanted the world to know it had a renewed vitality, and dramatic architecture in its churches, both inside and out, was one of the ways the Popes wanted to prove that."

Just when I want to run him out of town—or, at least, never see him again—he surprises me and makes sense. I'm getting too old for these mood swings. "Francesco, I'm proud of you. I couldn't have said it better."

Borromini smiled a tiny smile—more of a smirk, really. *That felt good—I've got to have some victories.* "Where do you think I heard it?"

Cardinal Spada stared at the exterior of the church. "I see your point about the unfinished dome. Those rough bricks need to be stuccoed—right now the dome looks like a ruin. On the other hand, the bell tower is extra sumptuous. It certainly is dramatic and underscores your point about what the Church is looking for in architecture."

"What are the people of Rome saying about the campanile?" Borromini asked. A homebody, he never received feedback—except from Giuseppe—and he really cared.

Francesco, you should know that it's as controversial as all your work. Romans, I fear, are too provincial to understand you. You are the future—I have always believed that, which is why I have supported you lo these many years. I just wish you weren't such a handful. "They love it," he said. *I know how to make Francesco happy.* "Tell me how you did it. How did you get the diverse sections appear to the eye as a logical whole? You have achieved what I call, as an architectural dilettante, vertical continuity."

One way or another, I notice Virgilio gets 'architectural dilettante' into every conversation. He must need reinforcement—or he is bragging. In any case, I don't like the way he's sort of pretending he's an architect. He's not an architect. "The sections may appear radically different but they are, in fact, interrelated. Painting the stucco white helps give the impression of smoothness when you stand down here in the street." *That should fix him.*

"That is all well and good, but I don't know of another architect who could combine flaming torches, exaggerated scrolls, continuous circles, columns, caryatids, buttresses, and heaven know what else, and make the result pleasant to the eye, fun to look at, and dramatic, all at the same time. On behalf of the Church, I thank you."

Borromini combined a half laugh with his half sigh. *How can I get mad at this man?*

—

"Francesco, shall we go into that bar on the corner," Cardinal asked. "We'll have a coffee—and I want to show you some sketches I've made for a memorial chapel for my family in San Girolamo della Carita. I want you to build it."

Borromini came off his high in record time. "You designed a chapel and you want me to build it?"

"Is there a problem here?" Spada was truly surprised at the reaction.

Borromini studied his patron for several minutes and then did the only thing he could do. He told the truth. "Is there any other way to see it?"

Chapter CXXIX

Beyond Michelangelo

The Castelli Romani describes a region south of Rome, which consists of a number of small towns and villages nestled in the Alban Hills. To escape the scorching summer heat, Romans have journeyed to this bucolic countryside for thousands of years. In fact, during his tenure as Pope Urban VIII, Maffeo Barberini created a summer residence in Castel Gondolfo. Perched high above Lake Albano, the air is clear and crisp in Castel Gondolfo, and the views from the charming, tiny village are spectacular.

Alexander and Bernini stood in front of a decaying church across the square from the Pope's summer palace. "As you can see, Cavaliere," the pontiff said, "the land drops dramatically toward the lake. Knowing you as well as I do, however, I'm not worried about that—you will undoubtedly turn the site problems into assets, just like you are doing at Sant' Andrea."

Bernini squinted; imagining the site after the old country church would be torn down. The master drifted off as he spoke—a situation Alexander observed many times in the past. The Pope listened quietly; he was always fascinated when he had the opportunity to watch the Cavaliere's mind at work.

"The façade of San Tommaso di Villanova—as I understand you will call the new church—must relate to your papal residence, but must also be subservient to it. How will I accomplish that juggling act? I see a rather plain front—painted stucco perhaps—featuring pilasters, instead of columns. I will use the Tuscan Order for simplicity. Let's see, what else. I will design a Greek Cross plan, with four equal arms, dominated by a towering dome. This approach will enable me to give the church a more elaborate interior, even though it's only a country church. After all, it does have the papal imprimatur on it."

"And the rear of the building," the excited Alexander asked. "What would that look like?"

"As usual, it appears you are way ahead of me Your Holiness. The rear elevation. I'll design the rear elevation to be as interesting as the front of the church. Actually, as you hinted, the site cries out for dual exteriors, so to speak. Since the church will sit on the highest point in the area, I want it to look attractive and dynamic from great distances, as well as from this piazza."

—

The Pope and Bernini approached the medieval town of Ariccia, which lies near Castel Gondolfo and is equally famous for its views and porchetta.

"Soon," the Pope said to Bernini, "in addition to our family's palace, Ariccia will be famous as the home of another spectacular Chigi church. We shall call it Santa Maria dell' Assunzione. That is, if you enjoyed designing San Tommaso way out here in the country."

"When do we start, Holy Father?"

"Good. We will have to remove a number of these houses—as we did for the piazza in front of Saint Peter's—because I would like to have a large piazza in front of the church."

This commission is going to be a much bigger challenge than San Tommaso. "The first thing that strikes me," Bernini said, "is even though this site is spectacular—high up here on the edge of this extinct volcano—we will need to find a way to integrate the church into the fabric of the community. This is a problem we didn't have in Castel Gondolfo."

The Cavaliere walked the site for more than an hour while the Pope waited patiently in his carriage. Bernini came bouncing back.

"Wings," he said. The astonished pontiff was too surprised to speak. Bernini continued. "We'll place a wing on each side of the church. Large wings, about the size of the church, which will follow the curve of the church but will be separated from it by wide, interesting corridors, or alleyways. The wings will have the effect of integrating the church into the town, plus they'll give a warm feeling to the overall project."

"Cavaliere, that is exciting. Tell me about the interior? What do you envision for the High Altar?"

"Your Holiness, I think you know that since my study of the Pantheon, I prefer a dome totally dominating the interior—like in Sant' Andrea and San Tomasso. Also, like in those two churches, the cupola will be highly decorated and highlight the church. As for the High Altar, I see it as a spectacular focal point, with a large fresco that will be the only color in the church. The painting will depict the Assumption of Mary into heaven, of course. I'm thinking of using Guglielmo Cortese to paint it."

"Interesting," Alexander said. "Out of curiosity, did you consider using Pietro da Cortona again? He did such a masterful job for us in the High Altar of San Tomasso—his representation of the Crucifixion blended in so beautifully with your architecture and sculpture."

"That's the problem," Bernini replied. "In Aricca, I see the High Altar as a spectacular focal point. I need a riot of color and Pietro may be too subtle for the effect I need."

—

On the ride back to Rome, the Pope studied the remarkable artist.

"It feels good to be in your company, Cavaliere. You are a true genius, in every sense of the word. Incredibly, just watching your mind work makes me feel good all over. But may I ask you a personal question? Are you sure you can take on all of the commissions I have for you? How do you do it?"

"Holy Father, if I added up all of the time in my life dedicated to eating and sleeping, I doubt that all of my inactivity would total more than one month."

"Why, Cavaliere? Why have you worked so hard all your life?"

Bernini answered without hesitation. "You just said it, Your Holiness. To make people feel good. Since I was a little boy, that's all I ever really wanted to do. Make people feel good all over—mentally, physically, and especially spiritually. Normally, of course, I achieve this through my art."

Bernini paused a minute to think and then passionately continued.

"Fittingly, Holy Father, you feeling good by merely watching my mind at work has taken my dreams to a higher level."

Chapter CXXX

Beyond Michelangelo

A somber Father Giovanni Paolo Oliva waited for Bernini. He studied the Cavaliere's library. *There must be thousands of volumes here—this collection is bigger than mine. I wonder when he finds time to read books.* "Ah, there you are Cavaliere," said the refined and cultivated cleric. He was taller than most, and was one of the few men in Rome without a beard. His black hair was starting to turn gray and was brushed back over his large ears and away from his full nose.

"I wish we could discuss the books and other pleasant things at length, but I bear bad news. Your friend Jules Mazarin is dead at fifty-nine years of age. In France, of course. I'm sorry to be the one to bring you the tragic news, but since Jules was a Jesuit and I am the vicar general of the Jesuits, the obligation fell to me."

Bernini fell into a chair; he was in shock and unable to talk. Father Oliva understood and made no attempt at small talk. Bernini slowly regained his composure.

"I guess," the Cavaliere said, "I guess I can call him Giulio Mazzarini again, like when we were young and on the town. How sad." *At least he lived his short life to the fullest. People should only know. Secretly marrying the Queen and siring the King—I wonder what those proud people of France would do if they knew their beloved French King Louis XIV had an Italian father.*

Father Oliva broke GianLorenzo's reverie. "I know how close you two were, but have you stayed in touch with Jules?"

Bernini tried his best to put on a good face. "Constantly. I received a letter from him last week. He was all excited about some laws he'd managed to impose. He said they would help the ordinary citizens of France. He was like that."

"He was like that, wasn't he?" Father Oliva said, nodding and smiling in the difficult situation. "Actually, he turned into a real Francophile. Did he say anything else important in his letter?"

"He asked me, once again, to go to France—to join him and live there."

My God, that would be a tragedy for Italy. "What did you say?"

"Naturally," Bernini said, "I declined his invitation. Why would I go to France? I'm 100% Italian."

Bernardo rushed into his uncle's house and found him in bed. He shook Borromini as vigorously as he felt he could, considering his age and station.

"Wake up uncle, wake up. Please. Please wake up."

Borromini tried to focus. *It looks like Bernardo, but why is he screaming at me? He never did that before.*

Bernardo continued shaking his uncle.

"Wake up. Please. A disaster. Cardinal Spada died today. I was certain you'd want to know right away. Wake up, please."

"What?" Francesco rubbed the sleep out of his eyes. "What? Am I dreaming? Did I hear Virgilio died?"

"Yes, today. I'm sorry, uncle. I know how close the two of you were. More than a patron, wasn't he? He was your protector and friend and . . ."

"I'll miss him but Virgilio was a hard man to work with. He thought he knew more about architecture than he really did. He actually designed his family's chapel and then wanted me to build it."

"Uncle, is there anything I . . ."

"Plus, I think he secretly liked that Bernini person."

Chapter CXXXI

Bernini and the Pope watched workmen dismantle the last of the scaffolding in the apse of Saint Peter's. Alexander fell to his knees and prayed. The Cavaliere followed.

"I am overwhelmed," the pontiff said. "Finally, after nine years, the 'Cathedra Petri,' as I call it. This is clearly one of the most complex and unprecedented projects in history, Cavaliere, and you did it. How? That is a mystery to me. Those four bronze figures of the Church Fathers appear to be effortlessly and miraculously carrying the shrine containing the sacred chair, yet they are so large."

"Over sixteen feet high," Bernini said. "And thanks to you, the shrine is now in proper perspective."

"A small contribution, at best," Alexander said. "For me, what pulls your masterful group together is the blaze of gilt-bronze rays and angels that radiate from the yellow glass window—that previously useless and ill-placed window. The sunburst is so powerful it seems to light up the entire basilica. It is a divine light, containing the Dove of the Holy Spirit. It is a divine light and the source of papal infallibility."

"Exactly the illusion I intended to create," a pleased Bernini said.

GianLorenzo had work to do and was anxious to leave, but the pontiff sat, mesmerized. The Cavaliere, of course, waited patiently.

The Pope continued. "The honoring of the actual chair of Saint Peter naturally excites me, but I am most pleased that the basilica is now basically complete for the benefit of the faithful. Truly, Cavaliere, you are a genius—a prodigious genius."

When he heard the words 'prodigious genius,' Bernini quickly sat down—his legs felt like cooked spaghetti. *Mister Carracci, I know you're in heaven and can hear the Holy Father. Gratifying, isn't it? How could you have been so right about me and so wrong about your own personal well being?*

Chapter CXXXII

Bernini paced up and down the portico of Saint Peter's waiting for the Pope. *I'll never get over the fine job Carlo Maderno did designing this porch for the basilica—he made it an honor for me to design the floor. Considering the wear it receives, it's holding up beautifully. I wonder why His Holiness wanted to meet down here.*

"There you are, Cavaliere," Alexander said. "Thank you for coming. Please, follow me."

The pontiff led Bernini to the right side of the portico, turned left and started walking up a set of rickety stairs.

"Be careful, Cavaliere. This is not the safest set of stairs in the world, although they are among the most important—which is why they are called the Scala Regia, or Royal Staircase. As you know, these are the stairs we Popes take from the Vatican Palace to Saint Peter's, and vice-versa. They are so bad, Innocent X usually had to be carried up and down them in a litter. I wanted you to ascend them to see for yourself how uncomfortable, gloomy and downright perilous they are."

Bernini followed the Pope up the stairs and into a large, beautifully decorated room. *Ah, the Sale Ducale.* "This is more like it," the Cavaliere said. "Civilization."

Alexander chuckled at Bernini's choice of words. "It's hard to believe how ugly these two rooms looked before you renovated them five years ago. When I'm receiving my flock in this room—you know how much I enjoy meeting with the faithful—I often reflect on the outstanding job you did."

"You will recall," Bernini replied, happy to discuss yet another success, "it was necessary to keep the beam between the rooms for structural reasons. So the key was disguising the remaining portion of the wall."

"Disguise?" the Pope said. "Disguise? The billows of marble drapery look like they are silk, and the putti look like they are actually putting the drapery in place. It's more than a disguise—it's an ingenious way to create one large room out of two small ones. Plus, the use of marble is staggering in its beauty. Enough of that. I didn't invite you here to discuss the Sala Ducale. It's about the Scala Regia. I want you to rebuild it."

"Holy Father, I . . ."

"Before you answer, I want to be honest with you. Innumerable predecessors of mine have tried to improve the stairs, but the reality has proven too much for any architect to handle."

"As we climbed," Bernini said, "I noticed the wide entrance narrows and the existing walls are not parallel. Also, there is no light. What's the reason for that?"

Alexander smiled a knowing smile. "The stairs pass under, or abut, the walls of the Pauline Chapel and even the Sala Regia—which is the largest meeting room in the Vatican. Obviously, these are important rooms and are much too precious to jeopardize. The Scala Regia is a structural problem and challenge second to none. Cavaliere, may I be perfectly honest with you? I know of the bell tower fiasco."

Bernini couldn't help showing his displeasure—he felt like throwing up at the very mention of that disaster.

The Pope noticed and continued quickly. "I mention that fiasco because several of my elderly advisors, who don't know the facts, think it was your mistake that caused the cracks in the façade. They are urging me not to entrust this delicate commission to you. Naturally, I am disregarding their bogus concerns. What do you say?"

"Holy Father, I am over sixty years old. At this point in my life and career, I am not interested in jeopardizing anything, much less a structure I love, and a friendship I cherish."

"What are you saying," the confused pontiff said. "Are you saying you will or won't accept the commission?"

"Of course I will do it. I relish the challenge. Permit me to state it this way. If you want to see what a man can do, you must give him a problem. The highest merit goes to the architect who makes use of a defect in such a way that if it had not existed, one would have to invent it."

—

Three years later Alexander and Bernini stood at the bottom of the Scala Regia.

"I must confess, Your Holiness, this was probably the most difficult commission I've ever undertaken, and yet, in a way, it may be my least defective work."

"To me," the Pope said, "it is a triumph—artistically, of course, but also as an illusion. The way you camouflaged the narrowing of the steep, dark stairs by diminishing the columns in size and bringing them closer to the walls as they go up—well, it's inspiring."

"The illuminated landings help the illusion," Bernini said, "but the hardest aspect was the structural problem, just as you predicted three years ago. Remember? I can tell you disaster lurked every day as we shored-up the walls of the rooms over the staircase's vault. That was some delicate situation. My father once said, 'when you tell the truth, it's not bragging,' so I'm going to tell you something honestly. If I had read that someone had accomplished this, I would not have believed it."

Chapter CXXXIII

F ather Oliva, the new Superior General of the Jesuits, listened in disbelief as the Pope, obviously troubled, spoke to him in somber tones.

"Padre, here is the reason I sent for you. As you know, France is on the verge of establishing a National Church. We need look no further than across the channel at the Church of England to know how disastrous the ramifications could be. We must stop this so-called Gallican Movement. As I analyze this situation the Church finds itself in, I have concluded that you are the only person I can turn to for help."

Father Oliva studied the Pope. *This gentleman appreciates the finer things in life and doesn't need these kinds of problems. Neither do I.* "I'm flattered that you sent for me, Holy Father, and I like to think my Order is important—even powerful—but in a matter such as you have mentioned, the Jesuits would be a minor consideration at best."

The Holy Father sighed. *He doesn't want to get involved. I don't blame him, but unfortunately, I have no choice.* The pontiff pressed on. "Who is the one person who can stem the tide of Gallicanism and secure the position of the Catholic Church in France?"

"The Most Christian King, Louis XIV, of course."

"Of course. For the twenty plus years Cardinal Mazarin was in power, he ran the country with an iron fist, so the Church was in a strong position in France. Since the Cardinal died a few years ago, however, young Louis has not appointed a successor; rather he is acting as his own Prime Minister. While this is unprecedented, it is also real. Obviously, the Church must now shore up its position with the King."

Father Oliva waited—as a young cleric he had learned not to rush bad news.

Alexander continued. "I dispatched my nephew, Cardinal Flavio Chigi, on a diplomatic mission to France. He recently returned to Rome with disturbing news. The King wants Cavaliere Bernini to go to France and be 'at his disposal.' And then, this very day, I received this letter from Louis. I'll read it to you:

> Most Holy Father, having already received by order of Your Holiness two designs for my building of the Louvre from a hand so distinguished as that of the Cavaliere Bernini, I should think

rather of thanking you for this favor instead of requesting still another favor of you. But since it regards a building that for many centuries has been the principal residence of the kings who are the most zealous in all Christendom in the support of the Holy See, I believe that I may apply to Your Holiness in all confidence. I entreat you then, if his duty to you permits it, to command the Cavaliere to come here in order to finish his work. Your Holiness could not grant me a greater favor in the present set of circumstances. I will add that it could not be made to anyone who feels more veneration or more warmth than I,

Most Holy Father.
Paris, 18 April, 1665.

Your Most Devoted Son,
Louis"

Father Oliva was stunned. *That is an amazing letter but my instincts tell me the Louvre isn't the point.* "Do you really believe getting Bernini to France is about the Louvre?" Father Oliva asked.

The Pope contemplated the question for some time before responding.

"I believe the King has a much more subtle intention. In my opinion, he wants to make a dramatic point to the world, which would be something like this, 'Now that I am personally in charge of my country, see what I have been able to accomplish; I have attracted the most renowned artist in the world to France, and away from his patron'."

Father Oliva was stunned once more. *Can Louis XIV have so much ambition he wants to undermine the papacy? No wonder the Holy Father is depressed.* "I gather you want me to talk the Cavaliere into going to France. I will be happy to accommodate you, Your Holiness, but with all due respect, I don't think I can succeed. His close, personal friend Jules Mazarin tried many times, and even the young King's father, Louis XIII, tried. All to no avail."

"I understand those efforts were to entice Bernini to move to France, not go for a visit."

"The distinction is well taken, Your Holiness, but there is more. A few days ago, GianLorenzo received a personal letter from the King asking him to go to France, but he still won't budge."

Alexander perked up. "Are you certain? I'm surprised the Cavaliere didn't tell me about that. Do you know what the letter said?"

"I have the letter with me—Caterina gave it to me since I am the Cavaliere's Personal Confessor. I'll read it to you:

> Signor Cavalier Bernini,
>
> I have such a special esteem for your merit that I have a great desire to see and to know more closely a personage so illustrious if my intention is compatible with your service to the Holy Father and with your own convenience. My desire moves me to dispatch this special courier to Rome to ask you to give me the gratification of undertaking the journey to France on the propitious occasion of the return of my cousin, the Duke of Criqui, who is my special ambassador. He will explain to you in greater detail the urgent reason that causes me to wish to see and discuss with you the fine designs that you have sent me for the building of the Louvre. For the rest, as I have told my cousin, I will make my good intentions known to you. I pray God that he keep you, Signor Cavalier Bernini, in His holy care.
>
> From Lyon,
> Written in Paris, 11 April, 1665.
>
> Louis

Alexander smiled. *Louis is cleverer than I thought.* "Do you know if Bernini answered the King's letter?"

"He did not," Father Oliva said. "He asked me what I thought he should do and I told him I needed to think about it. Now, coincidently, you sent for me and we have this conversation." The cleric looked deep into the Pope's eyes. *What a dilemma—I'm torn between love of county, love of Church and love of friend. I've got to get out of this if I can.* "May I respectfully ask why you think I can succeed where all the others have failed?"

Beyond Michelangelo

"There are a number of reasons. First of all, you are one of Bernini's most intimate friends. Secondly, he respects you as the Head of the Jesuit Order. Most important, as his Personal Confessor, you occupy a unique place in his life—which has become, as you know, increasingly religious oriented. Add to that, he even asked your opinion about whether he should go. Padre, I know you to be a very intelligent man. I'm sure you are more than capable of thinking of an argument that will convince the Cavaliere to make the journey."

"You flatter me, Holy Father, but Bernini is sixty-seven years old and can be stubborn—after all he is half Neapolitan. I think it will take more than my arguments to convince him."

"Funny you should say that because I neglected to mention one thing. I have scheduled a secret meeting with his delightful wife, Caterina."

Chapter CXXXIV

Bernini grumbled to himself during the entire trip home from Ariccia. *I probably wasted more time today—going back and forth to the country—than I have the rest of my entire life. What a disaster.*

"How was Ariccia, darling? Caterina said to her exhausted husband. "Sit right down. For a little change, I grilled you a piece of rabbit to eat with your fruit salad."

"What a waste of time," Bernini said. "Alexander asked me to look things over in Ariccia, so I thought there was a problem. Turned out, everything was fine—the workers weren't even expecting me."

"The Pope. He was here earlier today," Caterina said. "He asked me to keep his visit a secret, but you know me—I have no secrets from you, sweetheart."

"For Alexander to meet with you behind my back," the surprised Bernini said, "he must have had something of major significance on his mind."

"The Holy Father wants me to talk you into going to France," Caterina said. "That's what he came to tell me. He maintained that it's important to him, and the Church, and you would be doing both of them a personal favor if you went."

"What did you tell the Holy Father?" Bernini asked cautiously.

"I told him it was your decision."

Bernini dug into his rabbit without responding. *I should have predicted my darling's response—she always says the right thing.*

Caterina continued. "Before you decide, why not talk with Father Oliva? Aren't you seeing him tomorrow night?"

On the way out of the Villa Borghese after the concert, Bernini and Father Oliva passed a number of the Cavaliere's early masterpieces, including the Flight From Troy, Rape of Proserpina, David, and Apollo and Daphne.

"What thoughts go through your mind when you see these marvelous pieces?" Father Oliva asked.

Answering just loud enough for the group following him to hear, Bernini said,

"Oh, what little progress I have made in art, when as a youth I handled marble in this way."

The next day, the Cavaliere's comment was the major topic of discussion throughout the city of Rome.

—

Father Oliva put it off as long as he could, but finally decided to meet the issue head on.

"The Holy Father is putting incredible pressure on me to talk you into making the journey to France. He has a myriad of reasons I won't go into—suffice it to say he is determined to grant this favor to the King."

Bernini tried to look at his friend with an objective eye. *Why would he want me to make this perilous journey at my advanced age? He must be under enormous pressure of some kind.* "Padre, you really want me to make this trip, don't you. No need to answer, I know you do. So does Alexander. I'm not sure about Caterina. Let me ask you one question—how important is it to you that I go to France?"

Father Oliva stopped, took a deep breath and spoke slowly and passionately.

"I think," he said, "you should go to France . . . even if it kills you."

—

"How was the concert dear," Caterina asked.

"You should have come," Bernini said. "The Villa Borghese never looked better, the music was downright exciting, and it was fun seeing some of my past work."

"Then why do you look so sad?"

Bernini took his wife in his arms and kissed her passionately. "Because I don't see how I can leave you and the children and go to France."

"What did Father Oliva say?" Caterina asked, returning the kisses.

I am certainly not going to upset my darling. "He said it was up to me."

"Poor baby," Caterina said, extricating herself from her husband's powerful arms. "Let me make sure I understand exactly what is happening here. Alexander VII, the Pope, is asking you to do him a personal favor by going to France. If you say yes, that is grant him, the Pope, his personal favor, this would allow the Pope to grant the King of France, Louis XIV, the personal favor he is requesting of the Pope, which is your presence in France. Am I close?"

Bernini plopped his wife down. "And you say you like to watch my mind at work."

"Well, darling, I don't think Popes and Kings are in the habit of asking personal favors. If they were asking me, I would be honored."

"It is an honor, isn't it? Besides it would be fun to meet the boy."

"And, if it were me, I'd say yes with as much style and grace as I could muster. To meet who?"

"Sweetheart, you say hello and good-bye with style and grace. I also had a secret, but now that Giulio is dead, I guess I can break the vow I made to him. Giulio Mazzarini, that is Jules Mazarin, was secretly married to the Queen, and is the father of Louis XIV, King of France."

GianLorenzo looked at his beaming wife and returned her warm smile.

"It appears that I'm finally going to meet Giulio's son."

—

Letter:

Pope Alexander VIII to our Louis, Most Christian King of the French, most beloved in Christ the Son.

Nick J. Mileti

    Cherished son, the noble Duke Criqui, your Majesty's spokesman, has delivered your message to us and has very earnestly requested that we should grant the presence in your kingdom of our dear son Cavalier Bernini for three months. Although this request would scarcely be granted because his assistance is now necessary for the construction of the Vatican colonnades and for other requirements of St. Peter's building program, nevertheless, because the magnitude of our love for you overcomes all, we have granted it with a glad heart. So we bestow on Your Majesty the Apostolic Benediction especially brought forth from all the sentiment of the paternal heart.

    Given at Rome in Santa Maria Maggiore with the seal of the Fisherman's Ring, April 23, 1665, in the eleventh year of our pontificate.

Chapter CXXXV

Bernini's entourage, which was financed by Louis XIV, consisted of nine men—the Cavaliere and his son, Paolo; two assistants, Mattia de' Rossi and Giulio Cartari; three servants; and two representatives of the King.

When dawn broke on the beautiful spring day of April 25, 1665 (the Pope lost no time in dispatching his charge) every inch of Via delle Mercede was overrun with Romans. Rich, poor, male, female—the entire city turned out to bid farewell to its most famous, and beloved, citizen. The people who couldn't fit onto the Cavaliere's street lined the route to the Porta del Popolo, and even spilled up the Via Flaminia.

The members of the entourage waited astride their horses, while a carriage, with the two young French drivers, awaited the Cavaliere. The Frenchmen watched the trip's final preparations with haughty indifference. "Don't these people know we have food in France? They're bringing enough to feed our army." "Who is this old man, anyway? I never heard of this GianLorenzo Bernini. What kind of name is that?"

Because of the crowd, Caterina and the children said their tearful farewells inside the house. When Bernini finally appeared outside, the spectators burst into sustained applause and screamed at the top of their lungs. "You servants better make sure he eats decent food—not that French glob." "Don't let that King seduce you with money or titles or women. Ha, ha." "They using knives and forks yet?" "Cavaliere, please dress warmly—I don't think they have heaters in France."

"Those Romans are a boisterous bunch," one of the brassy Frenchmen said as the entourage began inching its way through the adorning crowd. "Disgusting," said the other.

Bernini overheard. *I'd be worried if they weren't boisterous.*

—

On the long trip north, Bernini and his group were treated as royalty—in fact, every town and every noble family tried to out do each other with receptions and honors.

"This is all nice," the Cavaliere said to his son, Paolo. "But we must be careful. If we stay in every town as long as they all want us to, we'll never get to Paris, which means we'll never get back to Rome."

The days blended together as the group moved north through the Italian countryside. They stopped only once for business—to inspect Bernini's work on the Chigi's family Chapel of Our Lady of the Vows, located in Siena's cathedral.

Eighteen year old Paolo was proud of himself. "I may only be an apprentice sculptor," he bragged to his father, "but of the four statutes, I can tell that you personally carved the Saint Jerome and Mary Magdalen. They are spectacular."

Bernini was proud of Paolo, but like his own father, he pushed his son along.

"Very good, Paolo. Now, which of my assistants carved the others?"

The youth blushed and shifted from one foot to the other as he thought. "I'm sorry, father," he stammered, "I guess I have a lot to learn."

Bernini put his arm around Paolo. "I didn't mean to embarrass you, son. That ability will come with time. The Saint Catherine is by Antonio Raggi and the Saint Bernard is by Ercole Ferrata. Shall we move along? It's time we resumed this interminable journey." *I've been working too hard—I don't even know how to talk with my sweet son.*

—

"Where do all of these people come from," one of the Frenchmen asked Paolo. "Doesn't anyone work in Italy?" "They just stand there, staring at the old man," said the other.

Paolo grabbed the reins and stopped the carriage. Bernini watched with interest.

The youth screamed at the Frenchmen. "What's the matter with you two stupid fat heads? These people have turned out to see my father. If either of you had a brain in your head, you'd realize they are curious—they've probably never seen a world famous person. That's why they line the roads. And 'just stand there.' And 'stare.' Don't you two pathetic creatures realize whom you are accompanying to France? You better show more respect for Cavaliere GianLorenzo Bernini or you'll end up walking back to Paris."

The Cavaliere motioned for his son to join him in the carriage. Paolo latched his horse to the coach and jumped in.

"Son," Bernini said. "Don't you think you were a little hard on them?"

Paolo took a few minutes to cool down before he answered. "No I don't father. I'm proud of you and I don't care who knows it. Did you hear what they said about the Italians? What's wrong with those Frenchmen, anyway?"

Bernini laughed out loud. "They're Frenchmen." he said, with no concern that the drivers might overhear him. "That's their problem."

Paolo loved Bernini's attitude. *Father always cuts through the superfluous—he's like a lighthouse beacon to me, no matter how rough the sea, he always directs me to a safe shore. I've been afraid to ask him but this might be a good time.*

"Father, what do you think of these gawking crowds? Don't they bother you?"

The Cavaliere looked at his young son with a combination of love, respect and concern. *Paolo's a sweet boy, but he harbors a touch of naivety. Time to have some fun—I hope he can handle it.*

"I feel," Bernini said, "like a traveling elephant."

—

The two Frenchmen bet the rest of the entourage that the old man would never make it across the treacherous Alps. "The mountains," they bragged, "are menacing and the transit is tortuous."

When Bernini heard about the wager, instead of being upset, which the party was certain he would be, he urged everyone in the group to put every last scudi at risk.

At daybreak, the travelers gathered, but no Bernini. As if programmed, the Cavaliere appeared—sitting in a litter held aloft by four tall, muscular, menacing-looking servants.

The Frenchmen were flummoxed.

Bernini couldn't help grinning. "Young Louis XIV sent them. All four of them. Now let's hurry along, Paris awaits."

"This isn't fair," one of the Frenchmen complained to Paolo.

"Don't look at me," Paolo replied. "He's your King, not mine."

The entire population of the border town of Le Pont-de-Beauvousin turned out to welcome the entourage.

An elderly, distinguished looking man approached the travelers. "I am the District Representative of the King of France, His Majesty Louis XIV. Welcome to France and our humble border town. Our Master has instructed us to attend to you in the way that it is customary in the case of Princes and Ambassadors. Every town on your journey from here to Paris has been similarly officially notified. It has been commanded by His Majesty,"

"This is going to be fun," Paolo whispered to his father.

"Considering how far we have journeyed," Bernini scoffed, "it's the least the King can do."

A royal coach joined the entourage on the outskirts of Paris. A handsome nobleman, in his mid-fifties, exited the carriage and approached Bernini, who immediately jumped down from his coach. The two men shook hands.

"Welcome to France, Cavaliere," the Frenchman said. "My name is Paul Freart, Sieur de Chantelou. The King has appointed me to see to all your needs while in our country. Naturally, I consider this assignment a singular honor, and I will do everything in my power to make your visit comfortable and memorable."

Chantelou presented his official welcome in French, but since Bernini didn't speak French, he didn't understand a word the man said. Bernini answered in Italian.

"It has been a great honor for me to be called to the service of a King of France. As well as this, the Pope, my lord and master, ordered me to come here. But had there been no more than these considerations I should have still have been in Rome. The chief and main cause of my leaving home was that I heard that the King was not only a great Prince, but also the greatest gentleman in his kingdom. This report made me curious to get to know him, and stimulated my wish to serve him. I lament that my talents are not proportionate to this honor, nor do they correspond with the estimate people have of me."

Reaction to Bernini's speech:

Paolo: *My father would have been the greatest diplomat of all time.*

The Two Frenchmen: *I feel like throwing up.*

The Rest of the Entourage: *These poor French people—they have no chance.*

Chantelou: *The Cavaliere probably rehearsed that speech for a week. Still, his modesty surprises me.*

"Cavaliere Bernini," Chantelou said in Italian, "your words are as beautiful as your works of art—and I believe I have seen most of them during my visits to Rome."

"I can see," Bernini said, "that you speak perfect Italian. That indicates your distinguished monarch is thoughtful. That pleases me."

"Thoughtful of you, yes," Chantelou said. "In fact, my instructions are to treat your stay in France as a royal visit. Now, if you are prepared, I will escort you to Paris—it is only a few miles up the road. Oh, one thing. Would you mind if I kept a diary of your visit?"

—

Bernini and his entourage arrived in Paris on June 2nd, 1665, six weeks after leaving Rome.

Chapter CXXXVI

Nick J. Mileti

JUNE 2, 1665.

As my first entry, I will note our distinguished guest's physical appearance.

Bernini is thin, of medium height. His skin is on the dark side but his complexion is clear. He is almost bald on top, and his hair is thinning—as it inevitably does for all—but what remains is pure white, and wavy. His eyelashes are long, his forehead is high and his large dark eyes resemble those of an eagle. I observed him intimidate one of his assistants with a glance.

Not unexpectedly, Bernini has an assured manner and fiery temperament. I asked him if he objected to my inquiring into his age. He replied not at all, that he was sixty-seven years old. I told him he appeared very vigorous for his age, which seemed to please him. He added that if I didn't mind, he would like to walk as much as possible while in France, as he was fond of walking and felt half his age whenever he went for a brisk stroll.

The King has provided the entire party with lavish accommodations, which appear to be satisfying. Four highly trained servants—in addition to the three the Cavaliere brought from Rome—were made available to Bernini on a twenty-four hour basis.

The Cavaliere asked me if I would mind if his majordomo was put in charge of his culinary needs. Naturally, I consented to this unusual arrangement, although I first pointed out that the typical guest in France was grateful for the opportunity to partake in our cuisine. Bernini responded that he had peculiar eating habits with which he did not want to bother our chefs. I think he was merely being polite when he said that.

Bernini asked to meet with His Majesty, but since the King is not in Paris, I recommended that the Cavaliere rest for the remainder of the day. This first night, Jean-Baptiste Colbert, the Superintendent of the King's buildings, left Saint-Germain—where the court was ensconced—and presented himself to Bernini. The short meeting was cordial and plans were made for an in-depth tour of Paris the next day. The Cavaliere suggested they set out at daybreak. Colbert reluctantly agreed to the early hour.

JUNE 3, 1665

The first thing the Cavaliere commented on was the security. He said he appreciated the fact that all of the doors were guarded.

Colbert arrived—appearing half-asleep—and proceeded to give Bernini a tour of Paris. The Cavaliere was interested in the Gothic architecture of Notre Dame and Sainte-Chapelle. An in-depth tour of the Louvre was conducted later in the day. When I asked him what he thought of the King's residence, he replied that the existing work at the Louvre was of little consequence.

JUNE 4, 1665

Colbert arrived at seven this morning with two coaches-and-six. The entire party proceeded to Saint-Germain to meet the King. The two-hour ride was uneventful.

We were all waiting in the anteroom, as the King reportedly was not dressed. To the astonishment of everyone, the King—apparently unable to suffer the delay before seeing him—peered from around a curtain and searched the room trying to decide which one was Bernini.

The Cavaliere, who noticed the slight movement of the curtain said, "That is the King." When asked how he had been able to recognize the King, never having seen him before, he said, "I recognized in my first glance at that face a grandeur and a majesty such as could only be that of a great King."

Shortly thereafter, Bernini and his party were shown in for their audience with the King. Bernini repeated—word for word—what he said to me upon arrival, and then, regarding the Louvre, he said to His Majesty:

"I have seen, Sire, palaces of Emperors and Popes which are to be found in Rome and on the route from Rome to Paris. But for a King of France, a monarch of our own time, there is need for something greater and more magnificent than any of these. Let no one speak to me of anything small."

"Very good," the King said to the nobleman standing at his side. "Now I see that this is indeed the man as I imagined him."

The King then addressed Bernini. "I have a certain fancy to preserve the work of my predecessors, but should it be impossible to build on a grand scale without demolishing what they have left, let it be done. As far as money is concerned, there need be no restriction." I noticed that several of the courtier's winced.

The remainder of the day, Bernini met the other members of the Royal Family—the Queen Mother; the Queen, who is Spanish; and the King's brother, Monsieur and his wife, Madame, who is the daughter of King Charles I of England. I noticed that Bernini paid particular attention to the Queen Mother, Anne of Austria.

I found it strange—although the Cavaliere did not—that the King's brother, Monsieur, did not discuss the work Bernini was to do on the Louvre but rather asked him if he would have time to do a portrait of the King. Bernini replied he would make time if the King himself requested the bust.

JUNE 9-JUNE 19, 1665

Bernini has been working on his third set of Louvre drawings for the last ten days. Evidently Colbert nixed the first two proposals over the past year or two.

Colbert studied the present drawings in great detail and raised innumerable issues, all of details. I fear the Cavaliere's Italian blood has reached the boiling point, because Bernini said to me: "Colbert's critical observations are of greater number than the stones required to build it." Colbert is not making my task any easier.

JUNE 20, 1665

Second meeting between the King and Bernini. As usual, thirty or forty others were present.

His Majesty studied the new elevation for the east wing of the Louvre. His enthusiasm was remarkable. As he looked at the drawings, he commented to the assembled group "This is not only the most beautiful drawing ever made, but also the most beautiful that ever could be made. I am delighted that I asked the Holy Father to grant me the Signor Cavaliere. No one other than he would have been capable of this."

The King turned to Bernini and said, "I had high hopes of you, but your work has surpassed my expectations." Bernini replied, "Sire, inasmuch as you have not seen the buildings of Italy, you have remarkably good taste in architecture."

The King's courtiers were shocked at this remark and expected the King to severely reproach Bernini. Instead, His Majesty replied that while it was true that he had not seen the buildings of Italy, he had examined the indifferent designs for the Louvre submitted by French architects, so he was able to appreciate the merits of Bernini's. The members of Bernini's party greatly enjoyed the repartee. It seems as if there is a rivalry of sorts between the French and the Italians.

As the Cavaliere was preparing to take his leave, His Majesty surprised everyone, except Bernini, by requesting that he undertake a portrait bust of him. Bernini readily agreed, but said he would need twenty sittings of two hours each. The first gasps that filled the room were overwhelmed by the second set of gasps, which occurred when the King agreed to the sittings. The courtiers surreptitiously whispered among themselves that they had never heard His Majesty agree to sit for any artist, much less agree to twenty sittings of two hours each.

I overheard Bernini tell his son Paolo that this convinced him that the bust was the real reason the King wanted him to come to France. Paolo asked his father why a marble portrait could be so important. The Cavaliere pointed out to his son what a coup getting him (Bernini) to France was for the young Louis XIV—that this makes him more important than the King of England. I understood what he meant, because I knew that Bernini had refused to journey to England and sculpted the bust of Charles I from a Van Dyke painting.

Paolo asked him whether he would continue working on the Louvre drawings. Bernini laughed and answered of course. When Paolo asked him why, the Cavaliere said why not. I'm being paid and I don't have much else to do here in France.

JUNE 21, 1665

Today was a day of mixed emotions for Bernini. He told me that he was pleased to get on with the portrait of the King, as sculpture has always been his first love and the King was an intriguing sitter. He was displeased, however, that since his time in France was so short, he had no time to get a block of marble from Italy, and had to make do with what was already cut and happened to be in Paris.

I took him and Giulio Cartari—his assistant in sculptural matters—to seek out an appropriate block of marble. We walked along the River Seine, to the Tuileries and the Val-de-Grace. The Cavaliere selected three blocks, which he requested be delivered to him the next day.

I asked Bernini what he thought of the Tuileries Palace. He said it was a colossal trifle whose articulation resembled a troupe of tiny children. I also asked him what he thought of the church of Val-de-Grace. He said the dome looked like a little cap on a big head.

JUNE 22, 1665

The blocks of marble have not arrived and Bernini is upset. He sent for Colbert, but since he was out of the city—with the King at Saint-Germain—his assistant Charles Perrault reported to the Cavaliere. In no uncertain terms Bernini evidenced his displeasure that the blocks of marble had not arrived as ordered. He pointed out to Perrault that this would never happen in Italy.

Perrault's excuse was that Bernini was to do a full-length statute of the King, not a bust. The Cavaliere pointed out—calmly at this point—that this was the first he had heard of this matter. Perrault replied that Colbert had written of this idea to some minor functionary.

Again, I could see Bernini's Italian blood boiling. He exploded, saying to Perrault "No. It has to be a bust, and for more reasons than one. First, because that was what was agreed. Secondly, because a bust permits of refinements which are not feasible in a full-length statute. One is intended to be shown in a room, the other in a long gallery. A bust is to be seen from close quarters, a statute from a distance. It therefore needs to be seven or eight feet high, and there is not even enough good marble in Paris for a bust, let alone a statute."

He told me later that he believed that Perrault, directly, and Colbert, indirectly—for whatever reasons—were committed to undermining him.

I can see that the Cavaliere is no easy target. He wrote Colbert regarding Perrault and also asked permission to return to Saint-Germain tomorrow to sketch the King. He explained that he expected Perrault to retrieve him at daybreak. I felt he took an instant dislike to Perrault.

JUNE 23, 1665

Upon our arrival in Saint-Germain, we discovered the King playing tennis. His Majesty waved to Bernini indicating he should make himself at home. Bernini sat at the side of the tennis court and sketched until the game was over.

Following lunch and a siesta, the Cavaliere was shown into the King's apartments where he joined the King who was about to give an audience to the English ambassador. He sketched throughout the meeting. Everyone present admired the drawings, particularly His Majesty. He said: "Very good. This is the best and most faithful likeness that has ever been done of me."

As we departed, we happened upon a nurse with the infant Dauphin. Bernini commented that the first son of the French King was too fat. Upon hearing of these remarks, the court reacted badly. They seem to be keeping track of his numerous snide comments, which I believe to be merely tactless.

JUNE 24-27, 1665

Bernini working on the clay model for the bust of the King. Nothing for me to do.

JUNE 28, 1665

Back to Saint-Germain for another sketching session with His Majesty. Bernini learned today that even though the King uses me as an interpreter, he knows more than his share of the Italian language. Here is how it happened:

Bernini was sketching the King, who was presiding over a meeting. Suddenly, the King's eyes met those of the Cavaliere's. "Sto rubando" (I am robbing you) Bernini said. His majesty immediately responded: "Si. Ma e per restituere (Yes, you are robbing me, but only in order to give it back).

JUNE 29, 1665

Today Bernini mentioned his love of music and plays—he said he has a theatre in his home, which astounded me—so I took him to see the Salle Neuve. As soon as he saw it, he said it was "disproportionately long and has poor seating."

When I told him that I'd been to see a play there the previous week and was disappointed in the acoustics, plus most of the action couldn't be seen, the Cavaliere immediately asked what did I expect when the proscenium was only 32 feet wide, but the stage had to be 140 feet deep. I was amazed that he could recite the exact measurements utilizing his naked eye.

JUNE 30, 1665

Only two blocks of marble were delivered today. Bernini was not pleased with the quality of either.

JULY 1, 1665

Bernini showed the clay model of the bust to Colbert. Colbert was his usual, effusive self when addressing the Cavaliere.

JULY 6, 1665

Bernini's assistant began blocking out the piece of marble the Cavaliere had chosen. Bernini was concerned that he would not be able to produce a bust of the highest quality due to the low quality of the French marble.

I took the Cavaliere to see some drawings belonging to the painter, Mignard. Bernini studied the drawings for some time and then made a surprising statement. He said that Raphael's talent was so great that his first thoughts, expressed in his drawings, were among the most beautiful things in the world, and that in general drawings by the greatest masters were, in a way, more satisfying than the finished works.

JULY 8, 1665

An extended visit to the Royal Armory. Bernini studied every suit of armor, and made numerous sketches of several of them. He said he plans on incorporating a suit of armor into the portrait. When I inquired why, he replied it was for symbolic reasons.

JULY 14, 1665

An exciting day for me. I watched Bernini himself begin working the marble. His son, Paolo, cautioned me not to interrupt his father when he was cutting marble. Cartari told me not to break the Cavaliere's concentration for any reason. Rossi suggested I stay home when the maestro was carving.

Beyond Michelangelo

JULY 15, 1665

Bernini working on the marble. Colbert came to see the one-day's progress. He noted its majesty and degree of resemblance to the King. I believe the Cavaliere was relating to the obvious insincerity of Colbert's premature praise when he surprised me with a conspiratorial look before returning to his sculpting. I think he likes me a little.

I have today heard that malicious rumors are circulating in Paris about Bernini's brashness, including an incredible one. The court is saying that on the Cavaliere's first audience, the King himself realized that Bernini was prejudiced against all things French.

JULY 19, 1665

After several more days of intense cutting, we journeyed back to Saint-Germain for the fifth and last sketching session, which turned out to be a highly unusual one. Bernini said he wanted to draw the King in a different way. He asked the King to sit down, and then he got down on his knees and drew him from there.

JULY 22, 1665

Bernini is highly agitated today due to the events surrounding the altar at Val-de-Grace, which he had been commissioned to design by the Queen Mother. He is convinced his design will never be used; that a cabal of French architects is out to prevent any project of his from being consummated.

He said that the French were fickle. He told me that Pope Urban VIII, Maffeo Barberini, when he was still a Cardinal, had dissuaded him from coming to France; that things were started here with enthusiasm, but this enthusiasm only lasted as long as straw took to burn; and that after appreciating and encouraging someone for a year or two they would then drop him—and that the one who was best at intrigue was always the most successful, even if devoid of ability and talent. He said he now realized what Cardinal Barberini meant.

I did not tell the Cavaliere what Colbert told me. Colbert said: "I would willingly have paid 200,000 ecus for Bernini's design of the baldaquin in the church of Val-de-Grace if only it could have been the work of a Frenchman."

JULY 25, 1665

The Cavaliere was scheduled to visit, after many delays, the famous art collection of Eberhard Jabach, but the visit had to be canceled because we were informed that Jabach had gone to the country. The King's coach, in which we normally traveled, was already at his door, and Bernini was furious. He equated the situation with the week's delay in the delivery of the marble. "It is not just he," he said. "It is the fault of the nation. There is no punctuality in France." I replied that we are not all the same, and did not mention that Jabach was German.

As an alternative, I suggested that we go to my home to view my collection of paintings by Nicolas Poussin. Bernini got down on his knees in order to examine more closely the Seven Sacraments Poussin had painted for me some twenty years ago. The Cavaliere was surprised, and I believe pleased, when he learned that I was Poussin's principal patron. I believe it is for that reason the Cavaliere said, with great emotion, that he likes Poussin because he works with this (pointing to his forehead), and that I had shown him the merit of an artist who makes him realize that he is nothing.

At times like this, it is difficult for me to believe that this diplomatic man is one and the same as the non-diplomatic one I so often see. Bernini is a complex man.

JULY 27, 1665

Bernini asked for a piece of taffeta, which he wanted to use as a model for the drapery he planned for the bust. Bernini said the marble was stale and he was not sanguine about it holding up to the chisel for the cutting of the drapery. He said he wanted the drapery to float and this undercutting might necessitate extensive use of the drill.

JULY 29, 1665

Colbert visited the workshop once again and said the bust was already such a good likeness, he did not think live sittings would be necessary. Displaying his quick mind, Bernini replied: "There is always more to be done if one wishes to do it well. Up to this point I have drawn on my imagination, and have only rarely had recourse to the sketches, which I made. I have relied principally on what is here (he patted his forehead) where I have the idea of His Majesty. Otherwise I should be making, in effect, a copy and not an original. But all this is very painful to me. In commanding his portrait the King could not have asked of me anything more laborious. Nevertheless, I hope that the result will be the least bad of all the busts that I have done. In this kind of portraiture mere resemblance is not sufficient. One must express what goes on in the heads of heroes."

I wonder if Colbert is really trying to keep Bernini from the King, which the Cavaliere suspects. There is no question that there is incredible jealously of the famous Italian in the French court.

JULY 30, 1665

Rode in the carriage with Colbert. On our way to visit with Bernini, Colbert was in a foul mood and expressed displeasure with the Cavaliere in several regards. However, when we entered Bernini's studio in the Louvre, Colbert adjusted his expression to his usual smile.

AUGUST 8, 1665

Because the King and his court are moving back to Paris from Saint-Germain, Bernini and his party were moved today from their quarters in the Hotel de Frontenac to the Palais Mazarin, a short distance from the Louvre. The Cavaliere was given Cardinal Mazarin's old rooms, which were more luxurious than those he vacated. Unexpectedly, the Cavaliere started to reminisce about his life-long friend Giulio Mazzarini, as he called him. The Cardinal's death was obviously a great blow as his eyes were filled with tears during the entire discussion.

AUGUST 9, 1665

Numerous demands are being made on Bernini, both public and private. Colbert said the King wanted the Cavaliere to advise him on the training of young artists, and for him to take an active part in the French Academy he, the King, was planning for Rome. The private requests range from new buildings to staircases for existing buildings. I notice that Bernini graciously accommodates every demand, even though he is confident nothing significant will come of his plans in this country.

AUGUST 11, 1665

His Majesty arrived at Palais Mazarin for his first sitting. He said he had come directly from Saint-Germain, without partaking of lunch. Bernini gave His Majesty a fresh pear, which the King eagerly devoured. Only half-a-dozen courtiers, including Colbert, accompanied the King. They were once again shocked at the unprecedented informality between Bernini and the King. I calculate that the Cavaliere himself has worked on the bust ten full days. All, especially the King, praised it vigorously.

AUGUST 12, 1665

Two of the courtiers, Le Tellier and de Lionne, called upon Bernini today. After a bit of small talk, they told the Cavaliere that the reason Colbert was unexpectedly present at the sitting yesterday was to impress the King with his devotion to duty. Bernini did not acknowledge these remarks. Rather, he talked about the bust and explained the object of the live sittings.

He said: "As regards the face, it is for the King and myself to finish the work. He has put me in the state where I see him in my mind's eye, in the image which I have formed and printed on my imagination. I have drawn him in council, as you have seen, and speaking in his natural manner without having to keep still or submit to anything. If I had not done this, or if I had sketched him seated, he would have appeared constrained, and the image would have lacked vivacity. Since then I have not even used my drawings, not wishing to copy my own work but to create an original. They were only made to saturate me with the image of the King."

Bernini concluded by stressing the difficulty of marble portrait sculpture. He pointed, out as proof, that his idol, Michelangelo, had never been willing to undertake it.

AUGUST 14, 1665

The Cavaliere was in a good mood at the sitting today and amused His Majesty's young courtier's by stalking stealthily round the King. This was an incredible sight, considering the age and stature of the great artist, and even the King had difficulty in not laughing.

AUGUST 19, 1665

Today Bernini supplied Colbert with more drawings of the Louvre. The Cavaliere has spent considerable time on Louvre drawings and said to me that he hopes and prays that the bulk of that work is now behind him.

AUGUST 21, 1665

His Majesty arrived today for his sitting, accompanied by forty courtiers. The Cavaliere said nothing about the difficulty in working around such a large crowd, but after the King departed, Bernini protested to me, saying: "They have the King all the time, but grudge me even half an hour with him."

AUGUST 23, 1665

At today's sitting, Bernini told the King that it was very difficult to give a natural lightness to his hair because of the difficulty of undercutting the stale marble. The Cavaliere said that French builders and materials are entirely inferior to those in Italy. His Majesty refrained from commenting.

After the King left the studio, Bernini was in a talkative mood. He pointed out that a man dressed all in one color seems bigger than one whose clothes are of different colors. He said that in one of his sculptures the head seemed too small, though it was in fact correct for a work of that kind, namely one-ninth of the total height. He said he thereupon re-measured the Antique sculptures, the Antinous, and the Apollo Belvedere, but found they were no different. Finally he realized that it was a piece of drapery over the shoulder of his figure that produced this effect. When he reduced it the proportions appeared correct.

Before we left the Louvre today, Bernini requested to see the King's bedroom, in order to better understand his subject. The Cavaliere glanced at the ornately embellished room and then said at once: "The decorations are that of a woman's room." Since the room was previously that of the Queen, Bernini was technically correct. Fortunately, the King was not present, but the courtier's who heard Bernini held this comment against him, and were pleased to inform the King of it.

AUGUST 24, 1665

Today a young Englishman who was visiting and studying in Paris called on Bernini. His name is Christopher Wren and he is determined to become a great architect, even though he is already thirty-three years old. After saying the most flattering things possible, Wren asked the Cavaliere in such an earnest way to see his designs for the Louvre, Bernini acquiesced. The Cavaliere told me later that he liked the youngster's enthusiasm, that nothing great had ever been achieved without enthusiasm.

I happened upon the young man the next day and he showed me a letter he had written to his friend, Doctor Bateman. The part regarding Bernini said 'Mons. Abbe Charles' introduced me to the acquaintance of Bernini who showed me his designs of the Louvre and of the Kings statute . . . Bernini's design of the Louvre I would have given my Skin for, but the old reserv'd Italian gave me but a few Minutes View . . . I had only Time to copy it in my Fancy and Memory; I shall be able by Discourse, and a Crayon, to give you a tolerable Account of it.'

SEPTEMBER 3, 1665

Bernini told me he is extremely pleased with how the King's hair finally turned out, and he asked me to explain his achievement to His Majesty. If beautiful things need verbal assistance, I am honored to be the spokesman, but I was truly surprised at this request.

I met with the King later in the day and delivered the message in what I hope were subtle tones. His Majesty then commented: "Bernini does not praise much." I replied that as far as I could see, the Cavaliere was an honest man, sometimes to a fault. The King then asked me point blank whether Bernini had said that his bedroom was that of a woman. I replied that that was a malicious misunderstanding.

SEPTEMBER 5, 1665

Bernini was invited to address the Academy today. His remarks were received with extraordinary enthusiasm and I repeat them here.

"I put forward the suggestion that the Academy acquire plaster casts of all the finest Antique sculptures, bas-reliefs and busts to serve for the instruction of young artists. In this way they will form an idea at the beginning of what is beautiful, and this will remain with them afterwards for all their lives . . .

"It will only be their ruin if they are put to draw from nature as soon as they begin their instruction. Natural appearances are almost always poor and lacking in nobility, and if the imagination of the young is fed on nothing else they will never be able to produce fine and grandiose effects, since these are not to be found in nature. Those who study nature must already be in possession of sufficient discrimination to be able to recognize its shortcomings and be able to correct them. Young artists with no experience are not capable of doing this . . .

"To illustrate this point I tell you that there are sometimes objects in nature which seem to be in high relief but which should not be so depicted; while there are others that should be but do not seem to be. Those who know how to draw will shut their eyes to whatever they show them which should not be included, and will incorporate what should be, but which may not show. And this I tell you once again, the young artist is not capable of doing, as the idea of the beautiful is not at his command . . .

"When I was still very young I often drew from the Antique. Then, when I made my first sculptures, I went back, whenever I was in doubt concerning anything, to the Antinous. Each time I saw this work I noticed beauties which I had missed until then, and which I never should have noticed had I not myself been a sculptor. For this reason I always advise my students and other artists not to devote all their time to study but to continue their own work concurrently. They should alternate production with copying—you might say pass between the active and the contemplative—and in this way great and marvelous progress comes about."

A young painter said he read recently that a painter should not show his work as soon as it was finished, and what did Bernini think of that. The Cavaliere said: "It is an academic question whether a painter should show his work as soon as it is finished or if he is not better advised to put it on one side and then to study it again before exhibiting it to the public. Annibale Carracci had the habit of showing his work immediately in order to discover it's faults—if it were too dry, or too hard, or had some other shortcoming—and therefore to correct them."

SEPTEMBER 13, 1665

Today's sitting was more interesting than usual, as the large crowd would attest. The King was arranging himself in his customary way when Bernini approached him and gently parted the locks of hair, which were arranged, which is the fashion, over the brow. In a quasi-authoritative manner, which the King knew was a joking manner, the Cavaliere said: "Your Majesty is a King who must show his forehead to one and all."

Within a day, the entire court followed that hairstyle, which is now known as 'The Bernini Modification.'

SEPTEMBER 15, 1665

Rossi, who had received a letter from Italy, informed Bernini that his wife, Caterina, was ill. The Cavaliere said he would leave today to get home to her, but I dissuaded him, pointing out that he was almost finished with the King's bust, and that it would be a shame to waste the entire trip, which had begun in April. I also said, from what he had told me about her, his wife would make the same recommendation. Bernini reluctantly agreed.

SEPTEMBER 22, 1665

His Majesty today asked Bernini why he is not referring to the numerous sketches he has made. The Cavaliere replied: "I prefer to make a copy of reality, not a copy of a copy. In fact, Sire, it is my opinion that all the delight of our senses is in imitation."

I was pleased that the King asked him what he meant by that because I was also puzzled. Bernini replied: "For example, consider the great enjoyment that comes from seeing a fine painting of a rancid and loathsome old woman, who in living and breathing flesh, would nauseate and offend us."

His majesty was delighted with Bernini's insight, and said: "Then I cannot wait to see your imitation of me."

SEPTEMBER 30, 1665

When I arrived today, the Cavaliere showed me a number of drawings he had recently made. I counted seven in all, which Bernini said he intended to give as gifts. He said that in Rome he made three every year, which he presented as gifts.

OCTOBER 4, 1665

Tonight the entire party attended a Palace Ball, thrown by the King in honor of Bernini who will soon be leaving Paris. Every important person in France was present for this command performance, including numerous smartly dressed French ladies. Throughout the evening, the guests were in awe of the Cavaliere and maintained a respectful distance.

Several of the courtier's, however, took advantage of the situation and bombarded Bernini with questions and requests for advice, and shockingly, even for his services of design. Bernini maintained his calm until a young Duke asked him to design lace for his wife's party gown.

This last request highly insulted the Cavaliere. He decided to leave the Ball forthwith, but on his way out of the ballroom a handsome military officer in full regalia accosted him. Bernini stopped out of courtesy. The gentleman said he had a question of major importance to ask him on behalf of his entire regiment, which had been discussing the matter. The room grew quiet, as the officer had spoken in a loud, challenging voice.

"Which are more beautiful, Italian or French women?" the officer asked.

Bernini, who was weary of the courtiers by this time, gave an extraordinary, devastating and unforgettable reply that still echoes throughout the ballroom.

"All are very beautiful, with this difference. Under the skin of Italian women runs blood, and under that of French women, milk."

The Cavaliere's footsteps resounded on the marble floor as he regally left the room, which remained in absolute, frozen silence. Until now, I have felt that the Cavaliere's comments, for the most part, have been uttered innocently, but this bon mot I question. It was so powerful and on target, I would not be surprised to learn that Bernini meant it maliciously. I will also be surprised if it is not quoted extensively in the years to come.

OCTOBER 5, 1665

Today was the thirteenth sitting. Bernini tapped the eyeballs of the King's marble likeness and then dramatically removed his work clothes.

"Hallelujah," he said. "The bust is finished."

The Cavaliere then made a moving speech. He extolled the King's virtues and the King's spirit, which he maintained were even more exalted than the King's position. His Majesty was deeply moved by Bernini's rare display of affection when, inexplicably, Bernini burst into tears and, to the confusion of His Majesty, and his courtiers, rushed out of the room.

The King rose from his chair and carefully examined his portrait. Although he had seen it in every stage, he seemed to be studying it anew. The King has been placed on a pedestal, with whirling drapery blowing to the right and the King's slightly raised head turned in the opposite direction. His face has a look of regal hauteur, bordering on arrogance, and is framed by a mass of intricately carved hair. The body has a silk collar and a hint of armor. Bernini has made the King look handsome.

Surprisingly, every courtier in the room was truly thrilled with the bust, but none more than the King, who proclaimed it the most outstanding marble portrait of all time. I agree with His Majesty, and can now understand why Bernini is referred to as the greatest sculptor who has ever lived.

OCTOBER 6, 1665

Bernini met with Perrault who was late for the meeting, which the Cavaliere took personally. The meeting concerned the Louvre, and Colbert's assistant raised numerous trivial matters. Seeing Bernini's Italian blood boil, I stated these matters could easily be settled several years hence. Perrault unwisely persisted, and, to my astonishment and disgust, said that he, and a hundred others, failed to understand why one of the pavilions in the Louvre plans was smaller than the other.

Bernini turned red. He replied: "I should like you to understand that it is not for the likes of you, Monsieur Perrault, to make objections of this kind. You may have some understanding of the uses of a palace, but the design is the concern of someone more skilled than you are . . .

"You are not worthy to brush the dust off my shoes. There will be no discussion about the matter which you have raised. His Majesty has approved the designs. I will complain to him, and I am going this very minute to Monsieur Colbert to inform him of the outrage which has been done to me. To a man of my standing, to me whom the Pope treats with friendship and affection, that I should be subjected to this. I shall complain to the King. I shall leave Paris tomorrow, and I don't know why I don't take a hammer to my bust after the insult that has been done to me."

Everyone present, including the Cavaliere's son, tried to calm Bernini, to no avail. Finally, to the great relief of Perrault, who feared for his career, Bernini agreed to go upstairs and the Cavaliere graciously forgot the incident. I don't believe Perrault realizes that Bernini has designed several palaces in Rome for the nobility.

OCTOBER 7, 1665

Bernini is like a caged rat. He has very little to do and to fill his time, he occasionally even helps his son Paolo with his marble relief of the Infant Christ. Paolo has been carving this small piece since he arrived in France, and it is to be a present to the Queen when they depart.

OCTOBER 10, 1665

On behalf of Louis XIV, Colbert made yet another request of Bernini to remain in France. This time he pointed out that arrangements have been made for his son Paolo to marry a noblewoman who had a substantial dowry. Colbert said the lady in question was not only beautiful, but that she was also willing, even anxious, for the coupling. The Cavaliere told me that he and Paolo discussed this generous offer at great length, but decided that France was not for either of them.

OCTOBER 11, 1665

Bernini had previously repeated, to the King and Colbert, the substance of the lecture he gave to the Academy, both of whom specifically requested him to do so. Today he said he had forgotten to include a recommendation and asked me to deliver it to them. I found it amazing that with all of the things on the Cavaliere's mind, he was still thinking about a speech he made over a month ago.

The paper said: "As advice in general to those who draw from nature I say, be on your guard, and examine the model carefully. Make the legs long rather than short. A fraction more will increase their beauty, and one less will make them seem heavy and lumpish . . .

"Make the shoulders of a man broad rather than narrow, as indeed is usually the case in nature. Make the head rather too small than to large. In the case of women make the shoulders a little narrower than they really are, since God gave breath to the shoulders of a man with a view to strength and labor, and breath of hips to women to enable them to bear us. Make the feet small rather than large, as you see them in beautiful models and in Antique art . . .

"Stance is of the greatest importance. Most men, unless they are very old, put their weight on one leg only. Naturally the shoulder on the side of the weighted leg should be lower than the other and if one arm is raised it will be the one on the side opposite the weighted leg. Otherwise the result is ungraceful and unnatural. In looking at the finest Antique statutes I have always found that this prevails."

OCTOBER 12, 1665

I now have a better understanding of how brilliant Bernini is. What caused me to have this insight was the Abbe Butti. Today the Abbe told me that he always doubted whether Bernini's design for the Louvre would be carried out, and he still doubted it. He also said that Colbert had always been against Bernini, but to date the King's decision in favor of his work had prevailed. The Abbe was confident Colbert would eventually succeed in scuttling Bernini's plans.

Bernini took this pronouncement philosophically. He said that the French are by nature, inconsistent (happily excluding me), the Prince (Louis XIV) young and impatient, the peace precarious, and therefore one should certainly not undertake vast projects (in France).

OCTOBER 17, 1665

The King conducted the ceremony of laying the foundation stone for Bernini's design for the Louvre. The event was not remarkable except for one fact. The commemorative plaque contained Colbert's name but not Bernini's. I met with Colbert at the end of the day who told me that in spite of today's ground breaking, he feared that after Bernini left France, things would not go well for him at the Louvre.

OCTOBER 20, 1665

The day was spent in warm farewells. Whether the courtier's were friends or enemies of the Cavaliere, they were anxious to be seen in this context.

Bernini gave me a warm hug and kissed me on both cheeks. He then said an astonishing thing, which I will always cherish, as I know the Cavaliere is not one to extend lavish compliments. He thanked me for my many courtesies and then said:

"You saved my life in France. If it had not been for you, I would have returned home long ago. While I admire you as a connoisseur and diplomat, it is a different trait that has made you my friend. You are a man of your word, unlike these others, and that is a trait I admire the most. It is for this reason you are the only person I really liked and trusted in this entire country. Good-by my friend, I will miss you."

I told the Cavaliere the past four and one-half months had been the most wonderful experience of my life. Bernini and I both had tears in our eyes as his carriage made its way out of Paris, headed for his beloved Italy.

Beyond Michelangelo

OCTOBER 21, 1665

Today I met with His Majesty. Colbert was leaving when I arrived. After closing the door, his famous smile turned into a deep frown. After meeting with the King I knew why.

His Majesty said he'd sent for me to inform me that he was delighted with the way I'd performed my duties and that it gave him great confidence in me. Then he said an extraordinary thing. He said he was not pleased with his courtier's attitude toward Bernini, who, after all, was his distinguished guest. I was surprised he told me that.

More surprising, he told me that the nobles in his court so completely disgusted him in this matter of importance he planned to curtail their various powers in the future. When I respectfully asked him why, the King said that if the behavior he personally observed was any indication of how the nobles acted behind his back, he had better take care of the matter.

DECEMBER 17, 1665

I have been informed that Bernini and his party arrived safely in Rome on December 3 to a tumultuous welcome, a celebration unprecedented in a city known for its love of celebrations.

—

Alexander VII toasted Bernini—tonight the anisette warmed him and had its usual mellow taste.

"I am pleased beyond words to see you back in Rome, and to hear that Caterina is feeling better," the Pope said. "Perhaps the two events are interrelated."

"It does sound suspiciously like the way I often reacted before I met her," Bernini said. "Yes, I think Caterina is happy to see me."

"All of Rome is happy to see you—I have never seen such festivity."

"In my little way, I hope I was able to help the Church in its critical work around the world."

"I have heard from the King himself—as well as my sources in France. The King was extremely pleased with you, even if his courtiers were not. Yes, you definitely helped. I can see it in numerous ways and I thank you."

"Holy Father, speaking of the courtiers, it would be impossible for me to describe the pettiness of the French court. Thank God I don't see that kind of behavior by the men who surround you. My friend Giulio mentioned the pettiness—and the intrigue—several times, but I didn't grasp his true meaning until I saw it for myself."

"So I've heard. Now, Cavaliere, I know you are anxious to be with your family, but stay a minute or two more as I have exciting news. While you were in France, the Dominican's were digging a trench for a wall and discovered a small obelisk in the garden of their church of Santa Maria sopra Minerva."

"That is exciting. Was there any writing on it?"

"That is the most exciting part. My Egyptian expert tells me that by interpreting the hieroglyphics, he can state categorically that this obelisk symbolizes sunlight—the light of learning. The obelisk belonged to the Temple of Minerva that lies below the present church. Considering that this particular obelisk has been lying in the ground of Rome for thousands of years, perhaps it is a personal sign of some sort that it was discovered during my pontificate."

"What are you planning to do with the obelisk, Holy Father?"

"I want you to design a monument utilizing it. The Dominicans suggest that it be placed in front of their church, in Piazza Minerva, and be dedicated to my honor."

Chapter CXXXVII

Nick J. Mileti

Borromini suffered attacks of anxiety, depression and mild epilepsy on and off all of his life—which made the great architect ill tempered and difficult at times. In mid-June of 1667, Francesco had his worse attack: Violent convulsions and seizures. He grimaced and rolled his eyes in a menacing manner; his face was alternately composed and frenzied; he roared like a lion while his body twisted in grotesque ways.

Francesco Massari, Borromini's sixteen-year-old live-in servant, was terrified—he had never seen his master like this. He ran to the nearby house of Borromini's nephew, Bernardo, screaming for help. When they arrived back at his home, Borromini was lying quietly on the floor. Together, they carefully placed him on his bed. Bernardo wiped the sweat from his uncle's face and brushed his hair from his eyes.

"Drink some of this chicken broth," Bernardo said. "It's nice and warm and will make you feel better."

"Do you know anything about dreams?" Borromini mumbled.

"Were you dreaming, uncle?"

"I was just dreaming that that Bernini fellow was never born, and to celebrate that perfect Act Of God, I ate every dish of pasta in Italy. Now leave me alone, I'm hungry and I want to go back to sleep—to dream my beautiful dream again."

—

Bernardo went into Borromini's library and poured himself a large goblet of brandy. *I love this uncle of mine, but considering the direction things are moving, he's going to turn me into an alcoholic.* He walked around the high-ceilinged room, marveling at the thousands of books, which were mostly on architecture and the humanities. He took down a tanned goat-leather copy of Giorgio Vassari's 'The Lives of the Artists.' *I'll read him the section on his idol, Michelangelo—that never fails to cheer him up.* He placed the book back on the shelf. *I have a better idea.* Bernardo searched through a massive pile of architectural drawings and sketches and finally found what he was searching for—a set of drawings for Sant' Ivo alla Sapienza. *Uncle's greatest accomplishment—these never fail to please him.*

"Sit up uncle, see what I brought you" Bernardo said as he spread the plans of Borromini's bed.

Borromini glanced at the top sheet. "No, no, no. Not today. The way I feel today, I want to see the Sant' Agnese in Agone drawings. All of them."

Reluctantly, Bernardo retrieved the Sant' Agnese drawings and spread them on the bed. *This scenario again—my absolute worse nightmare.*

Borromini glanced at the top sheet. "This first set is not by my hand."

"I know, uncle. They are the plans of the Rainaldi's, father and son. You remember—they had the original commission from Pope Innocent X. Ah, here's your set. I notice your changes were considerable."

"Borromini managed a brief smile. "Perfect, aren't they? Do you know what happened next?"

How would I know what happened next—I've only heard this story a hundred times. "No, uncle, what happened next?"

"I out-foxed them—I quit the Sant' Agnese job before Prince Pamphili could fire me. Then, if you can believe it, the Prince rehired young Rainaldi—his father was dead by now—and the little snot changed all of my plans."

Bernardo laughed to himself. *I better not mention he did the same.* "That Prince is not a nice person."

"Hand me that final set of drawings," Borromini said, gaining strength from his anger.

"It's late, uncle. I must be off." *I don't know why I try, I never win this argument.*

"I said bring them to me, you imbecile. See those swords hanging there? I don't want to use one on you."

Defeated Bernardo handed Borromini the final set of plans—they were signed by GianLorenzo Bernini. *I know what he's going to say. He's going to say 'This is the ultimate humiliation. That Bernini person was hired to replace my replacement, whom I replaced. Have the Gods gone crazy? Or have I?'*

Instead, Borromini said, "I love you, Bernardo," and crashed into a deep sleep.

Chapter CXXXVIII

Beyond Michelangelo

The doctor completed his examination of Borromini and called Bernardo into the adjoining room.

"Absolutely no more work," the doctor said. *I don't know if anything can help this man.* "Your uncle needs rest and lots of it. Perhaps a change of scenery would help."

Borromini, his nephew Bernardo and his servant Massari left for Milan the next day. Bernardo's convincing line: "You can show us the buildings you studied when you lived and apprenticed there."

When the trio reached Florence, the sight of Michelangelo's works caused Borromini to begin to lighten up. In Bologna, he ordered two plates of pasta, which astounded his traveling companions, because Borromini was normally such a light eater.

"I'll never forget the other time I was here," Borromini said between bites. "It was fifty years ago. I was on my way to Rome to earn fame and fortune and . . ." The architect fell asleep at the table.

As Bernardo tucked Borromini into bed, he smiled lovingly at his uncle. "Do you know why I'm smiling, uncle? I'm happy because the further we get from Rome, the better you seem to be doing."

"I should be doing better, as you put it," he replied. "I'm getting further and further away from that Bernini person."

In Milan, the trio spent the first week enjoying the churches where Borromini worked as a young stonemason. They saw the gigantic Duomo, of course, and the petite San Giuseppe.

Borromini led a tour of San Lorenzo Maggiore. "This church was rebuilt when I lived here. Does it remind you of any church in Rome?"

"I'd say your San Carlino, uncle," Bernardo, the budding architect, said. "Except your little jewel has much more character and ingenuity."

To the wonderment of Bernardo and Massari, Borromini smiled for the first time in months.

—

Bernardo arranged a small reception for old friends and relatives. With great interest he watched Borromini talking with two of his fellow stonecutters from long ago; they were acting like a day hadn't passed since they'd seen each other.

Bernardo's joy was quickly tempered. *My God, those men look half uncle's age. I guess I'm too close to the situation but I didn't realize how fragile and aged uncle has become. Compared to his friends, his complexion seems pasty, and worse, his eyes look vacant.*

A young waiter serving Borromini antipasto recognized the guest of honor.

"Mister Borromini, I'm going to be a great architect like you someday. Would you sign this napkin for me please—so I can prove to my father that I met you? Thank you. I know you live in Rome now. So does the other person I'd like to meet—that genius Bernini. Do you know him? GianLorenzo Bernini? They say he decorated Saint Peter's basilica single-handedly, and his latest monument is an obelisk sitting on top of an elephant of all things. They say it's sublime—that's the word they used. Do you know him?"

Bernardo and Massari rushed across the room but couldn't reach the waiter in time to silence him.

"I hear Bernini is better than Michelangelo—some say he's even better than the master. Can you believe it? He's the only thing people in Milan are talking about. Him and his work. Have you seen that elephant and obelisk? Do you know him? This Bernini?"

Borromini, who thought he'd been dreaming, finally focused and leapt from his chair, sending tables, chairs, food and guests flying. He grabbed the waiter and began to pound his head against the wooden floor. It took four young, muscular laborers to subdue the aged, but charged-up, Borromini.

—

Beyond Michelangelo

Within an hour, on explicit orders from the Milan police, the three men were packed and heading south.

Bernardo and Massari alternated driving the carriage non-stop, setting a speed record for a Milan-Rome trip.

Borromini set a record for time spent in non-stop sulking.

Chapter CXXXIX

Beyond Michelangelo

When the three weary travelers arrived home, the exhausted Bernardo went home and straight to bed. Borromini ordered his servant to take him to Piazza Minerva.

"Signor, no," Massari said. "You must rest—the doctors will kill me if you don't get rest."

"If you don't take me there," Borromini said, "I'll walk. I don't care what you do."

The servant made the Sign of the Cross and relented. The unlikely pair rode through the dark and deserted streets in silence. When they reached the small piazza in front of the Dominican church of Santa Maria sopra Minerva, Massari stopped.

Borromini stared at Bernini's small monument with a combination of disbelief and horror. *An elephant—with personality and charm—balancing an obelisk on his back. And all my life I thought I was the innovative one.*

—

"For the love of God," the servant said, "you've been here over two hours, just staring. Please, let me take you home. I beg you."

Borromini ignored Massari. He stumbled down from the carriage and jumped on the monument. He caressed the elephant's trunk and legs; he kissed his floppy ears; he snuggled up to his tilted head, defying the eyes that seemed to be mocking him. He read the inscriptions. He glared. He muttered. He mumbled to himself. And then, without any warning, Borromini collapsed.

—

Getting his master into the carriage, home, out of the carriage and into bed demanded all of the strength and skill Massari possessed. Pleased that he finally had his master in his bed where he belonged, the young servant collapsed, fully clothed, into his own bed in the adjoining room.

"Where are you, you fool?" Borromini called out from his bedroom. "Bring me my drawings from the library. My sketches, too. Put them on the floor next to the garden door and then leave me alone. I don't want to see you any more tonight."

Massari was dumbfounded. *He's not asleep? What's keeping him going?* It took the young servant numerous trips to bring all of the architectural drawings and sketches into Borromini's bedroom. When he finished, he ran out of his master's bedroom and fell back into his own bed, fully clothed, and completely exhausted.

—

The smell of smoke jolted Massari awake. He ran to his master's bedroom and almost fainted from shock. There was Borromini, standing at the open garden door, dropping papers onto a bonfire, looking like he was preparing a fire to roast meat for supper.

The young servant ran to Bernardo's house screaming, "Help me. Come quick. This time he's gone crazy."

Bernardo found Borromini hunched over an open fire, feeding priceless drawings, one by one, into the leaping flames. He was humming a tune from a Monteverdi opera.

"Please uncle," Bernardo pleaded, "come lie down. You're in shock."

The pathetic man offered no resistance.

—

"Don't throw water on those drawings," Bernardo screamed at Massari. "What's the matter with you? We've got to save what we can, not ruin them more."

The two frantic young men stomped out the fire, their boots turning black in the process. When the flames were extinguished, they fell on the floor, totally drained.

"Something serious must have happened," Bernardo said. "Do you have any idea what could have caused him to commit this crime against humanity? Those drawings were one of a kind and priceless."

The young servant stared straight ahead, half in shock and half in fear. He drew imaginary patterns on the floor with his right foot. Bernardo noticed.

"It's something you did, isn't it? Tell me, or I'll kill you. I swear."

"I . . . I took him to see Bernini's new monument—that elephant and obelisk. He made me do it. I begged him but he wouldn't listen."

Bernardo grabbed Massari by the throat and squeezed as hard as he could. The young servant's face turned from pink to deep red to purplish. His eyes bulged and his body shook.

Borromini moaned. Bernardo stopped. He looked at his uncle and then at his victim.

"What am I doing?" he said aloud. Bernardo released Massari as suddenly as he'd attacked him. "Go to bed," he said. "I don't want to look at you."

―

Bernardo was only twenty-four years old, but he had been apprenticed to Borromini since he was a child. This made what he had to do a double nightmare.

Bernardo sifted through the ashes and took what he could salvage to his home. Shaking, he poured himself a large goblet of brandy, drank it down and poured another. He sat at his drawing table and started to clean each document he was able to save. Overwhelmed with sorrow, he sobbed unashamedly. Bernardo felt nauseous. He hurried to the bathroom and threw up. It didn't help. *This tragedy will haunt me the rest of my life. The world has lost a library of irreplaceable documents and I couldn't stop the genocide. Why didn't I stay with him?*

―

Borromini smiled as he tossed and turned in his sleep. He dreamt an obelisk knocked down Bernini, and before he could get up from the ground, he was stomped to death by a herd of elephants. Each elephant had personality and charm.

Chapter CXL

Beyond Michelangelo

The next morning, Borromini awoke refreshed. *My dreams are getting better—I think. I just wish I could remember them better. Let's see. Last night. Elephants and obelisks were crushing that Bernini man and . . .*

The thought of Bernini's Elephant and Obelisk monument triggered another violent attack.

Massari ran for the doctor. "At this point, the only thing I can prescribe is rest," the doctor said to the young servant. "Call in the priest. And one more thing. Mister Borromini must never be left alone. I fear he may try to hang himself."

—

That night, Borromini's mania became more intense and his condition deteriorated. About a half-hour after supper, Borromini sat at his desk, took out paper and pencil, and began to write his will. At three in the morning he was still writing.

"Signor Cavaliere," Massari called out from the next room, "you ought to put out the light and go to sleep because it is late and the doctor wants you to sleep."

Borromini's mind was a jumble. "But then," he said, marshalling his thoughts, "I will have to light the lamp again when I wake up."

"Put it out," the young servant said, "because I'll light it again when you wake up."

That seems right. Borromini stopped writing, put the paper and pencil on his nightstand, blew out the light and drifted into a dreamless sleep—his first in months.

—

About five in the morning, after only two hours sleep, Borromini woke up. *Where am I?* He tried to focus in the dark room when his hand brushed against the pencil and paper on the table next to his bed. *Now I remember.*

"Massari, I'm up," Borromini called out. "Please light the lamp."

"Signore, no," the young servant answered in accordance with the strict orders of the doctor. "The doctor wants you to sleep."

The servant's reply infuriated Borromini. The more he thought about his young servant denying him the light, the more enraged he became. He got out of bed and paced the floor. He moved back and forth, back and forth, for over three hours—working himself into a frenzy.

And then, inexplicably, Borromini's mood turned from fury to despair.

—

Borromini's eyes focused on a sword hanging among the consecrated candles at the head of his bed. He pulled the sword out of the scabbard, placed the hilt on the bed, put the point of the sword to his side and fell on it.

The force of the fall rammed the sword clean through Borromini's body—from one side to the other.

The wounded architect fell screaming to the floor. When Massari heard the frantic shouts he ran into his master's room. The young servant saw Borromini sprawled on the floor with a sword sticking in him, and panicked. He started screaming and running in circles. He found Bernardo's house like a homing pigeon—more by instinct than by design.

—

Bernardo pulled the sword out of his uncle's side with great care but then wildly threw it away. The missile came within an inch of Massari's head. *I wish I'd hit him. No, I don't mean that.*

"What happened?" Bernardo asked

Between sobs, the trembling young servant told Bernardo the story of the lamp.

A resigned Bernardo studied Massari. *That story is so bizarre, it has to be true. I really can't blame this youngster—and I'm glad I can't. Very glad. I was losing control.*

"Go." Bernardo said. "Go to your room and let me think."

Beyond Michelangelo

Disconsolate, Bernardo hurried to call the doctor, all the while trying to analyze the situation logically. *There is no way Borromini would try to kill himself merely because his servant wouldn't light his lamp. That could be a trigger maybe, but not tne cause. I hope some day I can come to understand what was going on in my uncle's brilliant, complex mind.*

Chapter CXLI

Beyond Michelangelo

It was a gray summer morning in Rome. The sun was behind the clouds, but in spite of the early hour, the searing August heat began to permeate the very fabric of the city. Bernardo was exhausted, mentally and physically. He'd stayed awake the entire humid night watching over Borromini, trying to understand why his uncle would try to kill himself.

Borromini stirred. Bernardo quickly filled a goblet with the clear broth he'd prepared during the night. "Here, uncle, drink this."

Borromini slapped at his nephew's hand, sending the broth all over the room. Undaunted, Bernardo tried again. "Please, uncle. Please. Just a little. Please."

Bernardo spooned some hot broth into his uncle's mouth. After spitting out the first few spoonfuls, Borromini started to drink the broth—which seemed to invigorate him.

"Remember that trip we took to Milan yesterday?" he asked.

"Don't try to talk . . ."

"No, no, I want to tell you something. Something important. Give me more of that broth."

Encouraged, Bernardo fed his uncle more broth. He wiped Borromini's chin and kissed him on the forehead.

"The trip was over a month ago, uncle, but what about it?"

Borromini got a far away look in his eyes. "Remember when we stopped in Florence?"

"That was the highlight of the trip for me," Bernardo said honestly. "Seeing Michelangelo's work seemed to energize you. Why was that?"

Borromini mulled the question over in his mind. "Michelangelo was my most valued inspiration—the one man I could emulate with absolute confidence, and . . ."

Borromini coughed violently, causing Bernardo to spill some broth on the blanket. He called for Massari to come in and clean it up. "Leave now," Bernardo told the young servant. "Stay with the priest and doctors in the next room." He spooned more broth. "You were talking about Michelangelo, uncle."

"When I saw Michelangelo's works for the first time in Florence—that was about fifty years ago—something magical happened. At that moment, I knew what I wanted to do with my life. I wanted to be a real artist. No, I wanted to be more. I wanted to be Michelangelo. Even better."

"Uncle, you are a better architect than Michelangelo ever was." *Even if it weren't true, I'd say it. But it is true.*

Borromini tried to acknowledge the compliment with a smile but was too weak to do it.

"I want to see Bernini."

Bernardo gasped. *I've never heard him say Bernini's name plain like that. It's always 'that Bernini,' or 'that Bernini person' or something similar.* "You're delirious, uncle. Have some more broth."

"Has your hearing gone bad? Do what I say. I want to see Bernini. I have to see him now. Before it's too late."

—

The bewildered Bernardo ran all the way to Bernini's palace. Caterina answered the frantic knocking on the front door.

"Mrs. Bernini? I am Bernardo, Borromini's nephew. I . . ."

"Come in, Bernardo," Caterina said. "You look dead tired. A cappuccino will warm you and I'll grill you a sausage—you look like you haven't eaten for some time."

"No. I mean don't cook. I mean I have no time."

"I'll call my husband."

—

Bernardo was shocked when he saw Bernini. *I know he's about the same age as uncle, but he looks half as old.*

"It's Bernardo I understand," Bernini said shaking his visitor's hand. "To say I'm surprised to see Borromini's nephew in my home would be quite an understatement—considering I haven't seen the man in some forty years. To what do I owe . . ."

"My uncle tried to kill himself last night."

"Oh my God. Is there anything I can do?"

"He wants to see you."

—

On the short ride through the early morning empty streets, Bernardo told Bernini about the tragic events. When they reached Borromini's modest home, Bernardo asked the priest and doctors to leave them alone with his uncle.

"Uncle, I'm here," Bernardo said. "Wake up, it's me. And look who else is here."

Borromini slowly focused on the two figures standing by the bed. "Bernardo, it's you. I was afraid you left me forever. Who is that with you?"

"Uncle, you asked to see him. It's Bernini."

Borromini shook like he was having another spasm. "Here? He's here? What's that Bernini person doing here? What's he up to this time?"

Bernardo was getting more distressed by the minute. *I hope I can live through this.* "When he heard you were sick," Bernardo said, "he wanted to see you. Uncle, please be nice to your visitor. He was nice enough to come to your side."

Bernini reached down and took Borromini's cold hand. "My wife and family are praying for your soul."

Borromini pulled his hand away. "I can pray for myself."

Bernardo was at a loss for words. Bernini took Borromini's hand once more and filled the awkward gap.

"Your church of Sant' Ivo. It's like no other and you can be proud."

Borromini coughed up and swallowed a mouthful of phlegm. "Bernardo, who is this holding my hand?"

"It's me, Francesco. Bernini. GianLorenzo Bernini."

Borromini's eyes widened. "Bernini? He's here?"

"What is it, Francesco? Bernini asked. "Why did you ask to see me? Do you have something on your mind you want to tell me?"

Borromini swayed back and forth. "Bernardo, if you see Bernini, I want you to tell him something. I want you to tell him I have seen every project of his in Rome. When nobody was looking, I'd go . . ."

Borromini clutched his chest and rolled his eyes.

"It's okay, Francesco," Bernini said. "Save your strength."

Borromini shook so uncontrollably he knocked the broth off of the nightstand. He was able to continue. "I used to pray that Bernini would fail but he wouldn't cooperate. He got better and better and I got more and more depressed. I've made my confession to God, you know that Bernardo, but I have to say these other things—I want to join Maderno and Michelangelo, my two idols, with a totally clear conscience."

Bernini felt like crying. *This is certainly the most unusual thing I've ever been through.* "Francesco, it's not necessary . . ."

Borromini continued. "Remember that Pope? The one before Gregory? You know, the Borghese. Paul V, that's it. Forgive me Lord, but that Pope was wrong. Bernini is not the Michelangelo of his age, he has moved beyond the master. Bernini has moved beyond my idol. Bernini has moved Beyond Michelangelo. Oh, this Bernini, this scourge of my life. And the bell towers. Bernardo, tell him I'm sorry I . . ."

Francesco Borromini sighed and closed his eyes. Bernardo called out for the doctors, but it was too late. The troubled architectural genius had succumbed to the injuries he inflicted on himself the previous day. The date of his death was August 3, 1667. He was sixty-eight years old.

Chapter CXLII

Bernardo couldn't shake his depression. He tried, but none of his sure-fire methods worked. *It's the combination of uncle's death and my stupidity that has me down. Like most, I thought Borromini hated Bernini because they had divergent personalities. Then I went through a period where I thought it was because uncle felt Bernini was taking advantage of him. But I eventually realized it wasn't either of those things. Nor was it because Bernini never showed Borromini any respect, or that Bernini received commissions uncle thought he should have received. No. Those are all logical reasons, but Borromini was not logical when it came to his rival. I'm glad he told me why he had his obsessive hatred for Bernini, because I never would have guessed the reason in a million years. Now that I know—it's so simple. Bernini surpassed Michelangelo in ability and Borromini didn't. To say it another way, Borromini hated Bernini because Bernini stole his dream.*

In a perverse way, Bernardo felt exhilarated. After a lifetime of wondering, he finally knew.

It was an awful realization.

—

Caterina finished slicing a bag of peaches, sugared them, and piled them on a plate for her husband.

"You have been so sad lately," she said. "Maybe these will make you feel better. What's bothering you, sweetheart?"

"It's nothing, really. It's just that I can't walk three feet without someone asking me what I think Borromini could have accomplished if he'd had my personality."

Caterina laughed and blew her husband a kiss across the table. "Everyone should have your personality. It's perfect—just like you are."

"I'm serious, honey. It's maddening. They ask what I think Borromini could have accomplished if he hadn't had that irrational, all-consuming hatred of me. What am I, a Borromini scholar?"

"I understand, dear. What do you say to the pests?"

"Frankly, I'm getting more and more tempted to point out the man was deranged. I mean it. I think he was mentally unbalanced. But I don't say those things. Why? Because I remember my father's advice never to speak ill of another artist."

Caterina didn't attempt to hide her admiration as she beamed all over. "So what do you say, darling?"

"I say I didn't know the gentleman as a person. I say as an architect, he was adequate, he just didn't know when to stop."

Caterina whistled. "That's strong. May I tell you something truthfully? I've heard that Borromini was a genius, but he would have accomplished substantially more if he would have directed his energies into positive channels."

Bernini nodded. "I, for one, would certainly have appreciated that."

Chapter CXLIII

In the thirteen years after Francesco Borromini's death, GianLorenzo Bernini continued to produce artistic masterpieces of extraordinary creativity and beauty.

—

Alexander commissioned Bernini to design his tomb, which was to be located in Saint Peter's. The Pope, kneeling in prayer, is surrounded by statutes symbolizing his virtues—Charity, Prudence, Justice and Truth. Unfortunately, the location for the tomb was burdened by a pre-existing door, which could not be sealed off. Bernini, in his usual creative way, turned the problem into an asset by designing the figure of death lifting a swatch of marble drapery to reveal the door. The Cavaliere had turned the offending door into the door to heaven.

Fabio Chigi died May 22, 1667, after serving twelve years as Pope Alexander VII.

—

One month later, sixty-seven year-old Giulio Rospigliosi was elected Pope, serving as Clement IX.

The new Pope was an old friend of Bernini's. Earlier, the duo had collaborated on comic operas—the art form the pontiff invented. Rospigliosi wrote the operas, and Bernini designed the sets and did everything else.

During the first night of Clement IX's pontificate, the Pope told the Cavaliere he had a problem. "My insomnia is dangerous to my health," he said, "and the only thing that induces sleep is running water. Sadly, the Belvedere Fountain beneath my chambers is broken, and the engineers can't find the problem."

Bernini investigated and reported to the pontiff that he fixed the fountain. What he really did was design a funny looking machine with a wheel that moved and struck paper globes. The movements of the wheel against the paper created a sound exactly like that of an abundant fountain with running water. That night, the Pope slept comfortably. The next day, when he learned of the Cavaliere's trick, the pontiff exclaimed to his aides, "Bernini's genius always expresses itself in little things as well as great."

The Ponte Sant' Angelo was the only bridge that led to Saint Peter's. Clement IX commissioned Bernini to renovate the old bridge and to add ten Angels to it.

The Cavaliere introduced iron grillwork to the bridge, which allowed pedestrians to see the Tiber River below for the first time. As for the Angels, Bernini personally designed all ten of them. He assigned eight to be carved by his most capable assistants and sculpted two personally. The Pope was so overwhelmed by the two Angels Bernini carved, he took them into his private collection—he didn't want them ravaged by the weather. When the pontiff suggested to Bernini replacements be carved and mounted on the bridge, the Cavaliere himself sculpted a second 'Angel with Superscription.' "It is my desire," he said, "to have a statute from my own hand join the other nine Angels on the old Roman bridge, to welcome the pilgrims to Saint Peter's."

The Pope was understandably astounded by the Cavaliere's accomplishment: At the age of seventy, Bernini had personally carved three over life-size marble statutes in the space of two years—a feat a young artist would have trouble duplicating with ordinary results, much less producing three acknowledged masterpieces.

—

Gabriele Fonseca was a Portuguese doctor who was the first to prescribe quinine—which had recently been discovered by Jesuit Monks—as a cure for malaria. He commissioned Bernini to carve his bust. Within a square of colored, variegated marble, Bernini created a powerful, spiritual work, leaning a life-like doctor Fonseca forward, gazing toward heaven with piercing, pleading eyes that say to God, "If anyone deserves to be with you, it is me." The doctor's left hand his pledges his heart and his right clutches a rosary. Bernini integrates the bust perfectly into the Fonseca Chapel, which he previously designed in the centrally located church of San Lorenzo in Lucina.

—

Honoring a commitment he made on his trip to France, Bernini allowed the students of the French Academy in Rome to carve the equestrian monument he designed honoring their King, Louis XIV.

The Cavaliere was so surprised, and devastated, by the lack of quality in the work of the French students, he adamantly refused to forward the statute to France.

—

After serving only 2 ½ years as Pope Clement IX, Giulio Rospigliosi died on December 9, 1669.

Four months later, seventy-nine year old Emilio Altieri was elected Pope. In honor of his predecessor, he chose to serve as Clement X.

—

At his advanced age, it was not practical for Clement X to think in terms of major artistic projects, but his nephew did. Cardinal Altieri commissioned Bernini to redesign the family chapel in San Francesco a Ripa, the Franciscan church in Trastevere, to honor the beautification of a relative, Ludovica Albertoni. Her cult had been recently sanctioned and she had been beautified.

The Blessed Ludovica Albertoni was the daughter of a noble Roman family. Decimated by the death of her husband, Ludovica took the vows of the Franciscans and devoted the remainder of her life to serving the poor of Rome. Like Teresa of Avila, Ludovica Albertoni experienced a vision at her death. For this reason, Bernini used the concepts he utilized in the Cornaro Chapel and took them to their logical conclusion—which was to show physical death and spiritual awakening simultaneously. The Cavaliere achieved this near-impossible goal by employing a number of stratagems in his execution of Ludovica's statute: He slightly twisted her body; he parted her lips; he turned her half-closed eyes toward the heavens; he had her right hand clutch her bosom; and he even wrapped her body in provocative drapery.

As with Saint Teresa, the Cavaliere was criticized for the sexy appearance of the Blessed Ludovica Albertoni—except this time, the statute was more sensuous, so the carping was more virulent. "I don't mind," Bernini's wife Caterina said. "Truth be known, I'm thrilled, because in essence, these jealous people are calling my seventy-three year-old-husband sexy. And I agree with them one hundred percent. Moreover, I predict the Blessed Ludovica Albertoni will become one of the most renowned statutes ever carved."

Several years before Bernini remodeled the Altieri Chapel and carved the statute of the Blessed Ludovica Albertoni, the Cavaliere's brother, Luigi, brutally raped a young boy behind some scaffolding in Saint Peter's (this is the same brother GianLorenzo tried to kill many years earlier).

As thanks to Clement X, for his assistance and kindnesses in the unfortunate matter, Bernini accepted no fee for his services on the pontiff's family's chapel.

Actually, the waiving of his notoriously high fees was becoming a trademark of the Cavaliere's later life. One striking example was the church of Sant' Andrea al Quirinale, where Bernini labored for a dozen years and where, as he told his son, Domenico, "This is the only piece of architecture for which I feel special satisfaction from the depth of my heart; often when I need rest from my troubles I come here to find consolation in my work."

—

Surprisingly, the elderly and parsimonious Clement X commissioned Bernini to design the Altar of the Blessed Sacrament in Saint Peter's—which he wanted complete in time for the Holy Year of 1675. The assignment was doubly surprising to the Cavaliere, because, incredibly, the commission originated 44 years earlier under his patron and mentor, Urban VIII, and even though each successive Pope renewed it, it was not funded until now.

Bernini designed a sumptuous group—a tabernacle, flanked by two kneeling Angels—that consists of marble, gilded bronze and lapis lazuli. The Cavaliere perfectly integrated the sweeping, pre-existing altarpiece by Pietro da Cortona, thereby creating a spectacular concetto of sculpture, architecture and painting.

Ironically, the Chapel of the Blessed Sacrament is situated behind iron gates designed by Francesco Borromini fifty years earlier.

—

In 1673, a tragedy of monumental proportions struck Bernini and his family. Caterina—his wife, mother of his children, confidant, advisor, lover, and friend of 35 years—died at the tender age of fifty-six years. The seventy-five year-old Cavaliere collapsed.

Dominico, Bernini's oldest son, took over, as was expected of any first-born male. "I don't want to be disrespectful, father, but is that what mother wanted you to do when you were depressed? Collapse in bed?"

"You know it isn't," the Cavaliere replied. Bernini studied his eldest. *I've always loved Dominico, but I had no idea how smart he was.* "Bring me a goblet of Caterina's favorite wine, and hurry. I have much work to do."

—

Bernini carved a powerful, but unusual, half-figure marble statute of his patron, Clement X, which captivated Rome, because of its startling, and loving, accuracy. Shortly thereafter, Clement X, the seventh Pope Bernini served, died August 22, 1676.

Two months later, Benedetto Odescalchi was elected Pope, and chose to serve—in Bernini's eyes, ironically—as Innocent XI."

—

In April of 1680, one of Bernini's rivals astonished Rome by starting a malicious whispering campaign against the eighty-one year-old-master. The rumormongers claimed that when Bernini embellished the piers at the Crossing of Saint Peter's some fifty years earlier, he caused a crack, "which was going to cause Saint Peter's to collapse at any minute."

Dominico scoffed at the ridiculous charges, but they upset his father considerably—because the Monsignor in charge of maintenance of Saint Peter's issued a quick report agreeing with the gossips. "Father," Dominico said, "don't you know the Monsignor accepted a substantial bribe to write that report?" "That may be," the Cavaliere replied, "but the report is still out there."

To put the scurrilous charges to rest, the Pope immediately ordered an independent trio of architects to give him a written, informed report. While the investigation was being conducted—the three experts studied every plan and drawing on record and spent considerable time on the site—the Pope commissioned the Cavaliere to repair the Papal Chancery, parts of which appeared ready to collapse.

Bernini attacked his latest commission with vigor, climbing around the scaffolding like a man possessed. Dominico begged him to slow down.

"This attack," he said to his energized father, "has no more validity than those previous attacks on your bell towers."

Bernini wouldn't listen to his son. "I can do no less," he said, "than what is required by the standards of good service to my Pope, to the job and to my reputation. I want to give what is necessary, even if I pay for it with my life."

—

Bernini's words were tragically prophetic. He started to lose sleep, slowly weakened, and within a few weeks, due to exhaustion, came down with a fever. The aging genius's condition deteriorated daily. Always the realist, Bernini recognized the end was near and made plans accordingly. Turning his room into a shrine, he had a makeshift altar made—which he had set up at the foot of his bed.

On November 15, 1680, Bernini suffered a stroke that left his right arm paralyzed. "It is only proper," he said, looking death in the face and laughing weakly, "that the arm that worked so hard in life should rest a little." In fact, the royalty, clergy, assistants, pupils, and family gathered around him were all astounded by the Cavaliere's spirit and ongoing sense of humor.

Eventually, near total paralyses stole Bernini's speech and most movement. In his usual efficient manner, the Cavaliere had anticipated this, so he devised a system of eye movements with his nephew, the Oratorian Father Marchese. When the padre explained the system to the others, the loved ones who were gathered at his bedside were also able to understand what their hero was saying.

As the end approached, Bernini gave a benediction to each of his nine surviving children and received the Pope's blessing. Father Marchese asked the Cavaliere if he had anything more to confess. Bernini indicated he did not.

The padre than asked him if he wanted to discuss Francesco Borromini.

"Who?" Bernini asked.

—

On November 28, nine days short of his 82nd birthday, GianLorenzo Bernini died of an apoplectic stroke.

Beyond Michelangelo

Rome wept at its loss. Learned men composed eulogies, sonnets, lyric poems, erudite verses, and the most heartfelt poetry any person in Rome had ever heard. There was mass mourning throughout Italy. Tens of thousand tried to attend the great man's funeral. In fact, Bernini's internment in Santa Maria Maggiore had to be postponed to accommodate the throngs that came to pay their respects.

—

Two months after the Cavaliere's death, the investigating architects issued the written report Innocent XI had requested. The detailed report completely and conclusively exonerated GianLorenzo Bernini, to the delight of every right-thinking person in Rome—but, of course, not his pathetic rivals.

—

"Cavalier Bernini was not only the best sculptor and architect of his century, but to put it simply, the greatest man as well."

Cardinal Pietro Sforza Pallavincini

BIBLIOGRAPHY (PARTIAL)

(*THE*) *ART OF GIANLORENZO BERNINI: Selected Sculpture*, exhibition catalogue, edited by MEZZATESTA, Michael, Fort Worth, 1982

AVERY, Charles, *Bernini, Genius of the Baroque*, London, 1997

BALDINUCCI, Filippo, *The Life of Bernini*, Rome, *1682*, translated by ENGGASS, Catherine, University Park & London, 1966

BAROQUE ARCHITECTURE, SCULPTURE, PAINTING, edited by TOMAN, Rolf, Germany 1998

BARZINI, Luigi, *The Italians*, New York, 1964

BAUER, George C., *Bernini in Perspective*, New Jersey, 1976

BERNINI, Domenico, *Vita del Cavalier Gio. Lorenzo Bernino, descritta da suo figlio*, Rome, 1713

BLUNT, Anthony, *Borromini*, London, 1979

BORSI, Franco, *Bernini*, New York, 1984

BOUCHER, Bruce, *Italian Baroque Sculpture*, London, 1998

BURBAUM, Sabine, *The Rivalry between Francesco Borromini and Gian Lorenzo Bernini*, dissertation, Germany, 1999

BUSSAGLI, Marco, *Bernini*, Florence, 2000

CARERI, Giovanni, *Bernini: Flights of Love, the Art of devotion*, translated by LAPPIN, Linda, Chicago, 1995

CELLINI, Benvenuto, *Autobiography*, Italy, c.1558, translated by BULL George, London 1998

CLARK, Kenneth, *Civilization*, New York, 1969

CONNERS, Joseph,

Alliance and Enmity in Roman Baroque Urbanism, Romisches Jahrbuch der Bibliotheca Herziana, XXV, 1989, pp 207-94

Virgilio Spada's defence of Borromini, Burlington Magazine, CXXXI, 1989, pp 75-90

Speccio di Roma barocca, with RICE, Louise, Rome, 1991

Borromini and the Marchese di Castel Rodrigo, Burlington Magazine, CXXXIII, 1991, pp 434-440

Virtuoso Architecture in Cassiano's Rome, Cassiano Dal Pozzo's Paper Museum, London, 1992, volume II (Quaderni Puteani 3), pp 23-40

A Copy of Borromini's S. Carlo alle Quattro Fontane in Gubbio, Burlington Magazine, 137, 1995, pp 588-99

Borromini, Hagia Sophia and S. Vitale, Architectural Studies in memory of Richard Krautheimer, edited by Cecil Striker, Mainz am Rhein, 1996, pp 43-48

Borromini in Oppenord's Sketchbooks, Ars naturam adiuvans. Festchrift fur Matthias Winner, Mainz am Rhein, 1996, pp 598-612

Il Libro dei conti della Avery Library della Columbia University, in Piranesi e l'Aventino, exhibition catalogue, edited by JATTA, Barbara, Milan, 1998, pp 86-94

Francesco Borromini: La vita 1599-1667, in Borromini e l'universo barocco, exhibition catalogue, edited by BOSEL, Richard and FROMMEL, Christoph, Milan, 1999, pp 7-21

Un teorema sacro: San Carlo alle Quattro Fontane, in Il giovane Borromini: dagli esordi a San Carlino, exhibition catalogue, edited by KAHN-ROSSI, Manuela and FRANCIOLLI, Marco, Lugano, 1999, pp 459-95

Poussin detrattore di Borromini, in exhibition catalogue, Atti del Convegno Internazionale su Borromini, 2001

CHRISTIE'S SALES CATALOGUE, *An Important Sculpture by Bernini*, New York, 1990

EFFIGIES & ECSTASIES: Roman Baroque Sculpture and Design in the Age of Bernini, exhibition catalogue, edited by WESTON-LEWIS, Aidan, 1998

FAGIOLO, Maurizio, with CIPRIANI, Angela, *Bernini: The Creator of the Baroque*, Florence, 1981

FRANCESCO BORROMINI AND ROME: Through the Images of Franco Tibaldi, exhibition catalogue, edited by BOTTARI, Francesca, Rome, 1999

(THE) GENIUS OF ROME, exhibition catalogue, edited by BROWN, Beverly Louise, London, 2001

GERRARD, Mary, *Artemisia Gentileschi*, New Jersey, 1991

GIAN LORENZO BERNINI: Regista del Barocco, exhibition catalogue edited by BERNARDINI, Maria Grazia and DELL'ARCO, Maurizio Fagiolo, Milan 1999

GOULD, Cecil, *Bernini in France: An Episode in Seventeenth-Century History*, London, 1981

HASKELL, Francis, *Patrons and Painters: A Study in the Relations Between Italian Art and Society in the Age of the Baroque*, London, 1963

HIBBARD, Howard, *Bernini*, London, 1990

ITALIAN BAROQUE (MUSIC) MASTERS, various authors, London, 1997

IMPRESSARIO, THE, an unfinished play by Bernini, translated by BEECHER, Donald, and CIAVOLELLA, Massimo, Canada, 1994

LEPROHON, Pierre, *Rome*, Geneva, 1977

LIFE AND THE ARTS IN THE BAROQUE PALACES OF ROME: Ambiente Barocco, exhibition catalogue, edited by WALKER, Stefanie and HAMMOND, Frederick, New Haven and London, 1999

MAGNUSON, Torgil, *Rome in the Age of Bernini, Volume I*, Sweden, 1982; *Volume II*, Sweden, 1986

MARDER, T. A., *Bernini and the Art of Architecture*, New York, 1998

MARTIN, John Rupert, *Baroque*, London, 1991

MCBRIEN, Richard, *Lives of the Popes: The Pontiffs from St. Peter to John Paul II*, San Francisco, 1997

MCPHEE, Sarah, *Bernini and the Bell Towers: Architecture and Politics at the Vatican*, New Haven, 2002

MONTAGUE, Jennifer, *Roman Baroque Sculpture, The Industry of Art*, New Haven, 1992

MORRISSEY, Jake, *The Genius in the Design: Bernini, Borromini and the Rivalry that Transformed Rome*, New York, 2005

PETERSSON, Robert, *Bernini and the Excesses of Art*, USA, 2003

POPE-HENNESSY, John, *Italian High Renaissance and Baroque Sculpture*, New York, 1985

PORTOGHESI, Paolo, *The Rome of Borromini: Architecture as Language*, translated by LA PENTA, Barbara Luigia, New York, 1968

SCRIBNER, Charles III, *Bernini*, New York, 1991

SKETCHES IN CLAY FOR PROJECTS BY GIAN LORENZO BERNINI, edited by GASKELL, Ivan and LIE, Henry, Cambridge, 1999

SPADA, Virgilio and BORROMINI, Francesco, *Opus Architectonicum*, Rome, 1647, published 1725

TRIADO, Juan-Ramon, *The Key to Baroque Art*, UK, 1993

VASARI, Giorgio, *The Lives of the Artists*, Florence, 1568, translated by BONDANELLA, Julia Conaway and Peter, Oxford, 1991

WALLACE, Robert, *The World of Bernini*, USA, 1973

WITTKOWER, Rudolf

Bernini: The Sculptor of the Roman Baroque, London, 1997

Art and Architecture in Italy, 1600-1750, USA, Hamondsworth, 1958

BVG